Prisoners of a Pirate Queen

Marshall J. Moore

Atoll Press, LLC

marshall@marshalljmoore.com

For Jimmy.

I can't count the memories I have of listening to your music with my dad on boats he named after your songs. Thanks for being the soundtrack to my childhood.

I hope you two are trading fishing stories up there.

1

"Have I ever told you how much I love the theatre, Cap'n?" Ophelia Price, first mate of the pirate ship *Bloody Angel,* asked as she touched two fingers gingerly against the false nose she wore.

"You have a time or two," acknowledged Quint Thatch, better known across the Archipelago as Captain Redbeard. This was in fact a significant understatement; he'd lost track of the number of times Ophelia had dragged him along to some terribly-staged melodrama whenever they were in port for more than a day. "Didn't the makeup artist tell you the prosthetic's going to fall off if you keep on touching it?"

"Right," Ophelia said, jerking her hand away from the bulbous fake nose. "Sorry. It's just *fun*, pretending you're someone else."

"It is odd to see you like this," her captain admitted, eyeing her. Like him, Ophelia was dressed in the purple uniform jacket of the Imperial Navy, her thin stripe of loose blonde hair covered up beneath the double layer of a bicorn hat and a brown wig. A foundation of makeup concealed the tattoos that ordinarily would have peeked out of her collar and sleeves, making her already-fair complexion look unnaturally pale beneath the tropical sun overhead. "You look...blank."

"Aye," Ophelia agreed, and winked at him. "But at least I ain't wearing two beards in this heat, mate."

Quint's hand was halfway to the fake beard he wore over his real one before he recalled the makeup artist's warnings about touching their prosthetics. He lowered his hand self-consciously, avoiding Ophelia's knowing smirk as they marched towards the wooden stage.

It was a broad wooden platform of the sort used by theatrical productions who had no need of a backstage and were comfortable performing outdoors, exposed to the elements. Behind it the cool blue waters of Amell Bay glittered with reflected sunlight. From where they stood Quint could just see the ships docked in the harbor below, directly behind the steep, straight slope of the hill upon which the stage stood.

He tried not to look at the ranks of uniformed Navy officers they marched past, each dressed in their purple jackets and standing at attention in neat rows before the stage. Guards stood stationed all around the periphery of the open square, muskets resting conspicuously against their shoulders. This was not the largest gathering of Imperial Navy officers he'd ever encountered at once, but it certainly merited placement in the top three.

"So far so good," Ophelia breathed, glancing over her shoulder at the towering ramparts of Fort Amell looming behind them. "At least, nobody's come running outta the fort yet shouting about how we ain't actually Commodore Goosegrow and Admiral Merryfeather."

"So far," Quint agreed. He resisted the urge to fidget with his stolen uniform, disliking the unfamiliar weight of the commodore's golden epaulettes at his shoulders or the numerous medals pinned to his chest. "Assuming neither of us gives the game away."

"You just gotta get more into character, Cap'n," Ophelia reassured him out of the corner of her mouth. "Remember, you're a stuffed waistcoat here to hobnob with your equally stuffy peers. Walk like you've just made a mess in your breeches."

Quint stifled his laugh with a fist pressed against his mouth, passing it off as a coughing fit instead.

"Vigo in place?" he asked once he'd recovered himself.

"Aye," Ophelia said as they mounted the steps onto the stage, where a dozen chairs had been erected for the highest-ranking officers attending the day's ceremonies. "Assuming that stagehand's spare keys are any good, he should be ready and waiting for the signal."

"The coins we slipped her were good enough," Quint remarked as they took their seats. No one else wearing an admiral's or commodore's uniform had arrived yet, so for the moment they were alone onstage, staring out at a sea of purple jackets. "And I doubt her production company pays her well enough anyway."

"And they call us the thieves," Ophelia grinned ruefully.

Other men and women began to filter onto the stage, each of their uniforms bearing rank insignias of captain or higher. The youngest of them looked to still have a good two decades on Quint and Ophelia, but none paid the two newcomers any mind beyond polite greetings as they took their seats.

"Game ain't given away yet," Ophelia whispered.

Quint nodded his agreement. Their scheme had relied upon the fact that, of the dozen or so high officers invited to the day's ceremonies, all were from different fleets flung across the vast reaches of the Empire. Odds had been good that many of them had never met in person before. Yet the Empire prized good breeding in its ranking officers—so much so that Quint had elected to wager his whole plan on the assumption that none of the admirals, captains, or commodores would dare be so boorish as to admit to not knowing who they were.

He allowed himself a slight smile, imagining the confusion of the *real* Commodore Goosegrow and Admiral Merryfeather when they awoke from the drunken stupor he and Ophelia had left them in. By which point they would, of course, be leagues and leagues away, with a strong breeze in their sails and the Crown Jewels safely stowed away in their hull.

Quint's gaze drifted upwards, towards the towering shadow that was Fort Amell. He and his crew had already stolen the Crown Jewels from the stronghold's supposedly impenetrable vaults months ago, before circumstance had forced them to relinquish them into the Navy's custody. It was a truly daring pirate who managed to pull off such a successful heist the one time. But twice?

That was the stuff from which legends were made.

A band near the back of the square struck up a drumbeat, a rapid martial rhythm that snapped every sailor and soldier in attendance into an upright posture. Quint and Ophelia did their best to straighten themselves from the slouches they had sunk into.

The drumbeat echoed off the walls of the fort above. Soon it was joined by the first bombastic chords of the Imperial anthem. Quint found himself holding his breath as a troop of Navy officers came marching down from Fort Amell's gates, down the center of the aisle formed by the soldiers standing at attention and towards the stage.

Quint's own attention was fixed on the woman striding proudly at the head of the procession. She was tall and long-limbed, her curling dark brown hair pulled back from her face and bound in a high bun. Her purple uniform and golden epaulettes were a pleasing contrast to her mahogany features, and though her face was schooled into a model of military dignity, Quint recognized the slight twist to her lip that meant she was fighting down the urge to smile.

Vanessa, he thought, a pang of longing piercing him. He forced his lingering feelings down, knowing she would not be similarly pleased to see him here today.

The opposite, really.

"Hey, loverboy," Ophelia said, nudging him with her elbow and pointing. "There's Rusty."

Quint looked where she pointed. A few paces behind Vanessa marched a shorter, considerably more bedraggled figure in threadbare clothes, flanked on either side by a pair of intimidatingly broad-shouldered Navy guards.

Rusty "Rustbucket" Russell, formerly a member of Quint's crew turned mutineer, had certainly seen better days. His ordinarily scrawny features had turned alarmingly gaunt, while his beard—typically tied into a tight orange braid—hung wild and scraggly from his chin. The bright sun reflected angrily off the shiny dome of his scalp. A pair of iron manacles bound his wrists together, and someone had tied a cotton gag across his mouth.

"Looks a little worse for wear," Ophelia observed. Quint nodded his agreement, a guilty twist in his gut at the thought that he was at least partially responsible for Rustbucket's current state. True, Rustbucket's mutiny against Quint had led him directly to the predicament he now found himself in, but still. He was part of Quint's crew.

Not anymore, Quint reminded himself, forcing his gaze away from Rustbucket. On Vanessa's other side marched another pair of Navy guards, these ones flanking not a prisoner but a prize: a heavy wooden chest bearing an impressive number of locks. Within lay the Imperial Crown Jewels.

Soon, Quint promised himself, that chest and all its contents would be in his possession once more. And this time neither Vanessa nor Rustbucket would be able to foul things up.

The procession reached the stage and mounted it, Vanessa in the lead. Quint shrank back into his chair as she passed, and for a moment he swore her eyes passed over him, then darted back. A cold thrill crept along his spine at the possibility that she'd seen through the disguise. How would she react—

At the far end of the stage, someone cleared their throat. Vanessa's momentary gaze left Quint, fixing instead upon an elderly, bewhiskered admiral. The man's uniform bore so many medals that he'd probably sink any vessel he stepped aboard smaller than a frigate. Vanessa's heels clicked together as she gave an exactingly precise salute.

"Rear Admiral Stetson," she said, her back straight enough to put a flagpole to shame. "Commander Vanessa Delacort of Her Imperial Majesty's ship *Valiant,* reporting."

"At ease, Commander," the aged admiral squeaked, his voice high and reedy as he returned the salute. Vanessa lowered her hand but remained at attention.

"You were dispatched to seek out the renegade pirate styling himself Captain Redbeard," Rear Admiral Stetson continued, raising his voice loud enough to carry across the assembled onlookers, "and to recover the Imperial Crown Jewels which he stole from this very fort."

From where he sat onstage, Quint could actually see the murmur of consternation rippling through the assembled sailors and their officers. The Navy had expended what Quint considered a gratifyingly significant effort to hush up his theft of the Crown Jewels, rightfully fearing the damage to their Empire's reputation that such a scandal might cause. That Rear Admiral Stetson had just confirmed the inevitable scuttlebutt surrounding the manhunt for Captain Redbeard sent a ripple of shock through the watching crowd.

"I have, sir," Vanessa said, saluting once more. There was a slight crinkling about her eyes. It was an expression he knew well—not a smile, exactly, but the satisfied look from across the chessboard she got just before pronouncing checkmate.

"Show me," Rear Admiral Stetson ordered.

Vanessa obeyed, producing a ring of keys from her jacket and meticulously unlocking the chest's locks, a process which stretched on for nearly a minute. Quint supposed that, considering the trouble she'd gone through in order to retrieve them from him in the first place, he couldn't fault her for the increased security.

Not that it would do her any good.

Finally, the last tumbler clicked into place and the final latch opened. Vanessa glanced to Stetson, who nodded, and threw open the chest.

This time an audible gasp echoed through the crowd as the Imperial Crown Jewels lay exposed and glittering beneath the bright tropical sun: the Pearl Knife, the Emperor's Carcanet, the Queen Mother's Rings, and countless other official regalia belonging to the Empire's head of state. The gemstones each were inset with were mined from across the islands, representing the tribute the Empire enacted upon its subject isles. Each of the Crown Jewels was priceless in its own right, but together they formed a potent symbol of the Empress's dominion over the Archipelago.

And Quint Thatch was going to steal them all.

"Rear Admiral," Vanessa said, coming to her feet with another salute. "I present to you the Imperial Crown Jewels, and commit them to the safekeeping of Fort Amell."

"As I commend you for your valiant actions in retrieving them," Stetson said, smiling thinly. "I understand you have apprehended the criminal responsible for their theft?"

"I have," Vanessa said after a brief hesitation. She turned to the bulky guards flanking Rustbucket and gestured them forward. Rustbucket offered no resistance, though he frantically shook his head from side to side and did his best to protest around the gag in his mouth.

"This is the pirate styling himself Captain Redbeard?" Stetson asked, squinting at Rustbucket, whose beard was little more than a wild tuft of orange sprouting from his chin.

Vanessa hesitated again, then gave a curt nod. "Aye, sir."

"Thought he'd have a bigger beard," Stetson muttered, barely loud enough for Quint to hear. He turned back to the waiting crowd, gesturing as he did so for Vanessa to shut the lid of the chest and locked it. There was an audible sigh of disappointment from the spectators as the glittering Crown Jewels were hidden from sight once again.

"Captain Redbeard," Stetson said, allegedly to Rustbucket but clearly intending for his words to be heard by every soul present. He unfurled a parchment scroll and began to read in his high, quavering voice. "For your many and sundry crimes against Her Majesty the Empress and the Empire she controls, including but not limited to the following: Piracy, Conspiracy, Rebellion, Shipjacking, Impersonation of a Cleric, Theft, Fraud, Smuggling..."

Quint tuned out the list of his crimes, which was long and not remotely close to comprehensive. Instead his gaze was fixed on where Rustbucket and Vanessa stood center stage, the chest containing the Crown Jewels beside them.

"They couldn't have found their mark better if they were professional actors," he murmured approvingly to Ophelia. "You ready to ditch this shindig?"

"Aye, Cap'n," Ophelia nodded, grinning.

They stood in unison. The heads of the other high-ranking officers turned to stare curiously up at them, as did many of those still in the audience.

"...Evasion of Taxes," Stetson droned on before them, oblivious. "Gross Indecency, Petty Theft—"

"Begging your pardon," Quint said, loudly clearing his throat. "But I object to that last. Weren't nothing petty about it."

Every eye in the square was on him now. And, though he was no actor, Quint Thatch found himself enjoying the spotlight.

Out of the corner of his eye he saw the faces of those assembled upon the stage craning towards him, their expressions shocked and disbelieving—none more so than Rustbucket, who looked up at Quint as if his former captain were the Angel of Justice in all his terrible glory. Or Vanessa, who was staring at Quint with a mixture of recognition and the dawning horror of someone who'd just come home to find their family dog had made a mess on the carpet. Her mouth shaped his name.

"I *beg* your pardon, sailor," Stetson said, his high voice growing positively shrill as he recovered the power of speech. "Who exactly do you think you are, that you can interrupt official Imperial matters of state—"

"Ain't it obvious?" Quint grinned as he tossed the bicorn hat from his head and yanked off the fake beard, eliciting a gasp from somewhere in the audience. He sketched a courtly bow and said, in a voice that resounded off the walls of the fort above: "I'm Captain Redbeard, mate."

Someone in the crowd screamed. Nearer at hand, one of the admirals muttered to a commodore, "that's hardly more of a beard than the bald one's got."

Quint ignored them both. He'd only been growing it a few months, after all.

What he couldn't ignore were the unfriendly gazes of the guards stationed nearest the stage as they lowered their muskets from their shoulders.

"None of that!" Ophelia called to them, her hands flying to her coat and pulling out a pair of matchlock pistols, which she levelled at the guards. "Let's let the man say his piece, eh?"

The guards hesitated, though Quint suspected their resolve wouldn't waver for long. Nor did he need them to.

He took a step closer, Ophelia moving beside him as carefully as if this were a dance long rehearsed, until the two of them occupied the same eight-foot square in the center of the stage as Rustbucket and the Crown Jewels.

"If you're *really* Captain Redbeard," Rear Admiral Stetson said scornfully, though he could not quite conceal the faint tremor in his voice, "than you surely must know that you're hopelessly outnumbered and outgunned. What exactly is your plan, here?"

"Thought that was obvious, too," Quint replied cheerfully. "I'm here to retrieve what I rightfully stole from you."

With that, he lifted his foot and stomped down twice upon the stage, sending a hollow *thwunk-thwunk* echoing across the square.

Nothing happened.

"Redbeard," Vanessa said, her voice low and disbelieving. Quint was briefly thankful she had not used his given name, which she alone of the gathered Imperials knew. "What are you—"

"Hold on," he said, and stomped twice more. Again, nothing.

"Guards!" Stetson shouted, waving both hands over his head. "Don't just *stand* there! Apprehend them!"

"Cap'n," Ophelia said, her face going white even under her makeup as the guards obeyed, levelling their rifles at the two pirates onstage.

"Just give me a—" Quint started to say, as beside him Rustbucket whimpered something unintelligible through his gag. Quint raised his foot to stomp a third time, only to hear a groan of ancient timbers creaking. Suddenly the stage shifted beneath Quint's feet, lurching like a ship caught in a gale, then fell away entirely, sending them tumbling down into darkness.

2

Fortunately, it was a drop of less than ten feet.

Quint's fall was cushioned by a bed of stale-smelling straw. He sat up to see Ophelia, Rustbucket, and the chest containing the Crown Jewels had also tumbled into the haycart which his crew had maneuvered under the stage in the small hours of the morning.

"Can't believe that worked," Ophelia said, dusting straw from her coat sleeves as she gazed up at the bright rectangle of light framed by the open trap door above their heads. Sounds of consternation filtered down from the stage, the Navy officers still reeling from the unexpected turn of events.

"'course it worked," a deep voice boomed as Vigo stepped into the light, grinning at them. The *Angel's* third mate was a robust, dark-skinned man whose hair and beard alike were braided with colorful beads. "Sorry 'bout the trap door, Cap'n. Damned thing wouldn't budge."

"Not the worst thing that could've gone wrong," Quint said.

As if on cue, Vanessa dropped from the stage into the cart. She landed in a crouch, a pair of iron manacles in her hands.

"Captain Redbeard!" she shouted, loud enough to be heard onstage. "By order of Her Imperial Majesty, you are hereby under arrest!"

She lunged at Quint, trying to clap the manacles around his wrists.

"Not this time," Quint said, jerking his hands out of reach. Vanessa lunged forwards again, only for Vigo to lean forward and pluck the cuffs from her with one burly hand.

"Hey!" she protested, grabbing for them.

Vigo raised the manacles to the light for a better look, well out of her reach. "You just...always have these on you?"

"They come in handy more than you'd think," Vanessa said, looking at Quint again.

"A woman after me own heart," Ophelia commented. "Good to see you again, Vanessa."

"You too, Ophelia," Vanessa said, not sounding like she meant it.

Shrugging, Ophelia picked up a coiled rope that had been left in the cart the night before, turned around and busied herself with tying the chest to the inside of the cart, her sailor's hands making quick work of the complex series of knots.

"Like I was saying," Vanessa said, "you're under arrest, Redbeard."

"Ness," Quint said, admiration and annoyance warring with each other in his voice. "We don't have time for this—"

"Like I'd just let you go after that stunt," she hissed. "What in the nine hells do you think you're doing, *Quint*?"

"Didn't you hear me up there?" he asked, plucking a stray bit of straw from behind Vanessa's ear as Vigo circled around to the front of the cart. With a grunt, the burly mate slid open the door to the understage, which was suddenly illuminated by the flood of sunlight. "I'm stealing back the Jewels. Besides, I couldn't let Rustbucket take all the credit for my success, could I?"

Still gagged, Rustbucket made a protesting noise. Vigo moved to the back of the cart beside Quint, pressed his hands flat against its rear.

"Or my crimes, neither," Quint added, and winked at Vanessa. "Besides, I did tell you I'd be seeing you soon."

"I didn't think it'd be *this* soon," she protested. "And speaking of your crimes—"

Further argument was forestalled by a silhouetted head appearing in the rectangle of light cast by the trapdoor above.

"Listen here, pirate!" Rear Admiral Stetson's high, piping voice sputtered. "There's thirty Imperial guardsmen converging on you as we speak. Now unhand Commander Delacort and come out from under the stage with your hands up!"

"After you," Quint gestured to Vanessa, who folded her arms across her chest and made no sign of moving.

"Fine," Quint sighed, and looked to Vigo. "Do you mind?"

"Not at all." The big mate's beads jangled as he shook his head from side to side, and gave Vanessa an apologetic smile. "Sorry, Commander Delacort."

His burly arms darted out with surprising speed as he lifted Vanessa from the cart, depositing her with unexpected gentleness on the ground before resuming his place behind the cart.

"Hey!" Vanessa shouted in protest, but before she could try to scramble back into the cart to arrest Quint, Vigo gave the cart a tremendous shove.

The cart's wheels groaned as it rolled forward. Quint threw himself low against the floor of the cart as they passed beneath the understage door. Ophelia slung an arm about Rustbucket's shoulders and did the same for him. Above and behind them Quint could hear the sounds of commotion as more admirals and commodores joined Stetson at the trapdoor, jostling for a better look.

"Be seeing you!" Quint called over his shoulder to Vanessa as the cart emerged from beneath the stage into the bright tropical sunshine. The wheels groaned forward over the flat ground at the edge of the square and kept rolling.

Right over the edge of the steep hill leading down to the harbor.

"Hold on!" Vigo yelled as the cart's front wheels dipped down, down, down. Quint's fingers gripped the cart's edges, his boots scuffling for purchase in the straw. Vigo gave a last push, then threw himself into the cart beside Quint as they fell hurtling at breakneck speed down the dizzyingly steep incline.

Steep but straight, Quint reassured himself as wind whistled past his ears, the blue waters of the harbor growing larger and nearer with every passing second. The ships docked there grew from toy-sized to life-sized with startling rapidity.

The cart bounced and rattled as it picked up speed, the tufts of uneven grass beneath its wheels turning the ride distressingly bumpy. Quint tore his gaze from the water to his fellow passengers. Ophelia was laughing, one foot braced against the chest, her arm thrown across Rustbucket's shoulders for the same purpose. Above the gag, Rustbucket's eyes were squeezed tight.

"Haaa-HAAAA!!!" Vigo boomed alarmingly close to Quint's ear as they hit a particularly obstinate mound of dirt, causing the cart's wheels to momentarily leave the ground altogether. Quint's stomach dropped into the region of his intestines, then overcorrected by attempting to climb out of his throat as the wheels crashed against the hillside once more.

This seemed like a better idea when we were hashing it out over drinks, the small part of him not preoccupied by sheer terror reflected. The harbor was growing larger with every passing moment, and Quint found himself suddenly, keenly aware of the sharp brown rocks sticking up from the shallows that lay between them and the docks.

"We're going too fast!" he shouted over his shoulder, the wind snatching the words from his mouth almost before they'd left his lips. "Doesn't this thing have a brake??"

"*Cap'n*," Vigo thundered over the rushing wind, his tone incongruously patient. "It's a *haycart*."

"I'm guessing that means n—" Quint started, then stifled a shriek as the cart gave a sudden, horrifying lurch upwards.

All his concentration was diverted to clinging on for dear life as the wagon raced up a sharp incline, a natural ramp in the hillside. The front wheels left the ground, then the rear, and suddenly they were flying. The hillside below their feet gave way to glittering blue waves lapping against jagged rocks, and for the briefest moment Quint found himself enjoying the feeling of weightlessness.

Then gravity reasserted its inexorable pull, dragging them towards the waiting waves.

"Hang tight!" Quint roared over the wind, the authority of his station as captain reasserting itself over his own fear. All four of the cart's passengers braced themselves as best they could, digging in the straw to find the little handholds Vigo had installed the previous afternoon. Ophelia held Rustbucket down with one hand since his manacles prevented him from doing so himself.

Hitting the water felt like being slapped by a giant, knocking the air from Quint's lungs. He sucked in a ragged breath, then pulled himself to his feet. The wooden timbers of the haycart's planks were a familiar comfort beneath his boots, though water was already beginning to seep through the cracks between the boards—the cart wasn't exactly seaworthy.

At least they'd landed nearer to the docks than the rocks. A two-masted schooner lay anchored not more than a dozen yards away, exactly as they'd planned.

"Nicely done, Cap'n," Ophelia said, pulling off her prosthetic nose and tossing it overboard before reaching over the edge of the cart and wetting her sleeve. She wiped it across her face and neck, wiping away the makeup she'd used to conceal her more prominent tattoos. "Plan went swimmingly, just like you said."

Quint was about to answer when Rustbucket let out a plaintive, muffled complaint.

"Right," Quint nodded, reaching over and untying the gag binding Rustbucket's mouth. "Sorry about that, Rusty."

Rustbucket shook his head from side to side, like a dog who'd just had his muzzle removed, then turned to face his former captain.

"What in the blazes are you *doing*, Cap'n?" he said, his tone colored with an odd blend of curiosity, incredulity, and admiration.

"Your grasp of the obvious seems to have weakened since we last parted ways, mate," Quint said, clapping a hand on Rustbucket's shoulder. "We're rescuing you."

"Or rescuing the Cap'n's reputation," Vigo offered, plucking a long-handled pole from the side of the cart and dipping it into the bay until it hit the seabed below. He began to pole them forward, towards the waiting schooner. "Since they think he's you, and all."

"And stealing back the Crown Jewels in the bargain," Ophelia said, shuffling out of her stolen admiral's jacket.

"I don't get it," Rustbucket said, frowning as his gaze tracked past Quint to the towering ramparts of Fort Amell. "Why take me with you? You could've just revealed yourself as Redbeard, then made off with the jewels while leaving me high and dry."

"Instead of down here and rapidly growing wetter?" Quint said as the cart sank ever lower, bits of straw floating up around his ankles. A few hundred yards away a pair of fishermen in a tiny rowboat were staring at them openmouthed, oblivious to the tugging at their lines. Quint gave them a jaunty wave, as if falling from the sky in a haycart into the bay were something he did regularly. "I wouldn't do that to you, Rusty."

Rustbucket's face scrunched up as if he'd just been confronted with a confounding riddle. "But I mutinied against you. Pointed a gun in your face and everything."

"You did," Quint agreed, shading his eyes towards a two-masted schooner that was cruising towards them from the nearest docks, "and I'm still sore about it. Just not sore enough to let you hang for it."

Rustbucket gulped audibly, manacled hands rising to his throat. "I...I appreciate that, Quint."

"Cap'n," Quint corrected, still focused on the approaching schooner. "No crewman of the *Bloody Angel* has danced the hangman's jig yet, Rustbucket. I don't intend for that to change."

"Unless you want to be a trailblazer," Ophelia said, shading her eyes and looking up at the hillside. "Speaking of trails, Quint..."

Quint followed her gaze to see a thick plume of dust rising from the winding switchback trail leading down from the fort to the harbor below. Some of the Navy troops gathered in the square must have elected to race to the docks, intending to cut the fleeing pirates off before they could board a ship and escape.

Good luck to them, Quint thought, turning away from the rising dust and the echo of hoofbeats across the bay. The sleek little schooner was nearly on top of them now, close enough to read the cheerful yellow letters on its prow: *MARIGOLD*.

"Not that I don't appreciate the sentiment," Rustbucket said dubiously as the schooner drew closer. "Rescuin' me, I mean. But whoever this boat belongs to is gonna turn us over to the Navy faster than you can say 'arrest.'"

"Probably," Quint agreed. "Thankfully, she's had a change of ownership."

As if on cue, a tall, gangling figure appeared over the *Marigold's* rail. "Ahoy, Cap'n!"

"Ahoy, Darby!" Quint replied, waving. Scarecrow-thin with a beaky nose and prominent spectacles, the *Angel's* second mate looked more like a clerk than a pirate. But he was as able a hand as any in Captain Redbeard's crew. "Permission to come aboard?"

"Posthaste," Darby nodded, stooping to toss a rope ladder over the rail. "Vigo alright?"

"Fine, love," Vigo called up.

"Then come aboard!" Darby called. "There's enough Navy ships in this harbor to make me feel like a shrimp in an eel's nest. The sooner we're away, the better."

"You heard your better half," Quint said, slapping the burly third mate on the shoulder. "Stop poling and abandon cart, mate."

"Aye-aye, Cap'n," Vigo chuckled. He tossed the pole carelessly into the bay. "Help me with the chest, Ophelia."

Ophelia did so, and together they hauled both themselves and the treasure up the rope ladder and onto the *Marigold.* Quint heard a heavy *thunk* as the chest hit the deck, followed by a softer collision as Darby wrapped his mate up in his arms.

"You came from all the way up there?" Darby asked, looking incredulously up at the hilltop, then down to the rapidly sinking cart. "In *that?*"

"Right into your waiting arms," Vigo said, resting his head against Darby's shoulder. "Besides, love. You agreed to this."

"I did," Darby admitted reluctantly, still staring at the hillside. "It seems steeper from down here, though."

"It wasn't so bad," Quint lied, nodding towards the ladder. "You next, Rusty."

"With these on?" he said, holding out his manacled wrists.

"You'll manage," Quint assured him. "Darby's got a set of lockpicks in the cabin. Once we're underway we'll get those off of you, but as things stand at the moment, we're on a bit of a tight schedule."

"I..." Rustbucket swallowed, then jerked his head in a nod. "Aye, Cap'n. And...thank you."

"Thank me once we're out of here," Quint said, watching the plume of dust approaching the harbor. "We haven't outrun the storm yet."

No fewer than half a dozen Navy ships lay anchored in the harbor, their sails furrowed. The largest was a massive ship of the line, which to Quint's mind wasn't so much an oceangoing vessel as it was a floating fortress. But neither the massive warship nor the four frigates berthed beside it could be easily readied for departure in the time it would take the pirates to sail the *Marigold* out of the bay and away from Fort Amell.

No, Quint thought as he turned and began to haul himself up the rungs of the rope ladder, *it's the sloops they'll send after us.*

Or at least that was the hope. If any of the frigates managed to get underway before they were over the horizon, this chase would be over before it had begun. Of the two sloops stationed at Fort Amell, only the *Unstoppable* was currently docked. Her sister ship, the *Immoveable,* was patrolling the waters past the headlands of the harbor even now.

"Cap'n aboard!" Darby called as Quint clambered onto the deck, pulling the rope ladder up after him.

"At ease," Quint said with a perfunctory salute, crossing the shifting deck and laying ahold of the ship's wheel. The feel of the wheel beneath his hands was a familiar comfort. "Now step lively, lady and gentlemen. Let's chart a course for Port Solace."

Wind filled the *Marigold's* sails, sending her cruising across the bay as the waves swallowed the sinking haycart. Ophelia took off her stolen admiral's hat and held it to her chest in mock salute.

"Guess it ain't true what they say after all," she remarked, glancing at Quint. "The captain *doesn't* go down with his cart."

"Not this captain," Quint agreed, turning back towards the *Marigold's* prow as he adjusted their course, putting Fort Amell in their stern as they steered towards open seas.

3

—•—

"Where is everyone?" Rustbucket asked, glancing about the deck as if expecting the rest of his erstwhile crewmates to emerge from belowdecks at any moment. "And for that matter, why ain't we on the *Bloody Angel?*"

"Even I'm not fool enough to try and raid Fort Amell in the *Angel* a second time," Quint said. "She's a tad more noticeable than this little schooner. And besides, this was just a rescue operation."

"Rescuing the jewels," Ophelia put in as she wedged the chest between the helm and the rail of the afterdeck, securing it against any sudden turns. "You're a bonus, Rusty."

"A rescue," Quint repeated. "The fewer involved, the better. We'll sail the *Marigold* to Port Solace, fence the jewels, then meet up with the rest of the crew there."

Rustbucket frowned, no doubt wondering how the rest of the *Bloody Angel's* crew would react to his return.

"Err, Quint?" Darby cut in. He pointed aft, towards the harbor. "We've got company."

Quint looked where Darby pointed. Sure enough, the Navy sloop *Unstoppable* had departed the harbor, its sails billowing as it raced towards them. Though the smallest class of the Empire's warships, even a sloop was half again as large as a schooner like the *Marigold*, and boasted sixteen cannons to the *Marigold's* meager complement of four.

"Figures," Quint muttered. "At least it's only the one."

"Why, though?" Rustbucket asked, frowning. "And why aren't we hightailing it out of here?"

He gestured towards the bow, which veered back and forth between the long arm of the headland sheltering the harbor and its open mouth. Quint had chosen to tack into the wind, driving the *Marigold* in a zigzagging line that took them steadily but slowly towards the mouth of the bay. The *Unstoppable*, in contrast, was bearing down on them directly. They had not caught up yet, but given time and momentum, the sloop's greater sail power would triumph over the schooner's.

"I thought the whole point of this escapade was to," Rustbucket continued, looking dubiously back at Quint. "I don't know, *escape?*"

"Which is what we'll be doing as soon as soon as the final member of this little expedition is safely aboard," Quint said. "We've slowed down so that she can catch up."

Rustbucket turned in a slow circle, scanning the horizon for any approaching ship nearer than the *Unstoppable*. None presented itself.

"Who—" he started, only to be interrupted by a loud splash as a gleaming, serpentine body erupted from the bay.

Droplets glittered like diamonds in the sun as the mermaid arced from the water, landing with surprising grace against one of the broad nets of rigging running up from the rail to the *Marigold's* mainsail. She wound both tail and arms through the holes in the rigging, stabilizing herself, before turning her huge dark eyes consideringly upon Rustbucket.

"Drown?" Lurk asked Quint hopefully.

Rustbucket shrieked and darted for the *Marigold's* rail. Before he could throw himself overboard and onto the mercy of the pursuing

Imperials, Vigo grabbed him by the arms and hauled him back onto the deck, murmuring something soothing in Rustbucket's ear. Meanwhile Darby began lashing down anything on deck that still remained unsecured, readying them for the true chase now that all members of their partial crew were aboard.

"No drowning him, Lurk," Quint said, shaking his head as he joined Darby in tying a loose barrel to the mainmast. "He's still part of the crew, more or less."

"How *much* less?" Lurk asked, undeterred.

Rustbucket shrank away as far as Vigo's hold permitted. His one previous encounter with Lurk had nearly ended in his own drowning, and only Quint's merciful intervention had stayed the mermaid's webbed hands.

In fairness, Quint reflected, as Lurk's overlong tongue snaked hungrily out from between her sharklike teeth, the mermaid's appearance had not softened any in the intervening months. Her blue-gray scales were now adorned in several places by tattoos, courtesy of Vigo's skillful needlework. Most of these were of abstract design, though a few bore stylized representations of subjects the mermaid would have found familiar: a coral-covered anchor, a pair of sea turtles, and even a broad oblong shape which had perplexed Quint until Lurk had told him it was meant to be the *Bloody Angel*, as viewed from below. One of the rayed fins jutting out from the side of her head was also decorated with a handful of gold hoops, though at Lurk's own request the earrings had been kept small in order to reduce drag while swimming.

"You're..." Rustbucket sputtered, staring hard at Lurk as she craned lower from the rigging, cocking her head questioningly to one side. "You're...*clothed.*"

"Only a little," Lurk said, sounding somewhat abashed. She plucked self-consciously at the tight-fitting vest she wore across her narrow chest. Another of Vigo's designs, it bore numerous pockets, each fastened tight with several brass buttons. "It helps me carry things while I'm in the downbelow."

"Speaking of," Ophelia called, striding towards them from where she'd been standing in the bow and handing Quint a brass spyglass. "I found that other sloop off to starboard. Here."

Quint raised the spyglass to his eye, scanned across the horizon until he glimpsed the *Immoveable's* white sails peeking up from above the far side of the cape that made up the eastward boundary of the harbor. It was making for the mouth of the bay, sailing at an intercept course. In a straight line, Quint couldn't help but notice.

"You did what I asked?" Quint asked Lurk, lowering the spyglass and returning it to Ophelia. Behind her, Vigo had produced his lockpick set and was busy freeing Rustbucket from his shackles.

"Aye-aye," she said, splattering Quint with salty droplets as she nodded vigorously. "Just like you showed me."

"Well done, mate," Quint said, reaching up to give Lurk an affectionate shoulder squeeze as he performed some mental calculations. Based off the *Immoveable's* current course and approximate distance, the *Marigold's* heading and how long it would take the pursuing *Unstoppable* to close the distance between them...

"It's going to work," Quint said aloud. *Barely,* he refrained from adding. "Full sail with the wind behind us, mates. Enough tacking."

He turned the wheel, angling the schooner so that her sails strained against their lines with the full force of the breeze filling them. The pirates aboard held tight against rigging and rail as the *Marigold* jerked forward with the sudden increase in speed, her prow cutting through the blue waves. A broad smile broke across Quint's face as he steered them with a steady hand towards the mouth of the bay.

Angels above, he thought. *I love sailing.*

"Qu—" Rustbucket cleared his throat, tried again. "Err. Cap'n. She's getting closer."

Quint blinked. "Pardon?"

Rustbucket shrugged and pointed stern once more, towards the pursuing *Unstoppable.* She was fully underway now, her great square sails billowing as she flew across the waves after them.

Quint tamped down a mild surge of alarm at how much distance she had closed in so short a time. He did a quick check on his mental geometry, and arrived once more at the same conclusion.

We'll be fine, he assured himself. *So long as we hold to the course.*

Ophelia peered at the *Unstoppable* through her spyglass. "Got good news and bad news for you, Cap'n."

Quint tried to keep his attention on the helm. "Give me the bad first."

"Your ladylove's aboard."

"Vanessa?" Lurk leaned forward from her place in the rigging, motioning for Ophelia to hand over the spyglass. "I liked her! Is she going to join our crew?"

"Doubtful," Quint sighed. "The good news?"

"She's trying to talk to you," Ophelia said. "Telling us to stop."

"I don't know if that qualifies as good news."

"Take it from me, mate," Ophelia said, clapping him on the shoulder. "It's when your lady *stops* wanting to talk that you need to start worrying. Now, here. Keep those lines of communication open."

She pressed the spyglass to his chest. Lurk made a keening noise of displeasure in her throat.

"I'll let you look in a minute," Quint promised her, taking the spyglass as Ophelia moved to take his place at the helm. He trusted the *Marigold* in her hands as much as he did his own, if not more. "Let's see..."

The world contracted to the tiny circle of the spyglass's scope. It took Quint a moment to orient on the *Unstoppable,* but when he did he found himself sighting directly onto Vanessa.

She stood with legs set wide apart for balance. Loosened from its customary bun, her hair blew into her face, but she hardly seemed to notice. Above her head she waved a square flag divided into quarters, two black and two yellow.

"Full stop," Quint murmured to himself, lowering the spyglass. "Not on your life, Ness."

Or on all of ours, for that matter.

"My turn?" Lurk inquired, reaching her webbed hands towards the spyglass.

"Aye," Quint said, relinquishing it. "Actually..."

An idea struck him. "Rusty?"

"Aye, Cap'n?" Rustbucket started guiltily. A glance showed Quint that his onetime crewmate had been attempting to slip away towards the *Marigold's* prow, as far from Lurk as the limited space on deck permitted.

"There's a set of semaphore flags belowdecks," Quint told him. "Portside chest, right against the bulkhead between the stairs and the main cabin. Fetch it for me."

"Aye, Cap'n," Rustbucket said, giving Quint an automatic salute. He lowered his hand and stared at it, as though the appendage had done so of its own volition.

A few minutes later, the open chest full of brightly colored flags lay open at Quint's feet. He knelt over it, rummaging through them in search of the signals most pertinent to the conversation. Lurk "stood" beside him in the schooner's stern, her humanoid torso turning in a slow circle as she peered through the spyglass at the world around them, the rest of her serpentine body coiled beneath her.

"Everything's *tiny*," she giggled. "Ahoy, tiny ships! Ahoy, tiny town! Ahoy, small fort! Ahoy, teeny-tiny Vanessa!"

"Is she still waving the black and yellow flag?" Quint asked, selecting a blue-and-white checkered one and straightening.

"Aye," Lurk said after a moment, aiming the spyglass back towards the *Unstoppable* again. "The one with the squares. And she's making a face. Like *this*."

The mermaid lowered the spyglass and scrunched her face up as much as her features permitted, narrowing her enormous eyes into slits and puckering up her overwide mouth.

"Thanks, Lurk," Quint said, raising the checkered flag above his head and waving it. "Keep watching and tell me which flag she replies with next."

Lurk nodded, putting the spyglass to her eye again. "That's the kind of face humans make when they're mad, right?"

"That, or she ate some bad oysters," Quint said.

"Well she's making it again," Lurk said, glancing aside at Quint's checkered flag. "Only bigger. What are you *telling* her?"

"I'm telling her no," Quint said. A thought struck him. "You're sure she can tell what this flag is?"

Signal flags were carefully designed with bright, contrasting colors and clear, easily discernable patterns. But all communication invited the possibility of miscommunication. Quint wouldn't like to think that he was inadvertently telling Vanessa that the *Marigold* was carrying plague, for example.

"She should," Lurk said. "There's a man with a spyglass next to her telling her what ours is, just like I am to you. Wait, she's changing flags."

There was motion aboard the *Unstoppable's* prow as Vanessa traded out the black and yellow flag for another. The distance between the two vessels had lessened enough that he could discern the colors—white and red—but not enough to tell the pattern.

"Squares, like the last one," Lurk said after a moment. "Red ones and white ones. What's that one mean?"

"Means we're running into danger," Quint said, sparing a glance over his shoulder towards port. The white sails of the *Immoveable* were growing nearer and larger, though the low-lying sweep of the headland still separated her from the bay and the pursuit occurring within its sheltering waters.

"She's getting more flags," Lurk observed. "A purple one with a white stripe down the middle...the red and white squares again...now one that's a bunch of red and yellow stripes that aren't up and down or side to side, but kind of slanted..."

"Diagonal," Quint supplied, wracking his memory. Each of the signal flags had its own individual meaning, ranging from requests for assistance to simple directions to warnings of fire or illness aboard. But each one also had a letter assigned to it, allowing a skilled signaler to string together more complex ideas. "Purple means Navy ship; the white and red squares is U and the diagonal stripes are Y. She's warning us that the *Immoveable's* going to intercept us."

"We'll see about that." Lurk made a hissing sound, the sunlight glinting off her sharklike teeth. Quint fought the urge to shudder at the mermaid's laughter.

"Lurk," he said slowly. "I told you not to drown anyone—"

"I didn't!" she said, her spinal ridge rippling in agitation. "Honest. I did exactly as you asked."

"Alright," Quint relented, kneeling to fish for another flag. "Just making sure."

He rose, holding a flag identical to the one Vanessa had first used, quartered yellow and black.

"You're telling her to stop?" Lurk asked, glancing to the side as Quint switched to a second flag, a red X on a blue field.

"Aye, unless she wants to sink," Quint said, waving it. His arms were starting to grow sore, but he could rest once they were clear of danger.

The response, when it came, was scornful.

"Ship too small," Quint translated for Lurk's benefit as the mermaid reported the sequence Vanessa waved. "Cannons too few. Captain—*okay,* Vanessa, that's just rude."

"She's still making the mad face," Lurk pointed out. "What are you saying to her now?"

"Roughly," Quint grunted as he selected another flag, "that she doesn't have the heart to open fire on me."

"I hope not," Lurk said, lowering the spyglass. "How far can those cannons shoot?"

"Far enough that she's had a few minutes to shoot, and hasn't," Quint said, judging the distance as he waved at Vanessa, calling her bluff.

"Couldn't it be," Ophelia called over her shoulder from her place at the helm, "that Commander Vanessa Delacort's just a *tad* reluctant to open fire on a ship carrying the Imperial Crown Jewels?"

"Of course not," Quint said, shaking his head as he waved a flag emblazoned with a red heart on a white field. "It's because *I'm* aboard, and Vanessa and I are—"

Thunder rumbled across the bay. A moment later it was followed by a high whirring sound, then a terrifically large splash as a cannonball plummeted into the water not ten yards from the *Marigold's* stern.

Quint stared across the narrowing gap between the two ships. Vanessa stood in the prow of the *Unstoppable*, near enough now that Quint could plainly see her smug expression through the spyglass.

"You—" Quint sputtered, hardly able to get the words out. "You...you *shot at me!*"

Vanessa could not possibly have heard him, but her checkmate smile tugged at the corners of her mouth all the same. She gestured at one of her officers standing nearby, who handed her a brass speaking trumpet. A moment later her amplified voice was carried to him from across the wind and waves.

"Cute flags, Captain Redbeard," she said. "Your signaling leaves something to be desired, though. Unless you *meant* to tell me that your cabin is on fire?"

Quint blinked, looked down at the collection of flags he'd just been waving. Surely he hadn't...

"Cap'n," Ophelia said, frowning over her shoulder at him. "Were you waving the heart flag upside-down?"

Quint didn't answer.

"What's it mean upside-down?" Lurk asked, tilting her head to one side.

"Blazes," Quint groaned. He swallowed hard and looked back across the narrowing gap between their two ships as Vanessa raised the speaking trumpet again.

"Fortunately," she said, "we can provide rescue from any shipboard fires, *Redbeard,* on the condition that you stand down and surrender yourself immediately."

"Ophelia?" Quint asked, his voice low and urgent. "How are we doing?"

"Nearly out of the bay," she replied, not taking her eyes off their heading. "But that second sloop is getting close, Quint. It's gonna be a near thing."

Quint dared a glance starboard. The *Immoveable* was indeed bearing down on them, and as best he could tell they hadn't deviated from their previous course whatsoever. They'd have to adjust if they wanted to catch the *Marigold,* which was just now cruising between the headlands and out the mouth of the bay. *Almost home free.*

"Can we make it?" he asked.

His first mate's answer was immediate and unhesitating. "Aye, Cap'n. Angels willing."

"Angels willing," he murmured, returning his gaze to Vanessa. She was peering at him over the trumpet, a frown creasing her brow. Upon seeing that Quint was looking at her she raised it to her lips and spoke once more.

"Captain Redbeard, associates, and all other souls aboard the *Marigold,*" Vanessa called. "Strike your sails, stand down, and surrender yourselves to the mercy of Her Imperial Majesty."

In answer, Quint reached into the chest of flags and pulled out a black one emblazoned with a skull and crossbones. It wasn't the *Bloody Angel's* particular iteration of the Jolly Roger, true, but it left no doubt as to Quint's intentions.

Nor were those intentions lost on Vanessa.

"Fine," she replied. Something stirred in Quint's heart at the thought that she did not sound angry, so much as tired, and perhaps even a little sad. Yet her voice was firm as it came to him from across the waters: "Prepare to be boarded."

4

"Stand by to repel borders, Qu—err, Cap'n?" Rustbucket asked, appearing at Quint's elbow and looking almost pitifully eager to help.

Doubtless it's the prospect of swinging from the gallows that's lit a fire under him to get well clear of here. Privately, Quint wondered whether "impersonating a pirate" was a crime under the laws of the Empire, and if so, whether it applied to a pirate who impersonated a *different* pirate. If not, he surmised, then some judicial clerk in Fort Amell was likely penning the first draft of such a legislative proposal at this very moment.

Not that Quint Thatch intended to be around to find out. He looked up at the *Marigold's* sails straining with the force of the wind, then over his shoulder at the *Unstoppable* bearing down upon them, closer with every passing moment. Last of all to the *Immoveable,* her sails trimmed at an angle as she steered towards the mouth of Fort Amell Bay.

"You're sure we can make it?" he called to Ophelia.

"Provided Lurk's done her job, aye," Ophelia called back. Though her knuckles were white against the spokes of the ship's wheel, she spared a moment to flash Lurk a grin nearly as toothy as the mermaid's own.

A ripple of pride shuddered down Lurk's spinal ridge. "I did do my job!"

"Aye," Quint nodded. "Now we'll see how it plays out. Rustbucket, go help Darby trim the sails."

Rustbucket hurried off without a salute. Quint returned his attention to matters nearer at hand.

The three ships formed an obtuse triangle, with the *Marigold* as its center and the pursuing sloops at either arm. The *Unstoppable* had just passed the mouth of Amell Bay, closing steadily in on the fleeing *Marigold,* while the *Immoveable* was bearing down on them from just off their starboard bow.

Quint fought down the urge to swallow nervously. He trusted Lurk and Ophelia with his life, but it was going to be a near thing.

He bent down, plucked a red flag emblazoned with a black cross and waved it towards Vanessa.

"What's that one mean?" Lurk asked.

"Impending collision," Quint grunted as he waved the flag at the *Unstoppable.* "Brace for impact."

The *Unstoppable* was close enough now for him to make out Vanessa's frown. He saw her turn her head towards the *Immoveable,* make her own mental calculations of its angle of approach. She arrived at her conclusion with trademark swiftness, and within moments was waving a flag identical to Quint's at the *Immoveable,* which was now directly off the *Marigold's* starboard side and less than fifty yards away.

The *Immoveable* did not slow.

"Ophelia?" Quint yelled, the first audible note of fear creeping into his voice.

"We'll make it," she said, her own voice icy calm.

She held their course steady as the *Immoveable* bore down on them, unswerving in its course. Now it was close enough that the voices of the men and women on deck were carried to them by the breeze, and though Quint could not make out all they said the panic in their tones spoke volumes.

For a brief, surreal moment, Quint could have stretched out a hand and grasped the long wooden spar of the *Immoveable's* bowsprit.

Then they were past it, the larger vessel cutting through *Marigold's wake.* Quint looked up and found the *Immoveable's* commander staring back down at him, his expression a portrait of shocked dismay.

Then the two Imperial sloops collided.

A roar like thunder echoed across the bay as the *Unstoppable* rammed headlong into the side of the *Immoveable.* A cacophony of groans and cracks split the air as the timbers of both ships warped, twisted, and splintered under the force of the impact. The *Immoveable* gave a shuddering lurch towards the *Marigold,* and her unfortunate commander would have fallen from his ship onto Quint's had not one of his crewmen caught him about the middle and hauled him back onto the deck.

"Hang tight!" Ophelia yelled as the wave generated by the force of the collision came roaring at the *Marigold.* Quint had barely grabbed hold of the rail before it hit them, sending his feet flying out from under him. His hand tore free of the rail, taking a few splinters with it, as the *Marigold* pitched forward upon the sudden wave. It swept beneath the schooner and past it, dipping her stern so close to the water that Quint's back was drenched in a burst of spray.

Not how I pictured this ending, he thought as his hip hit the edge of the rail. He grasped for a handhold again, found none, and pitched headfirst towards the sea.

Slender but surprisingly strong arms wrapped around him, arresting his fall. They were followed swiftly by the coils of a serpentine body wrapping protectively about his torso, securing him to the *Marigold's* stern.

"No drowning!" Lurk chided, holding tight. The rest of her tail was draped along the edge of the ship's rail, providing a much-needed support.

"No drowning," Quint agreed with a gasp. He squeezed back, resting his head on Lurk's shoulder. Peering past her he saw that Ophelia remained at the helm, while Vigo had both Rustbucket and Darby wrapped tight in his arms, bracing himself against the foremast. "Thanks, mate."

"You're my pod," Lurk said, still in that chiding tone. But Quint did not miss the pleased ripple of her spinal ridge.

"Speaking of drowning," Ophelia said, turning the wheel slightly so that they were no longer fully in the wind, "take a look at our handiwork."

Quint did, shrugging free of Lurk's embrace as he surveyed the damage. The *Unstoppable* had collided with the *Immoveable* just behind her portside mast, turning the two ships' rigging into a hopelessly tangled mess of intertwined cables and splintered yardarms. The *Immoveable* was canted at a steep angle, making the two ships' masts look to Quint like a pair of trees who had gotten badly drunk and now leaned against one another for support.

"*I* did all of that?" Lurk asked in a hushed, reverent tone. "Just by cutting a few lines?"

"That's the thing about ships," Quint said, feeling dazed. It was one thing to plan such destruction, and another entirely to look upon his handiwork. "They can't steer without their rudders."

Lurk had not been idle while Quint and the others had undertaken their daring rescue of Rustbucket. By the time they'd piled themselves into the haycart, she had cut through the tiller ropes of every Navy vessel docked in Amell Bay, rendering their rudders useless. The *Immoveable* had been the last of these, by virtue of being the only vessel on patrol, but its crew had clearly not detected the sabotage until it was too late to avert course.

"They're getting in lifeboats," Ophelia observed, pointing to where the crew of the *Immoveable* were making their way in hurried but orderly lines to the waiting jollyboats. Loath as he was to praise the Navy on any count, Quint privately allowed himself a begrudging admiration for the lack of panic the two ships' crews displayed. Even in a crisis, they were conducting themselves with a composed dignity.

He could only hope that, on the far side of the *Immoveable*, Vanessa was doing the same.

"Not all of them," Lurk said, pointing a webbed hand. "Look."

Sure enough, several sailors looked to have been thrown overboard in the collision. Some clung to bits of flotsam, while others bobbed up and down in the waves, treading water as they tried to stay afloat. If any of them went under and didn't come up...

"Lurk?" Quint asked, turning to find the mermaid staring at him with her huge dark eyes.

"Drown?" she asked hopefully.

"Still no drowning," Quint shook his head. "In fact, could you actually do the opposite of drowning them?"

Lurk made a bubbling, dissatisfied sound in her throat. "*Quint.*"

"Lurk, mate," Ophelia said, squeezing the mermaid's shoulder. "They're all part of Vanessa's pod."

The bubbling sound stopped. Across the way the first of the *Immoveable's* jollyboats had just been lowered into the water.

"Oh," Lurk said slowly, after a moment of pondering. "And Vanessa's Quint's mate."

"*Was* Quint's mate," Ophelia corrected, ruffling Quint's hair. "But aye. Now go undrown the poor purple coats, would you?"

"Fine," Lurk said, still more than a hint of a pout in her voice. "But only because I like Vanessa."

She slipped overboard and into the water with hardly a splash. Quint watched as one of the Navy sailors struggling to keep his head above water was suddenly pulled under, his startled yelp turning into a gurgle as the waves closed in over his head.

"She wouldn't drown them after we told her not to," Quint said to Ophelia. Then thought it over. "Right?"

Ophelia shrugged.

Before Quint had further cause to worry, the sailor in question came rocketing up from the water, tossed by unseen webbed hands directly into the jollyboat. Shouts of surprise and consternation from his fellows turned to exclamations of relief as they realized their comrade had been rescued from the sea's embrace.

Quint watched with growing amusement as another sailor was dragged underwater, only to be hurled unceremoniously into the jollyboat moments later. And a third, and a fourth, as Lurk fulfilled her captain's request despite her own reluctance.

"We really should let her drown someone one of these days," Ophelia commented, also watching. "She's earned it."

Quint made a noncommittal noise.

"So," Rustbucket said, coming to stand on Quint's other side. "We setting off now, or—"

"Once Lurk's done," Quint said, nodding towards the jollyboats as Lurked tossed another Navy officer aboard. "So far we've managed to pull this caper off without killing anybody, and I intend to maintain that streak."

"Beggin' your pardon, Cap'n," Rustbucket said dubiously, "but if you think saving them'll make the Empire take it any easier on us..."

"It ain't about that," Quint said, shaking his head.

Rustbucket looked perplexed. “Why, then?”

“Ah, Rusty.” Quint combed his hand through his hair. “If you have to ask, you really don’t have any place in my crew.”

Rustbucket swallowed hard, avoided his captain’s gaze. “Listen, Quint. I know that I don’t deserve rescuin’—”

“You don’t,” Ophelia agreed.

Quint silenced her with a look, then turned his attention back to Rustbucket.

“Rusty,” he said, a hint of steel creeping into his voice. “You’re out of the crew. I didn’t want it to be that way, but you *mutinied,* mate. Pointed a gun at me, like you said—and more’n that, at Vanessa. At my *ma*, Rusty.”

“I—” Rustbucket started. Quint held up a hand, forestalling him, and Rustbucket jerked away as though Quint had slapped him.

For a moment Quint was tempted to do exactly that. The memory of Rustbucket’s pistol aimed straight at his ma sent anger boiling through Quint’s veins, down his arms and into his fingers, curling them into fists. No one would object to their captain hitting Rustbucket. Hells, most would probably think it was well-deserved.

But a captain was like a father to his crew, Quint’s own pop had always said. And Clarent Thatch had never struck anyone in anger, least of all his child or his crew.

“You broke my trust,” Quint said, and on that last word his voice shook for just a moment. “Threatened people I deeply care for. More than that, you broke the crew’s trust. Ophelia’s is about as warm a welcome as you can expect from any of them.”

Quint leaned in, affecting a whisper that Ophelia could certainly still hear, standing so near. “And between you and me, mate, this is her being downright *cordial* to you. You don’t wanna hear what she’s said about you in private.”

Rustbucket glanced at Ophelia, who was toying with one of the countless knives she kept hidden on her person, and shuddered. "Why save me at all, then?"

"Like I said," Quint shrugged, "ain't a member of the *Angel's* crew swung from a rope yet, regardless of current affiliation. And I ain't the sort to stand by and let another fellow suffer, no matter who he is."

As if to underscore this point, there was a frantic yelp from one of the jollyboats as Lurk tossed another drowning sailor in.

"We're going to Solace," Quint said firmly. "And after that, Rusty, you and I will never cross paths again. Understand?"

Rustbucket nodded. "Aye, Cap'n."

"Good." Quint returned his attention to the wreckage of the two sloops. By now an entire fleet of jollyboats bobbed in the waves to their stern, many of the sailors within noticeably sodden wet. No more remained overboard, treading water or clinging to flotsam.

"Looks like Lurk's nearly done," Quint said, nudging Ophelia. "Time for us to clear out of here."

"More'n time," Ophelia agreed, returning to her place at the helm and hollering across the deck to Vigo and Darby. "Oi, mates! Haul the sails to full and make for the open sea. I want this accursed fort beneath the horizon within the hour!"

"Aye!" Darby and Vigo called in unison. Rustbucket gave Quint one last imploring look, then hurried forward to assist the others before Ophelia could offer comment.

Quint looked back towards the wreckage of the sloops, hoping for a glimpse of Vanessa, however brief.

A plume of water splashed him as Lurk came rocketing up from the waves, rising on a column of spray as her powerful tail propelled her from the surface and up the side of the *Marigold,* but this time she held something damp and wriggling in her arms.

Not something, Quint corrected himself, *someone. Oh, no—*

Lurk landed against the *Marigold's* rigging, securing herself to the lines with one arm. With the other she dropped her unwilling passenger to the deck, spraying Quint with seawater in the process.

"Err," Quint told the new arrival as she sputtered at his feet. "Welcome aboar—"

"Quentin," Vanessa said with exaggerated calm as she rose, seawater dripping from her sodden clothes. "Bloody. Thatch."

Quint took an involuntary step back, felt his back bump up against the *Marigold's* rail. Vanessa advanced, peering at him through a curtain of sodden curls as she stripped off her soaked Navy jacket, looking half-crazed. She put her hands on either one of his shoulders and stared intently up at him.

"By order of the Imperial Navy," Vanessa said unblinkingly, "you and your crew are hereby under arrest."

5

Quint's response was drowned out by a yawning groan as one of the *Immoveable's* yardarms gave way, crashing to the waves below with a thunderous splash.

"You might find that a tad difficult," he said into the silence that followed, carefully keeping his arms clasped behind his back in case Vanessa had procured a second pair of manacles since their earlier encounter. "Considering present circumstances and all."

"Why'd you bring her aboard, Lurk?" Ophelia asked, glancing up at where the mermaid hung from the rigging.

"Quint told me to undrown everyone," Lurk said, scales rippling as she shrugged. "So I put them all back on their boats."

"You put Vanessa on the wrong one," Quint protested, trying to shrug out of Vanessa's grasp. *Angels above, but she's got a strong grip.*

"Oops," Lurk's smile was wide and innocent. A little *too* innocent, in Quint's estimation. But before he could question Lurk further Vanessa was shaking him by the shoulders, calling his attention back to her.

"Listen," she said, voice low and urgent. "You're going to have to capture me."

Quint blinked. "I beg your pardon?"

"Capture me," Vanessa repeated, jerking her head to one side. "Look."

Quint glanced aft and saw the small fleet of Navy jollyboats drifting in the waves. Some had already begun to row their way towards shore, but a fair number lingered in the *Marigold's* wake, eyes affixed on the confrontation unfolding between Quint and Vanessa.

No, he silently corrected himself. *Between Captain Redbeard and Commander Delacort.*

"See?" Vanessa said. "As far as they know you just sunk two Navy vessels and ordered your pet mermaid to kidnap the commanding officer of one."

Lurk's spinal ridge twitched agitatedly. "I'm not—"

"She's not a pet," Quint protested in unison.

"I know," Vanessa said impatiently. "But *they* don't. Now please, Quint. I need you to take me prisoner and make a big show of it while you're at it. Elsewise they'll think I was in cahoots with you this whole time."

Quint saw the sense in this. He'd undertaken this caper to rescue the Crown Jewels, Rustbucket, and his own reputation—and not necessarily in that order. What he hadn't intended to do was ruin Vanessa's life.

"We could just have Lurk return you?" he said, the suggestion becoming a question as he glanced up at the mermaid.

"Like hell," Vanessa said as Lurk shook her head wearily. "I'm not just gonna abandon the Crown Jewels to you."

"Plus we're not slowing down now!" Darby called from the *Marigold's* prow. "Not if we want to make it to Solace before the Navy sends someone else after us!"

"And that wouldn't allay suspicions," Vanessa pointed out. "Bringing me aboard and then throwing me back like a fish too small for the griddle. *So take me prisoner.*"

"Right," he nodded, and raised his voice. "Now listen here, you filthy Navy bilge rat—"

"They're too far away to hear us now," Vanessa said, shaking her head. "But they can see us just fine. Now please, Quint. I'm going to try and escape, and you're going to stop me and take me prisoner. Make it abundantly clear to every soul watching that I'm not coming willingly, because I'm not going to make it easy for you. Ready?"

"Aye," Quint nodded. "But—"

Before he could express his doubts Vanessa was darting past him, diving towards the ship's rail. Quint reached out and seized her around the middle, more out of reflex than any conscious intent.

Vanessa resisted, struggling against his hold with a surprising vigor, squirming and clawing to fight her way free.

"I thought—*ow*—" Quint wheezed as Vanessa's elbow connected painfully with his ribs. "—thought we—ow, *angels above,* that hurt—"

"I don't understand," Lurk said to Ophelia, as the two of them watched this play out. "Are they pretending to fight, or not?"

"Vanessa ain't pretending," Ophelia observed, using one of her knives to clean her nails as Vanessa finally broke loose of Quint's grip. During their struggle they'd reversed positions, so that Quint was standing between Vanessa and the ship's rail. "Not sure what the Cap'n's doing, though."

Currently, the captain in question was leaning away from Vanessa's left hook, which sailed half an inch past his face. "You could have broken my nose!"

"So fight better," she said, following the hook with a cross to the stomach that nearly doubled Quint over. "This has to look realistic."

"Realistic ain't the same as murderous," Quint protested, jerking his head aside to avoid Vanessa's next strike. Out of the periphery of his vision he saw that the jollyboats were indeed growing gradually smaller with each moment, though those aboard still seemed fixated on the violence unfolding aboard the schooner.

"You really gonna let her embarrass you in front of her whole crew, Cap'n?" Vigo called, grinning as he hauled out one of the *Marigold's* yardarms, adding to the schooner's speed.

"I—" Quint's protest was cut off as he narrowly avoided Vanessa's uppercut. "Alright, that's *enough*."

He grabbed her wrist before she could retract it for another strike, using his slight advantage in height to move around her and cross his forearm across her collarbone, still gripping her wrist and pressing her back against his chest. Vanessa retaliated with another elbow to his side, but Quint wrapped his other arm around her waist and wrapped his fingers about her upper arm, restraining her fully.

For a moment they just stood there, straining against one another. Vanessa was as competent a fighter as any Quint had met, but he had a good grip and superior leverage, keeping her from wriggling free.

"We done yet?" he murmured in her ear.

"Think so," Vanessa replied back, her voice low and breathy. Quint was suddenly aware of her back pressed against his chest, both of them breathing heavily. Of her damp, sea-smelling hair in his face, his hands on her wrist, her arm...

From behind them, Ophelia let out a low wolf whistle. "Good fight."

"Alright," Vanessa said, still breathing hard. "That'll do."

Her shoulders stiffened, and though Quint could not see her eyes he knew she must be looking out at the little fleet of jollyboats, the sailors aboard them now distant enough to look no bigger than dolls. "Now make it abundantly clear that you're going to take me belowdecks to some unspeakable fate."

"I would never—"

"*Quint.*"

"Right." He nodded, then spun her around so that they were facing one another. Water droplets sprayed from Vanessa's mane of hair as he caught her by the wrists and pulled her close, almost as close as they had once held each other in happier days. Vanessa gasped, her mouth forming a perfect circle.

Then Quint bent, grabbed her around the middle, and hoisted her over his shoulder. Vanessa's gasp turned into a startled "*WHAT*" as he stood, turning to face the onlooking jollyboats and their Navy crewmen.

"I'm taking this scurvy Navy wench prisoner!" he called, hoping that they'd be able to discern the intent of his taunting, even if he was too far away for them to catch the actual words. "And any of you that follow'll get the cat-o-nine tails, y'hear?"

"*Wench*?" Vanessa's muffled voice came from behind him, sounding equal parts bemused and indignant. Further back Lurk was asking Ophelia how many tails cats usually had.

"I'm bad at improvising," Quint said. His shrug elicited a squeak of protest from her, hanging from his shoulder as she was. Her sodden clothes were soaking through his shirt. "Now let's get you changed into something dry, wench."

⚓

"Cute ship," Vanessa commented as they descended belowdecks, glancing about at the narrow corridor adjoining the *Marigold's* four crew cabins. "Suppose the *Angel* would have been too conspicuous for your little stunt today?"

"Perspicacious as always," Ophelia said, causing both Quint and Vanessa's heads to turn.

"What?" the blonde first mate said in answer to their stares, a touch defensively. "I read books. Means insightful."

"I know what it means," the other two answered in unison.

"Where'd you get it, then?" Vanessa asked, touching a hand to the wooden bulkhead.

Quint gave her a look. "Is that a question you really want to know the answer to?"

"Hm." Vanessa shook her head; her hair still damp but no longer dripping. "Suppose not—"

"We stole it!" Ophelia said cheerily. "Belonged to a nice Trechtish couple, I think. Nicked it off them in Respite while her crew was ashore for resupply."

"I'm sure they were pleased to come back and find their ship vanished," Vanessa said, glancing at Quint. "You starting a fleet, then? Going to need a larger pair of boots, Admiral Redbeard?"

"Nah," Quint said, giving her an easy grin as they came to a halt in front of his cabin door. "My ambitions remain modest as ever, you'll be glad to hear. The *Angel's* going to meet us in Port Solace. Respite's less than half a day's sail from there, so it'll end up in the original owners' hands once word gets 'round that the *Marigold's* docked there."

"Uh-huh. And what does this nice Trechtish couple get out of their vessel's temporary theft and use in a criminal enterprise?"

"A very nice thank-you letter." Realizing how inadequate that sounded when said aloud, Quint hurriedly added: "Plus a sack full of doubloons for their trouble."

"Say what now?" Ophelia asked.

"It'll come out of my share," Quint reassured her as he opened the cabin door and stepped inside. Vanessa followed him in.

"It better," Ophelia said. She looked at Vanessa, then at her captain, then back to Vanessa. "I'll run and get you some dry clothes, Vanessa. Welcome aboard."

She turned and shut the door behind her, the sound of her footfalls retreating down the corridor, leaving Quint and Vanessa suddenly and unexpectedly alone together.

Silence stretched between them, neither certain of what to say next. Quint was suddenly aware once more of her sheer *nearness,* somehow more intimate standing close to her in this dim and confined space than it had been when they were pressed against each other above. Down here there was no escaping the smell of her, the faint lingering aromas of jasmine and coconut not even the sea could wash away.

Vanessa was the first to break the silence.

"How does it always happen like this?" she asked, glancing around at the captain's cabin. It was more modest than Quint's cabin aboard the *Bloody Angel*, but the Trechtish tapestries hanging from the wall and the woven rug gave it a homey atmosphere. "Us ending up in your bedroom, I mean."

Quint barked out a laugh. "I guess whichever angels are watching over us appreciate symmetry."

"Wonder if they appreciate more than that," Vanessa said, and though her tone was deliberately casual something about the way she said it propelled Quint's heart into his throat.

He raised his hand, reaching for her face, to tuck a damp strand of curls behind her ear. The ship lurched beneath them as the *Marigold* hit a choppy patch of sea, and suddenly he was stumbling forward instead, hand still outstretched towards her.

"*Ow,*" Vanessa hissed as he bumped against her forearm, jerking her hand away as if he were a hot stove she'd just touched. Quint looked down to see a line of red against the white cloth of her sodden shirt-sleeve.

"You're bleeding," he said dumbly.

"Only a little," Vanessa said, thrusting her arm behind her. "It's mostly stopped by now."

"Mostly—" Quint shook his head. "May I see?"

Vanessa chewed her lip, then gave a short nod and thrust her hand towards him. She held her wrist slightly limp, like a queen proffering her rings for kissing.

Ringless though her fingers were, Quint had to fight the urge to kiss them regardless as he gently rolled up her sleeve. Vanessa bit back a gasp of pain as he peeled the sodden garment away from her skin, revealing a long but shallow cut that ran nearly from wrist to elbow.

"Oh, Ness," he murmured, guilt twisting his gut. She had been lying about the bleeding having mostly stopped. "Was this...did I...?"

"Not during the fight," she said, shaking her head. "Probably when I went overboard. Only noticed it when you got me in that hold."

"I'm sorry," Quint said, still peering at the cut. It was shallow enough not to require stitching, but it was still bleeding quite a bit. "Let me play doctor?"

Vanessa snorted and sat heavily on the bed. "If you insist."

After a brief rummage through the cabin's medicine chest, Quint returned with a strip of bandages and a bottle of amber liquid. The bed creaked as he sat beside her and uncapped the bottle, filling the cabin with the sharp sting of alcohol.

"Rum?" Vanessa asked, quirking an eyebrow. "How stereotypical."

"Tequila, actually," Quint said, turning the bottle so that the label faced her. "The aged variety, straight from Gypsum."

"Decent stuff," Vanessa said, proffering her arm. "Seems a shame to use it for disinfectant."

"Nothing but the best for you," Quint said, offering a wan smile. "If it makes you feel any better, we'll have a drink afterwards."

"I'll hold you to it," Vanessa said. "Now hurry up before this arm starts to rot."

Quint obliged, carefully pouring a thin stream of alcohol into the cut. Vanessa let out a sharp exhale through her nose, but other than a muscle twitching in her throat remained perfectly still as he set the bottle on the bedside table and began bandaging her arm.

"You'll be repaying the *Marigold's* owners for the tequila, then?" she asked, filling the silence. "The aged kind isn't the cheap stuff, you know."

"I'll leave them a *large* sack full of doubloons," Quint promised. Vanessa let out a short laugh.

"Speaking of doubloons," she said. "You have to know that there's going to be an even bigger manhunt to get the Crown Jewels back than there was last time, aye? Every Navy ship and privateer in the Archipelago is going to be looking for Captain Redbeard. Especially now that you've kidnapped a Navy officer."

"Think they'll still be more put out about the Jewels than you," Quint pointed out. "No offense. Besides, the kidnapping was your idea. Mostly."

An idea was forming, one he hardly dared voice. "Unless..."

"Unless what?"

"Unless it's not a kidnapping," Quint said, "but a defection."

"A defection," Vanessa repeated, looking up at him nonplussed. He stared at her intently, until realization dawned across her face. "Quint, you don't mean—"

"You could join us," Quint said, all in a rush. "Sail with us aboard the *Angel*. Be a part of the crew, be my—"

"Be a pirate," Vanessa said quietly. Whether the good sort of quiet or the other kind, he couldn't tell.

"Would that be so bad?" Quint asked, concentrating on tying off the bandage instead of meeting her eyes. "Sailing wherever your fancy takes you, your crew all folk you care for instead of whoever some Admiral muckity-muck assigns you? Able to do as you please, eat and drink as you please, love—"

"Quint." She pressed a finger to his lips, and for a moment he could taste the sea on her. That more than anything was what silenced him.

"It's a nice dream." Vanessa gave him a sad smile. "But that's all it is. I've got my path and you've got yours, and wishing otherwise won't make it so."

If wishes were fishes, Quint thought, recalling his father's favorite song. "I...suppose not."

Another silence stretched between them. Quint reached for the bottle of tequila and offered it to her. Vanessa accepted, throwing it back without hesitation.

"Quint?"

"Yes?" he asked, his mouth strangely dry.

"I'm..." Vanessa looked at him, then down at the bottle in her hand. "I'm glad you're growing your beard out again. It suits you."

"Thanks," Quint laughed, rubbing at the coarse, coppery hairs on his chin. "Ness?"

She swallowed another mouthful of tequila. "Mm?"

"I'm sorry." Quint did not look at her as he spoke the words, but he still meant them. "For ruining your big day."

Her laugh was not as bitter as it might have been. "Trust me, Quint, my commendation was an afterthought."

"How do you mean?" he asked, frowning.

"I mean that the Navy was so enthused about my recovery of the Crown Jewels and apprehension of 'Captain Redbeard' that they decided to go all-in on making an event of it." She grimaced. "I was stuck in Fort Amell for months while the call went out for all those captains, commodores, and admirals to assemble for the ceremony. You have no idea how many meetings I had to sit through listening to my superiors bicker about cutlery arrangements and which of their great-grandnieces-in-law deserved an invitation to the celebratory ball afterwards."

"You can always count on the Empire to find the most wasteful way to spend your taxes," Quint said, and was gratified when Vanessa did not object.

"I'll admit, this wasn't how I pictured finally getting out of Fort Amell," she said, glancing around at the snug confines of the modest cabin. "But honestly, it's nice being back at sea. Even aboard a pirate ship."

"I might have rescued you sooner," Quint said, rubbing at his beard, "only I had to let this grow back in. Nobody would believe I was the *real* Captain Redbeard if I was still baby-faced."

Vanessa raised an eyebrow. "It's been months, and that's all you've got to show for it?"

"I've been trimming it," Quint said, a little more defensively than he'd intended to. "And it takes longer to grow than you'd think. Besides, we didn't get word about your big shindig until a few weeks back."

Vanessa smirked. "You certainly added some spice to what was otherwise going to be a very dull affair, truth be told."

Now it was his turn to laugh. "Still. I did kind of steal your thunder."

"You did at that."

"You won't be in too much trouble?"

Vanessa shook her head and handed him the bottle. "Not after our little performance up top. Hells, if anything they might commend me for taking decisive action."

"Well," Quint said, sipping at the tequila. It was somehow at once spicier and sweeter than the rum he was more accustomed to. "If they give you a medal for it, I promise not to ruin the ceremony this time."

"Mm." Vanessa turned to him, leaned in ever so slightly. Her eyes fell upon the queen chess piece tattooed on his forearm. Quint shivered as she delicately traced its outline with one finger, the sensation pleasantly ticklish.

"If they do, I'll be looking for you in the audience anyway. Just in case."

"And I'll keep a cabin ready for you aboard the *Angel*," he said. "Just in case."

Vanessa's response was interrupted by a knock at the door. Before either of them could answer it flew open, revealing an expectant Ophelia holding an armful of clothes against her chest.

"Oh," she said, surveying Quint and Vanessa with an expression of undisguised disappointment. "I figured you two would be naked by now."

6

Quint launched himself from the bed as if it had suddenly caught fire, the burning in his cheeks indicating they'd turned as red as his hair. "We weren't—I mean—"

"Ophelia." Vanessa frowned up at the tattooed pirate from the bed. "Is that why you took your time getting me fresh clothes?"

"Would've taken longer if I could," Ophelia said, shrugging. "Only I came back here and the only noises through the door were you two *talking*. Was expecting—"

"We know what you were expecting," Quint said, his flush deepening.

"Right," Ophelia nodded, looking between them. "So why isn't the boat a-rocking any more than usual, then?"

"Thanks for the clothes, Ophelia," Vanessa said, rising from the bed and taking the proffered bundle from Ophelia. "Do you mind?"

"'Course not," Ophelia said, turning and starting to shut the door behind her. Vanessa gave Quint a pointed look, and he hurried out after his first mate.

⚓

"You're a bleeding idiot, Cap'n." Ophelia said once they were in the corridor.

"Thanks," Quint said. "How do you figure?"

"Snug cabin, comfy bed, open bottle of quality tequila, Vanessa's big brown eyes." Ophelia gestured at him. "Yet here you are, on the wrong side of that door, fully dressed."

"She's not particularly pleased with me right now," Quint protested, but it sounded weak even to his ears.

"Mm." Ophelia chewed her lip, then turned to Quint as they came to a halt outside her own cabin door. "Permission to speak my mind, Cap'n?"

Quint raised an eyebrow. "Has my saying no ever stopped you?"

"Nope." Ophelia ran a hand through her blonde stripe of hair. "Couldn't help overhearing the tail end of your talk. Did you really mean what you said to her? About reserving a cabin aboard the *Bloody Angel* if she ever decides to turn coat?"

"She won't," Quint said, shaking his head. "I already tried, but she wasn't—"

"Quint," Ophelia said, her voice gone dangerously quiet. "Did you *mean* it?"

Startled, Quint met her eyes, and found anger and hurt in her gaze.

"What if I did?" he asked, regretting how defensive the words sounded even as they left his mouth.

"Then," Ophelia said, the crease between her brows indicating she was choosing her words carefully, "I'd have to ask whether you ever intend on consulting the rest of the crew before you hire on someone new."

"Consult—" Quint shook his head, bewildered by the shift in conversation. "What, like put it to a vote?"

"Maybe." Ophelia folded her arms across her chest, leaned against her cabin door. "You've gotten into a habit of bringing on new crew, without consulting those of us who've been with you long enough that we should have some say."

"Like who?" Quint asked reflexively, but Ophelia had anticipated the question.

"Lurk, most recently," she said, counting off on her fingers. "Before that it was Chuck and Lex, and before them Rustbucket. And now you're doing the same thing with Vanessa. Offering a place to her aboard the *Angel* without giving anyone else aboard a chance to voice their objections."

"Objections," Quint repeated. "But you and Vanessa are *friends*—"

"*I* don't have a problem with her signing on," Ophelia said, which only mystified Quint further.

"Then why are we even having this conversation?"

"Because." Ophelia drummed her fingers on the hilt of one of her favorite knives. "It shouldn't be solely your call who joins up. You may be captain, but the rest of the crew deserves a say in who they share the galley with, who they bunk with. Who they'll have to trust when their backs are up against a wall. Elsewise we end up with another Rusty situation on our hands."

Quint grimaced. "I suppose I'm not always the best judge of character."

"You're right about folk more often than you're not," Ophelia said, reaching out and tousling his hair. "And the lapses are only because you're so quick to see the best in people that it sometimes leaves you blind to their faults."

"Guilty as charged," Quint admitted, then frowned as a thought struck him. "If we *were* to put it to the crew...there's more'n a few who wouldn't be so quick to warm to the thought of a Navy commander signing on."

"Like as not," Ophelia agreed. "But they should at least be able to tell you as much themselves, instead of being informed by their captain that his lover's going to be joining us."

"Former lover," Quint corrected, eliciting a raised brow. He scratched his beard, thinking it over. "Can I ask where this is coming from?"

"Depends on whether I've still got your permission to speak my mind, Cap'n."

"I don't recall retracting it," Quint said, spreading his arms as wide as the narrow corridor allowed. "Lay it on me."

Ophelia brushed her hair from her eyes. "You collect people."

Quint blinked. "I what people?"

"Collect them." She tugged at her open collar, revealing the pair of soaring frigatebirds inked above her heart. Quint had the same tattoo, in the same place. "I was the first, I s'pose, or at least the first since you left home. But I've watched it happen to other folk since, again and again."

"Watched *what* happen?" Quint asked, thoroughly bewildered.

"Watched folk attach themselves to you," Ophelia said, a hint of exasperation creeping into her voice. "You draw them in without even meaning to. Outcasts, renegades, oddities—once they find you they cling to you like a remora to a manta."

"And that's a problem?" Quint asked, raising his palms placatingly to show he was genuinely asking.

"It is when the community you build ends up centered entirely around yourself," Ophelia said. "Angels' sake, when was the last time someone other than yourself brought a new crewmember aboard? And *don't* say Rustbucket's cousins."

"They weren't crew," Quint objected. Ophelia narrowed her eyes. "But I see your point."

"Good." Ophelia let out a long exhale. "Look, it's just...lonely, when every single person you know is closer to your best friend than they are to you."

Guilt pulled at Quint's heart. "I...I didn't know you felt that way."

"I don't always," Ophelia said, shrugging. "And I care just as much for our little crew of rogues as you do, mate. But if anything ever happened to you, I don't know that they'd stick around for me the way they do for you."

Quint had no answer for that, and they lapsed into a contemplative silence.

"There someone you have in mind?" Quint asked after a while. Ophelia looked at him. "Someone you might want to bring into the crew, provided the rest of us get to vote on them?"

She laughed and combed a hand through her hair. "I honestly hadn't given it serious thought."

"Might be nice to have someone to snuggle up to in your bunk," Quint suggested, wiggling his eyebrows at her.

"Please," Ophelia snorted. "If I wanted to bring every lass I've shacked up with into the crew, I'd be able to man a ship of my own. Or woman it, as it were."

Quint chuckled. "I'm serious, though. I mean, if Vanessa were ever to change her view on the subject..."

"*And* if the crew agreed to take her on," Ophelia reminded him. "You might be needing a double miracle there, mate."

"Aye," Quint agreed. "Might as well make it three, then. Beseech the angels that Ophelia Price settle down with a nice girl.'

"If the best compliment you can pay a woman is that she's 'nice,' then I want no part of her," Ophelia snorted. "Give me one who's smart, adventurous, daring. Someone *fun.*"

"You do have a type," Quint remarked. He glanced over his shoulder at Vanessa's cabin door, still shut. "I suppose we both do."

"We do at that," Ophelia said ruefully. "Unfortunately, Estelle's no more interested in turning pirate than her sister is."

"You never know," Quint said, rubbing his beard. "Folk can change their views. On things and people both."

"Like pirates," Ophelia agreed. "And piracy."

"Precisely, mate," Quint said, clapping a hand on Ophelia's shoulder. "Maybe when all this is over and the Jewels are safely fenced, we take a voyage to Tourmaline? Even if Estelle's not there, her dads can point us in the right direction."

Ophelia's cheeks colored. "I don't...you think the rest of the crew would go for that?"

"Tell you what," Quint said, and squeezed her shoulder. "We'll put it to a vote."

"I'll hold you to it, Cap'n," Ophelia winked, putting both hands on his shoulders. "Now, why don't you go back in there and see what your lady love thinks of the idea of a visit home?"

Quint blinked. "What, right now?"

"No time like the present," Ophelia said, turning him around. "I'll even make sure the rest of the crew stays busy up top so that you two have plenty of time to, ah, *discuss.*"

Giving him a gentle shove, she turned and trotted up the stairs to the deck, leaving Quint to stare at the closed door of his cabin, wondering whether or not he should knock.

Go in and tell her, a part of him urged in a voice that sounded not unlike Ophelia's. *Let her know how you feel, while there's still time.*

Quint took a deep breath and raised his fist, still staring at the door. He had faced cannon fire and battled storms, yet somehow it felt that his heart had never beaten so fast as it did now.

He pressed his knuckles against the door so lightly that they made no sound. His heart ached to knock, to see her face on the other side and confess his feelings for her. To ask her if she felt the same, if she wanted to build a future together.

Only what if she said no?

He looked at his hand, then at the door. Somehow the thought of a future without Vanessa in it frightened him far worse than any mortal peril ever had, or could.

Quint lowered his fist, and turned away from the door.

7

—•—

After a dinner of steamed mussels, Quint drew the first watch of the evening.

The sun was just sinking below the horizon at his back as he manned the helm, the darkening sky before him streaked with orange and violet clouds. Soon purple dusk faded to black night, though the full moon hung low in the sky, its fractured reflection upon the waves casting the world in pale silver light broken only by the occasional dark patch of a distant island. Here in the southeastern latitudes of the Archipelago the isles lay clustered close to one another.

He was alone on deck, save for Lurk. The mermaid lay with her serpentine tail wrapped about the mainmast, her head resting atop her coils as she gently snored, wearied by the day's exertions. Vigo and Darby had retired early, since they had to rise before the sun for the morning watch, while Ophelia, Vanessa, and Rustbucket had taken to their own cabins.

Ophelia's words and Vanessa's kept chasing each other through Quint's head, weighing his longing for some kind of future with his onetime lover against the likelihood of her ever abandoning the Navy. As the *Marigold* sailed through calm seas beneath a moonlit sky, he indulged in idle fantasies of Vanessa trading her purple Navy jacket for a black flag. Of the two of them living the buccaneer's life, ranging far and free across the Eight Seas. Together.

It was a pleasant way to while away the lonely watch. But like all such dreams, Quint knew his fantasies would fade in the morning, leaving him only with the wish that things could be other than they were.

"If wishes were fishes," Quint half-murmured, half-sung beneath his breath. "Hey-ho, ho-hey..."

"*We'd all swim in riches!*" A voice squawked from overhead. Quint looked up to see a green parrot fluttering down from the yardarms to land on his shoulder. "*All live-long day!*"

"Ahoy, girl," Quint said, tickling Jimmy under her chin. The parrot made a soft cooing sound of satisfaction, leaning into his fingers. "What d'you reckon? You think Vanessa's likely to come around?"

Jimmy turned her head, looking behind him. "*Coming around! Hard to port!*"

"Yeah," Quint nodded, glad that *somebody* was finally agreeing with him. "I think she might, at that—ow!"

This outburst was on account of Jimmy having nipped hard at his ear, her beak tugging painfully at his earlobe. Quint cursed and tried to shrug her off, but his parrot only clung to him more stubbornly, tugging at him again.

"*Hard t'port!*" she crowed again through a mouthful of earlobe.

This time Quint obeyed, turning to his left and looking out across the *Marigold's* portside stern.

A ship cruised silently through the darkened waters, her four sails billowing in the nighttime wind. Though she was still several miles off, Quint could tell even from this distance that she was considerably larger than the little *Marigold*.

And worse, she was making directly for them.

"The Navy?" he said aloud, astonished.

They were less than a day's sail from Fort Amell; surely Lurk's sabotage of the frigates stationed there could not have been repaired so quickly. Perhaps, Quint tried to convince himself over the rising pulse of his heart, this was merely a merchantman charting the same route to Solace. Or if it *was* a Navy ship, maybe they were simply going to pass the *Marigold* by on their way to the important business of overtaxing the Empire's citizenry.

"Right," Quint muttered to himself. "And maybe it's crewed by a flight of angels coming to offer me a sainthood for all my virtuous deeds."

"*Sinners and saints,*" Jimmy crooned softly, peering up at her captain as if to tell him she knew exactly where he fell upon that moral spectrum.

"Quiet, you," Quint told her, but the rest of the rejoinder died upon his lips as the cloud obscuring the moon was blown aside by a sudden rising wind that set the *Marigold's* rigging to rattling. The world was once more bathed in a soft silver glow, the other ship's sails turning ghostly white as the flag above them fluttered in the breeze.

This flag was not the Navy's white eagle upon its purple field. This flag was a field of black, darker than the starry sky.

"Pirates," Quint breathed, and for the first time in his life the word sent a thrill of fear through him.

The flag flapped in the breeze, revealing the emblem blazoned upon it in full. Set against the black field was a grinning white skull, its brow adorned by an eight-pointed crown.

Quint knew that flag.

"Harps and bells," he swore, turning back around so swiftly that Jimmy went fluttering from his shoulder with a protesting squawk. "The Pirate Queen herself."

Jimmy landed on the portside rail, gazing out at the approaching vessel and then turning back to Quint. "*Sea hag?*" she inquired.

"That's the one," Quint said grimly, his hands tightening around the spokes of the helm as if he could urge the *Marigold* to greater speed through will alone. "But don't say it in her hearing, or she's like to roast you like a chicken."

"*Chicken*!" Jimmy repeated, shuffling from side to side. "*Cluck-cluck. Cap'n, chicken!*"

"In this case I certainly am," Quint said, looking over his shoulder. The other vessel was drawing steadily nearer, its four sails driving it across the waves with considerably greater speed than the *Marigold's* two.

"Jimmy," he said, fixing his attention on the parrot. "I need you to rouse the crew. All hands on deck."

"*All hands on deck!*" Jimmy repeated, standing as tall as her little body allowed, then launched herself from the rail before disappearing down the hatch leading belowdecks. "*All hands on deck! Stand by to repel borders!*"

"Hopefully it won't come to that," Quint muttered to himself, looking about at the horizon, unbroken save for the ever-growing shape of the other ship. "Naught but empty ocean...*ah.*"

There, to the southeast, off their starboard bow: a black lump rising against the stars, scarcely larger than the shadow of the other vessel. If the *Marigold* could make it there in time they might be able to lose Margherita's ship around the island's far side. It was a slim chance, but in Quint's line of work, you played the hand you were dealt.

The wheel flew beneath his hands as Quint turned the *Marigold* to starboard, adjusting course for the unknown island. By now he could hear the faint stirrings of the rest of the crew belowdecks, their muffled voices drifting up through the hatch.

Ophelia was the first one to reach the deck, her blonde swoop of hair hanging limply in her face, her eyes wide and alert despite the lateness of the hour. Her shirt was only tucked in halfway, but she had already donned the bandolier in which she stored the most obvious of her many knives.

"We under attack, Cap'n?" she asked as she laced up her britches. "Navy found us already?"

"Not yet," Quint said, gesturing towards the other ship. "And it ain't the Navy."

Ophelia's gaze found on the black flag. Her eyes widened. "Aw, shit. Rita."

"Old Marge," Quint agreed, wrinkling his nose at Ophelia's slightly more affectionate nickname for the pirate queen. "She can't know it's us, though. Can she?"

"Who knows it's us?" Lurk asked, startling Quint as she slithered soundlessly onto the aftcastle, looking out at the other ship. "Is that another pirate?"

"Sure is," Vanessa answered, joining them. She glanced at Quint. "Margherita Elena Rossini, self-proclaimed Pirate Queen of the Eight Seas."

"Pirates have queens?" Lurk asked, leaning towards the other ship with interest.

"Only the one," Vanessa said, patting the butt of a flintlock pistol thrust through her belt. Quint made a mental note to keep a tighter watch on the ship's weapon locker, provided they escape their current scrape. "And she's none too fond of anyone aboard this ship."

"Speak for yourself," Ophelia said, but the tight set of her jaw gave the lie to her flippant tone. She glanced at Quint. "Orders, Cap'n?"

By now the whole crew was on deck, Vigo and Darby already assuming their stations, listening for their captain's orders. Rustbucket hesitated between the aftcastle and the mainmast, clearly listening in on the conversation above.

"Full sail!" Quint called, raising his voice so that it carried across the deck. "Haul out the sails and set a course for that isle off the bow. With any luck we can make it to her far side afore—"

Fire flashed aboard the pirate queen's ship. Thunder rolled through the night, followed a moment later by a high whirring sound drawing swiftly nearer.

"DOWN!" Vigo roared, barreling over to Darby and throwing him to the deck. Quint reached out and wrapped his arm around Lurk's shoulder, pulling her down with him as he sank to the wooden boards below.

A splash broke the still night, startlingly close at hand. Quint felt droplets prick the back of his neck as he rose, helping Lurk up.

"Arm the cannons!" Ophelia yelled. But the *Marigold* had only four, all mounted upon the bow, useless against a pursuing enemy.

"Fire at will!" Jimmy agreed, fluttering up from belowdecks. *"All hands on deck, fire at will!"*

"BELAY THAT!" Quint bellowed, drawing the attention of every eye aboard the *Marigold.* He took a deep breath and continued at a more even tone. "That was a warning shot. We'll only get the one."

If they were within range of Margherita's cannons, then the chase was over before it could begin. Which meant they had only one chance at escape.

"We're going to attempt a parley," Quint said, his clear captain's voice holding his crew's attention. "Vigo, Darby, Rusty. Strike the sails. If we keep running she's going to put a hole in us."

"Aye, Cap'n," Darby saluted, then hurried away to pull on one of the ropes. Quint hauled on the helm, adjusting course so that they would no longer be sailing directly for the island. It was the clearest way of signaling to Margherita that they were no longer attempting to flee.

"We're not going to fight them?" Lurk asked, tail lashing across the deck. She sounded disappointed.

"Definitely not," Quint said, then realized who he was talking to. "But I have a task for you, Lurk."

Her dorsal ridge stood straight on end, quivering with anticipation. "Aye, Quint?"

"Get clear." He pointed towards the dark spot of land, which now lay directly to starboard, perhaps a league off. "Swim to that island and rest there for the night. When morning comes—"

"Wait." Lurk's ridge flattened against her head, her huge eyes reflecting the moonlight. "You mean...leave?"

"I..." Quint swallowed down what he'd been about to say. Lurk had already been separated from her family once. Now that she had found a second in the form of the *Bloody Angel*'s crew, what would it cost her to be forced away from them once more?

"Lurk," Vanessa said, coming to stand beside Quint. "He's not telling you to leave. He's just got a mission for you to carry out."

"A mission?" Lurk's ridge rippled, though she still sounded doubtful.

"Aye," Quint nodded, realizing that he *did* have an ulterior reason for sending her away to safety. "The *Bloody Angel* and the rest o' the crew were set to rendezvous with us at Solace in two days. Once they get there and realize we're nowhere to be found, they're going to start looking for us."

He pointed starboard, towards the unknown island. "And you'll be here waiting for them to come this way. It's right on the path between Solace and Amell, so they'll pass by before you know it. Once they do you can tell them how we got captured."

Lurk's gaze drifted over Quint's shoulder. He fought down the urge to look back at Margherita's approaching vessel, which was now close enough that he could hear the indistinct shouts of her crew echoing across the water. "They're going to *capture* us?"

"All of us except you," Quint said, fighting down his rising impatience. He reached down and took Lurk's webbed hands in his own, her scales smooth and slick beneath his fingers. "Please, mate. I need you to do this. We'll be alright."

Lurk's eyes were as big as the moon and black as the night. "You promise?"

Culturally, mermaids placed tremendous weight upon the value of promises. One's given word was held as a sacrosanct, inviolate thing, to be kept no matter the cost. And while Lurk was an exceptional member of her species in many ways, in this regard she was no different than any other mermaid.

Quint squeezed her hands. "I promise. Now go, while there's still time."

Lurk's spinal ridge remained flattened against her skull, but she squeezed back. Then, moving with serpentine speed, she turned and slithered over the starboard rail and disappeared.

Quint turned back, just in time to see the other pirate ship bearing down upon the *Marigold.* She loomed over them, so huge and so close and coming on so fast that a spike of fear lodged itself in his heart at the thought that she would plow right through them, reducing the *Marigold* to kindling.

Then the pirate queen's vessel turned sharply, her size belying her agility as she veered away from the collision at the last moment, pulling up alongside the *Marigold.* So little distance separated the two ships that Quint could practically reach out and touch the other's hull.

"Evenin', lads and lasses," a voice called down from the deck above.

Quint craned his head upwards, as did the rest of his crew. He found himself staring into a pair of huge, empty black eyes that swiftly revealed themselves to be the barrels of two pistols, aimed directly at his face.

"Captain Redbeard," the woman holding them said, and smiled. "You stole my ship."

8

"Don't tell me you're still sore about that," Quint said, the twin barrels of Margherita's flintlocks glaring down at him with blind hostility. "It wasn't so much theft as a joyride, and that was *years*—"

"Not that time," the pirate queen said, the jaunty white feather sticking out of her hat quivering as she shook her head. "More recently."

Quint opened his mouth, then closed it. "The...oh, harps and bells. Not the *Marigold*?"

"You didn't know?" Margherita cocked her head to one side, an amused smile tugging at her lips, which were already creased with laugh lines. She was a handsome woman in her late middle age, but her wavy hair was still raven-dark save for the shock of white running through it.

"It was supposed to belong to a nice Trechtish couple," Quint protested weakly, glancing at Ophelia. "Right?"

"Yeah," Ophelia said slowly. There were two high spots of color on her cheeks as she looked up at Margherita.

"Ja!" A second head peered over the rail of Margherita's ship; a round-cheeked and ruddy-faced woman whose blonde hair was pulled back into looping braids. She gave them a cheerful wave, though the cruelly-curved hook that capped her forearm somewhat undercut the friendliness of the gesture.

"Ja," she said again in an unmistakably Trechtish accent. "The *Marigold* is technically the property of myself and mine husband, but Captain Margherita is her true captain."

"Right," Quint groaned. "Pirate Queen, a hundred ships to her name, all of that."

"Don't forget the 'lover in every port' bit," Margherita added. Her guns remained trained on Quint, but her gaze darted to his first mate. "Evening, Ophelia. I see stealing my knife wasn't enough for you. You had to upgrade to my schooner?"

"It's a nice knife," Ophelia said defensively. She patted one of the sheathes protruding from the bandolier slung across her chest, the handle protruding from it inlaid with emeralds. "Nice little ship, too, for that matter."

"Both of which you'll be returning to me shortly," Margherita said, unamused. "No one steals from the pirate queen with impunity."

"Look," Quint said, raising his palms—something he supposed he should have done upon the appearance of those two pistols staring down at him. "Don't suppose we can chalk this up to a misunderstanding? Your ship's in as good a shape as it was when we nicked her, minus a few mouthfuls of tequila."

By now other pirates of Margherita's crew had appeared along the rail, leaning over it to peer down at the smaller vessel and its crew, more of them aiming weapons at the *Marigold* than not. Quint's last pronouncement elicited a chorus of stifled gasps and muffled groans from among them.

"You drank the boss's tequila?" asked one big fellow so heavily armed with flintlocks, cutlasses, and knives that his silhouette against the starry sky looked like that of a porcupine preparing for war. "Angels have mercy on your soul, son."

"We were going to pay you back!" Vanessa protested, one hand drifting towards her hip.

"None of that," Margherita chided, turning one of her guns on Vanessa. Vanessa's hand froze, inches away from the pistol in her belt. "Hands where I can see them."

Vanessa complied, raising her palms. Margherita cocked her head to one side, peering more intently at her.

"Déjà vu," she said after a moment, half to herself. "I've pointed a gun at you before, haven't I? Commander...Delacort, was it?"

"I suppose I should be flattered you remember me," Vanessa said through gritted teeth.

"You left a strong impression," Margherita acknowledged, glancing between Vanessa and Quint, her guns aimed steadily at them both. "Surprised you two managed to patch things up after that trouble back on Tourmaline. Redbeard here convince you to trade in the purple coat for the black flag after all, then?"

"Hardly," Vanessa shook her head, a denial which stung more than Quint had expected it to. "He's taken me prisoner, if you must know."

"I'm surprised he managed it," Margherita said, her brow arching. "Spirited thing like you."

"Look," Quint said, ignoring the jibe and giving Margherita his most ingratiating smile. "We just needed to borrow a ship that wasn't the *Angel* for a few days. We were even planning on making sure it found its way back to the owners, eventually. No harm's been done, so why don't we go laugh it off over a bottle of—"

"Tequila," Margherita said, all trace of amusement gone from her voice. "The very fine, very expensive tequila that was about the best thing I got out of my second marriage."

"Fine enough to shoot a man for?" Rustbucket spoke up, surprising everyone with this sudden display of boldness–himself included.

"You I would shoot for free, Rusty," Margherita said, snuffing Rustbucket's short-lived courage as she turned one of her pistols on him, the other still on Quint. "Though I would prefer not to waste the powder, if I could help it. But all this misses the mark."

She turned her attention back to Quint, the feather in her hat swaying in the breeze. "It is not about the ship, or even the tequila, although I *am* rather upset over that. It is the principle of the thing."

"You and your principles," Quint said through gritted teeth.

Margherita ignored him. "Were I to let you go, word would get around about how you nicked one of my ships from under me and drank my finest liquor, to boot. Surely you must understand that I cannot permit such an insult to my reputation to go unanswered."

"Pirates and their reputations," Darby muttered.

Vigo put a hand on his partner's shoulder. "You're a pirate too, dear."

"Reputation is the one treasure none of us can give up," Margherita shrugged. She nodded her head to one side, and a moment later two of her crew unfolded a rope ladder over the rail of her ship. It landed with a hollow sound against the *Marigold's* deck. "Though one would think that any pirate worth the name would at least make sure he isn't stealing from anyone who can do him a world of hurt."

She smiled at Quint, showing even white teeth. "*Especially* someone who would already pay good money to see him tarred and feathered."

As if in response, Jimmy let out an irate squawk and flapped noisily from Quint's shoulder onto one of the yardarms above.

"Now," Margherita said, as the first of her crew began to clamber down the rope ladder. "All of you stand against the starboard rail, if you please, and keep your hands on your heads. If any of you so much as thinks about reaching for a weapon I'll put a shot between your shoulders before you can say—"

"Parley," Quint said, raising both his hands as high above his head as they would go. "As captain of this ship, I invoke the right of parley on behalf of my crew—"

Margherita's answer came at the speed of lead. Flame licked from the barrel of her pistol as the shot whirred between Quint's raised hands, flying into the darkness beyond the *Marigold's* starboard rail.

"Parley's for pirates who abide by a code," Margherita informed him, holstering her spent pistol and drawing another without ever breaking eye contact. "Not for two-bit thieves like you, Redbeard. Now turn around, or the next bullet's going to be a few inches lower."

"Two-bit?" Quint fumed, but he complied, keeping his hands up as he turned and marched to the starboard rail. The others followed his lead; Ophelia on his right, Vanessa to his left. Behind him he heard the footfalls of Margherita's crew hitting the deck, spreading out to secure the *Marigold* with a disciplined efficiency any Navy captain would envy.

"Quint," Vanessa hissed, keeping her gaze straight ahead so that Margherita's crew would not know they were speaking to one another unless they drew close enough to overhear. "How secure are the Jewels?"

"Doesn't matter," Quint said, giving the slightest shake of his head. "This ain't a big ship. She'll find them sooner rather than later."

Further discussion on the topic was cut off by the prodding of a sword point against Quint's lower back.

"Keep your hands up," Margherita said from behind him, "and turn around slowly."

Quint did, flashing what he hoped was a reassuring smile at Vanessa as he turned, finding himself at eye level with the tip of the lustrous white feather.

"Welcome aboard, Marge," he said, lowering his gaze to the diminutive pirate queen. She was short and curvy, though her lined and sun-weathered face attested that she'd spent as many years before the mast as any pirate worthy of the name. "Permission to ask a question?"

"Not if you insist on calling me that," she said, laying the tip of her cutlass against Quint's breastbone, dark eyes flashing.

"Point taken," Quint said. *Literally.* "Margherita."

"Better," she said, gesturing with her free hand. Several of her crew hurried forward, patting down Quint and his companions and confiscating whatever weapons they found. *They'll have their work cut out for them with Ophelia,* Quint reflected, sparing a glance at his first mate. The bandolier of knives comprised only a small fraction of the blades she wore at any given time, even when roused straight from bed.

"How'd you find us?" Darby asked, returning Quint's attention to Margherita. "We didn't know this schooner was yours when we stole it, and it's not like we left a note saying where we were headed—"

"You didn't need to," Margherita said, feather swaying as she shook her head. "I've been around the islands a few times in my life, boy. Enough to know that there ain't such a thing as coincidence."

"I don't follow," Quint said, truthfully.

"What Captain Margherita means," the Trechtish woman said, glancing over as she patted down Vanessa with one hand, "is that the Navy announced they were to sentence Captain Redbeard for his crimes, and then my *Marigold* goes missing shortly before the sentencing date, and not far off from Fort Amell, either."

"No coincidences," Margherita said, glancing up at the *Marigold's* sails. Quint followed her gaze and kept going, until he saw a tiny green head peering down from over the rail of the crow's nest. *Jimmy.*

"Judging from the lack of holes in the sails," Margherita said, returning her attention to the deck, "your little escape was a success. I assume your second theft of the Crown Jewels was as well?"

Quint opened his mouth, trying to think of a lie, but none would come.

He was saved from answering by Vanessa's sudden about face, her jaw dropping. "How did you know—"

"That he stole them again?" Margherita snorted, turning the cutlass towards Vanessa. "As if the infamous Captain Redbeard's ego would prevent him from doing any less. Not to mention you would not be aboard his ship, *Commander,* unless it was in pursuit of some mission for your precious Navy. Recovering the Crown Jewels, say."

Vanessa's eyes flashed. She might have taken a step forward had the Trechtish pirate not clapped a sizeable hand on her shoulder, holding up her hook in a gesture that was both a caution and a threat. "Easy, Commander," she murmured.

"Look," Quint said, throwing caution to the wind and stepping in between Margherita and Vanessa so that the pirate queen's cutlass lay pressed against his ribs instead of hers. "You've proved your point, Margherita. I stole a ship from you, so you tracked me down, stole it back, and took the score of a lifetime with you as interest. Your reputation remains intact, I've been chastised for crossing you, and you get the Crown Jewels. Dump us on that island yonder—"

He jerked his head towards the dark shape behind him, where even now Lurk was hopefully taking shelter. "—and all's square between us."

For a long moment there was silence, save the soft sighing of the breeze across the deck.

"Square," Margherita said, her voice dangerously soft. "If that were all that lay between us, Redbeard, you and I might be square. But I'm not so old that I've started to forget all the other times your path and mine have crossed."

"If you're referring to the dolphin incident—" Quint said hurriedly, but was silenced by the sword tip rising to his throat.

"Malachite." The pirate queen spoke the name like a curse. "Fully a third of the Navy fleet anchored there. Two of their flagships drydocked for repairs. The hottest, driest summer anyone could recall in living memory, and a populace ready to boil over after years crushed beneath the Imperial bootheel."

Vanessa made a sound in her throat, but Margherita's attention was focused wholly on Quint. She took a step forward, adjusting her grip on the cutlass so that its blade lay across his neck, rather than its tip. One flick of her wrist was all it would take.

"I was so *close,*" the pirate queen murmured, an ocean of rage and regret in those four words. "So close to a *real* rebellion. A spark that would set every ship in Malachite aflame, and spread across this Archipelago faster than the Empire could hope to stamp it out."

"Until us," Ophelia said, her tone uncharacteristically serious.

"Until you," Margherita agreed, eyes locked on Quint's. "Until a shortsighted, greedy thief with delusions of greatness decided he'd rather try and steal a Navy frigate than sink it."

She looked expectantly at him, waiting.

"To be fair," Quint said, mouth dry, "you didn't tell me you were planning to light the harbor on *fire*."

"I didn't trust you," the pirate queen fired back, her nostrils flaring. "Still don't, and with good reason. You led that fleet on a mad chase, right after I struck the match. All the Navy lost that day was one of the flagships in drydock—they managed to douse the flames before the other burned. I meant to cripple the Empire at Malachite. Because of you, all I did was bloody its nose."

"He didn't know," Vanessa said. Quint did not dare look at her, but he could hear how fast and breathily she spoke. "He was just doing what pirates *do*. If you want revenge for Malachite, it should be against me."

"Because you stopped me from lighting the last fuse?" Margherita asked, still looking at Quint. "Any Navy lapdog would've done what you did in that position."

"If that's true, why'd they promote me to commander for it?" Vanessa let out a strained laugh. "I'm the one who stopped you, not him—"

"Ness," Quint said softly. "It's alright."

Quint stared into Margherita's eyes, hard and cold as the steel at his throat. His whole world seemed to teeter upon the edge of her blade.

"Please," he murmured, determined to make his final words worthwhile, if these were indeed his last. "Just don't hurt the others."

Margherita continued staring at him, her expression unreadable.

Then the sword left Quint's neck, returning with a soft sigh to the scabbard at Margherita's hip. Quint inhaled deeply through his nose, biting his tongue lest she have a change of heart.

"Captain Redbeard," Margherita said, raising her voice so that every soul aboard the *Marigold* could hear. "You and all your crew are now my prisoners. Offer no resistance, and you'll be treated with as much courtesy as I can manage. Resist, and I'll send you to whichever of the hells your angels have weighed your sins against."

She turned away from them, feather bobbing as she strode towards the stairs leading from the aftcastle to the maindeck. Quint's hand rose to his neck, massaging the thin cut that had formed there. Vanessa shrugged out of the Trechtish woman's grip, placed her hand on Quint's shoulder, her fingers digging in hard.

"What are you planning to do with us?" she demanded, causing Margherita to pause at the head of the stairs. "Turn Redbeard and his crew over to the Empire? Hold us all for ransom? Use us for target practice?"

"Any of those would be a waste of your lives, Commander Delacort," Margherita said, turning so that her proud features were in profile to them. "I have something much more worthwhile in mind for all of you."

"What's that?" Quint asked, his voice shaking. Now that the moment had passed, it was beginning to register how narrowly he'd escaped his end.

A slow, cold smile spread across the pirate queen's face. "You're going to help me end an Empire."

9

Stunned silence greeted this proclamation, broken moments later by the last sound Quint had expected to hear in its wake: Vanessa's laughter.

"How you planning to manage that?" she asked, her voice shot through with a bitter mirth. "Like you said, your plan fell apart at Malachite. I doubt you'll fare any better this time around."

"Sometimes failure is the greatest teacher," Margherita said, unruffled. It occurred to Quint that, now that she'd decided against killing them on the spot, the pirate queen was making a deliberate effort not to be baited. "In the case of Malachite, my failing was in trying to lay a trap in the heart of the enemy's territory. But happily, you've delivered me a way to rectify that mistake."

"Angels," Vanessa swore, putting it together just before Quint did. "You're going to use the Crown Jewels as bait."

"You're quick, Commander," Margherita said, smiling widely. "Not just the Crown Jewels, though. I imagine when word spreads that Captain Redbeard has stolen the Jewels and taken a Navy officer prisoner, her superiors will jump at the chance to recover the Jewels, rescue her, and put an end to a persistent piratical annoyance in one fell swoop."

"I like to think I rate a little higher than annoyance," Quint said, his mind racing. "But it's not going to work."

"And why's that?" Margherita asked, brows lifting towards the rim of her hat.

"Because every Navy ship within a hundred leagues is going to be scouring the seas for the schooner that fled Fort Amell," he said, nodding in the direction of that distant island, which by now was well beneath the horizon. "The moment any of them sights the *Marigold* we're going to be boarded, and then everyone on this ship and yours who's not named Vanessa is going to dance the hangman's jig."

The islands comprising the Archipelago were beyond count, but here in the southeastern reaches they were densely clustered together and heavily populated, with all but the smallest boasting at least one small hamlet or village. Word of the Crown Jewels' theft would spread across the islands like an algae bloom.

"We were going to fence the Jewels at Solace," Quint continued. "Conniving Connie was our contact. If we set out now we can make it there before anyone on Solace hears about Amell. I'll even cut you in—"

"You're not in a position to negotiate, Redbeard," Margherita remarked, her tone matter-of-fact. "And I'm not concerned about money, just the Empire. Hurting them, and avoiding them."

She cast her gaze southwards, where no islands broke the uniform black of the horizon. "Which is why we'll take the *Marigold* the long way around the Archipelago."

Quint's heart dropped as he realized what lay in that direction.

"Harps and bells, Margherita," he swore. "You're not going to take us into the Sea of Tears?"

"*Down, down, down to the Sea of Tears!*" a scratchy voice sang out from the yardarm high above, prompting every head on deck to look upwards. "*To drown, drown in a sea of fears!*"

"Is that a bird?" the Trechtish woman asked, peering hard into the rigging. "Or perhaps a ghost with a sore throat?"

"It's not a ghost, Tarja," Margherita said wearily, as though her hook-handed crewwoman commonly assumed ordinary sounds were the result of supernatural forces.

"Look," Quint said, recalling Margherita's attention to himself. "As far as anyone knows, those southern waters are the end of the world. I've never heard of anyone in the last hundred years venturing further than a day or two into that sea and coming back to tell about it."

"Perhaps you should get out more," Margherita remarked, giving him a grim smile. "I've braved that stormy stretch of ocean before, in ships smaller'n this one. The Navy won't think to look that way, and even if they did, they wouldn't dare risk one of their precious warships on such a tumultuous voyage."

"A voyage that could kill us all, easily," Quint said. "You're willing to take that risk?"

"What's life without a little risk?" Margherita said, shrugging.

"At least take the bigger ship, then," Darby said, desperation tinging his voice as he nodded towards the larger vessel. "It's sturdier than the *Marigold*, and faster. Better odds—"

"No." Margherita's refusal was flat. "The *Wildflower*'s already engaged upon an errand of equal importance, and I know better than to put all my eggs in the same basket. We'll cross the Sea of Tears, and we'll do it in the *Marigold*."

She turned, her feather waving softly in the breeze, and called up to the deck of the *Wildflower*. "Ahoy, Glennon!"

The heavily-armed silhouette appeared over the rail again. "Aye, Cap'n?"

"You've command of the *Wildflower*," his captain called up. "I'll be taking—hmm, let's say a dozen of the crew and sailing the *Marigold* south."

If the thought of taking a smaller vessel into the infamously deadly Sea of Tears gave Glennon any cause for concern, he didn't voice it. "Aye, Cap'n. You sufficiently provisioned for the voyage?"

"Doubtful," Margherita said, chewing her lip. "Take an hour to load her up with the necessary supplies, then we'll part ways. I'll reconnect with you on Pyrite in a month's time, after you've delivered the *Wildflower's* cargo safely to its destination."

Quint exchanged a glance with Ophelia, wondering if her previous dalliance with Margherita might give any clue as to the nature of the unnamed cargo. Whatever it was, it would have to be of incredible value for Margherita to risk losing both the Crown Jewels and her own life rather than endanger it. But Ophelia could only shrug.

"Aye, Cap'n," Glennon replied. He threw a salute and then disappeared from view.

Margherita returned her gaze to her prisoners. "Now, let's get you lot settled in. It's going to be a long voyage."

Quint considered refusing, but before he could so much as open his mouth to retort Margherita's hand was on the hilt of her cutlass.

"Fine," he said, shrugging. His arms were beginning to feel quite heavy after so long with his hands raised. "Down, down, down to the Sea of Tears."

From above them came a flutter of wings, flapping hard and fast away from the *Marigold,* towards the dark shape of the island lying off their starboard bow.

"*Sea of Tears!*" a hoarse voice croaked from across the water, fading swiftly into the distance. "To *drown, drown in a sea of fears!*"

Silence followed in the wake of that ominous pronouncement, broken only by Rustbucket's low mutter:

"I really hate that bloody bird."

10

The *Marigold's* brig was a small, cramped cabin at the farthest end of the belowdecks corridor, set well away from the others. It had neither bunks nor hammocks, only a few stray clumps of straw scattered about the floor.

"Could be worse," Quint said, wrinkling his nose as he tried to ignore the room's musty, pungent smell, which seemed to be equal parts sweat and other, less savory excretions. He rubbed his wrists, working some feeling back into them now that they were no longer roped together. "They could have chained us up."

"We will if you misbehave," Tarja added brightly. The large hook-handed pirate had evidently drawn first watch for guard duty, though at the moment she seemed more interested in chatting with them through the barred window of the brig's door. "The chains are already in place."

Sure enough, one wall of the brig was lined with chains of varying sizes, all of them worn and pitted but of clearly sturdy construction. Vanessa moved to the bulkhead and hefted one, noting that the manacle dangling from it was more appropriately sized for someone's neck than their wrists.

"All of this down here," she said, looking from Quint to Ophelia with one eyebrow raised, "and none of you figured that this ship belonged to another pirate?"

Quint and Ophelia exchanged a look.

"We figured it was used for transporting large animals," Ophelia said after a moment, waving a hand in front of her face. "On account of, y'know. The smell."

"The one with the cockatoo hair is right!" Tarja added brightly. She gestured with her hook at the chains, while Ophelia ran a hand self-consciously through her swoop of hair. "We often use the *Marigold* to smuggle larger beasts. Bears, snakes, tigers, that sort of creature."

"Snakes?" Darby yelped, rising abruptly from the pile of straw he'd been sitting on, looking wildly around as though he expected cobras and vipers to come slithering out of the cracks between the floorboards.

"Tigers," Vanessa repeated, more dubiously.

"Ja, tigers," Tarja nodded cheerily. "Cute when they are small, a bit more trouble once they are bigger. Is how I lost this." She gestured demonstratively with her hook. "And worry not about the snakes, my bespectacled friend. We only carry the big ones. Pythons and anacondas, that sort. Much too large to hide in so small a room."

Darby exhaled and resumed his seat. Vigo patted him on the shoulder.

"Unless," Tarja amended, scratching her head with the tip of her hook, "one of the last ones laid eggs in here, and they hatched. Has been known to happen."

Quint had never seen Darby come to his feet so fast.

"Is that how Margherita's been financing her operation?" Quint asked Tarja. The pirate queen's self-proclaimed title was not an empty boast; the *Wildflower* and the *Marigold* were only two of the many ships under her command. The source of her seemingly inexhaustible resources had long been a mystery to him. "There's plenty o' puffed-up governors and viscounts who think owning some fearsome beast is a fun way to show off how much wealth they've got. Margherita's one of those that supplies them, then?"

"You have things reversed, friend Redbeard," Tarja said, shaking her head. "Captain Margherita takes the beasts *from* such men."

"She frees them?" Quint asked, his brow furrowing.

"Ja!" Tarja beamed. "Mine husband and I, animal husbandry was our business back in Trecht. Most of the poor beasts, they are only cubs, or have spent so long at the hands of bad men that they will not know how to be wild. But there are certain islands across the Archipelago where friends of ours run sanctuaries for the unfortunate creatures. To these we take them so that they may have better lives than they would as some rich man's trophy."

"And Margherita does all this...why?" Quint asked, confused. "You can't tell me she's got a soft spot for animals. She doesn't even have a pet."

He thought with a pang of mingled concern and affection of Jimmy, winging out across the black waters towards the lonely island. Hopefully she and Lurk would reunite with one another there, and the *Bloody Angel* would find them sooner rather than later, angels willing.

"Captain Margherita is of the opinion," Tarja said, pride lifting her chin, "that no creature deserves to be caged."

This proclamation was met with a chorus of protests from the imprisoned pirates.

"Excepting those who have wronged her," Tarja amended. "Meaning no offense, I am certain."

Whatever she was about to say next was cut off by the sudden forward lurch of the deck beneath their feet.

"Looks like we are underway," Tarja said brightly. "Please make yourselves comfortable, ja? It will be a long voyage."

She turned away from the door, humming a Trechtish lullaby under her breath as she settled into her seat in the corridor outside. Within the brig itself, silence reigned, save for the sound of some bit of flotsam outside knocking rhythmically against the hull.

"So," Ophelia said, pursing her lips. "We're heading into the Sea of Tears."

Quint nodded.

"Angels above," Rustbucket swore. "We're all going to die."

"That's true of everyone," Vigo pointed out, frowning. "But there *does* seem to be a markedly higher chance of doing so in the Sea of Tears, if even half the stories of that place can be believed. Ships sunk by sudden storms, devoured by krakens, struck down as if by the wrath of the angels themselves..."

"Sailors' stories, dear," Darby said, putting a hand on Vigo's arm. But he looked similarly troubled. "Though those waters *are* famously treacherous, and the weather at that latitude is unpredictable at best. There can't be more than four or five known voyages to have sailed the Sea of Tears and returned alive, and none of those within the last half century."

"Margherita claims to have done it," Quint said, looking upwards as if he could see the pirate queen striding the deck above them. "Or at least she's confident enough that she can that she's steering into the eye of that storm, and taking all of us with her."

"She's not the only one," Ophelia said, giving Quint a look he couldn't quite name. "Captain Wolf did it, too."

Quint opened his mouth, shut it. Captain Wolf's voyages across the Sea of Tears had been one of his late father Clarent's favorite bedtime tales to regale a young Quint with. He couldn't count the number of times he'd drifted off to tales of Wolf's adventures in those distant uncharted waters, whether navigating between whirlpools and sailing into typhoons, or fleeing from a lonely island that turned out to be the back of a titanic leviathan before it could sink and take the famous pirate and his crew down with it.

Growing up, Quint had always assumed these were simply the bedtime stories his pop had chosen to put his young son to bed, exaggerated and fantastical as they were. Except, as he'd discovered mere months ago, Clarent Thatch had actually *been* the legendary Captain Wolf, his disappearance in the prime of his career merely a cover to ditch his infamous moniker and settle down for the quiet life of a tavern keeper with his wife—Lola Thatch, Quint's ma.

And while, like any sailor, Clarent's stories had been prone to exaggeration, none of the tales he'd told his son had been outright fabrications. Quint had his ma's word on that.

Which meant that his pop really *had* braved the Sea of Tears, and lived to tell the tale.

"You're right," he said, slowly, as whatever was outside knocked against the hull again. Vigo leaned his head against the bulkhead, listening. "It's possible. Even so, I don't like our odds. But we ain't lost all hope, yet."

"Lurk," Vanessa said a moment later, but Quint shook his head.

"She doesn't know where we're going," he said. "But Jimmy heard. Hopefully they both got clear and ended up on that island close by."

The others nodded, save for Vigo, who had closed his eyes and seemingly fallen asleep.

"And the rest of the *Bloody Angel* crew was planning to rendezvous with us on Solace in a day or two," Darby said, putting the pieces together. He adjusted his spectacles. "So when they pass this way looking for us, Lurk can make contact, and then Jimmy can tell them where we've gone."

"Won't do them much good if they can't sail the Sea of Tears," Ophelia pointed out.

"But they'll at least know what happened to us," Quint pointed out. He rested his head in his hands, suddenly feeling immensely tired. "And at least they'll take care of Lurk. Practically tore my heart out, sending her off like that. She's probably alone on that island right now, trying to think of what she can do to help—"

"She's not," Vigo said, opening his eyes. He turned his head, looking at Quint. "Lurk's here."

"Here?" Quint asked, unable to resist the ridiculous urge to look around the brig, as if the mermaid would come slithering from behind one of the other prisoners.

Then the knocking came again, and he understood.

In a heartbeat they were all crowded up against the hull, pressing their ears to the wood as they felt more than heard the vibrations of something knocking against the *Marigold's* hull—or rather, someone.

"She told me a few weeks ago that she wanted a way to talk to us," Vigo explained as he rapped his knuckles against the timbers. "While she was underwater and we were belowdecks. So I've been teaching her Nylish Code."

"Really?" Quint blinked. "I've been trying to show her how to read, but it's been slow going."

This had not been due to any failure on Lurk's part as a student, nor even Quint's as a teacher, but rather to the fact that books tended not to be waterproof, which somewhat limited Lurk's available reading materials.

"She took to code faster," Vigo nodded, listening as the knocking reply came. "Think it's something to do with how mermaids talk through that underwater singing of theirs. Translating speech into something else musical wasn't as much as a jump for her as letters were."

"That makes sense," Quint said. "What's she saying?"

"That she's alright," Vigo said, methodically tapping out a reply. "That she didn't go to the island like you told her, but...well. Lurked about, listening." He paused as Lurk added something in a long series of thunks, then looked back at his captain. "She apologizes for not staying to try and save us."

"Tell her she's nothing to be sorry for," Quint said, shaking his head vehemently. "Tell her that she did what was right, and that she's to make for Ember Bay at once."

They did not have to wait long. Lurk's reply came in the form of a long tap and a short one, followed by three long.

"She says no," Vigo said, then cocked his head to listen as Lurk continued knocking. "She says that we're her pod, and that she's not giving us up so easily."

Quint found it hard to speak over the lump that had suddenly formed in his throat. He swallowed it down. "She can't keep swimming alongside the *Marigold* forever. I won't have her wearing herself out that way."

Vigo relayed the message, then listened for its reply, which was longer than any of Lurk's previous responses. "Lurk says that there's plenty of barnacles and such growing on the underside of the hull for her to hold onto. And when she gets tired, she can climb up to the prow and hang off of the figurehead. Ain't none of Margherita's crew going to see her there unless they're standing right on top of the bowsprit."

"Alright," Quint said, running a hand through his hair. He began to pace the cramped confines of the brig. "Seeing as she won't be dissuaded, at least tell her to keep out of sight. I won't have any of Margherita's crew messing with her."

"Aye, Cap'n," Vigo said, beginning to tap out Quint's instructions.

"And under no circumstances is she to come aboard the *Marigold* unless one of us makes it abovedeck," he continued, not liking the thought of what would happen if one of Margherita's crew caught Lurk sneaking down to the brig to rescue them. Surprising though his rival's apparent soft spot for large snakes was, Quint doubted that sympathy would extend to serpentine mermaids attempting a jailbreak. "Tell her to hold tight—literally—and wait for us to give her a signal."

"You've got a plan, then?" Vanessa asked, glancing over her shoulder at the door. The Trechtish humming continued unabated.

"Not quite," Quint amended, turning to Ophelia. "Or at least not yet."

"Don't look at me," Ophelia protested, raising both her hands. "I don't know whether any of you noticed, but Margherita's still sore at me for nicking her favorite knife."

"What was that about, anyway?" Vanessa asked.

"Ah." Ophelia cleared her throat, looking embarrassed for one of the first times that Quint could recall. "You know how after a night together, some folks give the other party something to remember them by?"

"Souvenirs," Vanessa said. She frowned. "Or trophies, in this instance."

"I like knives!" Ophelia said, more than a little defensively. "So the last time Rita and I—"

"Wait a minute," Vanessa said, eyes narrowing. "Did you take something of Estelle's, too?"

"I never." Ophelia shook her head. "Your sister doesn't have any knives, or at least she didn't while we were back on Tourmaline. How is she, by the way?"

"Speaking of knives," Quint interrupted, impatient to move the conversation away from lost loves. "Do you still have any on you?"

"Nope," Ophelia said gloomily, patting her sides. "Doubt you noticed in the commotion of being captured, but that redhaired lass did an impressively thorough search of my person. Even found a blade or two you don't know about, Cap'n. S'pose Margherita told her where to look."

Quint blinked, trying hard to banish the image that conjured.

"Much as I hate to admit it," he said slowly, "there's not a lot we can do at the moment except sit tight. Whatever scheme Margherita has in mind is going to involve making sure the Navy knows where we—and by extension the Crown Jewels—are. A baited trap's no good if the bait's hidden."

"You're saying we should just wait until she's ready to spring her ambush?" Ophelia asked.

"I'm saying we wait until we all disembark at our final destination," Quint corrected. "Wherever that may be. Once we do, we'll get the lay of the land and figure out how we're going to wriggle out of this with Lurk's help."

He paused long enough for Vigo to convey this through the hull, then translate Lurk's response. "Says she's ready and waiting for your signal, Cap'n, however long it might take."

"Likely quite a while," Quint said, but before he could elaborate further there was a polite cough at the door, followed by the clang of metal on metal.

"Begging your pardon," Tarja said, knocking politely on the bars of the cell door. "But Captain Margherita is asking for the one called Ophelia?

All eyes turned towards Ophelia, who stood and crossed to the door. "What's Rita want with me?"

"I asked as much," Tarja said, frowning, "but she would not tell me. Will you come?"

"Aye," Ophelia said, not looking at Quint. "Let's hear what she's got to say, then."

Quint blinked. "Ophelia—"

Tarja opened the door, and Ophelia stepped through it without so much as a backwards glance. Tarja locked it behind her and gave the others a cheery wave. "I shall be back shortly, friends! Please do not get up to any trouble in my absence."

"No promises," Quint muttered, but they were already gone, their footsteps echoing up the corridor towards the captain's cabin.

"What did she want Ophelia for?" Darby asked, frowning at the locked door.

"I've a few ideas," Rustbucket muttered. "Though none of them bode well for us, I'll tell you that."

"Stow that talk," Quint said automatically. Ophelia was capable and persuasive, and while he doubted she would be able to convince Margherita to set them free, it could not hurt for her to try.

"In the meantime," he said, sinking against the wooden bulkhead and gathering enough straw to form a makeshift pillow, "I suggest we all get some shuteye. It's been a long night, and I have a feeling we'll want to save our strength for whatever's next to come."

"Good call, Cap'n," Vigo agreed, leaning his head against the far wall. He slung one arm about Darby's shoulders, and with the other began tapping out a message to Lurk.

"Tell Lurk goodnight for me," Quint said, lying down and trying to get as comfortable as the hardwood floor allowed. Around the brig the others did similarly, each clearing a space for themselves in the piled straw.

Quint had only just closed his eyes when one of the floorboards beside him groaned. He opened his eyes to see Vanessa settling herself down beside him.

"You think Ophelia's all right?" she asked before he could comment on her choice of sleeping arrangement. "I mean, going alone to Margherita's cabin and all."

"I'm not too worried for her," Quint said, which was halfway true. "If there's anyone on the *Bloody Angel* who can handle the so-called pirate queen, it's Ophelia."

"Better her than you, I suppose," Vanessa said. "Or me."

Quint laughed, though there was little humor in it.

They lay there in silence for a while, heads pillowed by the straw, side by side. Across the brig Rustbucket had already begun to snore. Vanessa stirred, uncomfortable.

"You want me to move over?" Quint asked her in a whisper.

"No," she whispered back.

"If you want this spot I can move—"

"Quint." Still soft, but firm. "This brig isn't that large. Either I get closer to Rusty and his snoring, or I interrupt Vigo and Darby's cuddling, or I stay where I am, so that at least you're blocking a little bit of the noise."

"Makes sense," he said, then laughed as a thought occurred to him.

"What?"

"It's not my fault this time," he said, staring up at the wooden ceiling.

"What isn't?"

"Us ending up in bed together. Or in straw, I guess."

Vanessa laughed softly and rested her hand on top of his. "I'll take full responsibility for this one."

They lapsed into a comfortable silence once more. Vanessa's hand remained atop his, her palm warm but calloused as any sailor's. Quint did not mind.

"I'm sorry, you know," he said after a while. Out in the corridor Tarja had resumed her post, her soft humming a gentle counterpoint to Rustbucket's snores.

Vanessa stirred beside him. "For what?"

"Getting you into this mess," he said, staring up into the dark. It was easier to talk like this, without looking at one another. "It's my fault you're here."

"Ah. Right." Vanessa nodded, causing her curls to tickle his cheek. "Because it was your idea to take me prisoner aboard this ship. The first time, I mean."

"I could've just thrown you overboard," he pointed out. "Lurk could've made sure you got picked up by the Navy in those jollyboats. That way you wouldn't have been aboard when Margherita captured us."

"I do admit that I enjoyed being your prisoner much more than hers," Vanessa said. Her fingers lightly tapped a rhythm against his, which he suspected was a piano scale.

"Or before that," Quint pressed on, unwilling to let himself be so easily absolved. "Instead of snatching the Jewels again. I should've just counted myself lucky that things worked out the way they had, instead of tweaking the Empire's nose—"

"And if you had?" Vanessa propped herself up on one elbow, looking down at him in the dim half-light spilling in through the bars in the brig door. "The Crown Jewels would be securely back in an Imperial vault by now, and Rustbucket would be swinging from the noose. Mutineer or not, you were never going to let that happen to him."

"No," Quint admitted. "He's my crew, or he was. But—"

"Quentin Thatch." Vanessa tucked a stray curl behind her ear, frowning slightly as she peered down at him. "I'm a grown woman. I made my choices, so I've got to live with them. And if those choices mean I'm the prisoner of a vindictive self-proclaimed pirate queen, well." She pursed her lips, the light casting interesting shadows across her face as she stared down at Quint. "At least I'm in good company."

Quint was seized with the sudden, overwhelming urge to reach up and pull her to him, to feel those soft lips on his, just as he had all those years ago.

Because that ended so well for you both the last time, some small, hateful part of himself murmured. *Or did you already forget what she said, when you parted ways on Tourmaline?*

He had not forgotten. *And things are different now,* he tried to tell himself, but too late. Vanessa's pursed lips had deepened into a frown. She laid back down, still beside him, but their hands no longer touching.

"Ness—"

"You're right," she said, rolling over so that she was lying on her side, her back to him. "We've an ordeal ahead of us. Best get some sleep."

"Aye," Quint said, feeling as if an invisible fist were squeezing his throat. He rolled over, the straw itching him where it touched his bare skin. "I...goodnight, Ness."

"Goodnight, Quint."

Silence. Quint felt the weight of all that had transpired that long day weighing down on him; the frantic heist and flight from Fort Amell, the thrill of Vanessa so close to him once more, the rapid turnaround of Margherita taking them all prisoner. Weariness reached up, dragging him inexorably towards sleep, but he could not let himself rest yet. Not before saying what needed to be said.

"Ness," he whispered, half-drowsing, into the dark. "I'll get us out of this, somehow. I promise."

But the soft, even cadence of her breathing told him Vanessa was already fast asleep.

11

"Well?" Quint asked Ophelia when she returned late the following morning, well after the rest of them had finished their scant but surprisingly flavorful bowls of porridge. "What did Margherita have to say?"

"'bout what?" Ophelia asked, stifling a yawn.

"Oh, I don't know," Rustbucket spoke up, scowling over his empty porridge bowl. "How about letting us go free? Maybe about not using us as bait in some scheme to trap the Navy? Anything like that?"

"We didn't really get around to any of that," Ophelia said, rubbing sleep from her eyes as she sat cross-legged on the floor. "Margherita wasn't much interested in talking, if you follow me."

Quint's stomach lurched in a way that had nothing to do with the rocking motion of the *Marigold* beneath his feet as he recalled his earlier argument with Ophelia; her dissatisfaction with always going along with whatever he wanted.

"So she just invited you to her cabin for a tumble?" he asked, hoping he sounded teasing rather than anxious. In truth, he hoped it truly had been nothing more than an amorous connection.

"Mostly," Ophelia said, running a hand through her hair—badly mussed, Quint couldn't help noticing. "She also offered to let me sign on with her an' her crew, if I wanted."

Quint had feared as much, but to hear it said aloud felt like someone had kicked him in the belly. "Generous of her. What'd you say?"

"What do you think?" Ophelia asked, waving her tattooed arms about the brig's cramped confines. "I'm back here, ain't I?"

"Fair point," Quint said. He paused. "Thanks."

"For what?" Ophelia asked, staring hard at him. "Harps and bells, mate. I had a fun night, but not so fun that I'm gonna turn coat on you."

"I know," Quint said quickly, yet the uneasy feeling in the pit of his stomach refused to dissipate. Now that the subject of Ophelia's defection had been raised, he did not think that Margherita would let the matter rest so easily.

"Tell me you at least managed to get ahold of one of her knives," Vanessa said, glancing towards the door, which was now being guarded by a bored-looking balding pirate.

"Afraid not," Ophelia said, a touch sheepishly. She rubbed her wrists, which were still red and chafed. "I was a little, uh. Distracted."

"Are you alright?" Vanessa said, taking Ophelia's hand and studying the marks on her wrist. "Did she tie you up again?"

"No," Ophelia said, then corrected herself. "I mean, aye, but only 'cause I asked her to."

"Right," Quint said, thinking that was more than he needed to know. "Well, maybe you'll be luckier next time."

"If there is a next time," Ophelia said with a shrug. "She wasn't too happy with me refusing to sign on."

"Speaking of luck," Vigo said, coming over and sitting on the floor across from Ophelia, Darby in tow. He produced a deck of cards from his vest and began dealing them out as Quint and the others folded their legs beneath them and sat, forming a loose semicircle. "This is as good a way to pass the time as any. I suggest we all save our strength, and pray to the angels that we make it across the Sea of Tears in one piece."

"And if the angels aren't listening?" Rustbucket asked, scooping up his hand as Vigo finished dealing.

"Then we'll just have to trust our own good luck, won't we?" Quint asked, picking up his own hand. He schooled his face into a neutral mask, looked down at his cards. Ace, Empress, Emperor, Knave, and ten, all of the crown suite: a royal flush.

A winning hand, Quint thought. *About time fate dealt me one of those.*

He only hoped that his luck would hold.

⚓

Quint's luck held for exactly one week.

Or close to a week, anyway. The passage of time was a slippery thing down in the brig, below the waterline. Without the sun or stars the movement from day to night grew swiftly difficult to discern. Their only clue as to the passage of time was their own internal clocks, and the steady rotation of Margherita's crew through their shifts guarding the prisoners. And mealtimes, of course.

Meals which were, Quint had to admit, surprisingly palatable. Good, even.

"Is my husband's cooking," Tarja confided on the third evening, passing several bowls piled high with rice through the slot at the bottom of the brig door. "You must eat with your hands, I am afraid. Captain Margherita does not trust you not to stab me, should I give you utensils."

"I'd *prefer* not to stab you," Quint said, taking a bowl and passing it down the line they'd formed at the door. Tonight's course was shrimp and rice, topped with pepper sauce and served with a side of pineapple rounds. "Though since you're between me and my freedom, I can't promise I'd never do it."

"Understandable," Tarja said, unoffended.

Deciding to change the subject, Quint looked down at the bowl in his hands. "Your husband's cooking isn't exactly traditional Trechtish cuisine, is it?"

"Who cares?" Ophelia objected, already shoveling food into her mouth. "Stuff's delicious."

"I will be sure to tell Frederick you said so," Tarja said, beaming. "And you are right, friend Redbeard. This is a Ziltarian dish. My Frederick is well aware that Trechtish fare is an...acquired taste. Happily, he enjoys the challenge of cooking recipes which actually use spices."

"Angels bless 'im for it," Ophelia said around a mouthful of shrimp.

And despite their present circumstances, Quint couldn't find it in himself to disagree.

Tarja was far and away the friendliest of their captors, but to Quint's surprise the rest of Margherita's dozen crewmen and women aboard the *Marigold* were similarly interested in their prisoners' welfare. Initially Quint had advised his own crew to be on guard against talking with their jailers, lest doing so complicate their eventual escape. But Vigo's deck of cards could only hold the group's attention for so long, and with scant little else to do, they soon fell into a habit of conversing with their guards.

There was Ginger, a chipper young redhead who spoke brightly and fondly of her parents and six siblings back home on Opal, and who had immediately taken to calling Quint "cuz" on the grounds that, given their similar coloring, they must be somehow distantly related.

Then there was Simon, a perpetually cheerful young man who would occasionally slip them sweets when none of his crewmates were looking, and spent his time on watch with a pair of knitting needles or darning socks. Quint had tried to figure out a way to steal those needles and use them as lockpicks, but so far the opportunity had not presented itself.

Frederick, ship's cook and Tarja's husband, turned out to be a small, gnomish fellow with thick spectacles, a wispy beard, and an avuncular smile. Delighted at the positive reception his cooking had received, he eagerly asked after each of the *Bloody Angel* crew's favorite meals, promising to do his utmost to recreate them as best as the *Marigold's* limited provisions would allow.

The quietest of their captors was Adewale, a slender umber-skinned young man who seldom spoke to them, but whiled away the hours of his guard duty plucking at a mandolin, its bright refrains echoing through the *Marigold.* His shift was usually the one after Ginger's, and Quint could not help noticing the way she would linger in the hall before reluctantly returning to her other duties.

They were not bad folk, in Quint's estimation, or at least no worse than his own crew of renegades and miscreants. Had circumstances been different, some of them might have even fallen in with the *Bloody Angel* instead of Margherita.

She alone refrained from guard duty, which Quint suspected was as much due to their mutual dislike as it was in deference to her station as captain. Angels only knew what would happen if Margherita herself had to spend hours on watch, with Quint having nothing better to do with his time than needle her.

"She'd probably needle you right back," Vanessa had commented over breakfast one morning, which was porridge sprinkled liberally with bits of dried fruit. "With her cutlass."

"And miss out on using me to lure the Navy into some convoluted scheme?" Quint asked, blowing on his porridge. "Her fuse ain't that short."

"Speaking of whatever she's planning on doing with us," Vanessa said, pausing with her bowl halfway to her lips. "What—"

The rest of her sentence was cut off by the sudden tilting of the floor as the *Marigold* listed sharply to one side, sending everything in the brig sliding towards the inner wall—the prisoners included.

Quint reacted without thinking, dropping his bowl and seizing hold of one of the chains bolted to the wall. Porridge sloshed onto the floor as he reached out and grabbed Vanessa's hand. She held on tight, her boots scrabbling against the floorboards. Their bowls careened towards the wall and splattered against it, smearing dripping trails of porridge across the wooden panels.

The rest of the prisoners went sliding past in a confused pile, landing awkwardly against the wall which was nearly halfway to becoming a floor instead. Vigo had wrapped his big arms around Darby and Rustbucket, shielding them both from the impact, while Ophelia had managed to wedge herself against one of the barrels lining the wall at the last moment.

Then the ship righted itself, rocking back into its original position. The floor became the floor again, to the prisoners' collective relief. The bowls clattered to the floorboards, though most of the porridge remained on the walls.

"Quint?" Vanessa said.

"Yeah?"

"You're squeezing my hand a little too hard."

Quint looked down, realized he was still holding her hand in a vice grip.

"Sorry," he said, flushing, and forced his fingers apart. Vanessa relaxed, but did not let go.

A clanking against the bars of the window caught their attention.

"Begging pardons," Tarja said, grimacing from the other side of the door. "But could one of you lend a hand, seeing as I have only the one?"

Evidently she'd wedged her hook between the bars when the ship had tilted, but was having some difficulty extricating herself now that they were right-side up again.

"I've got it," Ophelia said, rising to her feet and crossing to the door, one hand braced against the wall in case the ship shifted suddenly again.

"Many thanks, friend cockatoo," Tarja said as Ophelia examined her hook. "I suppose I could just take it off, but it is a pain to get back on the arm."

"Not a problem," Ophelia said. "Let's get you unstuck."

A moment later Tarja's hook was once more on the corridor side of the brig. Only then did it occur to Quint that they might have found some way to use the situation to their advantage—perhaps taking Tarja prisoner, or at the very least stealing her hook and using it to pick the brig's lock. Yet none of them had thought to do anything of the sort—captives though they were, it seemed a poor way to repay the friendly Trechtishwoman for her kindness towards them.

"Apologies for the turbulent waters," Tarja said, blissfully unaware of Quint's current line of thought. "We—"

The ship lurched beneath them again, this time in the opposite direction. No longer caught off guard, the prisoners managed to duplicate Quint's earlier trick of seizing hold of the chains bolted to the walls.

"We are entering the Sea of Tears proper," Tarja continued from the corridor, having managed not to get her hook stuck this time. "Is going to be very choppy sailing, I am fearing."

As if to emphasize her point, the floor jumped up as the *Marigold* crested an unseen wave, sending Quint's heart hurtling towards his throat.

"For how long?" Rustbucket demanded, a tinge of panic crawling into his voice.

"For quite a while," Tarja said, and though she had recovered her usual cheery tone something about it felt forced. "I would advise each of you to ready yourselves for a rough time and say a prayer to your angels. We're heading into a storm."

⚓

In the twenty or so years since he'd first signed on with a tall ship, Quint Thatch had sailed in every sort of weather imaginable, from driving hurricanes to tranquil breezes, arctic gales to stiflingly hot doldrums. He'd experienced the worst of rough waves and unpredictable winds the Eight Seas had to offer.

Until now.

Had he been abovedeck, things might have been different, but the experience of being trapped inside the *Marigold*'s brig while the schooner battled the storms outside was among the worst of Quint's life. It felt as though some vindictive giant had crammed them into a box, then plunged that box underwater and given it a vigorous shaking.

Never once in his thirty-five years had Quint been seasick, but this voyage was putting that record to the test. Several times he was nearly sick, and managed to force it down only with a significant effort. Not all of the others were as lucky, however, and the brig soon began to smell even worse than it had before.

"At least there hasn't been much vittles for us to lose," Rustbucket offered as a silver lining while he patted Ophelia's back. It was a gesture Quint suspected she would have resented, had she not also been visibly forcing herself not to be sick. Her record was nearly as unblemished as Quint's, and she was determined to keep it that way.

"Some silver lining," she retorted instead, closing her eyes and breathing in through her nose. "I miss Frederick's cooking."

"We all do," Vanessa nodded, looking forlornly towards the brig door. Margherita had ceased to station guards there, requiring every available hand on deck to keep the *Marigold* afloat. Their visits from their captors had lasted only long enough to slide the day's victuals under the door, which were now reduced to hardtack, grog, and thin strips of jerky.

"How is Lurk holding up?" Quint asked Vigo, desperate for a real silver lining. "She still with us?"

It was a question he'd been asking on an almost hourly basis, unable to shake the deep and abiding fear that their mermaid crewmate would be washed away by the unmerciful waves.

Vigo grunted and tapped the wall, holding Darby tight against him with his other hand. They waited tensely for an answering knock, as there had been an hour previously.

None came.

Again Vigo pounded his fist against the wall, harder and more insistently. Still nothing.

"She's got to still be there," he said, his voice rising an octave above its usual deep rumble. "She—"

The *Marigold* lurched forwards, sharper and longer than all the rest combined. Quint's heart climbed its way up his throat, and he was seized by a terrifying and insane image of the *Marigold* shooting beneath the waves towards the ocean floor as if it had been fired from a cannon—

A tremor ran through the hull, a great grinding groan as if the ship were a titanic beast roaring in unspeakable pain. The sound seemed to go on forever, its vibrations traveling through Quint's limbs to shake his very bones—

A *CRACK* filled his ears. Louder than thunder, louder than cannon fire, louder than the trumpets of all the angels in all the heavens. It sounded like the world was being torn apart.

The sound faded, leaving in its echo a roar like a raging river.

"Quint!" Vanessa shook his shoulder, shocking him from his stupor, and pointed at the brig door. "Look!"

Water was seeping in beneath the doorframe.

In a heartbeat the prisoners were pressed against the wall, pounding against the door, reaching their hands out through the bars, shouting for Tarja, for Margherita, for the angels to take mercy on them. Chill water came pooling about their feet, rising with terrifying speed past their toes, over their ankles—

"Stand back!" a familiar voice shouted. Tarja's face appeared on the other side of the bars, her blonde hair plastered wetly against her brow. It looked as if she had swum the corridor to get here, which Quint supposed was not far off from the truth.

"Away from the door, please!" she shouted, holding up a ring of keys hanging from her hook. "I cannot open with you all there!"

"Do as she says!" Quint shouted, in the commanding voice of Captain Redbeard. "Everyone away from the door!"

They complied, backing away as Tarja selected the proper key from the ring, which seemed to take an agonizingly long time.

"The *Marigold* is sinking," Tarja said, unnecessarily. By now the water was past Quint's knees. "Follow me out!"

The dull *clunk* of the key turning in the lock was the sweetest sound Quint had ever heard, though the screech of the door opening on its unoiled hinges was a close second. Tarja stood with her hand thrust against the door, holding it open.

"Move!" she and Quint both shouted at the same time. He gestured his crew forward, urging them past him and into the swiftly rising waters of the corridor. "Out, all of you!"

Vigo and Darby rushed past and into the corridor, pulling Rustbucket along behind them. Ophelia followed, sparing Quint a brief glance on her way out the door.

"Quint—" Vanessa started, but he shook his head.

"Go! I'll be right behind you."

She nodded and went. Quint stepped forward, wading through the water that was now up to his waist, into the corridor where Tarja waited with her hand pressed against the door. Ahead lay the stairs to the deck, transformed into a waterfall. He had a brief glimpse of Vanessa struggling her way up those stairs, Ophelia pulling her onto the deck—

The *Marigold* shuddered and tilted to one side, slamming Quint against a bulkhead. His shoulder screamed in complaint, but he fought it down. Tarja's feet went out from under her, sending her sliding towards the stairs, which now were somehow beneath them. She thrust out her hook, caught it on the railing, and hauled herself bodily up the stairs by means of her considerable strength, pausing only to stretch out her hand to Quint as he came hurtling after her. Her fingers felt slick but warm.

She hauled them both onto the deck. Wind whipped at Quint's hair as he turned, gaping at a world that was water on all sides: flooding the deck, lashing down from the sky, towering above them in a mountainous wave. On the far side of the deck the *Marigold's* crew had piled into the schooner's jollyboat.

Nor were they the only ones, Quint was glad to see, watching as Ophelia helped Rustbucket over the edge of the jollyboat. Only Margherita and Vanessa remained aboard the *Marigold*, the concern etched upon both their faces turning to relief as they caught sight of Tarja making her way across the shifting deck, and Quint at her heels.

"Quint!" Vanessa's voice was scarcely audible above the roaring storm as she started towards him, an arm upraised to ward off the worst of the sheeting rain. Quint tried to yell for her to turn back, to retreat for the safety of the jollyboat, but then Tarja yelled something he could not hear above the angry howl of the wind. She pulled insistently at his arm, but her fingers slipped, and suddenly he was loosed from her grasp.

Not a prisoner anymore, some absurd part of himself whispered, but could find no joy in it, for the big pirate's feet had gone out from under her, sending her tumbling towards the rail.

"*TARJA!*" Margherita's cry was a hoarse bellow, louder than Quint would have believed possible from a woman of her stature. Out of the corner of his eye he saw her racing across the deck towards Tarja, hot on Vanessa's heels.

But Quint was closer, and already diving after Tarja as the *Marigold's* starboard rail slammed into the Trechtish pirate's middle, her momentum sending her tumbling over the rail and into the storm-wracked sea below.

Or nearly. Rushing towards where she'd fallen, Quint saw the small, gleaming curve of Tarja's hook digging into the wooden rail.

"Hang on!" he shouted, or tried to. He bent over the rail to see Tarja doing precisely that, her legs dangling above the hungry waves. Quint thrust out his hand, yelling for Tarja to take it.

With a mighty grunt she did, though it felt like she was about to pull his arm from its socket. Quint gritted his teeth against the pain and pulled, but for all the good he did he might as well have been straining to lift a mountain. The ship rocked beneath him, threatening to spill him over the edge alongside Tarja.

"I've got you!" Arms wrapped themselves around his middle, pulling him back onto the rain-slicked deck, Vanessa's soaking curls tickling the back of his neck.

"Hold tight!" This from Margherita, appearing at his side as she reached both arms over the rail, wrapping them around Tarja's wrist.

It took all their combined strength, yet they managed to haul Tarja back onto the deck, the four of them collapsing into a panting, wheezing pile. Beneath them the *Marigold* shuddered, water rushing up from the hatch they'd exited only moments earlier.

"Jollyboat," Quint managed between gasps for air. It was still there, waiting for them with Ophelia in the prow, staring fixedly at them with an expression of naked anguish.

Quint was halfway to his feet when a shadow fell across the deck. He looked up just in time to see a wave the size of the world come barreling towards them.

Captain Redbeard had not even a chance to scream before he was washed overboard.

The Sea of Tears swallowed him up, dragging him down into its cruel embrace where all was dark and cold. He could neither thrash nor struggle against its crushing grip. Oblivion rose to envelop him, dragging him down into a darkness deeper than the ocean depths.

The last thing he remembered before the blackness claimed him was a pair of smooth and scaly arms wrapping around his chest.

12

The first thing Quint became aware of was a throbbing headache, dragging him mercilessly back into the world of consciousness. The second was the grainy texture of wet sand against his skin, coarse and cool beneath him. The third thing was a comfortable weight around his hips, pressing him down so that the sand molded itself to the contours of his back and shoulders. It felt somehow familiar, and not at all unpleasant.

Something trailed across his face, its touch ticklish and feather-light. That too was familiar, as was the gentle warmth of someone's breath upon his lips.

Quint's eyes felt as though they'd been weighed down with sandbags, but he forced them open.

A pair of eyes were staring into his, huge and very pretty, the deep brown color of rich soil. They widened as they saw him looking back.

"Quint?" Vanessa's voice. And her eyes, evidently. And—as he was suddenly intently aware—her lips, mere inches from his own.

He opened his mouth to answer, but instead of words what seemed like half the Sea of Tears came rushing out in a choking, coughing fit.

Vanessa recoiled, avoiding the worst of it as Quint turned his head away and retched up what felt like more seawater than any one person should have been able to swallow.

"Sorry," he wheezed once the choking fit had passed, turning back to Vanessa. His throat was raw and stinging. "I—"

Again he could not complete the thought, but only because Vanessa's arms were suddenly around him, pulling him up from the sand and into a crushing embrace. He clung to her like a drowning man to a piece of driftwood, her thick dark curls once again tickling his face. Instead of her usual jasmine-and-coconut scent, she smelled of salt and brine, not wholly unpleasant.

"Quint." Her voice was a muffled, choked sound in his ear. "Thank the angels you're alright."

"Aye," he managed hoarsely. He was having some difficulty drawing in a breath, and not because of his near drowning. "Er, Vanessa?"

"Mm?"

"You're choking me a little."

"Sorry." Her arms left him, and Quint propped himself up on an elbow to keep from falling back to the sand. Vanessa sat back in a crouch, framed against a sandy beach turned gray by the brooding clouds overhead. Behind her the ocean roiled and churned with whitecaps, lit by occasional streaks of lightning lancing towards the far horizon. The storm that had drowned the *Marigold* had not yet abated, but the worst of it had passed, seemingly.

"Are you quite done?" a weary voice asked. Quint looked around to see Margherita sitting perched upon a driftwood log a few feet away, her olive complexion looking decidedly pale. One leg was stretched straight out in front of her, her heel digging a divot in the sand. "Since it looks like your kiss of life wasn't needed after all, I mean."

Vanessa coughed and stood, offering Quint a hand.

"Tarja," Quint said, accepting her hand and coming to his feet as thunder boomed across the waves. "What happened? Is she—"

"I am fine, friend Quint," came a familiar Trechtish accent. Quint turned to see her come striding from the line of trees, tying up her breeches one-handed.

"The others," Quint repeated, looking out to sea. He shivered. There was no sign of the *Marigold* above the whitecapped waves. "Did they...?"

"They made it to the jollyboat," Vanessa assured him. "I caught a glimpse of it casting off just before we went under. Everyone was still aboard."

"Thank the angels," Quint said, a stab of guilt running through him. Ophelia had been forced to make the terrible choice to leave him behind, lest by lingering she endanger the entire crew. He hoped that she had made it ashore, and that she was not berating herself for making that call. It had been the right choice.

He was about to ask Vanessa whether there'd been any sight of the jollyboat or its passengers when a serpentine shape came rising up from the surf, bounding ashore with her arms tucked in tight against her sides in a way that reminded Quint of seals, though Lurk was of course far thinner than those happy creatures.

"Quint!" she said, coming to a stop in front of him, her spinal ridge quivering happily. "You're awake! Vanessa kissed you, then?"

Quint tried to think of something to say, but found he could only make a choking sound.

"Must not have worked," Lurk said, lips pressing together in a mermaid frown and turning to Vanessa. "Do you want to try again?"

Behind him, Margherita let out a snort. Vanessa's cheeks colored, and she ran a hand through her damp curls.

"I'm alright," Quint said hastily, coming to her rescue. "Just swallowed a bit more ocean than I'd prefer, is all."

"You're not supposed to do that," Lurk said, lips still tight. "You would've swallowed a lot more if I hadn't undrowned you."

"Undrowned?" Quint repeated, then remembered the scaly arms that had wrapped themselves around him like angel's wings.

"Angels bless the day I took you into my crew," Quint said, putting a hand on Lurk's shoulder. Lurk's spinal ridge quivered with what he thought might be pride, while out of the corner of his eye Quint saw Margherita and Tarja exchange surprised glances. "You saved my life today, mate. Thank you."

"All our lives," Vanessa amended, glancing over her shoulder at the other two. Tarja waved her hook at Lurk, beaming, while even Margherita managed to muster a grudging nod. "Thank you, Lurk."

"You're my pod," Lurk said modestly, but her spinal ridge was standing fully upright now. Her dark eyes flickered to Margherita, sitting on the driftwood log with her leg held straight in front of her. "Well. They're not. But I thought you'd want them undrowned too, even though they took you prisoner."

"For which we are very humbly grateful," Tarja said, nudging Margherita in the rib. "You see? I told you there was a serpent hiding somewhere aboard the ship!"

Quint raised an eyebrow at Lurk, who'd grown adept enough at reading human expressions to shrug. "When I got tired of holding onto the hull I'd climb up to the prow and coil around the figurehead."

"And you said I was seeing things," Tarja said to Margherita, grinning. She stood and gave Lurk a bow in the traditional Trechtish style. "Thank you for saving us, friend...Lurk, you said?"

"My landfolk name," Lurk nodded, pointing a finger at Quint. "Quint gave it to me."

"A pleasure," Tarja said, straightening from her bow. "I am Tarja, first mate to Captain Margherita Elena Rossini, who is sitting on that log."

"Apologies for not coming over," Margherita said, lifting her hand in a wave, then gesturing towards her outstretched foot. "Twisted my ankle while I was crossing the deck to help this lot."

"Legs are stupid," Lurk opined, not for the first time. "If you four had tails you could have just swam away, like I did."

"If only," Quint said. "Speaking of getting away...did you see what happened to the jollyboat after we went under?"

For Lurk to have rescued all four of them from drowning and then swam them to shore, the *Marigold* must have gone down relatively nearby. But in a storm of such ferocity the jollyboat could easily have capsized, or foundered against the reefs that must surely ring this shore.

"Aye," Lurk said, to Quint's unfathomable relief. She gestured further up the coast, in a direction that might have been north, based on what little sun managed to pierce the slackening storm clouds. "There's a strong current running that way, following the shore. They got swept up in it."

"Do you think..." Quint paused, trying not to let on how deep his worry ran. "But they were all in the boat? Everyone?"

"All of them," Lurk confirmed, and though her expressions were difficult to read Quint thought he saw realization dawn behind those black eyes. She reached out a webbed hand and rested it on his shoulder. "They're fine, Quint. The weather started getting better almost right after I undrowned you."

She was right, he realized, glancing up at the slate-gray sky. That he could even do that much without being pelted with fat raindrops was testament to the improving forecast.

Now that they were no longer in immediate peril—from drowning, anyway—and now that he was reasonably assured that the others were still alive, Quint took a moment to examine his surroundings for the first time.

They'd washed ashore on a narrow spit of rocky shore, bordered on either hand by steep, imposing cliffs the color of rust. Lurk had deposited them on what looked to be the only strip of sandy beach sandwiched between those rocky promontories, further raising Quint's estimation of his mermaid crewmate.

The waters beyond this narrow cove were green and choppy, stirred up by the storm which still sprayed spiteful raindrops upon the beach. Perhaps a hundred yards from shore lay a line of white breakers, marking the reef which separated them from the open sea. Flotsam churned in the waves, littering the rocky shore with snapped mastheads, splintered timbers, and ragged bits of rigging—all that remained of the *Marigold.*

Nearer at hand the churning surf pounded relentlessly against the sand and rocks, racing so far up the beach that it sloshed over Quint's and Vanessa's waterlogged boots and nearly reached the roots of the pandanus and palms that marked the transition from beach to dense jungle.

"We on an island?" Quint asked, peering into the gloom beneath the pandanus branches. With the clouds it was all but impossible to see more than a few yards within. "Or did we cross the Sea of Tears and find whatever austral continent lies on the other side?"

"Island," Lurk said immediately. When Quint raised an eyebrow she shrugged. "It's hard to explain to landfolk. Something in the way the currents and tides interact with a small piece of land, or a big one. And this one's definitely on the smaller end."

"So the jollyboat couldn't have gotten too far," Quint mused, glancing up at a slight gap in the clouds. The storm made it difficult to gauge precisely, but he guessed it was a little before noon. "If we set out now—"

"We?" Margherita repeated, raising an eyebrow. "I don't recall dying and making you captain."

"I *am* captain," Quint said, jabbing a thumb at his chest before remembering that Lurk was the only soul upon the beach who might consider him as such.

Margherita scoffed. "Don't recall freeing you, either, *Captain* Redbeard."

"You got a pair of manacles on you?" Quint retorted, but was cut off from further speech by Vanessa's hand on his arm.

"Is this really the time?" she asked, giving both him and Margherita a pointed look.

"Friend Vanessa is right," Tarja nodded, sitting heavily on the other end of Margherita's driftwood log. Margherita winced as the shift in weight lifted her slightly from her seat. "We have a saying in Trecht: Even the king of rats is still living in the sewers."

"I've seen worse sewers," Margherita said, glancing towards the trees overhanging the beach. "But I take your point."

"In that case," Quint said, thrusting his hand towards Margherita, "I propose a ceasefire. No fighting , no imprisoning each other, no tying anyone up."

Margherita stared at his hand. With her hair plastered against her head and her feathered hat presumably somewhere on the seabed, the pirate queen of the Archipelago looked diminished, almost vulnerable.

Hand outstretched, Quint waited. So did Tarja and Vanessa, eyes darting between the two pirate captains. Lurk was preoccupied with scanning the narrow beach, doubtless searching for the fire they'd decided to cease.

"Fine," Margherita said at last, taking Quint's hand with a grimace that suggested it cost her to do so. "Truce accepted, Redbeard."

"Thanks," Quint said. "You can call me Quint, by the way."

Margherita's sour expression grew guarded, doubtful.

"What?" Quint asked with a crooked smile. "You didn't think Redbeard was the name my parents gave me, surely?"

"I suppose not," Margherita said, her gaze rising from his hand to his face, studying him intently. "Not with that scrawny patch of stubble, anyway."

"Stub—" Quint started, touching two fingers to his chin. "Look, I've been growing it out, alright?"

"Alright," Margherita said, sounding dubious. "Quint. Huh."

"Now that we've established a cessation of hostilities," Vanessa said, looking like she was trying quite hard not to roll her eyes, "can we get back to the business of finding the others?"

"I'm not getting very far on this leg," Margherita said, gesturing down at her ankle. She flexed it experimentally, then winced with a hiss of indrawn breath.

"May I?" Quint asked, kneeling on the sand beside her as Margherita gave a grudging nod. He pried her boot off as slowly and carefully as he was able, then gently probed her ankle and foot with his fingers.

"There's no break," he announced once he was certain of that fact. "Think you just twisted it in the wreck. Sprained it, at worst."

"Good," Margherita exhaled, but she was frowning. "In the long term, at least. But I doubt I'll be doing any hikes to wherever the others washed up."

"I can find them," Lurk said suddenly. All four humans looked at her. "Whatever part of this island they ended up on. I can swim there and let them know you're alright."

"That's a good idea," Quint said, though a chill of apprehension gripped him. "But if they got swept away by a current—"

"*Quint,*" Lurk said, in that exaggeratedly patient tone she took whenever she was explaining some facet of aquatic life to him that she thought was supremely obvious. "I'll just swim around it."

"Right," Quint said, unable to shake his protective instincts. "But be careful, you hear me? And come right back—"

But Lurk had already thrown him a webbed-fingered salute, then turned and slithered down the beach, back into the waves. Her serpentine form snaked through the water, then was lost to sight. Quint sent a silent prayer after her.

"So," Tarja said as the rain finally slackened off entirely, looking brightly between Quint and Vanessa. "How long have you had a mermaid in your crew?"

13

Lurk returned far sooner than Quint had expected.

It was an hour or so past sundown, the stormy sky now a clear night filled with stars. The three pirates and Vanessa had taken shelter from the wind blowing in from the sea beneath a rocky overhang, sitting with their backs against the stone and warming their hands against the fire they'd built with the driest bits of driftwood they could find.

"If we just had a bite to eat," Quint was saying, patting his growling stomach, "then things might be downright comfo—"

He was interrupted by a splashing breaking the otherwise rhythmic pounding of the surf, and a moment later by the sound of his own name.

"Quint!" Lurk called in her high, musical voice as she glided up from the shallows and into the ring of light cast by their little fire. Not for the first time, Quint found himself grateful that the mermaid was his friend; the sight of her rising from the waves and slithering straight for them with water dripping off her scales might have been alarming in a different context. Judging by the way Margherita and Tarja instinctively flattened themselves against the rock, they thought similarly.

"Ahoy, Lurk," he said, leaning forward to greet her. "You found them, then?"

"Aye!" she said brightly. Now that she was within the little overhang Quint saw she was carrying something over her shoulder. "And I brought you something!"

She slung down her burden, revealing it to be a length of netting that must have come from the *Marigold*. It hit the sand with a clatter, and Quint saw that it looked like it was full of small, oblong rocks.

"Mussels?" he asked, lifting one to the firelight.

"And oysters," Lurk said happily, popping one into her mouth without even breaking the shell. An audible crunching filled the little overhang, her sharklike teeth flashing with each bite.

Quint's stomach gave an insistent growl, and he dove in, passing the oysters and mussels to the others.

"None for me," Margherita shook her head, grimacing. "I had a bad experience with some snails once. Haven't been able to eat anything with a shell since."

"You certain?" Vanessa asked, splitting open a mussel with a practiced motion and slurping it down. "We might not get another meal for a while."

"I can always bring you more," Lurk offered, the firelight reflecting in her huge eyes, which widened with sudden remembrance. "Oh! And I found this."

She reached into the bottom of the net and produced a soppy, dripping bundle, out from which poked the battered remains of a feather that might once have been white.

"Here," she said, holding it out for Margherita. "I thought you might want it back."

Margherita hesitated, then nodded and held out her hand.

"It's a little wet," Lurk cautioned, demonstrating her mastery of understatement as she handed over the sodden hat.

"I'll, uh. Wait for it to dry before I put it on, then." Margherita said, setting the hat carefully atop a nearby rock. She cleared her throat and nodded to the mermaid. "But thank you."

"And thanks for dinner, Lurk," Quint said. Tarja nodded her agreement, stifling a belch with her hook. "But I'm more concerned about the rest of the crew. Where are they? Are they alright?"

"They're fine," Lurk assured him, gesturing a webbed hand vaguely towards the jungle. "They are on the farther end of the island, at a place where a river empties into a broad lagoon."

"That's good," Quint said, relieved. They wouldn't run short of fresh water, in that case. "How are things between them? I mean, between Margherita's mates and ours."

Margherita went very still but said nothing, only stared intently at Lurk.

"Well," the mermaid said after a moment's consideration. "Nobody's put each other in shackles yet."

"An encouraging sign," Vanessa said. "They're working together, then?"

"Aye," Lurk nodded. "Last I saw them, they were busy building shelter."

"Smart," Margherita said, glancing up at the rocky ceiling of the overhang. "Who's taken charge? With me and Tarja over here—"

"Ophelia," Lurk said without hesitation. "That is, Vigo was in charge of building the shelter. But Ophelia was the one making choices, telling everyone what to do. That sort of thing."

"Good," Quint said, glancing at Margherita. The older pirate's face was unreadable, but he wondered if she too had noticed that it was two of his crew who had stepped up to fill the void in leadership. "Did she have any message for us?"

"For either of us?" Margherita asked, leaning forward.

"She did," Lurk said, then popped another oyster into her mouth, forcing them to wait while she crunched noisily. Quint had a nagging suspicion she was doing so on purpose.

"Ophelia says," Lurk said once she'd swallowed down the oyster, shell and all, "not to worry about the rest of the crew. There's fruit trees where they are, and they've got fresh water from the river."

The mermaid made a face at that, evidently finding the idea of freshwater distasteful.

"And you mentioned they were building shelter," Vanessa nodded, "but what about the jollyboat? Could they sail it around the island?"

There was another, unasked question beneath that one. Victims of other shipwrecks had survived for astonishingly long stretches of time in lifeboats no larger than the *Marigold's* jollyboat, enduring monthslong ordeals fraught with hunger, storms, and sharks. Quint did not relish the idea of undertaking such a perilous voyage.

"No luck there," Lurk said, her spinal ridge flattening briefly. "Jollyboat overturned while they were crossing over the reef into the lagoon. Everyone made it to shore, but the boat itself is sunk."

"So no chance of them coming to pick us up," Quint said, glancing at Margherita's ankle. He and Tarja had ventured into the jungle while Lurk was away, coming back with a young green sapling they'd cut into a splint for the injured pirate queen using Margherita's cutlass. Somehow, she hadn't lost it in the shipwreck.

Excluding Tarja's hook, it was the only weapon they had. Quint did not relish the prospect of an overland trek through unknown terrain so lightly armed. Angels only knew what sort of beasts might be lurking in the jungle beyond their little strip of beach.

"I'll be alright," Margherita said, misreading his concerned look. She patted her splint. "Might not be running any races, but I'll be able to put enough weight on it to tramp through those woods."

"Are you sure?" Lurk asked, looking dubiously at Margherita's splinted leg, then at Quint's uninjured ones. "I don't know how far landfolk can walk."

"Far enough to get us to where Ophelia and the others are," Quint assured her. He looked around at the others. "Break camp and head that way at first light?"

"What camp?" Margherita snorted, but nodded her assent. So did Tarja and Vanessa.

"What if you run into something dangerous, though?" Lurk asked, and Quint was touched by the concern in her voice. "Like snakes, or land sharks, or—"

"Land sharks?" Tarja asked, leaning forward with evident interest.

"She means wolves," Quint clarified.

"Sharks are not wolves," Tarja frowned.

"And sea lions aren't lions," Quint pointed out, then returned his attention to Lurk. "We'll be alright, promise. Come first light, we'll head on across the jungle until we reach this river Lurk mentioned, then follow it downhill to the beach where the others are staying."

Vanessa toyed with one of her curls, staring into the flames. "Judging from how long it took for Lurk to swim to the others' encampment and back, we're looking at two days' hike at the minimum. More, if the terrain's bad, or if Margherita's leg slows us down."

"Don't you worry about me," Margherita said, narrowing her eyes.

"No one is worried," Tarja said soothingly, patting her captain's back. "If you do go too slowly, I will carry you on my back."

Margherita grimaced as Quint hid his smile behind his hand.

"I'll head back to Ophelia in the morning when you leave," Lurk said, glancing over her shoulder at the black ocean behind them. "Let her know that if it takes you more than four days to reach her she should send someone to look for you."

She turned, squinting her great dark eyes at the jungle. "Are you *sure* you'll be okay walking through that? It's an awful lot of trees."

"We'll be fine," Quint assured her, then added the two words mermaids held inviolate above all others. "I promise."

"Good," Lurk said, though her spinal ridge did not relax. Instead she shot a look at Margherita and Tarja. "You'd better both keep him safe."

"What about me?" Vanessa complained, though Quint could tell she was trying hard not to smile.

"I know *you'll* be fine," Lurk said, shaking her head. "But Quint needs watching."

Quint blinked, somewhat miffed by the implications in that statement.

"Worry not," Tarja said, waving her hook. "On my husband's life, I shall keep your captain safe from whatever dangers the woods have to offer no matter how many snakes, tigers, or land sharks I must wrestle."

Her accent made it difficult to discern whether she was joking, but Lurk nodded, satisfied, before turning her attention to Margherita. "And you?"

"What about me?" Margherita asked, raising an eyebrow. "I agreed to a truce, didn't I?"

"You did," Lurk acknowledged, though her dark eyes flickered down to the cutlass sheathed at the pirate queen's waist. "But Quint's been betrayed before."

"That's something we've got in common, then." Margherita looked at Quint, her face momentarily clouded by an odd expression that accentuated the lines of her face. Then it was gone, replaced by a cocksure, rather mocking smile. "Rest easy, Redbeard. You've got no cause to worry about me stabbing you in the back."

Only later that night, as Quint struggled to fall asleep over the atonal roaring of Tarja's snores, did he realize that Margherita had said nothing whatsoever about stabbing him anyplace else.

14

—•—

The sun had just barely poked its yellow head above the unseen eastern horizon when they began their journey to rejoin their fellows. After bidding Lurk farewell, they set off into the jungle, carrying only the clothes on their backs and the netting Lurk had used to bring them their dinner, now laden with coconuts gathered from the palm trees overhanging the beach.

As they walked, Quint's nose was filled with the mingled scents of flowers he could not name. This early in the morning, the air within the jungle was heavy and humid, though still cool. The canopy above was alive with the chattering, hooting calls of unseen birds greeting the sun. Their musical trills and caws were frequently punctuated by a branch breaking or the rustling of leaves as furtive creatures scurried through the undergrowth, though by the second hour they had seen nothing larger than an iguana lazily sunning itself upside-down on a tree.

There was no trail, but the ground underfoot was clear of mud and mostly free of tree roots, and for the first few hours they made good time, even with Margherita's injury. The pirate queen herself took the lead, the bedraggled feather in her hat bobbing along as she hacked furiously at any overhanging vine or trailing creeper that made the mistake of coming within the reach of her cutlass. Tarja followed after, using her hook to clear the path of any vegetation that survived her captain's wrath.

Despite their easy progress, the pirate queen's anger seemed to grow with every hour, building in a way that reminded Quint of the tremors of the volcano in whose shadow he had spent the majority of his childhood. Yet where Ember Bay's periodic eruptions had been mild, restrained bursts of ash and dust, Margherita's mounting rage was clearly building to an explosion of considerably greater violence.

It came just after noon, when they found themselves confronted by a thicket of closely-spaced bamboo trees, the largest of them as thick around as Tarja's arm. Margherita attempted to chop her way through them with brute force, yet the sturdy bamboo proved more resistant to her efforts than the vines or creepers had.

"I am so *sick*," she growled, punctuating each syllable with a swing of her cutlass, followed by the dull *thunk* of steel biting into green bamboo. "Of—"

Thunk.

"—this—"

Thunk.

"Thrice-damned—"

Thunkthunk.

"—angelsforsaken—"

Thunk thunk, thunk thunk.

"Island!" the pirate queen howled, putting all of her weight into the last swing.

The cutlass bounced off the bamboo, leaving hardly a nick. Tarja yelped and threw herself aside as the sword went spinning from Margherita's grasp. Quint threw his arm across Vanessa's shoulders, pulling both of them out of the spinning blade's path as it flew past, missing them by mere inches. It landed in the mud behind them, a prominent notch a third of the way down its blade.

"Cheap Tourmaline steel," Margherita muttered to herself, turning to stomp over and retrieve it, but Quint barred her path.

"I don't know what you think this island did to offend you personally," he said, unable to keep an edge from his voice, "but maybe trying to deforest it one tree at a time ain't the best way to conserve our energy, eh?"

"Quickest way from one point to another is a straight line," Margherita said, glowering up at him. "I'd rather cut my way through this jungle than leave my crew alone a minute longer than I have to."

"They're not alone," Quint objected, moving to block her as she tried to get around him to retrieve her cutlass. Easily done, considering Margherita's injury and the disparity in their heights. "Ophelia's leading them, remember?"

Beneath the brim of her hat, Margherita's scowl deepened. "And that's supposed to set my mind at ease?"

"She's my first mate," Quint said, indignant on Ophelia's behalf.

"She's too young for command."

"Ophelia's the same age as me," Quint said, before recalling Ophelia's confession many years past that she had signed her Navy enlistment papers with a birthdate two years older than she actually was. "Or near enough as makes no difference."

"Exactly," Margherita sneered.

Now it was Quint's turn to scowl.

"I thought you *liked* Ophelia," he objected, knowing even as he spoke the words that he was opening a can of worms. "Seeing as you keep taking her to bed whenever we run into each other."

Margherita's eyes narrowed, and over her shoulder Tarja tried to hide a gasp with her hook. Vanessa put a warning hand on his arm.

"I *do* like Ophelia," Margherita said, and now there was a dangerous calm to her voice. "But liking someone and trusting them to helm your ship ain't the same thing."

Quint briefly considered pointing out that they had no ship for anyone to helm, before dismissing the idea of nitpicking Margherita's choice of metaphor as childish. "Not sure what's got you so worried. I've left her in charge of the *Bloody Angel* plenty of times."

"That's *exactly* what's got me worried," Margherita said, jabbing a finger into his chest. "You're both just making this up as you go along."

"Making what up?" Vanessa interjected before Quint could voice his opinion that practically everyone everywhere was simply improvising their way through life in precisely the manner Margherita described.

"Piracy," Margherita said, frowning at Vanessa as if that should be self-evident. "Neither him nor Ophelia ever had anyone teach them the ropes of the corsair's life. They just sort of fell into it when they deserted the Navy."

"It's not exactly the kind of career that requires an apprenticeship," Quint said, his anger ebbing away in favor of a bemused curiosity. "I mean, sure, we made some mistakes along the way while we was learning the trade. Sunk a few ships, pissed off a few of the wrong folk, woke up in someone else's clothes..."

Vanessa was looking dubiously at him, so Quint hurriedly changed tact.

"But we figured it out as we went," he continued. "It ain't an amateur pirate that could steal the Crown Jewels right from under the Navy's nose."

"Crown Jewels which are currently lying somewhere on the seabed," Margherita reminded him. "Thanks in part to your leadership."

"Thanks to your capturing us," Quint countered, heat rising in his voice. "If you hadn't—"

"Margherita," Tarja said, placing her hook between them. "Friend Quint. We have a truce if you recall?"

Quint looked down at his hands, found they had balled themselves into fists.

"Aye," he said, forcing himself to unclench them. "I recall."

"As do I," Margherita said, folding her arms across her chest and drumming her fingers against one bicep. "My point, *Quint,* is that there are things you've never learned about the pirate's life. Things I've offered to teach Ophelia. More than once."

That stung more than it should have.

"And yet she's declined each time," Quint countered. Behind him Vanessa bent and picked up Margherita's cutlass, wiping the mud from the blade with the hem of her shirt. "Must not be that tempting an offer."

"It's because she feels she's got some unpaid debt to you," Margherita said, grinding her teeth. "Even though you're just a lowdown, selfish thief who doesn't give half a rat's wet fart about anything other than getting rich—"

"I care about other things," Quint objected, feeling heat rise in his cheeks. His anger was desperately seeking an outlet, so rather than risk breaking their fragile truce, he shouldered past Margherita and into the dense grove of bamboo. "My crew, for one."

"Aye," Margherita said, hurrying after him as he picked his way between the slender bamboo shoots. "Caring for the gang of like-minded cutthroats and villains you drag into your greedy schemes. Most altruistic."

"I'll just, uh, hold onto this, then," Vanessa said, tucking the cutlass into her belt and following after them. So did Tarja, though given her greater bulk she moved more slowly between the densely-clustered bamboo. With a conscious effort, Quint forced himself to slow down. It would do no one any good for them to become separated.

"Pretty rich of you to accuse me of villainy," he said, bending a bamboo shoot out of his path, "when you were planning on using Vanessa and me as live bait just a few days ago."

"Bait for the Empire," Margherita retorted, as if that made it alright.

Quint released the bamboo, sending it whipping towards her. Short as Margherita was, it sailed right over her head, earning him a contemptuous snort.

"Right," Quint said, grinding his teeth. "The Empire, which is definitely just waiting for a heroic pirate queen to light the spark of rebellion that'll send it all up in flames. Certainly not an institution with the weight and wealth of centuries and cannons behind it."

Vanessa made an uncomfortable sound but said nothing. For several minutes there was no sound save the distant echo of birdsong, and the soft complaint of bamboo shoots being pushed aside as they made their way through the grove.

"You don't think it can be done," Margherita said, and to Quint's surprise she sounded more tired than angry. "Overthrowing the Empire."

"What gave you that impression?" Quint fired back, then shook his head. "There's always been an empire, and there always will be. No changing that."

"Actually," Vanessa said, frowning as she used the cutlass to lever aside a particularly resistant stand of bamboo, "the first Empress was Karina I, back in—"

"Not *the* Empire," Quint corrected himself, throwing an apologetic glance Vanessa's way. "But *an* empire. Before the one you serve it was the Jewel Confederacy, then the Arendt Kingdom, and so on, all the way back to ancient days."

A hooting call rang through the jungle, unlike any birdsong Quint had ever heard. They paused, eyes darting about the leaves overhead, but no creature revealed itself, and the call did not repeat.

"My point," Quint continued, suddenly feeling much wearier than the exertion of their hike alone warranted, "is that there's always going to be somebody in power, and that whoever it is probably ain't going to have what's best in mind for the little folk like us. Best to ignore them when you can and avoid them when you can't. No point trying to change the unchangeable."

"One might call that a coward's view," Margherita scoffed, but Quint found himself too tired to rise to the bait.

"Everyone's entitled to their opinion," he said with a shrug. "Mine is that it's a fool's errand to waste the lives of the ones I love on a hopeless fight. Better to live well while we've got time."

"I was taught differently," Margherita said, but then her scowl softened. "That it's better to fight for what you know is right than run from something just because it's hard."

"Uh-huh," Quint said, unimpressed. "Did your mysterious mentor also teach you to sail the smallest ship you had access to across the most dangerous stretch of ocean ever charted? Because if we'd taken the *Wildflower* across the Sea of Tears instead of that little *Marigold*, none of us would be stuck on this island in the first place."

Margherita did not answer for so long that Quint was almost tempted to believe that he'd won the argument. Ahead of them the bamboo grove thinned, revealing a grassy field gently sloping up to a low hillside. Through the gaps in the leaves Quint glimpsed the peak of a small mountain, smaller even than Ember Bay's lonely volcano.

"I knew what I was doing," Margherita said, so low that Quint thought she was talking to herself. Only when she glanced over her shoulder at him did he realize that the words had been meant for him.

"Meaning?" he asked.

"Meaning I'd rather risk my life than what the *Wildflower* was carrying," she said, tight-lipped.

Quint wanted to ask what sort of cargo the *Wildflower* was hauling to be worth more than the Crown Jewels, but the pirate queen was already hobbling out onto the grass, towards the mountain ahead of them. The breeze rustled the pinions of her hat's bedraggled feather.

"Come on," she called over her shoulder, all business now. "We should be able to see that river your mermaid friend mentioned from the top. And I'm sick of this jungle."

"As am I," Tarja said, looking relieved to finally stumble out into the open air. "Wait for me, Captain!"

She hurried after Margherita, looking like a bright and cheerful cloud trailing after the small, dark thundercloud that was her captain.

Vanessa drew up alongside Quint, still holding Margherita's cutlass. They exchanged a glance, both of them silently wondering how long this tentative alliance would hold.

15

The sun climbed high into the sky as they hiked steadily uphill, following the path of a narrow ridge that fell away steeply on either side. Through the trees they caught glimpses of densely-forested hills and valleys, bisected in places by brown cliffs and rocky canyons. Ahead of them the jungle rose steadily to the height of its central mountain, which was modest by Archipelago standards but towered above the hills surrounding it. Quint estimated that, given their current pace, they would likely reach its peak by sundown.

They traveled in a tight single file, Margherita leading, though she now picked her way carefully along the ridge, mindful of her injury and of the steep drop to either hand. Vanessa followed along, Quint behind her and Tarja taking up the rear. Each was sipping from one of the coconuts they'd brought along, which Tarja had pierced holes in using her hook. The rest she carried in the net slung over her shoulder.

"You know," Quint said, looking back at her and thinking of the mythical old man who rowed between islands delivering toys to children at each midwinter solstice, "you look a bit like Papa Kri carrying his sack."

"Aye," Tarja agreed, raising her coconut in salute. "Come to bring gifts to all the good boys and girls of the islands! So long as the gifts are coconuts, anyway."

"What, no baskets full of fishhooks for the naughty children?" Vanessa teased, citing the traditional gift for those whose moral performance during the year had been less than upstanding.

"Guess it depends on which of us has misbehaved the most," Quint said, glancing between the four of them. "We could really use some fishhooks while we're here, too."

"Do not look at me," Tarja shook her head. "I am not actually Papa Kri, though I am perhaps as big and as jolly."

"And I only ever found the hook basket outside my door the one time," Quint said, grimacing at the memory.

"What, that's a real thing?" Vanessa asked, frowning. "People on the islands actually give their kids fishhooks at solstice if they've misbehaved?"

"I forget sometimes," Quint said, wiping his hair from his face. Hours of marching beneath the tropical sun had plastered it to his brow. "You come from money."

"My dads kept us comfortable," Vanessa said, currently looking anything but comfortable.

"That's the kind of thing rich folk say when they're pretending they ain't rich," Margherita snorted. It was her first contribution to the conversation since they'd left the grove of bamboo.

"But for those of us less fiscally fortunate," Quint said, stepping in before tempers could rise, "the old 'fishhooks in your basket' at solstice is a time-honored means of letting your kids know they'd better shape up."

"And you got one of those," Vanessa said, a slow grin creeping over her face. "Having heard how you talk about your pop and having met your ma, I can't imagine them ever being that put out with you."

"That's because you didn't know me at fourteen," Quint said ruefully. "I was a right little nuisance that whole year. Guess my folks thought that the fishhooks might be a wake-up call to do better."

"Doubt it worked," Margherita muttered, loud enough for Quint to hear.

"It didn't, actually," Quint admitted. "I signed on with the Navy the following spring."

They hiked on in silence for another few minutes, the only sound the wind sighing through the trees.

"What about you?" Vanessa asked Tarja. "Papa Kri ever leave you a basket full of fishhooks?"

"Nah," Tarja shook her head. "We have different traditions on Trecht."

"Such as?"

Tarja thought a moment. "Well, the night before solstice, Cinder Criss—that is our version of Papa Kri—leaves chocolates in our shoes."

"Messy," Quint commented, thinking of how quickly such sweets would melt in the heat of the Archipelago, though he supposed Trecht's winters were a good deal colder. "When I was a kid my pop and his friends would take turns pretending to be Papa Kri each year. Come rowing up the harbor in a canoe and everything. Really went the extra mile to make it feel special for us."

"That is sweet," Tarja beamed, adjusting the net slung over her shoulder. "I have been Papa Kri a time or two myself, though the *Wildflower* is missing the canoe. Not that the little ones seem to mind—"

"Tarja," Margherita said warningly.

The big Trechtish pirate went even paler than usual and clapped a hand over her mouth, but too late.

"Little ones," Quint repeated, bewildered. He turned to Margherita. "You don't take *kids* aboard your crew—"

"Of course not," Margherita said with a firm, offended vehemence.

"Then—" Quint searched for another explanation of what children might be doing aboard a pirate warship, but Vanessa got there before he did.

"They're not crew," she said, something cold and flinty in her eyes Quint had never seen there before. "They're her cargo."

Belatedly, Quint realized that Vanessa was still holding Margherita's cutlass. But the pirate queen did not so much as twitch a muscle.

"Passengers," she corrected. "Them and their parents both."

"And how many of them agreed to book passage with you?" Vanessa asked, her voice deadly calm.

"As many as came aboard," Margherita said, holding Vanessa's gaze. "I'm no slaver, *Commander.*"

A muscle in Vanessa's jaw twitched; the slight emphasis on her rank had not gone unnoticed.

"That's why you weren't willing to risk the *Wildflower*," Quint realized aloud. "Because you had children aboard. Right?"

Margherita said nothing, but behind him Tarja sighed.

"Our secret is out, Captain," she said to Margherita. "In truth, I do not know why we bothered hiding it from these two. They are clearly sympathetic—"

"*She's* not," Margherita retorted, nodding at Vanessa. "She's Imperial. She wouldn't understand—"

"Try me," Vanessa said. "I'm more than my uniform."

Margherita took a step closer, near enough that if Vanessa decided to swing the borrowed cutlass it would pass right above its owner's head, neatly severing the quivering feather from her hat.

"Then prove it," the pirate queen said.

For a moment there was no sound save for the low moaning of wind through the grass. Quint felt suddenly, alarmingly aware of how narrow the ridge they were climbing was, and how steep its sides. Every fiber of his being was screaming out for him to interpose himself between the two women, yet he forced himself to stay still, knowing that a sudden move might shatter the fragile equilibrium between them.

Then Vanessa lowered Margherita's cutlass and held it out to her, hilt first. The older woman's brows lifted in the briefest flicker of surprise. She schooled her face back into its cool mask as she wordlessly accepted the proffered sword.

"Now explain," Vanessa said, still in that even voice Quint knew was her most dangerous. "Why were you willing to risk the lives of *children* by taking them aboard the ship of the most wanted pirate in the Archipelago?"

"They were Cuprite children," Margherita said, then paused, as if that were explanation enough. Or perhaps waiting to gauge Vanessa's reaction.

"Cuprite's part of the Empire," Vanessa said, and though her back was to Quint he knew her brows were furrowing. "Her people are Imperial citizens—"

"Not all of them," Margherita said softly, sheathing her cutlass.

Another moment passed, the wind softly moaning.

"You mean the separatists," Vanessa said slowly, as if the word were something unpleasant being pulled from between her teeth.

"That's the Empire's name," Margherita countered, adjusting her hat. "They call themselves revolutionaries."

"Freedom fighters," Tarja rumbled from behind Quint, cutting off Vanessa's retort.

Vanessa glanced over her shoulder at Quint, as though expecting him to weigh in.

"I've met a few Cuprite rebels," he admitted with an uncomfortable shrug. "They're folk like anyone else, just wanting to live the way they please."

"Aye," Margherita nodded. "It's been a decade since the Empire conquered Cuprite—"

"*Liberated,*" Vanessa corrected, seemingly unable to help herself. "Before the Empire they were tributaries of the Asturian Confederacy—"

"World of difference between sending a tithe yearly all the way back to Asturia and being directly under the Empire's thumb," Margherita spat. "Your precious Navy didn't land on Cuprite to *liberate* its people from their distant overlords, but to replace them."

Vanessa ground her teeth, but Quint put a hand on her arm before she could fire off a retort. She turned and looked at him, brows knitting in surprise.

"You asked Margherita to explain," he reminded her gently. "She's trying to."

Vanessa swallowed down her clearly mounting anger and returned her attention to Margherita. "And the separatists?"

Margherita drummed her fingers on the hilt of her cutlass, gazing past Vanessa at the dark blue line of the horizon.

"Ten years is too short a time for folk to forget how things were before," she said. "Too short to forget when they were their own masters. Does it really surprise you, Commander, that not all of them would lie down and accept the Imperial bootheel on their back so easily?"

Vanessa ground her teeth but, with Quint's arm steadying her, did not rise to the bait. "I suppose not."

"No." Margherita's tone softened as her gaze shifted from the horizon to Vanessa. "There were always those who sought to shake off the shackles of the Confederacy, but the Empire was—and is—a more demanding master, with its taxes and conscriptions and its greed for copper, of which Cuprite has mines in abundance. So resistance against their new oppressors swelled accordingly."

"The Cuprite Rebellions," Vanessa said, and for the first time Quint heard the faintest tremor in her voice. "They've sprung up on and off ever since they became part of the Empire."

"Oppression breeds rebellion," Margherita said, shrugging. "The ones you call separatists aren't protected by the same laws as the rest of your Empire."

"Because they forfeit their citizenship in taking up arms against the Crown," Vanessa said, a bitter smile crossing her features. "It's what they want, after all."

"A forfeiture that extends to their families," Margherita said. "To their spouses, their children, their parents. Entire villages, more often than not."

"That's—" Vanessa started, then stopped, that lone syllable full of uncertainty.

"I know," Margherita nodded, a trace of sympathy in the crinkling of her eyes. "Officially they're all listed as separatists or separatist sympathizers. As if it's reasonable to ask folk to turn in their brother, or their wife, or their daughter, for the sake of an Empire they never asked to join."

"You're saying that the Empire jails innocents," Vanessa said, not as doubtfully as Quint expected.

"Jails them, strips them of their property, and sentences them to hard labor in their island's copper mines." Margherita's every word was as sharply pointed as a knife. "If you don't believe me, Commander, there's an entire hold full of Cuprite refugees you can ask yourself, assuming any of us ever make it off this island."

A pause, no sound but the wind gusting over the ridge.

"I hope we do," Vanessa said, sad and thoughtful. "I'd have questions for them. And for my superiors."

"You might not like the answers they give," Margherita warned, but there was a curious expression hovering about her lips. Surprise, perhaps, or satisfaction.

"Doesn't matter," Vanessa said, shaking her head. "An uncomfortable truth remains the truth. And if what you say *is* true...there are people who will have to answer for it."

Margherita gave her a slow nod.

"Then for all our sakes, Commander," she said, something close to respect in her voice, "I hope we make it off this island."

"Then we had better hurry," Tarja said, glancing up at the mountaintop towering before them, and at the sun drifting steadily westwards. "I would like to be off this ridge before sundown."

Margherita nodded her agreement, then turned and continued onwards up the ridge. Quint and Vanessa followed after. For a while none of them spoke, each lost in their separate thoughts. Quint could tell by the line that had taken up residence on Vanessa's brow that she was still considering what Margherita had told them.

For his part, Quint could not picture Vanessa, with her implacable sense of justice and fair play, ever partaking in such an affront as the Empire's occupation of Cuprite.

"It's true," Vanessa said, so low that he could hardly hear her. Shaken from his reverie, he looked over to see her watching him, awaiting his reaction, or perhaps his judgment. "Isn't it? Everything she said. About the Empire, and Cuprite. About the Navy and what they did—what they're doing there."

"Vanessa," he said, seized by the sudden need to assure her that she was not like that; that she was the exception; the exemplar of what the Navy and its supposed values of honor and gallantry *could* be.

But then what was the reality? Perhaps that was better represented by the elderly and ineffectual Admiral Stetson, or by the flinty-eyed cruelty of Captain Gault, under whose merciless tutelage Quint had first learned to sail a tall ship.

Yes, Quint thought, his memories unwillingly turning back to the long-ago sight of a hollow-eyed child standing alone at the foot of a gallows. He could easily imagine the Empire ordering an entire village into forced servitude, laboring in the mines that should have been theirs by right.

Something of that dark memory must have surfaced in his expression, for Vanessa's own grew clouded.

"Oh," she said, and turned away from him.

"Vanessa," Quint repeated, reaching for her as if she were a rope slipping through his hands. "I didn't—"

"Don't," she said, curls bouncing as she shook her head. She turned back to him, forced a smile that did not reach her eyes. "Quint, I..I need some time. To think. Can you give me that?"

"Of course," Quint said, swallowing down the thousand apologies jostling for space in his head. He wanted to pull her to him, or failing that, to reach out and squeeze her hand. Both urges he resisted, sensing that she needed space as well as time. "As long as you need."

Vanessa's smile turned ever so slightly less forced. "Thank you."

Together they turned and continued following Margherita up the ridge, Tarja trailing along behind them. Quint silently vowed that he would give Vanessa as long as she required to work through what Margherita had said.

After all, if there was one thing they had in abundance here on these unknown shores, it was time.

16

The hike grew steadily steeper as they climbed along the sparsely wooded highlands, leaving the dense jungle behind them. Soon they heard the sounds of roaring water, and within an hour of their argument on the ridge they came to a frothing, fast-flowing river tumbling downslope from the heights of the mountain ahead of them. Their clothes were soon dampened by its constant spray, and Quint found himself wishing the sun were still directly overhead instead of sinking steadily towards the western horizon.

They'd long since drained the coconuts of their milk, and hours spent hiking under the tropical sun had left them parched. But the river flowed so fast that it was not until they rounded a bend where the water flowed more slowly that they were able to stop and slake their thirsts.

"Should we head downhill?" Tarja asked, kneeling at the water's edge. "The mermaid said the others were at the mouth of a river, ja?"

"We don't know if this is the only river on the island," Quint replied, nodding towards the mountain peak ahead. "If we head to the top we should be able to see enough of the place to know."

"That's more time added to our journey," Margherita objected, though she didn't sound as if her heart was in it. "More time before we get back to the crew."

"Who have managed fine without us so far," Quint reminded her. He dipped his cupped hands into the water and drank, reveling in the cool freshness of the mountain stream. "Besides, which will take longer: heading to the peak and finding our heading for certain, or going up and down each and every river we come across?"

"Point made." Margherita sighed, taking off her hat and fanning herself with it. She looked towards the mountaintop again. "Fine. We make it up there, figure out where the others have made camp, then head there at first light."

"Sounds like a plan," Quint said, nodding his agreement. He turned to Vanessa. "Bet the view from up top'll be spectacular, eh?"

Vanessa nodded distractedly, still lost in thought after their earlier conversation. The last few hours' hiking had been uncomfortably quiet. Vanessa had said little, clearly still mulling over Margherita's revelations, while the pirate queen herself remained cool in her interactions with her onetime prisoners. Quint had attempted several times to lighten the mood by breaking into well-loved old shanties, but only Tarja had joined in, and the big Trechtish pirate's singing voice was so off-key that Quint's enthusiasm had waned after the first chorus.

Once they'd all drank their fill, they climbed for another hour. The river was now a tumbling whitewater, in places so loud they had to shout to be heard above the frothing roar. They made their way in single file along a precarious game trail, the high cliffside of the mountain at their right, the roaring rapids to their left. The westering sun cast long shadows across their path, which fell from the trail onto the rapids beneath.

"We're nearly there!" Margherita shouted above the din, jabbing a finger forward and upwards. Quint looked where she pointed, and was surprised to see that the mountain's peak was not far off. Another hour's hard hiking, he guessed, and they would reach the top.

"Hold on," Vanessa said, breaking her long silence. She brushed her hair from her ear and tilted her head, a look of concentration coming over her face that took Quint back to the chess table where they'd first met. "Do you hear that?"

Quint listened. Above the moaning wind came the roar of falling water somewhere ahead of them, not far off. The river was still to their left, though by this point it was less a river and more a constant spray of foam that just happened to flow horizontally as much as it did vertically.

"Waterfall," Quint said, resuming the climb with even more careful steps. "If it blocks the trail we might have to turn back."

"Couldn't we find another route to the top?" Margherita asked, glancing upwards at the mountain peak, now less than two hundred feet above them. Quint was surprised to hear a hint of apprehension in her voice.

"Not before it grows too dark for us to safely climb," Tarja said, jerking her thumb over her shoulder at the sinking sun behind them.

Margherita sighed and continued along the trail. Several more minutes' climbing took them around a corner, revealing the waterfall.

It fell in a broad, foaming torrent from the heights of the peak above, plunging into a rocky pool that churned and frothed before flowing downhill to feed the river they'd followed all the way from the beach. The fading sunlight painted the falls golden, turning every plume of spray rising from the pool below into a rainbow.

"It's beautiful," Margherita breathed, and for the first time Quint agreed with her without reservation.

"But is it safe to cross?" Vanessa asked, shaking free of her fugue. The waterfall plunged directly across the path they'd followed, seemingly barring their final ascent to the mountaintop. Quint's stomach twisted in disappointment at the thought that they'd come all this way only to be turned back so near their goal.

"Safe, no," Tarja said, leaning farther out over the edge of the trail than Quint was comfortable with. She pointed her hook. "But doable, ja. Look."

Quint looked. Upon closer inspection, the waterfall did not fall directly onto the trail. Rather, its course was projected outwards by the lip of a rocky overhang that formed a sort of natural roof to the cliffside trail, which by now had grown quite narrow. Quint sent a silent prayer to his personal angel that it would widen again on the waterfall's far side.

"I will go first," Tarja said, as casually as if she had announced that she was going abovedeck for a spot of fresh air. The others turned to her as one, incredulous.

"Tarja," Margherita said, undisguised concern in her voice. "You weigh as much as Vanessa and I together."

"Exactly," Tarja nodded, as if glad her captain understood. "If I can make the crossing and not slip, so can the rest of you."

"And if you can't?" Quint asked, alarmed. Until now he hadn't realized how fond he'd grown of the big Trechtish pirate, and the thought of her risking herself in such a fashion made him feel as queasy as if he were standing on the deck of a storm-wracked ship.

"Then the rest of you will have to look for our friends without me," Tarja said, unconcerned. "And even were I to fall, the drop is not so terrible."

She waved her hook downwards. The plumes of spray partially obscured the surface of the pool, but it could not be further than twenty feet below them.

"Seems pretty far to me," Margherita muttered, glancing briefly downwards before quickly lifting her gaze back to Tarja. "And there's probably rocks at the bottom, too."

"Which is why we shall go slowly and carefully," Tarja said, then gently moved around the others until she was in the lead of their little group, pressing her back against the cliff wall and inching slowly along the trail, her palm flat against the stone. Quint was dismayed to see that her toes extended out beyond the edge, hanging in space above the rocks below.

"Tarja," Margherita said suddenly, her eyes fixed on her crewmate rather than the waterfall or the pool. The pirate queen swallowed so forcibly that it was audible over the pounding waterfall. "Be careful, you hear?"

"Ja, Captain." Tarja flashed her a bright, beaming smile, and resumed inching her way along the trail. Then she was gone, disappearing from sight behind the sheeting curtain of the waterfall. Quint held his breath, awaiting Tarja's reappearance on the far side.

It seemed to take far longer than it should, but finally Tarja emerged from the other side of the waterfall, her blonde hair plastered to her brow and water droplets glistening on her skin even from this distance. But she gave them a broad smile and waved them forwards with her hook, her hand still pressed against the cliff face.

"I'll go next," Vanessa said, evidently emboldened by Tarja's successful crossing. She turned to Quint and gave him a tight smile. "See you on the other side?"

"Aye," Quint nodded, fighting down the jolt of fear that coursed through him at the prospect of her slipping on the damp rocks. "Ness?"

"What?"

Quint opened his mouth, wishing for what felt like the thousandth time that they could have more time to work out what it was they meant to one another. That they could say the things they'd left unsaid for so long.

"Luck," he said instead, squeezing her hand. Silently, he resolved to say those things once they were safely on the other side of the waterfall.

"Thanks," Vanessa said, squeezing back. "You, too."

Then she was gone, making her way along the slick trail with steps as measured and slow as Tarja's had been. Quint took a deep breath as she disappeared behind the waterfall, releasing it only once she reappeared on the far side.

Vanessa waved to them across the space between, then turned and followed Tarja's path up the trail, leaving Quint and Margherita alone on their side of the fall.

"I'll go next," Margherita said, and pressed forward before Quint could voice any objection. When she reached the point where she had to press her back against the cliffside, she did so with her eyes closed.

Something about the terse, sudden way she'd declared her intent to cross made Quint uneasy, as if she'd been trying to convince herself to go more than announce it to him and Vanessa.

She's scared of heights, he realized. This assumption was soon proven as Margherita advanced slowly along the trail with her nose in the air, refusing to permit herself a downwards glance. Quint hesitated, wondering whether he should follow her, or if that would only make the crossing more perilous for them both.

Margherita gasped, a sound that somehow carried to him even over the pounding roar. Quint watched in fascinated terror as the pirate queen recovered her footing after a false step, her chest rising and falling in short, shallow gasps, eyes wide with terror.

His mind made up, Quint hurried after Margherita, edging along the path with his heels firmly planted on solid ground.

The stone was rough beneath his palms, and he fought to ignore the unsettling feeling of the trail growing progressively narrower beneath his feet. When he reached the point where his toes extended over empty space Quint turned his head to the side, seeking to focus on anything else.

Margherita, he saw, was creeping along with her eyes closed, her lips moving in a constant stream of what might have been prayers and might have been curses. The waterfall drowned out all sound, save for the blood pounding in Quint's ears.

She was less than an arm's length away, moving even slower than he was. Already they were as soaked from the spray as they had been from the shipwreck, the already perilous trail underfoot turned wet and alarmingly slippery. The opaque curtain of the waterfall plunged past not a foot from their faces, drenching them in its spray.

Tarja and Vanessa were nowhere to be seen, already having rounded a bend in the trail, doubtless scouting ahead for other dangers between them and the end of their road.

If anything happened to either Quint or Margherita, no one else would see it.

There was a darker implication to that realization, but before Quint could consider what it was a short, sharp sound cut through even the pounding roar of the waterfall. He whipped his head to the side, heart leaping into his throat with sudden fear.

Margherita's foot had slipped on the slick stone. Her eyes were wide open now, white with terror, her hands scrabbling behind her for any purchase she could find in a cliffside worn smooth by centuries of erosion. The feather in her hat waved frantically back and forth, buffeted by the spray as Margherita teetered, one foot lower than the trail, a breath away from slipping and pitching forward to be swallowed up by the raging waterfall.

Let her, some vicious and unworthy part of Quint whispered. *Let her fall, and you'll have one less enemy to contend with.*

But somewhere between the shipwreck and now, Quint had stopped thinking of Margherita as the enemy she had been at the start of this misbegotten voyage.

And besides, he was already reaching for her.

"Easy!" he shouted, the waterfall's roar swallowing his words as he thrust out his hand, catching Margherita under the shoulder. He lifted and pushed at the same time, pressing her against the stone wall long enough and hard enough for her to regain her footing.

They looked at each other, both panting hard, backs against the wall. Margherita's eyes flickered briefly towards the sheeting curtain of the waterfall, and when they returned to him he was struck with an absolute certainty that she knew the temptation he'd briefly felt.

Margherita nodded up at him, blinking hard to clear her vision from the waterfall's constant spray. Quint nodded back.

Then they continued along the trail, one slow inch at a time, until at last they were past the danger of the waterfall and onto more solid footing. Around the corner Quint could hear the muffled voices of Tarja and Vanessa waiting for them to reappear.

"Let's go," Margherita said, speaking for the first time since she'd decided to cross. "The others'll be wondering what's taken us so long."

Then she turned and pressed onwards, not waiting for Quint to follow. She would not thank him, he already knew. Nor would either of them speak again about what had nearly happened behind the curtain of the waterfall, away from the eyes of all save each other and their angels. They did not need to.

For a brief, terrifying moment, Quint had held Margherita's life in his hands. He had made a choice. Had their roles been reversed, would she have chosen the same?

It was a question he hoped would remain unanswered.

17

"Seems Lurk was right," Quint said, shading his eyes as he stared down from the mountaintop. "It's definitely an island."

They had reached the peak just in time to witness a truly stunning sunset, the sky turning a fiery orange that deepened in the east to a dark purple. The western horizon was a line of flickering gold, but the ocean that lay between it and the island's shore was a blue so deep it was nearly black.

A black ocean that stretched away in every direction, with no sign of land anywhere in sight, save for the isle upon which they stood. The mountain was not located at its center, as had been their impression from the rocky beach where they'd washed ashore. Rather, its peak stood at the extreme southeast end of the island, beyond which lay only a steep slope down to the rocky cliffs and the waiting ocean below. The rest of the island fanned out in a northwesterly arc from the mountain, the land falling away to the thickly forested hills they had spent most of the day climbing. From here the river looked like little more than a narrow ribbon winding through the trees before emptying into a distant lagoon on the island's northern shore.

"Not exactly good news though, is it?" Margherita frowned, coming to stand beside him at the lip of the bowl-shaped crater that crowned the mountain, and must have been a volcanic caldera sometime in the far-distant past. "If we'd discovered the northern tip of some larger landmass on the far side of the Sea of Tears, there'd have to be *someone* already on it. Someone we might be able to bargain with for food, or supplies—"

"Or they might have been cannibals," Tarja pointed out, joining them on the crater's rim. "Then we would have *been* food."

"That's grisly," Margherita said, throwing a fond look at Tarja.

"Not really," the blonde pirate said, shrugging her broad shoulders. "Not compared to being mauled by a leopard, anyway, or strangled by a Ziltar python..."

Shaking his head, Quint moved away from them and to Vanessa. She stood on the northern side of the crater's rim, hands on her hips as she stared across the Sea of Tears.

"You're facing the wrong way," he told her, gesturing towards the sunset. "Show's over there."

"I know," she said, sparing the most perfunctory glance westward as the bottom of the sun touched the horizon, before returning her gaze to the north. "But home's that way."

Home. The word sent a quiver of longing through Quint Thatch, both for the familiar creak of the *Bloody Angel's* timbers beneath his feet, and for the comforting din of glasses and dishware that filled his parents' tavern most evenings. Once he had struggled to reconcile these two longings for two very different places, but if recent events had taught him anything, it was that home did not have to be only one place.

More often than not, he thought, watching as the sunset painted Vanessa's profile golden, home was who you were with.

"Ness," he said, putting a hand on her upper arm. She stiffened, but did not pull away. "Watching the sea ain't gonna conjure a ship over that horizon, and you know it."

Her eyes remained fixed on said horizon. "At least this way I'll see it sooner."

"And do what?" Quint pressed, half teasing and half serious. "We've got nothing to signal with up here on the heights. Those down on the beach might, but we can't signal them, either."

Vanessa glanced over her shoulder, but it was as Quint had said: the crater behind them bore no vegetation larger than a few small ferns.

"I suppose that's so," she said reluctantly, looking up at him. The sunlight caught her eyes, illuminating their brown depths.

"Tomorrow might bring a ship," Quint said, hand still on her arm as he gently turned her westward. "Or a storm. But tonight, right now? There's a sunset."

They stood watching as the sun sank into the distant ocean, then beneath it. There was a moment of perfect stillness, as all the world seemed to hold its breath.

Then a flash of green glinted where the sun had been, in the place where the sea met the sky, before fading as swiftly as it had appeared.

"The green light!" Vanessa exclaimed, her fingers tightening over Quint's. "Did you see it, Quint?"

"Aye, I saw it," he nodded, smiling down at Vanessa's wonderstruck expression, then frowned. "Wait. Don't tell me you've never seen it before?"

She looked up at him, sheepish. "You'd think I would have by now, wouldn't you?"

"You're pulling my leg."

"Angel's honest, I swear." Vanessa's curls bounced as she shook her head. "Every deckhand and officer I've ever sailed with says they've seen it, but no matter how many sunsets I watched I could never seem to catch it. Until now."

"Well," Quint said, his smile returning. "At least that's one good thing to come out of this whole misadventure."

"One," Vanessa agreed, turning her gaze northwards. She went suddenly still, then pointed at the distant beach. "Look."

Quint followed her gaze. A thin column of whitish smoke was climbing steadily into the purpling sky, rising up from the northern beach—very near, in fact, to where the river flowed into the lagoon. Right where Lurk had said the others had made camp.

Quint let out a wild, joyful whoop as, without thinking, he threw his arms around Vanessa's shoulders. She turned to him, a grin plastering across her face, pulling him in tight, her laughter in his ear. Quint laughed too, relief flooding through him.

Soon they'd be back with their crewmates; with Ophelia and Lurk, Vigo and Darby, even Rustbucket and the rest of Margherita's crew. It felt like a weight had been lifted from him.

Vanessa pulled back, still laughing a little, though her hands remained on the small of his back, Quint's still around her shoulders. Her deep brown eyes looked into his, and Quint's breath caught. So did Vanessa's, her lips parting slightly.

Then a pair of massive arms draped themselves around both their shoulders, shattering the moment as Tarja pulled them both to her substantial bosom.

"There they are!" she shouted, pointing her hook at the curling smoke while also keeping Quint pressed firmly to her side. "All of our friends, down there and sharing a fire!"

"And probably eating well, too," Margherita remarked, drawing up alongside them and squinting towards the distant lagoon. "Your mermaid friend's probably gotten a feast ready for them."

"A feast we shall join in tomorrow night, or the one following," Tarja said brightly. "My Frederick at least will ensure that our return is an occasion for celebration. As is the present moment, I think."

She extended her arm, momentarily freeing Quint from her embrace, only for him to be swept back into it as she pulled Margherita into the circle of her arms. Quint stiffened as the shorter pirate queen was squeezed up against him, his thoughts drifting back to her too-specific promise not to stab him in the back.

Margherita did not stab him, but neither did she join in the hug, only awkwardly patted Tarja's bicep. For a time the four of them stood peering down the mountain at that lonely plume of smoke, wondering if their companions were looking towards the mountain, not knowing that their captains and friends were upon its heights. Only when the wind had begun to blow chill with the approaching night did they turn and descend back into the caldera.

With the high walls of the crater's rim above them, the mountaintop lay sheltered from the alpine winds. This permitted a surprisingly riotous growth of mosses and ferns, fed by the shallow pool at its center. A mountain spring, it flowed slowly towards the low northern lip of the rim, tumbling downwards to become the waterfall they had traversed scant hours ago.

They seated themselves in a loose ring besides the water's edge, drinking straight from the spring as it flowed from its underground source. Tarja was just passing out coconuts to serve as their evening meal when Vanessa, who had been kneeling beside the spring, let out a startled shout.

For a heart-stopping moment Quint feared that she'd been bitten by a snake—could snakes live at such a high elevation? The thought was quickly dispelled when he saw that, rather than backing away from the pool, Vanessa had plunged both her hands into its waters.

"Look!" she shouted, thrusting her hand into the air as the others gathered around her, alarmed by her sudden outburst. Something glimmered between her fingers, its metallic surface catching and reflecting the final rays of the sunset.

Like the sun, it was a golden circle.

Unlike the sun, it was emblazoned with a man's face in profile, crowned and stern.

"That's a doubloon," Quint said, unnecessarily.

"It is," Vanessa nodded, holding it up for the others to see. "Anyone lose a bit of change?"

They shook her heads. Quint had been stripped of whatever coin he carried when Margherita had taken them prisoner, while Tarja and Margherita had presumably lost their own coin purses in the shipwreck.

"But that means..." Tarja began, frowning.

"Aye," Vanessa said, a grim smile spreading over her features. "We're not the first ones to set foot on this island."

18

The fading light allowed them only a little time to examine the doubloon in detail.

"It's clearly been in the water a long time," Vanessa said as they passed it around the little circle they'd formed beside the pool's edge. "Look how worn it is. You can barely make out the face."

"Is definitely Imperial, though," Tarja said, peering hard at it. "You can tell from the crown. Eight points."

"For each of the Eight Seas," Margherita nodded as she passed it to her. She raised the doubloon to her lips, gingerly bit into its rim, then pulled it out to examine the slight indentation her teeth had left. "Real gold, too."

"And at least forty years old," Quint said, taking the coin from her and looking closely at it. "That's roundabout how long it's been since we last had an Emperor, rather than an Empress. Faded as it is, you can still see the beard."

He passed the doubloon to Vanessa, only to realize that the others were all staring at him.

"So I've read a history book or two," he said defensively. "No need to look surprised about it."

Margherita stifled a yawn, which Quint suspected was actually a laugh.

"That doesn't mean much, though," Vanessa said, holding it up for a better look. "These things stay in circulation for a long time."

"Ja," Tarja agreed, taking the coin. "I think I may have a few doubloons with such a face on them."

"So it could be more recent than that," Quint said, but Margherita shook her head.

"Doesn't matter," she said. She glanced at Vanessa, who nodded, evidently having come to a similar conclusion. "This island's not on any maps, which strikes me as a pretty clear sign that whoever left this here never made it home."

It was a sobering thought. Quint's imagination shied away from the prospect of spending uncounted years on this island, of growing old without ever returning home. Of his ma never knowing what had become of him, of losing her without the chance to say a final goodbye, as he had lost his pop.

It was a mistake he had sworn not to repeat. Silently, he resolved that they would find a way off this island, no matter what it took.

"Not necessarily," Tarja pointed out, breaking the pensive silence that had fallen in the wake of Margherita's gloomy pronouncement. "It might be whoever landed here was someone who sought to keep the knowledge of this place to themselves. A smuggler daring enough to brave the Sea of Tears, mayhap."

"Or a pirate," Margherita said.

Like Captain Wolf, Quint thought but did not say. The thought of his pop recalled the old man's tall tales of adventure in these southern latitudes, of Captain Wolf's supposed escapades to the unknown islands on the far side of the Sea of Tears.

Quint wondered whether he was, even now, following in his father's footsteps. Whether his pop too had once stood atop this very mountain, watching the sun sink into the ocean.

"It is getting too dark to look at it closely," Tarja said after a moment, reaching across their little circle to offer the doubloon to Vanessa, who passed it to Quint. The big Trechtish woman yawned, unsuccessfully attempting to cover her mouth with her hook. "And I for one am ready for bed."

"Or moss, as it were," Quint pointed out.

"So long as it is a soft place to lay my head," Tarja shrugged. "It is not every day that one climbs a mountain. Now, if you will pardon me, I will be sleeping where the sound of the waterfall will be louder than my snores."

Quint winced, recalling how the previous night's thin rest had been frequently interrupted by just such a commotion. "Thanks, mate."

"I'll make sure she doesn't roll over the edge," Margherita said, glancing after her first mate. She leaned in and admitted, a little self-consciously: "Truth be told, her snoring helps me drift off. It's like listening to the ocean."

"It's certainly loud enough," Quint agreed, smiling slightly. Somehow he did not think that Margherita would have confessed to such a thing before their experience at the waterfall.

The pirate queen waved goodnight, then set off after Tarja, trailing after her like a much smaller shadow in the dusk.

"Well," Quint said, turning to look at Vanessa. "That leaves us."

"It does," Vanessa agreed, looking up at him.

"Right." Quint cleared his throat and looked around the caldera. "I'll, um. Go find a place to sleep, then—"

"Here's good," Vanessa said, sitting on the mossy ground. She patted the spot beside her. "Come on down."

He hesitated, afraid to misinterpret. "Are you—"

"It's already getting chilly this high up," Vanessa said, hugging her arms across her chest. "We'll sleep warmer next to each other."

The warm breeze gusting down from over the lip of the caldera made Quint doubt that assertion, but he elected not to argue the point. His heart performed a frantic jig in his chest as he sat beside Vanessa, the moss springy and surprisingly soft beneath him.

"Harps," Vanessa said as she laid back, using one arm as a pillow. "I'd nearly forgotten what it was like to *enjoy* lying down."

Quint knew she was referring to their night spent on the rocky beach, and before that to their time in the storm-tossed brig of the *Marigold*, but he couldn't resist rising to the bait.

"I'll try not to read into that," he said, lying down beside her.

Vanessa snorted and punched him in the arm. "You're incorrigible."

"It's one of my better qualities," he agreed, resting his head on his own arm.

They lay there in silence for a while, though the cadence of her breathing told Quint that Vanessa was still awake. The caldera was full of the gentle sounds of water dripping from the rocks, and the quiet murmur of the pool drifting lazily towards the waterfall.

"There's isn't a chance she's lying, is she?" Vanessa asked, her voice quiet in his ear.

"Who?" asked a bewildered Quint, wondering if he'd fallen asleep and missed the beginning of the conversation.

"Margherita." Vanessa gestured vaguely in the direction the pirate queen and her first mate had departed to the caldera's far side. "About Cuprite. Everything that she said about the way the Empire treats the people there."

There was a note to her voice that was very nearly pleading.

"I..." Quint hesitated, choosing his words carefully. "I told you earlier, Ness. I've met a few Cuprite rebels. The story they told me about their island matches up with the one Margherita tells."

Silence. Quint's gut twisted, convinced that he had chosen precisely the wrong thing to say. He was about to apologize for being the bearer of such an unpleasant truth when Vanessa said, very quietly, "Then the Navy truly does have a lot to answer for."

"It does," Quint said. In another time or place, this simple admission from Vanessa might have been a victory in itself, but lying next to her, hearing the quiet tremor in her voice, all Quint wanted to do was comfort her. "That wasn't you, though. That was someone else—"

"Someone wearing the same uniform," Vanessa said, plucking at her sleeve as if she were still wearing the purple jacket. "Someone taking orders from the same collection of commodores and admirals that I get my orders from. I may never have thrown a Cuprite family into jail, Quint, but that doesn't mean I'm any less guilty than the ones who do."

"You'd never do a thing like that," he insisted, unwilling to let her berate herself for the crimes of others. "You're too..."

Vanessa looked at him, her brows raised with evident skepticism. "Too what?"

Too good, he'd been going to say, but what came out was: "Too principled."

"Principled." Vanessa gave a short, breathy laugh that held neither humor nor warmth. "You know that saying that a person doesn't know how brave she is until she's been scared? It's the same with principles, Quint. You don't know how strongly you'll stand by your convictions 'til you've had them tested."

Now it was Quint's turn to be skeptical. "You can't tell me you've never found yourself caught in a moral quandary before."

"Quagmires, more like," Vanessa said, giving him a bleak smile that quickly faded. "That's just it, though. I've taken part in...pacification efforts. Ones not too different from what Margherita described as happening to Cuprite. Fired on rebelling militias, chased down smugglers and insurrectionists. But now..."

"You're wondering if you were on the wrong side," Quint said quietly.

"That's just it!" He did not think Vanessa had meant to shout, yet her voice echoed around the caldera. She sat up, hugging her knees to her chest. "Things are never so black and white as Margherita paints them. I've seen the islands that are tributary to the Asturian Confederacy, or the ones that used to be Trechtish colonies back before they lost their holdings in the Archipelago. Hotbeds of poverty and corruption."

Two afflictions which the Empire was not immune to either, Quint thought, but he did not press the point. He had been to a few of the islands Vanessa described, and the levels of desperation and graft in such places were far beyond even the most backwater of the Empire's domains.

"Black and white," he repeated, rubbing the chess piece tattooed upon his forearm. "But you're hoping that you're a lighter shade of gray."

"Aye," she nodded, brushing her hair back from her face. "The Empire's not perfect, Quint. I *know* that. But I've spent my life believing that it's better than the alternative. That laws and paved roads and regular shipments of food are better than vice and neglect and want. That even with all its flaws, the Empire I swore to serve can be a force for good."

Quint sat up beside her, put his hand over hers. Vanessa looked down at it, then traveled upwards to his tattoo.

"But what if that's not true?" she asked, quiet and with a little tremor of fear Quint had never heard in her before. "What if I've failed every test of principle I've ever been put to, because I thought I was lifting people up from chaos and uncertainty, when all I was doing was adding to the weight pressing down upon their backs?"

She looked at him, and he could see the starlight reflected in the corners of her eyes. "What if I chose wrong?"

Quint did not answer at first, taking his time to weigh his words, to choose what it was he wanted to say with utmost care. Only when Vanessa turned away did he reach out and turn her face back to him, as gently as he knew how.

"Did I ever tell you why I decided to leave the Navy?" he asked, his thumb tucked under her chin.

"You..." Vanesa bit her lip, no doubt thinking back to the early days of their courtship on Tourmaline, when neither of them had known the other's profession. "There was something you said about not wanting to answer to foul-tempered Navy commanders or vicious captains."

"Aye," Quint nodded, grimacing. "One in particular, where the captain was concerned. The first ship Ophelia and I ever served aboard was the *Reign of Peace*."

Vanessa's eyes widened. "You were part of Captain Gault's crew?"

"Regrettably so," Quint nodded. For the first time in years, he permitted the old man's face to claw its way up from the depths of memory he had buried it in. Gault had been a creature seemingly carved from granite: all hard lines and sharp angles and flinty eyes, his only concession to vanity a thin pair of sideburns that served only to accentuate the stoniness of his features.

"You alright?" Vanessa asked, resting her hand on his knee.

"Aye." Quint took in a slow, steadying breath, reminding himself that his onetime captain was somewhere on the far side of the Sea of Tears, thousands of miles away, and in no position to do any further harm to anyone. Or so he hoped. "Just not someone I'm fond of recalling. Or the story, neither."

"If you don't want to tell me," Vanessa started, but Quint shook his head.

"It's alright," he said, forcing a smile. "Probably time I unburdened myself of it, anyway."

"I seem to have misplaced my clerical collar," Vanessa said, looking about the moss as if she'd just set it down. "But you can confess your misdeeds to me, if you like."

Quint's smile grew a tad less forced, then faded as he dredged up more unpleasant memories from the place of shame and guilt he'd kept them carefully stored away in.

"I'm sure you've heard the rumors," he began, adjusting his seat on the moss. "How Gault was as heartless a captain as ever plied the seas. About how he'd sooner send a crippled enemy vessel to the depths rather than deal with the hassle of taking prisoners, or how he dealt out twice the number of lashes for any infraction as Navy rules and regulations required."

Quint's hand rose to his shoulder, pressing down against the faint lines of old, old scars there, long since healed. "Or that old Gault liked to be the one holding the lash."

Vanessa made a sound halfway between a gasp and a growl. Quint was touched by her concern, but refused to allow himself to be derailed. This story's purpose was not to elicit Vanessa's sympathy for what he had endured in another lifetime.

"Point is," Quint said, shaking his head, "whatever you've heard of Captain Gault, the reality of the man was as bad as the rumor, or worse. Two years I served aboard that accursed ship, learning to sail a frigate under one of the hardest men ever to wear a captain's epaulettes."

"I'm surprised you stuck it out that long," Vanessa said. "You're not exactly the sort to stand by and tolerate that sort of cruelty."

"It's one thing when the cruelty's directed at someone else, and another when it's aimed at you." Quint shrugged. "And besides, I wasn't the sort of person I am now. Not yet. I thought I could tough it out, for Ophelia's sake, if nothing else."

There was no need for him to elaborate further. Vanessa knew well that Ophelia would have had nowhere else to turn to once she had abandoned her family for the Navy.

"What changed?" she asked instead, softly and a little afraid.

"One of those moral tests you mentioned," he said, forcing himself to speak lightly even as the memory of the child by the gallows came rising up like a revenant. "We were stationed on Jasper, assisting the local governor. 'Maintaining order and presenting a model of stability in the face of austerity and unrest.'"

Even now the old trite description tasted bitter in his mouth. He turned his head and spat.

"Austerity," Vanessa repeated softly. "This was during the famine years, then."

"Aye," Quint said. "There was a man. I don't...I never found out his name. He might've been anyone."

His throat felt raw, as if he'd been screaming, though his voice was little more than a hoarse whisper. He leaned over and drank directly from the mountain spring, letting its cool, clean waters whet his thirst until he could speak again.

"Just a man," he said, "like any other. I saw him one night, while Ophelia and I were on watch. There was a bakery right there on the wharf, and even with the austerity measures in place they had enough flour on hand to bake fresh bread every morning, which sold for a king's ransom while other folk starved in the streets."

"That's awful," Vanessa said, heat creeping into her voice. "You'd think that with all of their neighbors in need, the baker—"

"Would make a tidy profit," Quint said tiredly. "And believe me, she did. Anyway, this bakery was always locked up tight at night, and whoever had the watch aboard the *Reign of Peace* was also in charge of making sure no one broke in."

"But you let him," Ophelia guessed. "The man you mentioned."

"Aye." Quint cleared his throat. This next part was difficult. "He had a kid with him. A little boy. Might've been five or six, but looked younger. Hunger has a way of doing that when they're small."

"Wouldn't you and Ophelia have been punished?" Vanessa asked. "For letting him steal from the bakery?"

"If we'd have been caught," Quint said. "But Ophelia had already learned to pick a lock well before she signed onto the *Reign of Peace*. It wasn't the work of a minute for her to let the man inside, then lock the door behind him when he and his boy left."

He swallowed again, cleared his throat. "A week later there was a hanging."

"Oh." Vanessa's voice was very small.

"Fully twenty men and women," Quint continued. "All condemned for theft under the austerity laws. An example for anyone else who committed the crime of being hungry and poor, I suppose."

He opened his eyes, looking up at the distant stars as if the constellations might absolve him. As ever, they remained coldly silent.

"And there was the boy," he said. "Standing in the crowd, right near the front. Watching as they put a bag over his pop's head and pulled the lever. Kid didn't so much as scream. Just...watched. Like there wasn't enough in him for tears."

"Poor thing," Vanessa whispered. "And you...left, after that?"

"No." Quint laughed, the sound as hollow as the eyes of the child who had not cried. "Even after all that, I still thought that things could be fixed. That if I could bend the ear of Gault, or the governor, or anyone at all with the authority to do *anything...*"

He took a deep breath, forced himself to continue in a measured, even tone. "I was naïve, I guess. Next morning, I knocked on the door of Captain Gault's cabin, even though I didn't have a meeting scheduled with him and was much too junior a midshipman to go calling on the captain unannounced.

"I must have knocked at least four times before some fifth lieutenant whose name I can't even recall opened it, looking as surprised to see a lowly midshipman standing there as she would have been if I'd been the Empress Herself.

"And there they all were: Captain Gault, Commander Shelby, and all the lieutenants. Each and every one of them eating toast, fresh from the bakery. Gault laughing at something someone had said, crumbs spilling from his mouth and onto the floor."

He turned to Vanessa, desperate with the need for her to understand. "I knew, then. What I should've known the moment I saw that poor man swing. That the gap between those in power and those they're meant to protect is too wide to ever be bridged. That the Empire isn't there to protect its citizens, but to control them."

"That's when you decided to desert," Vanessa said.

"Aye," Quint said. "The plan itself came later—Ophelia and I concocted it while we were waist-deep in bilgewater—but that was the moment."

He lapsed into silence, feeling suddenly as exhausted as if he'd just hiked all the way down to the beach and back. He had buried those memories for a reason, and dredging them up again in this way had been an act of labor.

"I'm sorry," Vanessa said. Then, hesitantly, added, "At least Gault got his comeuppance, in the end."

Too little, Quint thought, *and too late.* His former captain's court-martial and eventual imprisonment had come years after Quint's own desertion, and had nothing whatsoever to do with the events on Jasper that had precipitated it.

"It's not about him," he said instead, shaking his head. "It's about that moment. The crumbs on his purple jacket, while folk starved in the streets just outside our hull."

Quint reached out, brushed one of Vanessa's curls behind her ear. "I only wore that jacket two years. You've had it on for more than half your life. That doesn't make you a bad person, Ness. It just means that you never had that moment."

Vanessa considered this, her brow furrowing. She looked so much like she had when they had first met across the chess table that Quint's heart lurched in his chest, heavy with unspeakable longing.

She looked up, her dark brown eyes peering intently into his green ones.

"What do I do," Vanessa asked, as uncertain as he'd ever heard her, "if that moment comes?"

Quint gave into his heart's insistent urging. He took both her hands in his, lifted them to his lips.

"You'll do what you'll always do," he said, with a certainty as unshakeable as the foundations of the island beneath them. "The right thing."

19

Whether from the exertions of their hike to the mountaintop or the emotional exhaustion of his conversation with Vanessa, Quint slept soundly and dreamlessly that night. When he woke it was to the distant trill of birdsong from somewhere far off, and to the faint lightening of the gray sky as the last stars winked out. To the pleasant warmth of Vanessa nestled against him, her head resting on his shoulder, her curls tickling his chin.

Without thinking, Quint leaned down and kissed the top of her head. Vanessa murmured something sleepily incomprehensible, refusing to be so easily dragged back into the waking world.

Smiling, Quint turned onto his other side, and found a tiny, wizened pink face staring into his own.

Quint blinked.

So did the beady black eyes. Then the puckered mouth peeled back, revealing sharp white teeth.

Quint screamed.

The monkey screamed back.

In a moment he was on his feet, pulling a bewildered and half-asleep Vanessa behind him. The monkey screeched again, clambering nimbly atop a nearby boulder so that it was roughly eye level with Quint. It was a smallish creature, not much larger than a cat, which made its weirdly human face and the way it stood on its hind legs all the more unsettling. Its fur was mostly black, save for a whiteness around the chest, face, and the tip of its long tail, which was thrashing back and forth with agitation.

For a moment Quint and the monkey stood staring at each other, both breathing hard.

"Quint, what—" Still rubbing the sleep from her eyes, Vanessa squinted. "That's a monkey."

"It is," Quint said, heart still hammering in his chest.

"That's why you screamed me awake?" Vanessa asked, wincing. "Because you saw a *monkey*?"

"One that was about an inch away from eating my face," Quint said, feeling defensive. The monkey smiled with all its teeth, which looked to Quint like as clear an admission of guilt as any.

"That's a myth," Vanessa said, peering over his shoulder at the simian perched atop the stone. "How'd it get up here, anyhow?"

It was a good question. But before Quint could speculate, Tarja and Margherita came hurrying over from the far side of the crater. Margherita's cutlass was in her hand, while Tarja was hurriedly affixing her hook to the stump of her arm.

"What is it?" Margherita demanded, pushing the brim of her hat out of her eyes as she rushed towards them. "Did someone—is that a *monkey*?"

"Ja!" Tarja said, her expression brightening as the monkey turned its beady black eyes on the newcomers. "It looks like it may be related to the white-faced monkey, which is common to the southern Archipelago."

"Are they docile?" Vanessa asked, still standing behind Quint.

"Oh, quite," Tarja said, putting hand and hook on her knees and bending to peer more closely at the little primate than Quint was comfortable with. "Most clever and friendly little creatures."

"Doesn't look terribly friendly," Margherita said dubiously, as the monkey stood as tall as its posture allowed and beat at its thin chest with its tiny fists. Its mouth made a perfectly round "O" as it loosed a series of surprisingly low hoots. Quint frowned, trying to place where he'd heard the sound before.

"They can be quite mischievous," Tarja allowed, "but they are no more dangerous than a housecat. Though how this little creature made it across the Sea of Tears—"

The monkey leapt at her.

Tarja recoiled, so that the monkey landed instead upon her shoulder, all four paws scrabbling madly for purchase. Tarja let out a bellow of dismay and spun, trying to shake the little primate loose.

Quint yelped. Margherita swore. Vanessa bent and picked up a rock, ready to crack a simian skull, should it come to that.

Now alternating between hoarse screeches and deep hoots, the monkey managed to brace its rear paws against Tarja's neck, even as she swatted at it. It pushed off and jumped, just as the Trechtish pirate's hook passed through the space where its tail had been a heartbeat earlier.

It flew through the early morning air, arms outstretched and fangs bared, straight for Margherita. The pirate queen froze, and despite the distance between them Quint found himself flinging his arm towards her, shouting for her to *move*.

It had the desired effect. Margherita ducked, dropping to the moss as the monkey collided with her hat, knocking it clean off her head. Hat and monkey both landed on the mossy banks of the spring's far side.

"You all right?" Vanessa asked, reaching down and pulling Margherita to her feet. The pirate queen rubbed at the crown of her head, a storm cloud crossing her features as she whipped around, just in time to see the monkey pawing at the battered garment that had cushioned its landing.

"Little bugger grabbed my *hat,*" the pirate queen said, her stormy expression turning thunderous. She took a step towards the monkey, who picked up her hat with both hands and placed it atop its head, enveloping the creature to the waist. "Give it back, you tiny thieving—"

A beady eye peeked out from under the brim of the hat and screeched at the approaching pirate queen, before disappearing back into the hat like a turtle withdrawing into its shell. Four legs and a tail sprouted from beneath the hat's brim.

Margherita dove for it, but the suddenly-ambulatory hat scurried away, clambering over mossy rocks with surprising speed. The four castaways gave chase, but before they could close the distance monkey and hat both scaled up and over the crater wall.

For a moment the monkey stood, silhouetted against the rising sun with Margherita's hat balanced precariously atop its head. It let out another series of low hoots, triumphant and more than a little mocking, before turning and scurrying down the other side of the crater.

The four castaways stood, blinking against the sunrise and staring at the place where the monkey had been. Gingerly, Margherita touched her head, and looked surprised to find that her hat was indeed well and truly gone.

"Did that really just happen?" Vanessa asked, voicing aloud what all of them were thinking.

"A monkey stole my hat," Margherita said, disbelief warring with outrage in her voice.

"I'm sure stranger things have happened," Quint said, wiping at his brow. He frowned. "Though to be honest, I can't think of any right now."

"Quite an exciting start to our morning," Tarja said, alone of the four of them sounding unperturbed. She looked brightly at the others. "Seeing as we are all awake now, let us not waste any more daylight! Our friends are waiting."

With that she turned and started towards the trail leading down from the mountaintop, humming one of her favorite Trechtish lullabies.

"Assuming the monkeys haven't gotten them first," Quint muttered, and followed after her.

⚓

Their hike downhill was mercifully far less eventful than their hike up.

They crossed back under the waterfall with even greater care and caution than they had the first time, then proceeded downhill with the river rushing beside them, the spray rising up beside them cooling them even as the sun climbed higher into the cloudless sky.

At first the mood had been somewhat soured by Margherita's grumpiness over the theft of her hat, for which Quint could hardly blame her—yet even her dour temperament lightened after they glimpsed another curling plume of smoke rising into the northern sky.

"They're getting breakfast ready for us," Vanessa joked; though their pace was better than it had been going uphill, the beach was still a full day's hike away.

"Let's hope it keeps until tomorrow," Margherita said, allowing herself a smile. "I like coconuts as much as the next lass, but there's something to be said for a varied diet."

"I'm sure Lurk's been keeping them well-fed on shellfish," Quint said. "And that lagoon's probably teeming with fish. Wouldn't be surprised if Vigo managed to rig some rods and reels together."

"He struck me as a resourceful fellow," Tarja nodded, carefully scratching at her neck with her hook. "But have any of your crew been poorly behaved enough to have earned a basket full of fishhooks?"

"Of course they have," Vanessa answered before Quint could. The other three turned to her and found her looking solemnly at Quint. "They're pirates."

They stared, each of them trying to read her stern expression. Vanessa stared back, until her mask slowly began to crack, a grin spreading over her elegant features.

Then all four of them were laughing, their mirth echoing across the hills, louder than the insistent murmuring of the river beside them. After the shipwreck and the waterfall and the utter absurdity of their tussle with the monkey, the divisions between pirate and Navy seemed unspeakably arbitrary, bordering on pointless.

They were all castaways now, without flag or country. There was something oddly freeing in that, Quint thought as he watched Vanessa and Margherita laughing together. A liberating joy in the lack of labels or barriers, forcing them to meet each other as they were, and not as their reputations or allegiances had made them out to be.

It was a thought he carried with him through most of the day's hike, their steady downhill progress easy enough to allow his mind to wander over their conversations of the previous days. Of the incident on Jasper that had driven him from the Navy, of Margherita's more personal vendetta against the Empire, of Vanessa's fervent need to have done some good with her service to both.

How strange, he thought, that all three of them thought of themselves as doing the right thing, and how stridently they disagreed on what the right thing was.

⚓

They pressed on until the sun dipped towards the unseen horizon, casting the jungle into a dim twilight, lit only by the golden reflections of the sunset glittering off the water. That night they made camp in a small hollow, near enough to the river that they could still hear its steady murmuring but far enough that only the most determined of crocodiles would disturb their privacy.

Even so, they took watches in shifts as the others slept. This had felt unnecessary both on the isolated beach with Lurk beside them, and on the distant mountaintop. But after the day's misadventures, having someone stand sentinel seemed not only prudent but necessary. They were upon a distant and untrod isle in strange seas; who knew what other dangers awaited them upon these farthest shores?

Margherita took the first watch, cutlass resting across her knees as she loudly vowed to make monkey steak out of any simian that came searching for another article of clothing to steal. Quint drifted off to the quiet rasping of flint against steel as the pirate queen sharpened her blade upon a whetstone she'd had in her pockets when the *Marigold* went under.

He was awoken several hours later by Vanessa gently nudging him. "It's your turn."

Yawning, Quint sat up, blinking around at the darkness. They had decided against lighting a fire that night, reasoning that all it would accomplish would be to serve as a beacon for any predators large enough and hungry enough to come investigate. The mysterious owner of the dropped doubloon aside, Quint could not imagine that anyone had visited this island recently enough for the local wildlife to develop a fear of those that went on two legs.

And besides, they were as far south as Quint had ever voyaged, the night air pleasantly warm, and doubly so when Vanessa had been dozing beside him.

"Anything to report?" he asked, coming to his feet as she sat down in the little patch of grass they were using as bedding.

"Lot of weird sounds," Vanessa said, shrugging.

She laid back on her elbows, looking up at him. "Goodnight, Quint."

"Night, Vanessa."

Quint was no stranger to the long, empty stretch of time that constituted a night on watch. A firm believer that no captain should be above the duties assigned to the rest of his crew, he had whiled away many such a night pacing the deck of the *Bloody Angel,* no sound but the soft sighing of wind through the rigging and the gentle lapping of water against the hull.

Here in this strange place the sounds were unfamiliar: the whirr and trill of insects for which he had no name, the scuffle of small creatures moving unseen through the undergrowth, and the throaty croaking of brightly colored tree frogs. Even the air felt different: thick and humid and still beneath the canopy, with none of the salt sting Quint thought of as the smell of home.

Without a fire, his eyes adjusted swiftly to the dark of deep night, though there was little enough to see. The hours ticked by as he paced in slow circles about the boundary of their camp, peering into the dense and tangled foliage beyond. Perhaps in response to the lack of external stimulus, his imagination conjured phantoms from the dark: packs of monkeys, each of them wearing miniature feathered hats, frigates and schooners sailing through the trees, Lurk swimming nimbly between the branches, Jimmy perched uneasily upon her back, and other, stranger visions no less ludicrous.

Once he even thought he saw a pair of eyes staring back at him, like two mirrors set in a shadow in the rough shape of a man. Quint took a step forward, but before he could say a word the apparition vanished into the gloom, nothing more than another errant fancy.

By the time the sky through the leaves turned from black to gray and the insect calls gave way to birdsong, Quint had forgotten all about it.

20

They heard the campsite before they saw it.

It echoed through the forest like a song, bouncing off the surface of the now sluggish river: the rhythmic beat of hammer and nails, the sigh of wood being sawn, and the chorus of voices raised in chorus together. The tune was familiar, but it took a moment to place it.

"Is that 'Blow the Man Down'?" Vanessa asked, wiping at her brow. They had been hiking most of the morning, the sun overhead beat down with oppressive midday heat.

"Ja," Tarja said, beaming as she pressed forward, cupping her hand to her ear. "And that is my Frederick leading the chorus, I think!"

They hurried onwards, hearts pounding with the eager anticipation of reunion. Their spirits leapt as they rounded a bend in the river and saw a small hill, just a little way up the beach from where the river emptied out into the lagoon. It was crowned with a grove of tall, spreading trees with broad trunks and wide branches, several of which had been cleared to make room for a collection of boxy wooden structures linked by a series of platforms and walkways.

"Is that—" Margherita murmured, her mouth falling open.

"A treehouse!" Tarja practically squealed, pressing on ahead of the rest of them. They drew nearer, close enough to pick out the individual castaways pacing about the treehouse platforms, or the large crowd of them near the base of one tree, hauling a makeshift crate upwards through a surprisingly elaborate pulley system.

"That'll be Vigo's work," Quint said, pointing it out to the others. "Man's a mechanical genius."

"Where'd the ropes and such come from, though?" Margherita asked, though she sounded impressed.

"Lurk must have brought them up from the wreck of the *Marigold,*" Quint guessed. "She's probably—"

"*Ahoy*!" They looked up to see Ophelia leaning against the railing of one of the treehouse platforms, grinning down at them and waving. "*Captains ahoy!*"

A jubilant shout rang through the trees, startling several birds that had been nesting in the highest branches. As they flapped into the morning sky with loud, protesting squawks, the castaways reunited.

Quint found himself swept up in a tide of hugs and handshakes and pats on the back, everyone rejoicing in the return of their wayward comrades. To his surprise and delight, Quint found that the *Marigold's* crew seemed just as excited and relieved to see him and Vanessa as they did their own captain and first mate.

With a delighted squeal, Tarja swept Frederick into a bear hug, lifting her husband up until his legs dangled off the ground. Meanwhile, Ginger stood on her tiptoes to peck Vanessa on either cheek. Quint found himself shaking hands with Adewale, while Rustbucket greeted Margherita with a stiff but correct salute.

"At ease, Rusty," Ophelia said, pressing her way through the crowd. She stopped in front of Quint, the morning sun shining on her tattooed arms, looking tall and strong and utterly at her ease. For a moment the captain of the *Bloody Angel* and his first mate stood there, looking at one another.

Then they were hugging, both of them pulling each other in tight and clinging to each other like drowning sailors to a piece of driftwood. No tears fell, but Quint could feel Ophelia's shoulders shaking, ever so slightly.

"You're all right," she said in his ear, low enough that the others would not hear.

"'course I'm alright," he replied, patting her back. Until now he had not permitted himself to worry for her, or for any of his crew. But now the relief of their reunion washed over him like cool water, quieting the turbulence of the anxieties he had kept carefully buried.

They drew apart, both grinning and a little embarrassed. Quint looked past her, up to the platforms on the trees. "Looks like you've kept busy."

"You know what they say about idle hands," Ophelia replied. She glanced over her shoulder at the treehouses. "You want a tour?"

⚓

The treehouses were accessible by a series of wooden rungs nailed against the tree trunks, from the look of them scavenged from the wreckage of the jollyboat. These also made up the planks constituting the flat wooden platforms, of which there were two: a broad lower one encircling the large main bunkhouse, and a second one accessible by a walkway set a little higher up in the canopy, which sported two separate, smaller treehouses.

"Main bunk for the crew," Ophelia said, gesturing at the larger structure. "We've been knitting together bedrolls out of palm leaves. Ain't the most comfortable, but better than lying on hard timber."

"How did you get all this wood, anyway?" Vanessa asked, glancing around. "This couldn't have all come from the jollyboat."

"Nope," Ophelia agreed, slapping a hand against the wooden frame of the bunkhouse door. "There's a grove of pines a little ways down the beach. Chopped down a few of them using a hatchet which Frederick had the presence of mind to grab before the *Marigold* went down."

"And you managed all this in three days?" Margherita asked, sounding impressed despite herself.

"I had good help," Ophelia said, shrugging modestly. "Darby's a master carpenter, Vigo's a genius when it comes to design, and Frederick keeps supply records in his head nearly as good as Bonnie Kate does in her ledgers. Mostly I let them make the decisions, told everyone to do as they said, and stayed out of their way unless they needed a hand."

"That's nine-tenths of good leadership," Quint said, throwing an arm around her shoulders. He glanced upwards at the smaller two bunkhouses. "What are those for?"

"Captains' quarters," Ophelia said, nodding between him and Margherita. "His and hers."

"And the crew was alright with that?" Vanessa asked, an eyebrow raised.

"They insisted on it, in fact." Ophelia brushed a strand of hair from her eye. "We all wanted to make sure you'd have a proper reception once you got here, so your cabins got priority. Next priority is adding walls to the main bunk, and roofs to both. The whole thing's a work in progress, but everyone's been pitching in."

"Even Rusty?" Vanessa asked, not yet convinced.

"Especially Rusty, actually." Quint must have made a face, for Ophelia raised her hands. "I didn't believe it at first, either. But he's been pulling his weight and then some ever since we washed up. Seems like a near-drowning might have prompted a change in perspective."

"Or a near-hanging," Quint mused. "You think this new leaf he's turned over is genuine?"

"Seems to be," Ophelia shrugged. "He's been...well, not friendlier, but quieter. Less bellyachin' or stirring the pot."

"Could just be self-preservation," Vanessa pointed out. "No one knows how long we'll be stuck here, and if things go bad even Rusty's going to want people in his corner."

"As captain, I'm electing to withhold judgment until I've taken his measure," Quint said, rubbing his beard. "Folk can change themselves for the better, provided they want to badly enough—what?"

"Nothing." Margherita shook her head, frowning a little. "You just looked a little like someone I used to know just then, is all."

"No sign of rescue yet, then?" Vanessa asked Ophelia, glancing through the branches at the blue lagoon.

"None," Ophelia said, shaking her head. "But it's only been a few days. And Lurk's been out swimming the edge of the reef or just beyond it most days."

"She can't go any further?" Margherita asked, frowning. "I mean, she does *live* in the water..."

"Not as far as the width of the Sea of Tears," Ophelia said, guessing at Margherita's intent. "According to Lurk, mermaids usually travel in pods. Safety in numbers from sharks and the meaner sort of whales, that kind of thing. And while she won't say as much, I think traversing that whole ocean alone is a little too intimidating a prospect for her."

"Makes sense," Margherita nodded, disappointed. "Besides, I suppose she'd be of more help to us here than out in the deep."

"Where is she, anyway?" Quint asked.

"She headed down to where you lot were washed ashore before first light," Ophelia said. "Told us she had a surprise in store. Should be back before too terribly long."

"She hasn't run into any crocodiles, has she?" Margherita asked, and Quint was touched by the naked anxiety in her voice.

"Crocodiles?" Ophelia frowned. "Definitely not. A few reef sharks, but those're a shy breed. Haven't given her any trouble."

"Right." Margherita leaned against the rail, looking down at the castaways sprawled across the roots, logs, and rocks below. The members of both crews chatted amiably amongst each other, sharing fresh-picked mangoes or trading drinks from the bottles and waterskins Lurk had apparently salvaged from the *Marigold's* wreck. "Any problems crop up between mine and yours?"

"None at all," Ophelia said, then blinked as Quint and Margherita both looked at her. "No need to be *surprised* about it, though."

"Sorry," Quint said, glancing at Margherita. "I just figured there'd be *some* resistance to one of mine being put in charge, is all."

"Nope," Ophelia said, a touch smugly. "Given that Rita and I have a history, they acclimated pretty quick."

"Leadership's a good look on you." Quint gave her a salute. "Should I start calling you Captain Price now?"

"Absolutely not, seeing as we've no ship for me to captain." Ophelia glanced thoughtfully about the treehouse. "Though seeing as we've established a settlement here, I'll accept alternative titles. Mayor, maybe, or queen..."

"Only room for one queen on this island," the pirate queen said, tugging at Ophelia's hand. "Though I suppose I'm open to discuss terms with rival claimants. Come on, blondie."

"Heavy is the head that wears no hat," Ophelia said, allowing herself to be led towards the upper platform where the two captain's treehouses lay. "We'll catch up with you lot later, I suppose."

Bemused, Quint waved them both farewell.

"So that's still going on," Vanessa said, watching as Ophelia pulled Margherita into their cabin.

"Apparently so," Quint nodded. "Ain't like there's a whole lot else to do here when you're not working, either."

"Guess not." Vanessa yawned, stretching both her arms over her head. "Angels. I hadn't realized how tired I was until now."

"Hiking in the sun all day will do that to you," Quint agreed.

"Mind if I take a nap in your cabin?" Vanessa asked. "It's a little more private than the main bunkhouse, even if Margherita and Ophelia are closer."

"Of course," Quint nodded. "Go on ahead."

Vanessa looked at him, her expression unreadable. "You're not tired?"

"Too excited at seeing everyone again, I guess," Quint shrugged. "You go on. I'll wake you before sundown, don't worry. Sleep well."

With a heavy sigh, Vanessa nodded and made her way up the rope bridge connecting the two platforms. Quint watched her go, unable to shake the feeling that he'd missed something.

"Cap'n?"

He turned around. Rustbucket's bald head poked up from the ladder leading down the trunk. "Lurk's back, Cap'n!"

Quint looked towards the cabin that was nominally his, but Vanessa had already disappeared inside. He turned his attention back to Rustbucket and summoned a cheerful grin.

"About time," he said, heading towards the ladder. "Lead on, mate."

21

"So," Quint said as he followed Rusty down the hill towards the beach. "I hear that you've been on your best behavior, lately."

Rustbucket grimaced. "No need to sound so surprised."

"Sorry."

"Don't be." Rustbucket rubbed his chin. Quint was surprised to notice that he'd shaved off his goatish little beard, though a slight patch of stubble remained in its place. "I know you were looking to be quit of me as soon as we reached Solace, but we ain't got there yet. So I figure I better pitch in an' pull my own weight while we're stuck on these shores."

"That's sensible enough," Quint admitted. "And what about after?"

"After we're rescued, you mean?" Rustbucket frowned and rubbed his head. "I've scarcely had time to give it much thought...hold up a minute."

He drew to a halt at the foot of the hill, where the grass gave way to gentle sand dunes before levelling out to the flat beach. "You're not offering me a place back on the *Bloody Angel,* are you?"

"...do you *want* to rejoin the *Angel*?" Quint asked, uncertain as the words came out whether or not he had intended to offer any such thing.

"Honestly?" Rustbucket looked up at his former captain, almost shyly. "I don't think that I do."

"Oh." Quint toed a line in the sand, uncertain what to say next.

"Oh, don't mope," Rustbucket snorted. "It ain't about you, Cap'n. It's about me. About who I turn into whenever the time comes to divvy up the loot. No matter how big the score or how generous the share, it don't ever seem to be enough for me. And I don't...it don't strike me as healthy for a body to *want* so badly."

He gestured at the sand dunes surrounding them, and the blue line of the Sea of Tears just visible beyond. "Especially when all the gold in the world isn't going to do any of us here any good."

"I understand," Quint said, though he didn't entirely. They made their way through the little valleys between the dunes, the warm salt breeze comfortably familiar on Quint's bare arms. "What will you do instead, then? Once we make it home."

"Honestly?" Rustbucket glanced up at him. "I think I'd like to go back home."

"To your family?" Quint asked quietly. He had met several members of the profligate Russell clan, who were as numerous and widespread as they were disreputable. The fact that Rustbucket was the one he liked best of them spoke volumes about the family's general character. "I know that your relationship with them can be...strained."

"There's a few of them who aren't complete reprobates," Rustbucket shrugged. "And I've got a few nieces and nephews who might appreciate having a wise old uncle around. Y'know, to teach them moral lessons and such."

"I'm sure they'll be glad for whatever wisdom you can impart."

"I learned from the best," Rustbucket said as they rounded the dunes. Lurk was slithering towards them, hauling a sealed wooden chest behind her. For a wild moment Quint thought it might have been the chest containing the Crown Jewels, before realizing that this container was much smaller than that one.

"Quint!" Lurk called, grinning her toothy smile at him. "You made it back!"

"Told you I would," Quint said, striding as quickly as the shifting sands permitted to reunite with her. Rustbucket followed after. "Let's give you a hand with that."

Quint seized one of the chest's handles, Rustbucket and Lurk the other. Together they hauled it down the beach, towards a smaller, secondary campsite under the shade of a grove of fruiting trees.

"That's our kitchen," Rustbucket said, nodding towards a firepit where Adewale was slowly turning a pig on a spit. "Wanted to make sure that where we ate was downhill and downwind of where we slept."

"Smart," Quint nodded, salivating as the smell of roasting pig drifted towards him. From within the chest they carried came the muffled sound of clinking glass. "What's in this, Lurk?"

"That drink Margherita likes," she said.

"Tequila?"

"Aye!" Lurk's ridge rippled. "Ophelia said that you and the others would get here today, and that we'd throw a party to celebrate. I offered to bring this back from the *Marigold.*"

"Lurk," Rustbucket said, chiding but resigned. "Think Ophelia wanted that to be a surprise."

"Oh." Her spinal ridge drooped guiltily as she turned to Quint. "Promise you'll act surprised when she tells you?"

"I promise," Quint told the mermaid.

⚓

"We're throwing you lot a party," Ophelia said, later that afternoon.

"What!" Quint forced his eyebrows to lift as far as they could, let his jaw drop. "For us? What a surprise!"

Ophelia sighed. "Which of them spilled the beans?"

"No one!"

"Quint Thatch," Ophelia said, brushing her hair back so vigorously that Quint thought she might pull a few strands loose in the process, "you are the worst liar I have ever met. Was it Lurk?"

"I promised her I'd act surprised," he said.

"Right." Grimacing, Ophelia glanced back over her shoulder at the two captain's bunkhouses. "Well, at least Rita and Vanessa can be properly surprised once they wake up."

"I won't tell them," Quint promised. He followed her gaze towards Margherita's bunkhouse. "You two picked things up again pretty quickly."

"Might be we did," Ophelia shrugged, not quite meeting his eyes. "There an issue with that?"

"No," Quint said quickly. "No, not at all."

"Good." Ophelia sounded relieved. "Because if you two are still at each other's throats, it's going to make living here a much bigger headache for all of us."

"We're not anymore," Quint admitted. "Not really. We got into some scrapes together on the way here."

"She didn't say anything about it," Ophelia said, glancing back towards the bunkhouse. "Though to be fair, we didn't waste much time in talking, neither."

"Suppose there isn't a whole lot else to do when you're stranded on a deserted island," Quint acknowledged.

"Nope," Ophelia agreed, and winked. "Though you're one to talk, mate."

"You've lost me," Quint said, frowning.

"Hiking across the island for three days with your sweetheart?" Ophelia's eyebrows performed a suggestive little dance. "You can't tell me that you and Vanessa didn't sneak away together for a quiet moment a time or two."

Quint blinked. "Me and Vanessa?"

"Stop playing coy," Ophelia snorted. "Every living soul on this island's seen the way you two look at each other. Rita's crew may not have the same awareness of the history between you, but even they could tell from the way you acted in the brig that *something's* up."

"Nothing's up," Quint insisted, his cheeks turning as red as his hair. "She doesn't...we haven't. Not since..."

"Since we washed ashore?" Ophelia looked appalled. "So the last time was back aboard the *Marigold*? Angels, that's far too long."

Quint avoided her gaze. "Longer."

Ophelia's frown deepened. "Back on Ember Bay? Harps and bells, mate, no wonder you two are acting so strange around each other—"

"Tourmaline," Quint blurted, meeting her gaze just long enough to see her eyes widen in shock before quickly looking down at his feet. "We haven't...Vanessa and I haven't been to bed together since Tourmaline."

"You slept in the same bed at the Queen's Arms," Ophelia objected, looking suddenly wary, as if Quint were pulling some convoluted prank on her. "Vanessa wouldn't let you out of her sight. *And* you told me she put you in manacles—"

"Not like *that*," Quint said. By now his entire face had turned the color of an awful sunburn. "I...we just talked, was all."

"About?" Ophelia asked, nonplussed.

"My pop."

"So." Ophelia ran a hand through her narrow swoop of hair. "The love o' your life—"

"Keep your voice down," Quint hissed, glancing over her shoulder. Mercifully, Vanessa was still in the bunkhouse, and hopefully still asleep.

"Vanessa Delacort," Ophelia continued, louder now, "your one true love, took you to bed. Handcuffed together. And you ruined it talking about your dead dad, angels rest his soul."

"No," Quint protested. "I mean, yeah, that's what happened, but you make it sound—"

"And then," Ophelia continued mercilessly, "the next time you cross paths, Vanessa *demands* you take her as your prisoner. Practically drags you into the *Marigold's* cozy little cabin, her all wet from the ocean, practically quivering—"

"No one was quivering!" Quint looked around to make sure no one had overheard his outburst, then turned his attention back to Ophelia and lowered his voice. "Look, we talked about it aboard the *Marigold*. Ness made it pretty clear that she and I had incompatible views of what the future would look like."

"Uh-huh." Ophelia looked at him flatly. "Did she explicitly say that her ideal future had no place in it for a steamy, illicit romance with a certain dashing-yet-impossibly-thick pirate?"

"Not in those words—"

"Did she specifically say 'no, Quentin Thatch, I could never get naked and dance the horizontal tango with you, however much I may want to climb your weirdly freckly body?'"

Quint wrinkled his nose. "Now you're just being hurtful."

"And you're deflecting," Ophelia said, folding her arms across her chest. "Look, Quint. She wants you. You want her. Stop complicating things for yourselves and be with each other."

"But the future—"

"*What* future?" Ophelia laughed sharply, gesturing towards a gap in the leaves through which Quint could just make out the volcanic peak at the center of the island. "We're stuck here, mate, for angels only know how long. Why waste time worrying about a future that may never come, when there's love waiting right in front of you?"

"Is that how it is for you?" Quint asked, the words slipping from him without consulting his brain. "You're in love with Margherita?"

"Of course I'm not in love with her," Ophelia said, rubbing her temples. "She's fun, don't mistake me, but she's no Estelle. I don't need to be in *love* to enjoy a good tumble, unlike some folk. Like I said, there ain't a lot to do around here, and I can think of worse company to pass the time with."

"And if we do make it home?" Quint pressed, half relieved to have deflected her attention from his own romantic troubles, and half fearful of what Ophelia's answer might be. "What happens when we get back to the Archipelago? If Margherita asks you to join her crew, would you tell her no?"

"I don't know," Ophelia said after a long moment, which was somehow worse than if she'd simply said yes. She turned, leaning against the railing of the treehouse platform, staring out at the glittering blue lagoon visible between the swaying branches.

"We've been together for a long time, you and I," she said. Quint listened, hardly daring to breathe, let alone speak. "And it's been quite a ride. But...I don't know, Quint. Sometimes I wonder. What it would be like if we weren't..."

"If you weren't my first mate," Quint said softly.

"No." Ophelia shook her head, her blonde swoop swaying. "I mean, yes, I suppose. But not in the way where I'd want to be part o' Margherita's crew, either. I want...I don't know. To stand on my own two feet. To just be who I am, without being defined against someone else."

She turned, looking at him, and though her eyes were free of tears Quint saw that they were red. "Does that make sense?"

"Aye," Quint said, nodding. "I...Ophelia. Once we make it back to the Archipelago. If you need to ..."

He cleared his throat, swallowing down the lump that had appeared in it. "You'll always have a place aboard the *Angel*. But if you want to leave, for a time. You don't need to ask."

"Really?" Ophelia's voice was smaller than he'd ever heard it.

"Really." Quint put a hand on her shoulder and squeezed. "You've my blessing, mate. Whatever you decide."

Ophelia pulled him in tight, her bony elbows digging into his sides, her lank blonde hair tickling his ear. He didn't mind.

"Thanks, mate," Ophelia murmured.

"Don't mention it."

"I won't," Ophelia said, releasing Quint from their embrace to hold him at arm's length, studying his face intently. "Provided you talk to Vanessa."

"I—"

She clapped a hand over Quint's mouth, silencing his protests.

"We only get the one life, Quint," Ophelia said, then twisted the knife. "You know that better than anyone. If you want to be with her, then be with her. That easy."

"I don't think—" Quint's reflexive protest withered under the sincerity of Ophelia's gaze. His voice grew small. "What if it's too late, and she doesn't want me?"

"Then at least you have your answer," Ophelia said, patting his cheek. "And the rest of us will finally have to stop pretending not to notice all the longing glances you two keep throwing at each other. Now, if you'll excuse me, I need to go find *my* paramour so that I can break the news to her of tonight's festivities."

She turned and strode up the walkway to the captains' platform, then stopped and looked back at him, head cocked to one side.

"For what it's worth, Quint," Ophelia said, "I think Vanessa will say yes."

"Really?" he asked before he could stop himself.

"Aye," she nodded, giving him a pitying smile. "But first you've got to ask."

22

—•—

Despite the limitations their situation imposed upon them, the castaways' party rivalled any Quint had attended back in the Archipelago.

There was food in plenty, for starters. While most of the crew had labored in constructing the treehouses, Ophelia had dispatched several of their most skilled survivalists to forage for food and hunt game—the crowning achievement of which was the pig Adewale had caught and speared, and was to serve as their main course. Quint believed that the mouthwatering smell of roasting pork drifting across the beach would have driven them all mad with hunger, had it not been for the other morsels on offer.

The foraging party had harvested a veritable feast of freshly picked bananas, mangos, and coconuts. Lurk's own scouting expeditions of the lagoon had revealed the best fishing spots along the beach, so there was no shortage of grouper or striped mullet. These they marinated in sea salt and lime juice, plucked straight from the trees overhanging the firepit.

Nor was that the only use they'd put the limes to.

"Lads and lasses," Margherita proclaimed, holding up a battered tin cup filled almost to the brim with a potent combination of lime juice, tequila, and an orange liqueur that had also been in the chest Lurk had fished up, "I give you the margherita!"

A rousing chorus of cheers echoed along the beach.

"But *she's* Margherita," Lurk said, frowning down at her tin cup.

"She's named the drink after herself," Quint explained, sipping at his margherita. The sting of alcohol was nearly masked by the sweet orange liqueur and the sour lime juice. It made for an oddly delicious combination.

"You landfolk are so strange," Lurk muttered, more to herself than to Quint. Nevertheless she took a sip of her margherita, which caused her spinal ridge to ripple in pleasure. "She *is* tasty, though."

"Aye," Quint agreed, raising both his cup and his voice. "To the margherita!"

Another round of cheering as the castaways threw back their cups, drinking long and deeply. They sat or stood in a loose semicircle about the firepit, which had been stoked to a blazing bonfire once the pork was served. Each castaway drank margherita from a tin cup and ate off a collection of battered but serviceable pewter plates—all of which Lurk had recovered from the wreckage of the *Marigold.*

"And to our new home!" Darby shouted, more than a little red in the face as he gestured towards the dark shape of the treehouse further up the beach. He leaned heavily against Vigo, who carefully took the tin cup from him before it could slosh. "To Margheritaville!"

"No," Quint said, loudly. "Absolutely not."

"That's a stupid name," Margherita herself said, shaking her head and smiling at him. "But what do you suggest? Quintton?"

"Angels, no," he snorted. "It sounds entirely too much like Quentin, for starters."

"And that would be very confusing," Lurk added helpfully.

"We could name it after you, friend Lurk," Tarja offered, waving her hook in the mermaid's direction. She'd capped the end of it with a piece of cork, Quint noticed, which seemed prudent considering the flush in her cheeks. "Perhaps Lurkland?"

"Land?" The mermaid bared her teeth in a grimace. "Ew."

"I think naming the island is a discussion we need to have when we're significantly more sober," Vanessa pointed out.

"Or significantly less," Quint countered, raising his tin cup in salute. "But seeing as we haven't gotten there yet, what say we play a game?"

This suggestion was met with another hearty cheer, and a volley of suggestions.

"Ring of Fire!"

"Quadruple Snakes!"

"Fishbait!"

"On Me Life I Never!"

"Nope," Quint said, rubbing his beard. "Last time I played 'On Me Life I Never' I woke up the next morning with my beard shaved off."

"You're lucky we didn't shear your head, too," Ophelia smirked. "What about the Hanging Judge?"

A unanimous, cheering assent greeted this suggestion.

"Alright," Ophelia said, looking about. "But if I'm going to play the judge, we'd better find me a wig..."

"What's this game?" Lurk asked, turning to Quint as the rest of the castaways set about trying to find a suitable costume for Ophelia to attire herself in.

"Hanging Judge?" Quint sipped his margherita, thinking how best to explain the game to Lurk. "Well...do mermaids have laws?"

"Not in the same way as landfolk do," Lurk said with a little shrug. "Ours are more like agreements the different tribes have promised to abide by."

"But that's close enough that you understand the concept," Quint said. Lurk nodded. "Well, a judge is the person in charge of assigning punishment for a person who's broken the law. Sentencing, it's called."

"Like drowning?" Lurk asked, her spinal ridge perking up with interest.

"Not usually," Quint said, lest Lurk become chosen as the Hanging Judge later in the game. "Anyway, the Hanging Judge is an old pirate game. One player is chosen to be the Hanging Judge. Then the rest of the players take turns pleading their innocence in the fact of the crimes the judge accuses them of."

"What crimes are those?"

"Piracy, mostly," Quint said, giving her a lopsided smile. "If any of the accused manage to successfully plead their innocence, they get to be the new judge."

Lurk considered this. "And if they lose?"

"The judge sentences them to whatever punishment strikes her fancy," Quint said, nodding in Ophelia's direction. "Observe."

Ophelia had procured a wig, albeit one that had until that point been a basket of woven palm fronds. She sat perched upon a pair of crates stacked one atop the other next to the bonfire, with a barrel placed beside them, which Lurk had brought ashore from the wreck of the *Marigold's* jollyboat. Considering the limited resources available to them, Quint was duly impressed with the facsimile of a judge's bench.

"Hear ye, hear ye!" Ophelia yelled, pounding her fist against her crate in lieu of a gavel. "This court is now in session, the Right Honorable and Exceedingly Fetching Judge Ophelia Price presiding."

"All rise!" shouted Tarja, who'd evidently elected herself bailiff. The assembled castaways did so, those sitting staggering to their feet with varying levels of difficulty.

"Right, sit back down," Ophelia said. "The court calls the accused to the stand: one Margherita Elena Rossini, self-proclaimed Pirate Queen of the Archipelago."

There was a chorus of cheers from the castaways, along with some good-natured booing from those pirates sober enough to recall that they were pretending to be a jury. Margherita swaggered up to the judge's bench with a jaunty wave and hopped up onto the barrel, her legs dangling over its edge. "The defense pleads not guilty, Your Honor."

"You're supposed to wait until I tell you what you stand accused of," Ophelia said, frowning down at her.

"Well whatever it is, I didn't do it," Margherita said, which earned her a laugh from the crowd.

"Quiet, you!" Tarja bellowed, thrusting her hook at her captain. The effect was somewhat lessened by the cork capping its point. "Or we hold you in contempt of court."

She turned to the judge. "Right?"

"Sounds right," Ophelia shrugged, and mimed unfurling a scroll. "Captain Rossini, you stand accused by this Imperial court—"

She paused to wait until the crowd's booing ceased. Quint noticed Vanessa taking a long pull from her tin cup.

"Accused," Ophelia continued, "of the following crimes: theft, piracy, murder, conspiracy, destruction of property, feeding a man's hand to a crocodile, et cetera. You still plead not guilty?"

"Aye," Margherita nodded, her smile wavering a little. "Especially to that last one. That really never did happen."

Ophelia blinked, as did Quint. Stories of the pirate queen's propensity for dismembering her foes had run rampant among the other midshipmen when they'd enlisted in the Navy together a lifetime ago, and none of their later encounters with Margherita had done much to dispel her reputation as vicious and vindictive.

Until now, Quint reflected, thinking of the gradually lessening hostility between them. She hadn't cut any pieces off him even before they'd been forced to rely upon each other.

"You mean you never chopped off old Montcrief's hand?" Ophelia asked, her palm frond wig coming askew as she tilted her head to one side.

"Oh, *that*." Margherita rolled her eyes. "One of those tales that gets added to with every telling, and each one making me more the evil witch and old Monty the guileless victim."

"So what really happened, then?" Vanessa asked, leaning forward with undisguised interest. Quint reflected that the tale of the pirate queen's dismembering of the infamous Captain Montcrief must have continued circulating when she was a midshipwoman, too.

"Answer the question," Ophelia ordered, levelling an imaginary gavel at Margherita.

"Short version," Margherita said, and though she still wore an annoyed frown Quint sensed she was enjoying the attention. "Monty and I were playing tonk. He cheated."

"And you were playing fair yourself?" Ophelia asked.

"Of course not," Margherita said, shaking her head. "I played better than him *and* cheated better. He got sour and called me on it, then pulled his knife. I pulled mine faster. The next thing anyone knows, his pinky finger's lying on the table and he's making a big hullabaloo about it."

"And the crocodile?" Ophelia asked, readjusting her wig.

"We were in the Ziltar swamps at the time," Margherita said with a shrug. "Can't spit there without hitting some species o' deadly reptile. As it happened, I was willing to call things square, but some o' Monty's mates took issue with his defingering and we got into a tussle. His pinky got knocked into the water in the commotion and swallowed up by a passing croc. The rest, as they say, is history."

"Wait," Quint called out, the pleasant buzz of tequila loosening his tongue. "I *met* Captain Montcrief, though. He's missing his whole hand, not just the one finger."

"Of course he is," Margherita snorted. "Damned fool went trying to get his finger back the next day, which worked out about as well as you'd expect. So Monty's spent the last quarter century telling anyone with ears to listen about how I chopped his hand off and fed it to a crocodile in front of his very eyes, like I'm some kind of fairy tale witch."

She paused, looking curiously at Quint, who realized he was staring at her. How much of his early interactions with her—hell, how much of their current interactions—had been informed by a story that, if Margherita was telling the truth, was almost entirely fictitious?

Judge folk by what you see of them, his pop's voice echoed in his head from a lifetime ago, *not what other folks tell you 'bout them. Reputation and reality are cousins, not twins—and distant cousins, at that.*

"Alright," Ophelia said, regaining her composure. "We'll rule out the dismemberment charge. But what defense do you offer in regard to the rest of the charges laid against you?"

"Character witnesses," Margherita said. "Tarja?"

The large Trechtishwoman folded her arms across her chest. "Apologies, Captain, but my testifying on your behalf would be a conflict of interest, as I am bailiff for this court."

"And mine," Frederick offered as Margherita's gaze fell on him. "Seeing as I am wedded to the bailiff."

Margherita looked at Quint, who grinned back at her. "You really want me giving character witness for you?"

"I s'pose not," Margherita said wryly. Her gaze swept about the bonfire circle, saw the merriment and mischief in the eyes of all the assembled castaways. Even those of her own crew were enjoying her time in the hot seat.

"Adewale," she called, beckoning him forward. "Tell Her Honor what a good captain I am."

Adewale approached the makeshift judge's bench, inclined his head to Ophelia. "Your Honor, it pains me to say that Captain Margherita is a cruel taskmistress. She drives us mercilessly as she sails across the Archipelago, scheming to destroy the Empire."

"Aye," piped up Ginger. "And she don't share her tequila, neither!"

"Objection!" Margherita called, levelling an accusing finger at the tin cup in Ginger's hand. "You're drinking a margherita right now!"

"Order in the court!" Ophelia shouted, banging her hand against the crate, to only partial success.

"ORDER!" Tarja bellowed, immediately quieting the crowd. She nodded to Ophelia.

"Captain Margherita Elena Rossini," Ophelia pronounced, her voice slow and solemn. "This court hereby finds you guilty of all charges, 'cept the one about dismembering folks. You are hereby sentenced to..."

The crowd leaned in, eager and anticipatory. Ophelia smirked, clearly savoring the moment. "*...community service.*"

A roar of approval from the castaways as Margherita hung her head in mock shame.

"To take the form," Ophelia called over the din, "of finding us a way off this bloody island! Or failing that, the building of a still so we can keep drinking after this tequila runs out."

"The punishment fits the crime," Margherita said gravely, and hopped off the barrel. "I'll start putting the still together tomorrow. Now, who's next?"

Ophelia's gaze travelled over the crowd and stopped. "The court calls to the stand the accused: Commander Vanessa Delacort of the Imperial Navy!"

A uniform round of boos, though Quint judged most of them to be in good humor. Vanessa endured them stoically as she strode to the bench and primly sat herself upon the barrel.

"Commander Delacort," Ophelia said, once more affecting a pompous, bombastic tone. "You stand accused before this court of—"

"Being an Imperial stooge?" one of Margherita's drunker crewmates jeered. To Quint's immense relief, Ginger and several others sitting nearby immediately hushed him.

"Nah," Ophelia shook her head, nearly sending her palm frond wig fluttering to the sand. She clapped a hand on it and continued. "You stand accused of theft. Namely, stealing the heart of Captain Redbeard, also known as Quentin Thatch, also known as the bloody love of your bloody life."

Quint looked resolutely into the fire, avoiding the gaze of every other castaway in the party. Beside him Lurk frowned, peering at his chest with a look of deepest concern.

"Further," Ophelia continued, "you stand accused of failing to return said heart, on not one but two separate occasions. Firstly, back in Ember Bay, where you somehow had the poor man in manacles yet failed to do what was needful with him."

A ripple of *ooohs* spread through the crowd, along with a low whistle or two. "And a second time back aboard the *Marigold,* may she rest in pieces, where despite the ardent efforts of this court you somehow kept your clothes on and your hands off each other. How do you plead?"

Almost against his will, Quint found his gaze drawn to Vanessa, and found her staring back at him, lips pursed and brows creased. She caught his eye and lifted her chin.

"Guilty," Vanessa said.

Hollering and wolf whistling rang along the beach as a flush climbed Quint's neck. Ophelia pounded her fist on the crates, recovering quickly from her surprise at Vanessa's admission of guilt.

"Let the punishment fit the crime!" the judge shouted with mock gravitas. "For so bold an act of theft upon the high seas, *Commander*, this court sentences you to live out the rest of your days as a pirate!"

The hollering and jeers immediately turned to cheers. Some of the drunker pirates even tossed their hats, a few of which landed perilously close to the bonfire.

"Oh, no," Vanessa protested flatly. "Anything but that. Especially since I'm already stuck here with all of you."

"Silence, pirate!" Ophelia yelled, grinning so widely Quint thought she might pull a muscle in her jaw. "Ordinarily we'd make you walk the plank—"

"What?" Vanessa frowned up at her, trying to tell whether Ophelia was joking. "I thought that was a myth."

"It's an initiation," Vigo said helpfully. "At least aboard the *Bloody Angel.* Quint's idea."

"Of course it was," Vanessa muttered. She shot Quint a glance, then quickly looked away.

"As this court was *saying,*" Ophelia continued, adjusting her wig. "Seeing as there's no plank to make you walk, go dunk yourself in the lagoon." She too glanced briefly at Quint, a glimmer of mischief in her eye. "The *far* end of the lagoon, mind."

"Aye, aye, your Honor," Vanessa said, throwing the least-correct salute Quint had ever seen from her. She threw another quick glance at him, then stalked away into the dark towards the beach.

"The court calls Captain Redbeard, also known as Quentin Thatch, to the stand!" Ophelia shouted.

Quint groaned, but allowed himself to be led to the bench by Tarja's firm hand. He sat on the barrel, the effort made somewhat awkward by the tequila buzzing pleasantly in the back of his head.

"Captain Redbeard," Ophelia said, smacking the crate. "You stand accused of being a right bloody idiot. How do you plead?"

"Um." Quint looked up at her. "Not guilty?"

"Objection!" Margherita shouted over her tin cup. "Only an idiot would think he could beat me at arm wrestling!"

"Pretty sure that's not how objections work," Quint pointed out, but Ophelia waved his concern away.

"Sustained," she said. "The court calls Captain Margherita Elena Rossini, pirate queen, skillful lover, and champion arm wrestler to the stand."

Margherita sauntered up, leaning against Ophelia's stacked crates.

"Captain Redbeard," the pirate queen said, "did you or did you not challenge me to an arm-wrestling contest, some fifteen years back?"

"Wait," Quint said, frowning. "Are you a witness or a prosecutor?"

She smirked. "Why not both?"

Quint looked to Ophelia, who shrugged. "The court's short on personnel. Now answer her question."

"Fine," Quint sighed, rubbing at his beard. "I admit to challenging you to the aforementioned test of strength. May I present two facts in my defense?"

Ophelia tucked a loose palm frond back into her wig. "Proceed."

"Fact the first," Quint said, counting them off on his fingers, "I didn't know who you were. Fact the second, who among us hasn't had a vast overestimation of their own capabilities at the age of twenty?"

"Counterpoint sustained," Ophelia said, slapping her hand against the crate. "What other evidence does the prosecution offer?"

"Well," Margherita said slowly, "It'd also take a real idiot to try and steal a Navy frigate from a harbor with thirty other ships docked there."

A hush fell around the bonfire, the onlookers suddenly uneasy as they sensed that the lighthearted game had become something more serious.

"You're referring to Malachite," Quint said, striving to sound unbothered. "To the time you hired me to sink the *Steadfast.*"

"I am," Margherita said, also sounding as if she were trying to keep her tone deliberately casual. "All you needed to do was plant the explosives, light the fuse, and get clear before she blew. Instead you stole the ship and set every other Navy vessel docked there after you."

She looked up at Ophelia. "Idiot."

Ophelia shifted on her crates. "Actually—"

"Actually," Quint interrupted, "there's a reason we didn't blow the *Steadfast* like you wanted."

"Because her hold was full of booty from the latest brushfire war with Asturia?" Margherita asked.

"No!" Quint objected, then corrected himself. "I mean, that part certainly didn't *hurt,* but that weren't all the *Steadfast* brought back to Malachite. Her brig was full of Asturian prisoners."

Margherita started, then glanced up at Ophelia for confirmation.

"Aye," Ophelia nodded. "They was packed together like sardines, and whatever officer held the key was ashore for the celebration."

"So we decided—" Quint looked at Ophelia and corrected himself. "*I* decided to abscond with the ship instead of blowing it to the sea-devil's locker, along with all the souls stuck inside."

Margherita stared at Quint as if she were seeing him for the first time, her mouth working soundlessly.

"An admirably noble motive," Ophelia said, filling the silence, "but not one that absolves you of the charge of being a right idiot."

"On which point the prosecution presents the following evidence," Margherita said, finding her voice again and grinning wickedly at Quint. "The incident with the dolphins—"

"That's fair," Quint said hastily, before the details of that particular misadventure could become widely known. He looked at Ophelia and allowed himself a rueful smile. "I have no defense."

"Then this court hereby finds the defendant guilty on all charges!" Ophelia said, to the crowd's approving shouts. She banged her hand against the crates. "For your crimes, you are hereby remanded to the custody of the Imperial Navy!"

"Wait," Simon called, frowning. "There's no Navy here."

"There's Vanessa," Margherita pointed out, gesturing past the fire circle and towards the lagoon.

"Quite right," Ophelia agreed, grinning wolfishly. "Captain Redbeard, you are hereby sentenced to be the prisoner of Vanessa Delacort for as long as this court sees fit!"

"Hold on a minute," Quint sputtered, forestalling the cheers and whistling that had already begun to break out among the castaways. "I'm already Margherita's prisoner."

Margherita shrugged. "I'll allow it."

Applause and cheers greeted this as the crowd of onlookers surged forward to hustle Quint off the barrel. As their rough hands seized him, Ophelia leaned down and murmured: "I better not see either of you back before sunup, mate. Y'hear?"

Then he was being hurried away, pushed out of the fire circle and onto the shifting sands of the beach. The half-moon glittered off the tranquil waves of the lagoon, permitting just enough light for him to make out the lonely trail of footprints leading away westwards.

"At least I'm in good company," Vanessa's voice said in his memory, and then Ophelia's: *"But first you've got to ask."*

Plucking up his courage, Quint set off along the beach, following the footprints left by the woman who'd stolen his heart.

23

Quint tried to tell himself that it was the headiness of the margherita, which had turned out to be a more potent beverage than anticipated, that was responsible for the odd lightness to his steps as he made his way down the beach towards the lagoon. Certainly he was too old for the sort of adolescent nervousness that had once set his fingertips to tingling the way they were now.

He came to a halt just above the lagoon's shoreline, the surf lapping softly against the sand. The waves were unbroken by Vanessa's form. Nor was she anywhere in sight, though a set of recent footprints did lead further away from the bonfire.

Quint followed them down the beach, rehearsing to himself what he would say once he caught sight of her. He debated whether a grand romantic gesture was in order, or whether a straightforward amorous proposal would better appeal to Vanessa's practicality. And if the former, whether he shouldn't have thought to gather up some flowers beforehand, or at least grab one of the bottles of tequila—

"Hey there, sailor."

Quint started, eyes darting about the moonlit beach until he caught sight of Vanessa. She sat only a few feet ahead of him, her hands folded in her lap and her back propped up against a palm tree.

He froze. *I didn't think she'd be sitting down.* Somehow this threw all his carefully rehearsed speeches into disarray. What now? Simply walk on, pretending he hadn't seen her, or run into the lagoon and try to cross the Sea of Tears on his own?

Mercifully, his common sense won out over either impulse.

"Angels," he swore, plopping onto the sand beside her. "I nearly tripped over you."

"Should probably watch where you're going, then," Vanessa teased. The dim moonlight and the stillness of the tranquil lagoon leant an ethereal quality to her countenance, like an angel drawn straight from scripture. "Don't tell me Ophelia sentenced you to walk the plank, too?"

"Nah," Quint shook his head, then frowned at her. "Though now that you mention it, your clothes are awfully dry for having just taken a dip in the lagoon."

"Maybe I went skinny dipping," she said, raising her chin.

"Without me?" Quint's mouth asked, disregarding his brain entirely.

"And why not?" Vanessa grinned at him. "Just because I waited for you last time on Tourmaline..."

"Your hair's awfully dry," Quint pointed out, recovering the power of speech. "For someone who's just gone skinny dipping, I mean."

"Fine, you've caught me," Vanessa said, raising both hands placatingly. "I wasn't about to jump in the lagoon in the dark. Not with this much tequila in my veins, anyway. I'm just waiting until it's been long enough that they'll believe I've dried off."

"Disobeying the judge's sentence?" Quint said, raising an eyebrow. "While I commend your newfound piratical approach to crime and punishment, you'll never be a real pirate 'til you've taken the buccaneer's baptism."

Vanessa laughed. "I don't think I'd make a very good pirate, Quint. I *like* rules, and ranks, and knowing what I'm going to do when I wake up every morning. I like the structure. It gives clarity."

"Are you saying I don't give my crew enough structure?" Quint asked, putting one hand over his heart in mock offense. "Because I'll have you know, we have a *mandatory* ship wide ninepins night every week."

"What, even at sea?" Vanessa snorted.

"*Especially* at sea," Quint confirmed. "The choppier, the better. The rolling deck adds to the challenge."

"Not exactly the kind of structure I meant," Vanessa said, shaking her head. But Quint caught the white flash of her smile reflecting the moonlight.

"Alright," he admitted, both palms raised. "Might be a pirate ship is a bit light on the rules and regulations. But that's part of the appeal, at least for me."

"Is it, now?" Vanessa sounded genuinely curious.

"Aye." Quint rubbed his beard, thinking how best to put into words something he'd always felt but never articulated. "I mean, for a lot of folk sailing the black flag is freedom from the law, or their families, or whatever else they're trying to leave behind. But to me it's always been about doing good where you see it. Not having to ask someone wearing more medals than you if you can feed a hungry family, or give folk a lift from a lonely little island to someplace better."

He paused. "Or redistributing the wealth of the Empire back to its citizens, come to think of it."

"Now I know you're full of bilge," Vanessa said, smacking him lightly on the arm. "You've only ever 'redistributed' Imperial coin to yourself and your crew."

"All of whom are proud subjects of Her Majesty the Empress," Quint countered.

“Hmm.” Vanessa gazed out at the moonlit waves, then glanced back at Quint. “So if Ophelia didn’t sentence you to a dip in the lagoon, what’re you doing down this end of the beach, anyways?”

“Ah.” Quint cleared his throat, wishing more than ever that he’d thought to bring one of the tequila bottles. “She, ah. Sentenced me to imprisonment for my crimes. And since you’re the only officer of the Imperial Navy on these shores...”

“Lucky me,” Vanessa said, nudging him with her elbow. “I don’t have any manacles on me this time, though.”

“Darn,” Quint said flatly, hoping the moonlight was dim enough that she couldn’t see the color rising on his neck.

Vanessa looked past him towards the distant light of the bonfire a mile back along the beach. “This coming hot on the heels of her sentencing me to a life of piracy for stealing your heart, too. Not a coincidence?”

“Probably not,” Quint agreed. He became suddenly very interested in the progress of a tiny hermit crab scuttling across the sand. “We, ah. Talked. Me and Ophelia. Turns out she’d been under the impression that you and I have been...

“Making love?” Vanessa suggested.

He looked up at her, flabbergasted.

“Harps and bells,” she said, one corner of her mouth curving upwards. “We’re both adults, Quint. Pick your jaw up off the sand.”

“Right,” Quint said, fixating on the hermit crab’s attempts to scale the toe of his boot. “Turns out Ophelia thought we’d been shacking up together since Ember Bay.”

“So what’d you tell her?”

“That we’d talked,” he made himself say. “You and me, I mean. But that we had different ideas of what the future would look like.”

"Hm." Vanessa turned her head, looking out across the lagoon, past the thin line of breakers marking the boundary reef separating them from the black leagues of the Sea of Tears. "The future's on the other side of that ocean, Quint. As long as we're on this island, there's only here and now."

"I know," Quint said, his throat suddenly gone dry. "Ophelia thinks the same. That's what she and Margherita..."

Vanessa turned to look at him, her gaze expectant.

Quint swallowed and shook his head. "But I don't want that. Not like what they've got."

"Oh." Vanessa's voice was flat, brittle. "I see."

"Ness, I—"

"I should be getting back," she said, distant and distracted. She rose to her feet, swaying only a little. Quint followed her up. His hand found hers.

"I don't want you just here and now," Quint heard himself say.

Vanessa turned slowly to him, her eyes huge in the moonlight. She did not speak, only waited.

"I don't," Quint said again, plucking up his courage from some secret well deep within himself. "I don't want to be with you because there's no future, or because it's convenient right here, right now. I want to have a future, and I want you to be a part of it. When I lost you the first time..."

His heart was racing like it did before a raid, but he pushed on. "It was like watching a ship sink, Ness. Something bold and beautiful being dragged down until it disappeared beneath the waves. A maiden voyage cut short. A horizon of endless what-ifs reduced to a shattered wreckage of might-have-beens."

"It was like that for me, too," Vanessa said, hardly louder than the surf beating against the sand. "But then we found each other again. Seems our ship hadn't sunk after all, just...run aground."

She looked down at his hand holding hers, at the chess piece tattoo on his forearm. "Why haven't we tried again, Quint?"

"I..." He forced himself to look her in the eye. "Because I need to know if what you told me was true. What you said when we parted ways on Tourmaline."

Recognition flickered across her face, along with something he could not quite place. Regret?

"That you didn't—" Quint shook his head, corrected himself as the memory that had lodged itself in his heart like a shard of ice came rising back to the surface. "That you could never love a pirate. Is that still true?"

Vanessa looked away, her mouth a tight line, but only for a moment. When she looked back her eyes caught his and held them.

"Quint," she said, very slowly and very softly. "I don't think that was even true when I said it."

His other hand found her hip, pulling her gently to him. Vanessa ran her fingers through Quint's beard, tugging his face closer to hers. She looked up at him, her eyes huge and luminous in the moonlight.

"Vanessa," he said, his voice coming out low and husky.

Vanessa answered without words, drawing his face down to hers. Her soft lips parted beneath his own.

Kissing her felt like coming home after a long voyage.

"Vanessa," he said again as she melted against him, filling his senses with her. Both their hands roved as they pulled at one another with a need at once desperate and gentle. Then less gentle as Vanessa planted both hands on his chest and pushed. Quint's back was suddenly pressed up against the hard trunk of the palm tree.

"Ow," he gasped, and laughed. She laughed too, the lines around her eyes crinkling as she looked up at him. Quint could read a thousand futures in those eyes.

Then he drew her closer, pressing his lips against hers again until there was no future, only a tender, endless now.

24

They did not talk much the following morning, as they walked back along the beach towards the main encampment. Nor did they need to, content as they were in one another's company. Quint felt—and suspected Vanessa did as well—as if last night had been some secret dream they'd shared, one they might wake from if they dared speak of it.

They did hold hands, though.

"Think they'll notice?" Vanessa asked, finally breaking the silence as they neared the remnants of the fire pit, where the detritus of last night's party lay strewn about the sand. The stacked crates Ophelia had used as her judge's bench lay toppled on their sides, the palm frond basket she'd used as a wig lying battered and forlorn beside them.

"What, that we were gone all night?" Quint grinned, rubbing his beard. "Don't think anyone's likely to miss that."

"Guess we'd better enjoy this just being between us while we can," Vanessa said, squeezing his hand.

Sure enough, others of the crew were already up and about as they drew closer to the grove, tending to the morning cookfires or collecting the refuse left by the previous night's celebrations. Quint and Vanessa found themselves on the receiving end of more than a few wolf whistles and catcalls.

"Think they've noticed," he murmured to Vanessa as Rustbucket trudged past them, a fishing net slung over one shoulder. He gave them both a look, grunted something that sounded like "finally," and continued towards the waterline.

"Let them," Vanessa said, leaning in and planting a kiss on his cheek. From somewhere amongst the grove of trees Quint heard Ophelia's clear, sharp whistle. "We don't need—"

She trailed off, eyes fixed dead ahead, mouth hanging slightly open. It was a look Quint hadn't seen on her since the last—and only—time he'd come close to beating her at chess.

"What?" he asked, frowning as he followed her gaze further up the beach, to the place where the river met the lagoon. Something glimmered there beneath the bright morning sun.

"It can't be," Vanessa breathed, finding her voice again.

But it was. The Pearl Knife, the Emperor's Carcanet, the Queen Mother's Rings, and all the rest lay in the chest he'd last seen them in, sitting propped open just past the waterline and shining as brightly as they had the first time Quint had stolen them from the vaults of Fort Amell.

There was a strangled shout from behind them. An instant later Rustbucket went barreling past, charging ahead in an unerringly straight line as if he'd been fired from a cannon, shouting "*TREASURE!!*"

"Oh *no* you don't!" Vanessa yelled, taking off after him. Quint stumbled along behind her, his hand still intertwined with hers.

"Vanessa," he panted as they raced along the beach towards the Crown Jewels, "wait—"

How'd the chest get unlocked, he wanted to say, but she was pelting headlong down the beach after Rustbucket, who had somehow maintained his lead on them despite their considerably longer legs.

"Mates!" he shouted joyfully. "Mates, we found the Jewels!!"

Out of the corner of his eyes Quint saw the rest of the castaways emerging from the trees, startled out of their hangovers by the unexpected commotion.

Vanessa was closing the distance to the Jewels, but Rustbucket reached them first. He skidded to a halt, sending plumes of sand flying into the air, then sank to his knees, plunging his hands into the pile of priceless treasures and lifting up a necklace studded with rubies the size of robin's eggs. This close, Quint saw that the many locks that had once bound the chest shut now lay in a ruin, as if something huge and heavy had smashed them apart.

"Rusty—" Quint managed, catching up to Vanessa and putting both hands on her shoulders. "Don't, it's a—"

Trap, he'd been about to say, but the words were drowned out by a geyser of water erupting from the surf, from which an enormous serpentine shape came crashing towards Rustbucket.

Lurk? was Quint's first thought, but the creature surging up the sand resembled Lurk only in general shape. It had to have been nearly twice her size, and the humanoid torso atop its coiling serpent's tail was ropy with muscle. But it had the same eyes as Lurk, huge and black and deep as the abyss, and—as it reared above Rustbucket and opened wide its mouth—the same savage shark's teeth.

"Mermaid," Vanessa squeaked, swaying against him as they both took an involuntary step backwards.

"NOPE!" Rustbucket yelled, his voice reaching an octave Quint would have found impressive under other circumstances. The ruby necklace fell forgotten from his hands as he scrambled backwards across the sands.

The massive mermaid raised a trident of bleached bone, longer than Quint was tall. Still backpedaling furiously, Rustbucket whimpered.

"*OI!*" Quint shouted, cupping his hands to his mouth. "Fish food! Find someone else to drown!"

The mermaid turned its head, trident still held aloft. A shiver wracked Quint's spine as those terrible eyes turned on him, but he stood his ground, Vanessa at his side.

Rustbucket wasted none of the time Quint's distraction had brought him. He stumbled to his feet and took off for the grove of trees.

Still looking at Quint, the mermaid turned cocked its head to one side, much as Lurk had done when she and Quint had first met.

"*Drown?*" it repeated in a voice as deep as the sea, eyes narrowing. Something in the way it pronounced the word suggested that it was not merely parroting back what Quint had said, but knew full well what it meant.

If it understands me, we might be able to parley with it, Quint thought. But he was given no time to open negotiations, for at that very moment the trees shook with the overlapping shouts of his fellow castaways.

They came charging down the beach, some armed with cutlasses and machetes, others with small knives or the tools they'd scavenged from the wreckage of the *Marigold,* a few with nothing more than their fists. Ophelia and Tarja raced at their head, Margherita not far behind.

"Back off, eel breath!" Ophelia bellowed, a cutlass in each hand, her swoop of hair flopping wildly from side to side as she pounded over the sands. Beside her, Tarja nodded her agreement, too red in the face to speak.

The mermaid's gaze returned to Quint, its great black eyes narrowing even as its mouth widened into a terrifying shark's grin.

"DROWN!" it roared, and thrust its trident into the air.

Behind it, the waters of the lagoon seemed to come to life, roiling and foaming as snakelike bodies breached the surface, like earthworms wriggling up from the soil after a rainfall. Enormous black eyes fixed upon Quint, and from dozens of throats came a high, keening chorus:

"*DROOOOOWN*!"

Then they came surging forward, crashing onto the beach like a wave made of scaly coiling bodies of deep blue and dark gray. Some were armed with short, vicious-looking javelins, others with long and jagged spears, though none were as intimidating—or as impressive—as the lead mermaid's enormous trident.

To their credit, the pirates did not back down from the sudden, overwhelming attack. Ophelia and Tarja reached Quint and Vanessa, Margherita and the others not far behind, all brandishing whatever weapons they had to hand, shouting and snarling at the hostile mermaids.

"Get behind me," Quint hissed at Vanessa as the lead mermaid raised his trident once more, trying to push her behind him.

"Like hell," she said, and stood her ground beside him. The mermaid's trident gleamed wetly in the sun, and began to fall.

"STOP!" A high, musical, blessed voice piped. "All of you stop this, *right now!*"

The lead mermaid's head jerked to one side, huge dark eyes widening. Its trident continued to fall, but Vanessa pulled Quint aside, and the three prongs buried themselves in the sand beside his feet rather than his chest.

"I said stop!" Lurk repeated as she emerged from behind the dunes, where she'd evidently been sleeping off the night's festivities. She slithered along the sand, coming between Quint and the mermaid who'd nearly stabbed him. There was a susurration of high, musical voices speaking in the mermaid's whistling language, cut suddenly short by the leader's upraised fist.

It cocked its head again, looking at Lurk with unmistakable surprise.

"Orders, Cap'n?" Ophelia murmured behind him as the lead mermaid said something to Lurk in their own tongue.

"Stand down," he said, loud enough for those castaways nearest to hear, but not so loud that the mermaids would take it as an interruption—or worse, a threat. "Keep your arms handy, but no one attack until and unless I say so. Not even if they strike first."

Nodding grimly, Ophelia took a step back, murmuring Quint's orders to those mates nearest her. Quint returned his attention to Lurk, in whose webbed hands all their fates now lay.

"Speak Landfolk," she said, interrupting the lead mermaid. "So that they can understand."

The other mermaid made a high, musical protest. Now that the danger was less immediate, Quint noticed it wore a necklace of coral pieces, and that there were curling barbels beneath its chin, giving it an almost bearded appearance.

"Landfolk," Lurk repeated, folding her arms over her chest. A ripple of irritation ran through the other mermaid's spinal ridge, which stood taller than Lurk's, and was a bloody orange red.

"They're my pod," Lurk said, mirroring her opposite's annoyance, and added what Quint presumed was the same statement in her own tongue.

The other mermaid blinked, its dark eyes turning from Quint to Lurk and back.

"You...are pod?" it asked. Its voice, while still high and musical, was deeper than Lurk's; a light tenor. Combined with the barbells and its spinal ridge, Quint was struck by a sudden suspicion that he had finally encountered a male of the species.

"Her pod?" The mermaid—or merman, rather—asked again, gesturing with its trident at Lurk. "The pod of—"

A long series of musical whistles like whale song, which Quint recognized as Lurk's true name.

"Aye," Quint said, finding his voice and nodding. "Lur—er. In Landfolk, her name is She Who Glides Through the Current to Lurk Unseen Amongst the Seaweed Groves."

"Crude," the merman said to Lurk. Unlike her, he spoke with a thick yet intelligible accent.

"It is not their fault they are not strong singers," Lurk said, spinal ridge bristling in what was either agitation or challenge. "But they are good folk."

"Landfolk cannot be good," the merman said dismissively. He glanced at Quint, then back to Lurk. "Why then have you taken them as your pod?"

Quint opened his mouth to speak but shut it at a glance from Lurk.

"I lost my pod," she said, and though the sadness in her voice was unmistakable she straightened, rising on her serpentine tail until she stood nearly as tall as the massive merman. "There was a terrible storm, and I was separated from my family. From my hatch mates and from my sires. I swam and swam until my strength gave out, then swam some more, until the great dark rose up to claim me."

A ripple of musical murmurs echoed from behind her, silenced once more by the merman's upraised fist.

"I have heard similar tales before," he said, showing his teeth. "Our people lost to wave or whale, only to be caught in landfolk nets and hauled aboard their great wooden turtles, their service bought in exchange for their lives."

He swayed atop his serpent's tail, leaning towards Quint. "Know, little landman, that this one may be forced to honor a promise drawn from her at the point of a spear, but I will not."

"Quint never forced anything from me," Lurk said, interposing herself between them. "He found me when I was lost and alone, and the only promise he ever asked of me was that I not drown him."

"Drown?" a mermaid's voice asked hopefully from the crowd, but was swiftly hissed back into silence.

"So you spared him," the merman said flatly, looking from Lurk to the motley assemblage of castaways behind her. "That does not explain how you came to be their—"

He made another musical sound, though this one was low and discordant.

"I am no one's slave!" Lurk said, drawing herself up so that her bared teeth were inches from the merman's. "These are my pod and my friends, and if you insult them again I will challenge you to—"

Quint could not translate the angry burst of mer-speak that followed, but its meaning was evident in the merman's unmistakable astonishment.

"You would fight me, little one?" he asked, blinking his huge dark eyes. "I, who in this distasteful land speech am named He Who Delves the Blind Depths to Prove His Mettle Against Whale and Squid?"

"I would fight your whole pod to protect my own," Lurk said, undaunted. Her spinal ridge stood fully upright, webbed hands raised like a boxer's fists after the first bell. She glanced past the merman at the rest of his pod, dozens strong. "Would any of you do less?"

Quint could not tear his eyes from the confrontation unfolding before him, but out of the corner of his vision he saw the other mermaids glancing at one another, their high and musical whispers scarcely audible above the crash of the surf.

"No," He Who Delves the Blind Depths to Prove His Mettle Against Whale and Squid said at last, his own crest drooping as his dark eyes moved from Lurk to Quint. "I could not. Nor will I spill the blood of a fellow mer over landfolk, however foolish I think it."

"Good," Lurk said, though she neither lowered her hands nor relaxed her ridge, which quivered slightly. *She's afraid,* Quint thought, his heart swelling with pride and fear for her. "Then you are welcome to rest in these waters, you and all your pod."

The merman—Squid, Quint could not help himself from thinking—snorted. "These have been our waters since long before you were birthed, little one. This island is the—" A keening, mournful mermaid sound "—of the Deep Shadows Pod, and has been since the first of our kind traded limb and land for scale and wave."

"Deep Shadows?" Lurk repeated, a new note in her voice. "The Deep Shadows pod that roams from the southern seas to the western Archipelago, and through it to the Great Reef?"

"We are," Squid said, a note of annoyance clear in his piping tenor even as his spinal ridge perked up. "These are the southern seas, obviously."

"Then you and I are kin," Lurk said wonderingly. "My mother's father was of the Deep Shadows."

She said what Quint presumed was her grandsire's name, and for several minutes the conversation devolved into the high, fluting sounds of mermaid language. Though Quint could not follow the exact words, he'd lived long enough in a small town to recognize the cadence of folk comparing family trees, trying to work out exactly how they were related.

"We're distant cousins," Lurk said of Squid when Quint asked. "Now stop interrupting, or I won't be able to keep them from drowning you."

"Pretty certain she's joking," Ophelia said in Quint's ear, though she did not sound certain at all.

Quint was barely listening, for there was a jostling among the crowd of merfolk. With their bloodlust allayed—or at least postponed—most had retreated back into the lagoon, watching as they bobbed in the waves. Despite the fact that their snakelike tails were hidden beneath the surface, this did not make them look any less alien.

But now one was pushing forward, winding snakelike through the crowd of others. Even before she slithered up from the waves and onto the wet sand Quint could tell this mermaid was old—her scales had lost the glistening sheen the rest of her kind possessed, and were criss-crossed with faded scars. There was a large chunk missing from her spinal ridge that looked like it had been bitten off, and when she opened her mouth and spoke in the mermaids' musical tongue Quint saw that many of her teeth were missing—though those that remained were as sharp as ever.

Lurk answered in the same language, her tone somehow cautious. The elder mermaid replied, then let out a soft hissing sound Quint recognized as laughter.

Lurk surged forward, her snakelike tail and the older mermaid's twining about one another, their coils locked in a tight embrace. Quint was struck by a surge of panic—what if they were fighting?—but Vanessa's hand found his and squeezed.

"Family reunion," she murmured.

Sure enough, Lurk and the elderly mermaid were now face to face, their webbed hands pressed flat against one another as they both spoke fast and high, overlapping each other.

"Who is she?" Quint asked Squid.

The massive merman looked down at him, showing all his teeth. "She is the father-sister of your...friend's...grandsire, who left us to join the Coral Gliders pod."

"Coral Gliders?" Quint asked.

“My pod,” Lurk said, disentangling herself from her elderly relation and slithering to Quint, the older mermaid following. “This is my...aunt, I suppose. You would call her She Who Guards Against the Shark and Serpent Without Fear. She knows my grandsire, who left this pod to join my foremothers’ in the Coral Gliders.”

She Who Guards must have followed this speech, or at least recognized a few words, for she added something in her own tongue. Lurk stared at her, asked something and was swiftly answered.

“What?” Quint asked.

“She remembers the Coral Gliders,” Lurk said, a tremor running down her spinal ridge. “Remembers my pod. And...”

She looked at Quint, her huge dark eyes pleading. “And she knows where to find them.”

25

"Are you certain?" Quint asked, a strange mixture of emotions welling up inside him. Excitement that Lurk might soon be reunited with the family she'd been separated from for so long, comingled with dread at the possibility of her departure.

Lurk inquired further, which She Who Guards responded to with something that might have been amusement. "She says that my pod and this one passed one another by only weeks ago. That they were on their way to the Great Reef."

Quint and Vanessa exchanged a glance. The Great Reef was a huge stretch of shallow water, practically a small sea in its own right, where corals grew in such wild abundance that most ships would rather skirt around it than risk running aground. The few islands dotting the Reef were little more than sandbars, and as such had little to entice passing ships to dare the maze of unseen hazards to weigh anchor upon their shores.

"Of course," Vanessa murmured, pushing her hair out of her face. "The angels themselves couldn't come up with a better place to keep humans out of."

"Might be the angels designed it," Ophelia pointed out, but Quint was not really listening to either of them.

"Lurk's family," he asked She Who Guards. "Her pod—you're certain that's where they are?"

The elderly mermaid must have understood more human speech than she spoke, for she answered the question without waiting for Lurk to convey her captain's meaning.

"She says they should be, unless disaster struck them," Lurk translated, pausing as her great-aunt continued. Whatever she said set Lurk's ridge to standing on end.

"Quint," Lurk said, turning to him with an astonished expression. "She says...they passed by my pod while they were swimming in opposite directions, not long ago. Two months. I...they're out there right now, at the Great Reef, or headed that way."

"That's incredible!" It was impossible to dread Lurk's departure when there was such ardent hope in her voice. Quint seized her webbed hands, ignoring Squid's looming scowl. "You can find them. See your family again."

"My family," Lurk agreed, a happy shiver rippling through her spinal ridge. "Mother and Father, and all my little sisters and brothers..."

She trailed off into the musical sounds of her siblings' names, but something about the way she said "Mother and Father" made Quint uneasy. He looked up at Squid, who was far and away the largest of the merfolk, his humanoid torso built like a champion wrestler's. Then at She Who Guards, whose frame was withered by age, yet still she stood taller than Lurk.

They were *all* taller than Lurk, Quint realized, looking out at the others of her kind bobbing in the waves. He had never thought much of his mermaid friend's slight build, but seeing her now, compared against her kin...

"Lurk," he said slowly, interrupting her recitation of her family line. "How old are you?"

She looked at him, spinal ridge stiff and chin upraised. "Old enough."

Lurk could not have known it, but that was precisely the same answer and body language that Quint had used to justify his signing on with the Navy to his ma and pop. He had been fifteen at the time.

"Angels above," he swore, paling beneath the tropical sun. "You're a *kid.*"

"Am not!" Lurk bristled, but further protest was cut short by Squid's hissing chuckle.

"She is young," he said, clearly amused. "Not child, maybe, but not full grown either. Obviously."

"Trumpets," Vanessa murmured, looking at Lurk. "She's a teenager."

"She's a kid," Quint repeated, only half hearing her as his eyes fell upon the designs he and Vigo had inked onto Lurk's scales: the sea turtles, the anchor, the stylized underside of the *Bloody Angel.*

"Angels forgive me," Quint prayed aloud, putting his face into his hands. "I tattooed a *kid...*"

"I like my tattoos!" Lurk protested. One webbed hand rose to the fins on the side of her head, tugging self-consciously at the little gold rings there. "And I like these. They all show that I'm part of your pod."

"My pod," Quint repeated, rubbing at his temples. He'd been seventeen when he and Ophelia had traded in their purple Navy jackets for the pirates' black flag, an age which seemed improbably young now. He had no idea how mermaid lifespans compared to human ones, but Lurk was visibly nowhere near fully grown.

"But now you can go back to your own pod," he said, looking at Lurk, and at She Who Guards standing behind her. "To your family. They can show you the way. Help you cross over the Sea of Tears, and through the Archipelago to the Great Reef. Until you come safe home."

Lurk blinked her huge dark eyes.

"Quint," she said, in the slow, deliberate tone one used when explaining to a small child that the burning stove was hot. "Home is where my pod is. Where my parents are, but also where you are. Home is never just one place. Don't you know that?"

Quint opened his mouth, closed it. He thought of the *Bloody Angel,* with which he had made his name as Captain Redbeard, and of Ember Bay, which had made him who he was, long before he ever raised the black flag.

"I know it," he said, reluctantly. "But if they leave, and you're not with them..."

"Then I'll find my family again," she said firmly, standing nearly as tall as Squid. She looked at the chieftain of the Deep Shadows pod, then back to She Who Guards, who was watching this with an expression of bemusement. "But...I think I need to go with them anyway. Just not as far as the Great Reef."

Vanessa caught on faster than Quint did. "Back to the Archipelago?"

"Aye," Lurk nodded, swiveling on her tail to peer out across the Sea of Tears. There were dark clouds above the distant horizon, promising rain later in the day. "I can make it across, with their help. From there I can get to Ember Bay, let Quint's ma know what happened, where you are."

"But the danger—" Quint started, still moved by some latent parental instinct awakened by the revelation of Lurk's true age.

To his surprise, it was Squid who interrupted.

"No danger," he said, shaking his head so vigorously that the curling barbels on his chin quivered. He pointed his trident at the Sea of Tears. "We make this journey many times. We know how to navigate the currents, to weather the storms. Shark and serpent will not dare challenge so many, and we keep our young and our sick at the center of pod, where they are safest."

"I won't be at the center," Lurk told the merman chieftain. "I'll be up front, with you. Once we reach the Archipelago you'll need me to guide us to Ember Bay."

A ripple of annoyance ran down Squid's ridge. "You are young for a navigator. And I have promised nothing, yet."

She Who Guards said something in the lowest, ugliest tone Quint had ever heard from a mermaid, her notched spinal ridge standing fully upright as she laid into Squid. To Quint's lasting surprise, the merman quailed beneath her tirade, shying away from She Who Guards as if she were twice his size, rather than half.

"She's really letting him have it, eh?" he asked Lurk.

"Aye, Quint," Lurk nodded, shooting him a toothy grin. "She's telling him what the rest of our kind would think if word got out that the Deep Shadows found a mer who'd been separated from her pod and didn't help her. How all merfolk would doubt their trustworthiness forever after."

"So they're obligated to help you?" Vanessa asked, furrowing her brow. "Even though you're from a different pod?"

"Sort of," Lurk said, shrugging as Squid shrank further beneath She Who Guards' atonal tirade. "If a pod comes across a lone mer without a pod, they have to at least offer to let her join, or help her find her way back to them. But seeing as I've already got a pod..."

"You're a unique case," Quint said, rubbing his beard. "They still have to offer to help you, but Squid's reluctant to. Because he doesn't see us as your true pod."

"Like you said," Lurk agreed. "I'm unique."

"That you are," Quint said, smiling at her. She Who Guards came gliding up beside Lurk, Squid following along behind, his proud red ridge drooping.

"Landfolk," Squid said, sounding abashed and a little sullen. He directed his words at Quint, who supposed that, as Lurk's self-appointed guardian, he was the nearest thing to the mermaid chieftain's opposite number among the castaways. "As chief of the Deep Shadows, I offer your companion She Who Glides Through the Current to Lurk Unseen Amongst the Seaweed Groves an invitation to travel north with us, back to the islands you call Archipelago."

"To Ember Bay?" Quint asked, looking at Lurk. But Squid shook his head.

"We offer to take her to the Great Reef," he said, also glancing at Lurk. "Or as far as she will go with us in that direction. Should she depart from us at any time, our obligation to her will be fulfilled."

"I can make it back to Ember Bay on my own," Lurk said, forestalling Quint's objections. "Once I'm across the Sea of Tears. And after I've told your ma where we are, I can ride aboard the *Bloody Angel* on the return journey."

"But you *do* promise to take her that far?" Quint asked Squid.

"Yes," Squid said, showing his teeth and standing straighter. "I, He Who Delves the Blind Depths to Prove His Mettle Against Whale and Squid, chieftain of the Deep Shadows pod, promise by salt and scale to guide She Who Glides Through the Current to Lurk Unseen Amongst the Seaweed Groves safely across the waters to the Great Reef, or however far she chooses to accompany us. I shall teach her the way of wave and current and storm, so that she may return safely to this place if she wishes. In return I ask only that she do her part when it comes to hunting for the pod's sustenance and the protection of our young. Do you accept my promise?"

"Aye," Quint started to say, but Lurk interrupted him.

"And do you promise not to drown any landfolk who are part of my pod?" she asked, glancing briefly at Quint. "Here or across the sea?"

Quint blinked, surprised and impressed. Squid had made it clear that he did not intend the Deep Shadows to accompany Lurk all the way to Ember Bay, but on the off chance they encountered the *Bloody Angel* before Lurk parted from the pod, she had just saved Quint's remaining crew from a highly unpleasant fate.

"I promise that too," Squid said, exasperation tinging his voice. "Will that suffice?"

Quint glanced at Lurk, who nodded, having no further addendums.

"Aye," Quint said, standing a little straighter, though the massive merman still dwarfed him. "I, Quint Thatch, captain of the *Bloody Angel*, accept this promise. And—"

He glanced behind him, at Ophelia and Margherita, at Tarja and Rustbucket. "I promise you that none of those you see here on this beach, nor the rest o' my crew, will ever raise a hand in anger against any merfolk ever again. I swear it on my pop's grave."

"Other landfolk have made similar promises before," Squid said, openly doubtful.

"Quint's not like other landfolk," Lurk said. "He keeps his promises."

Squid did not answer that, only stared at Quint as if he had lobsters hanging from his ears.

"Very well," the merman said slowly, folding his arms across his broad chest and bowing. "Your promise is heard, and accepted."

"Thank you," Quint said, mirroring the gesture. This seemed to satisfy the merfolk chieftain, for he grunted and gave a small nod of what might have been approval.

"Lurk," Vanessa spoke up, pointing at the Crown Jewels still glittering in the sunlight. "They fished those up from the wreckage of the *Marigold*. They don't...they're not planning on keeping them, are they?"

Lurk directed the question to She Who Guards, who gave Vanessa what Quint thought was a rather contemptuous shrug.

"She says no," Lurk reported. "That landfolk jewels are pretty, but useless. The Deep Shadows have no further use for them."

"In that case..." Vanessa closed the lid on the Jewels' chest. Vigo hurried forward, and together the two of them began hauling it further up the shoreline, towards the treehouses.

She Who Guards turned on her tail and pointed out across the Sea of Tears. She sang something, high and musical.

"What's she saying?" Quint asked Lurk.

"That if we're going to set out for the Archipelago, we need to leave with the tide," Lurk said, looking down at the surf washing gently over Quint's feet.

His heart sank. That left them scarcely more than an hour.

"Well," he said, forcing false cheer into his voice. "At least that'll give us enough time to say our farewells."

Lurk translated this for She Who Guards' benefit. The elderly mermaid nodded, then turned and retreated into the shallows, gliding away with long, lazy sweeps of her tail. She turned and called out something in her musical voice, then dove beneath the surface.

"What was that?" Quint asked.

"She said," Lurk said, confused, "to watch out for the ghost."

⚓

He was very nearly wrong about having enough time to bid Lurk farewell.

With the mermaids no longer threatening them, Quint had expected the castaways to slip back to the treehouses to sleep off their hangovers from last night's party. None did. Instead, they lingered by the shore, each of them wanting to offer Lurk well wishes for a safe journey, or their repeated thanks for having saved them from the shipwreck.

"They're all quite fond of her," Quint remarked to Ophelia, watching as Tarja said her goodbyes, which seemed to include a lengthy lecture on how best to wrangle saltwater crocodiles. It was advice he sincerely hoped the young mermaid would never need.

"Comes of saving their lives," Ophelia said. "And digging up supplies from the *Marigold's* wreck. And catching fresh fish. And her personality."

"Right," Quint said, rubbing his beard. "I suppose we raised her pretty well, didn't we?"

"Don't look at me, mate," Ophelia shook her head. "You took on the surrogate father role when you decided you wanted to be captain. Me, I'm more of the aloof big sister or fun aunt. Besides, if there's anyone you'd be raising up a kid with..."

She glanced at Vanessa, who stood chatting with Vigo, both of them having already bid their farewells to Lurk after returning from stashing the Crown Jewels in the treehouse. "How was last night, by the way?"

"It was..." Quint started, then trailed off, struck by a sudden realization that cast last night in a new light. Now that Lurk could make it across the Sea of Tears, their odds of eventual rescue had gone up dramatically. They might yet return to the Archipelago—and if so, they would be pirate and Navy officer once more.

"That bad?" Ophelia asked, wincing.

"No!" Quint said, shaking his head. "It's just..."

He trailed off, watching as the line of Lurk's well-wishers reached its end. To his surprise, Rustbucket stood there, hands clasped behind his back, looking down at his toes.

"Rusty," Lurk said, looking nearly as perplexed as Quint felt.

"Lurk," Rustbucket said to his toes. "Wanted...I wanted to say thanks."

"You're welcome," Lurk said immediately. She blinked. "For what?"

"For not drowning me, the first time we met, and in the shipwreck. And for all you've done for us since. I..." He spat into the sand. "Ah, hells, I'm no good at this."

"That's alright," Lurk said encouragingly. "I'm sure there's things you *are* good at. I just haven't seen them."

"Ain't so sure about that," he said, looking her in the eye. "I just...wanna say. We're lucky Cap'n brought you onto the crew. You're a better fit than I ever was. A better pirate, and a better friend."

Lurk pondered this.

"I don't know about that," she said at last. "I think whatever pod you fit with depends as much on who you are as who they are. If Quint's pod doesn't feel like home, maybe there's another one out there that does."

"Aye," Rustbucket said, casting his gaze across the Sea of Tears. "Maybe so. Be well, Lurk."

"You too, Rusty."

And then it was Quint's turn. He'd waited until he was the last, dreading the separation, yet now their parting was before him.

"Quint," Lurk said as he drew near to where she waited in the shallows, She Who Guards beside her. Squid had already departed for the far end of the lagoon, eager to lead his people out past the breakers into the open water. "Cap'n."

"Lurk," Quint said, looking past her at that crashing line of waves. "You're sure about this?"

"I can do it," she said with the total confidence of youth. She turned to look at She Who Guards, and smiled her sharklike smile. "I'll have help. And when it comes time to return, I'll know the way."

"Then you'll have saved us again," Quint said. "And this won't be goodbye. Just...until we meet again."

"Quint," Lurk said in that patient tone she used whenever he said something she found foolish. "That's what all goodbyes are."

Then, to his surprise, she wrapped her scaly arms around him and hugged him tight. Quint hugged her back, bemused and touched by her adoption of the human gesture of affection.

"May the winds be ever at your back," he murmured as she released him, knowing and not caring that the old sailor's blessing did not strictly apply in this instance.

"Warm currents and calm seas," Lurk replied. "Cap'n."

Then she was gone, turning gracefully about and gliding into the lagoon. Her long, sleek body cut through the water just below the surface, making for the white line of the breakers. Squid saw her coming and whistled something long and high. Quint had one final glimpse of Lurk leaping like a spinner dolphin from the surface, sunlight glinting off her scales as they cleared the breakers entirely, then plunged into the ocean beyond.

Then she and all the merfolk were gone, just as suddenly as they'd appeared.

Quint and Ophelia stood there, watching the waves. When he turned to look at her he was surprised to find Ophelia wiping a tear from her eye.

"They grow up so fast," she said.

26

"So," Quint said, catching up to Vanessa as the rest of the crew dispersed, heading back to the treehouses or to collect their scattered belongings from around the firepit. "Looks like we might make it off this island after all."

"Looks like," Vanessa agreed, her tone guarded.

"What..." Quint started, then realized he didn't know how to continue that train of thought. "Er, do you..."

That wasn't right, either, but Vanessa seemed to intuit what he wasn't saying.

"I don't know, Quint," she said, running a hand through her curls. "I mean...last night was..."

"Really nice," Quint said, then immediately cursed himself for that horrific understatement. "I mean—"

"I know what you mean." Vanessa shot him a tired smile. "It was a long time coming."

"Worth the wait, though?" Quint asked, hoping he sounded teasing rather than anxious.

"Most certainly," Vanessa said, tucking a loose strand of hair behind her ear. "But now...if we're going to make it home—"

What exactly a return to the Archipelago meant for their shared future was postponed by a high, piercing scream from the direction of the treehouses.

The castaways still milling about the beach in the wake of Lurk's departure froze, taken aback by the sudden cry, but Quint and Vanessa suffered no such hesitation. They broke into a run at precisely the same moment, racing across the dunes and up the hill as Margherita's voice cut through the early afternoon air:

"*ALL HANDS TO BATTLE STATIONS!*" the pirate queen bellowed. "*WE'RE UNDER ATTACK!*"

⚓

But by the time Quint and Vanessa reached the grove of trees and mounted the steps to the treehouse, the attack had already come and gone. Crates and barrels lay pried open or tossed on their sides, their contents spilled across the wooden platforms. Toolboxes lay upended, as did the bunks in the bunkhouses. It looked to Quint as though a tornado had torn through the grove, leaving the structure of the treehouses intact but sparing little else.

"Who was it?" he asked, panting a little as he clambered onto the wooden platform, eyes darting around for any sign of whoever had ransacked their modest little settlement. But there was only Margherita, dappled sunlight gleaming off the blade of her unsheathed cutlass.

"Not a clue," she growled, deep and throaty. Her eyes scanned the branches as she turned in a slow circle, as if the unknown vandals might materialize from among the leaves. "It was like this when I got here."

"So we're not under attack," Quint said, feeling more keenly than ever the absence of any sort of weapon at his hip. "We were raided—"

Margherita wrinkled her nose, but whatever contemptuous retort she was about to spit out was cut off by Vanessa shouldering her way past them both, making a beeline towards the upper platform where the captain's bunkhouses lay.

"The Jewels," Quint realized, his blood running cold. Margherita paled, the point of her cutlass drooping.

They turned and hurried after Vanessa, who veered into Quint's bunkhouse. As he ducked inside after her, he was struck by the incongruous thought that he hadn't even slept there yet, which somehow made its evident upheaval all the more insulting.

As with the main platform, anything not nailed down had been thoroughly rummaged through. Limes rolled across the floorboards, the crate they'd been stored in carelessly tossed in one corner. A small box of fishhooks had been upended onto the woven palm mat that served as a bedroll, while a collection of shells that Lurk must have dredged up from the seabed now lay scattered across the floor like caltrops.

All of this Quint registered only dimly as he joined Vanessa where she stood near the center of the room, staring dumbly down at an empty space amongst the wreckage, almost perfectly square.

"Is that—" he asked, though he thought he already knew the answer.

"Aye," Vanessa said, in a small voice that sounded lost and almost scared. "That's where we put the chest with the Jewels."

Quint felt as if someone had opened a trapdoor beneath him, which was something that seemed to happen to him with surprising regularity. He forced down the mounting panic and rubbed his beard, thinking.

"This wasn't random," he said, looking from the empty patch of floor to Vanessa. "Whoever did this was looking for the Jewels specifically."

"Which means they were watching the treehouses when Vigo and I brought the Jewels up from the beach," Vanessa said slowly, regaining a little of her composure with every word. Despite their circumstances,

Quint had to keep himself from smiling. If there was one surefire way to shake Vanessa loose from her daze, it was to present her with a puzzle in need of solving. "But they didn't follow us *into* the treehouses, else they would have known where to go first thing, rather than ransacking everything."

"Which tells us that they were in a hurry," Quint said, thinking hard. "They knew they only had a little time to search, while we were saying our farewells to Lurk."

How long had that taken, anyway? Quint thought it had been close to an hour, but he'd been so caught up in the dizzying rush of emotions revolving around Lurk's journey and their possible rescue that he couldn't swear to it. Angels, why hadn't any of them brought a pocket watch with them when they'd fled the sinking *Marigold?*

"Who could it have been, though?" Vanessa asked, turning to him with a pensive frown. "I mean...there's only so many of us shipwrecked here."

Rustbucket, an unworthy part of Quint thought, but he quashed it immediately, thinking back to their conversation amongst the dunes. Rustbucket had seemed sincere in his desire to turn over a new leaf, and Quint wasn't about to repay that sincerity with suspicion.

"We don't know that it was any of the crew," he said, trying to sound reasonable. "For one thing, we're all stuck here together. Why steal the Jewels when none of us are getting off this island alone?"

"Quint," Vanessa said, running an agitated hand through her hair. "It's the *Crown Jewels.* And they're pirates—"

"I'm a pirate," Quint pointed out, feeling as if she'd just struck him in the gut.

Vanessa's eyes widened, realizing what she'd just said. She opened her mouth, about to utter perhaps an apology or perhaps a rejoinder, only to be cut off by the creaking of boards behind them.

"It weren't no pirate that did this," Margherita said, darkening their doorway. "Leastaways, not one of our crew."

"How can you be sure?" Quint asked, turning to face her. Margherita stood in an uncharacteristically prim posture, both hands clasped behind her back.

"Because they left us a calling card," the pirate queen said, and extended a hand towards Quint and Vanessa.

Clenched in her fist was a crumpled, bent, tattered white feather.

27

"Don't suppose this could be somebody else's feather?" Rustbucket asked, turning it over in his hands.

The entire crew was gathered atop the treehouse's central platform, called to action by Margherita's warning of imminent attack. A few had stomped across the floorboards with storms in their eyes, swearing vengeance on whomever had laid waste to their newly built home, but most had been struck dumb with shocked disbelief. A few had looked close to tears at the hurt done to that which they'd all worked so hard to build.

And were already working to rebuild, Quint noted with no small amount of pride. Darby and Vigo had swiftly redirected the group's energy into cleaning up the mess their unknown adversary had made of their lodgings. Even now, as they passed the feather around while their leaders reported on what little they knew, most of the crew were busy sorting their scattered resources into organized piles while Frederick took careful inventory of what remained to them.

"You suggesting that it was a great big white bird that went and rifled through our things?" Margherita said, staring hard at him. Quint had the sense that she was not quite as ready as he had been to believe in Rusty's reformed character.

"Of course not," Rustbucket said, a flush rising in his cheeks even as he visibly strove to maintain an even demeanor. "I'm just sayin', we've seen a fair few birds during the time we've been wrecked here. Some of them must have white feathers."

"None like this," Tarja said, taking the feather from him and holding it up to the light. "That is, unless there is a flock of ostriches somewhere upon this island."

"Ostriches?" Vanessa echoed, sounding as perplexed as Quint felt.

"Ja," Tarja said, passing the feather along to her. "Big, magnificent flightless birds. There is a whole flock of them residing in one of the animal sanctuaries Frederick and I frequent. Whenever we stop by to deliver some unfortunate mistreated beast to them I always take a feather or two for Captain Margherita."

"Right," Quint said, trying to recover his footing as Vanessa passed him the feather. "Well, seeing as we got to the top of the mountain and didn't see any savannas, I think it's safe to say that this feather and the one the monkey stole are the same article."

This statement elicited more confusion than clarity; Quint realized too late that they had accidentally omitted their encounter with the monkey during their retelling of their misadventures across the island. By the time Margherita had recounted the unlikely theft of her hat, the conversation was growing dangerously close to being sidetracked once again.

"So you were stalked all the way back to camp by a monkey?" Ginger asked, frowning.

"And then why did it leave the feather behind?" Adewale pointed out. "And for that matter, where is the captain's hat?"

"Hold on," Ophelia said, and though she did not raise her voice, the chattering fell silent almost immediately. "Let's assume that both captains are right and it *was* this monkey that followed them down from the mountains. You said it was small?"

"It was," Margherita admitted, a touch defensively. "But it was *quick,* and when it came at me with those sharp little teeth—"

"Horrifying," Ophelia said with an appreciative shudder, which seemed to mollify Margherita somewhat. "But it was little, right? Small enough to sit on your shoulder?"

"I suppose," Margherita admitted, then realized where Ophelia was going. "Too small to carry the chest away by itself, you mean."

"Exactly." Quint glanced between Vanessa and Vigo. "It took you two to carry it back up the hill, right?"

"Aye," Vigo nodded, tugging thoughtfully at one of his braids. "Suppose one person might be able to carry it alone, but not very far, and not without taking a lot of breaks."

"And what about one person and a monkey?" Quint said, deciding that if someone were going to ask the obvious, absurd question, then it might as well be him.

"Or one person and several monkeys?" Margherita added, coming unexpectedly to Quint's aid. Or perhaps that was just because she had been the monkey's first victim.

"I think you're both overlooking the obvious," Vanessa said, pointing to the side of the treehouse platform. Eighteen heads turned to see the makeshift pulley system that they'd rigged to haul things up to the platform from below.

"Oh," Quint said. "Right."

"Explains how they got it down, anyway," Margherita said, looking glumly at her bedraggled feather. "Though not where they took it afterwards. I doubt that there's any tracks to follow, what with how the ground's so thick with roots."

"I'll go look," Adewale said, turning and clambering nimbly over the rail with a lifelong sailor's ease.

"Right," Quint said, fishing in his pocket. "There's also this."

He held up the doubloon, letting the dappled sunlight reflect off the weathered face of the long-ago emperor.

This did not have quite the intended effect. The crew exchanged glances, scratching their heads, or murmuring quietly to one another. Darby cleared his throat.

"You, uh, find some change in your pocket, Cap'n?"

"What?" Quint blinked and looked again at the coin in his hand. "No, of course not. We found this on the mountaintop."

It took a moment for the crew to fully realize the implications of that statement, but once they did it sent an excited chatter buzzing through them.

"On *top* of the mountain?"

"—means we're not the first—"

"Could be there's others here—"

"That's not all," Quint said, remembering. "The mermaid...priestess, or whatever she was. She Who Guards. She told me to watch out for the island's ghost."

"Ghost?" Tarja's eyes grew wide as she glanced fearfully about the branches, as if a menacing specter might choose that moment to materialize from among the leaves.

"There's no ghost, Tarja," Margherita sighed, rubbing at her temples. "Leastaways, if there is one, then it's material enough to try and make away with our loot."

Superstition being as common to pirates as black flags and copious amounts of rum, that inevitably set off another round of whispering as the castaways began comparing the various ghouls, phantoms, and other ghastly creatures they'd heard tale of in their voyages. Quint, who was by no means a skeptic, could have easily listed off fully a dozen spiritual beings reportedly corporeal enough to have made off with the Crown Jewels, yet he did not think that was what She Who Guards had intended.

"Hold on," Ophelia said, cutting through the commotion. All murmuring stopped as the crew turned to look at her, expressions at once expectant and obedient. Her crew, as much as they were his or Margherita's. The thought tugged at Quint's heart with a strange, wistful sort of pride, one he made himself carefully put away for later examination.

"Just because we ain't alone anymore," Ophelia continued, "doesn't mean the company's friendly. As evidenced by the recent uptick in theft on our otherwise crime-free island."

A ripple of uneasy laughter helped diffuse some of the tension. Ophelia glanced at Quint, who nodded, and then at Margherita.

"You have a plan in mind?" the pirate queen asked, the slightest of smiles playing on her lips.

"Aye," Ophelia said, raising her voice once more. "First thing's first. Let's take stock of what we've still got. Frederick, that'll be your department."

"Ja," the Trechtish quartermaster saluted.

"And we need to set a guard around the treehouse," Ophelia continued, gaining in confidence. "It's a stupid thief who robs the same house twice, but we're also the only neighbors our mysterious thief has got. Best to have watchers posted at all hours. Armed and in pairs, to make sure nothing else gets taken."

She glanced back at Margherita and Quint, both beaming. "Err. If that's alright with you lot."

"By all means," Quint nodded, but Margherita's faint smile had already diminished.

"All well and good," she said, "but if they *do* come back, we can't just sit around waiting to be raided a second time. We're not some wealthy merchant scow or the thrice-damned Navy. Present company excluded, Commander."

"Thanks," Vanessa said drily. "But I agree. We should search the island for whoever took the Jewels."

"And the Jewels themselves," Margherita added darkly. "I've still got plans for those."

Plans whose ultimate goal would be nothing less than the complete and violent dissolution of the Empire, Quint was certain.

"I'll go with you," he said. Though he and Margherita were on friendlier terms than they had been at the voyage's start, he was gripped by a strong intuition that the Jewels had the potential to drive a wedge between their tenuous alliance, unraveling all the progress they had made these last few days.

"Fine," Margherita said, shrugging. She looked to Ophelia. "Guess that leaves you in charge."

"Promise I won't burn the place down," Ophelia said, glancing about at the trashed remains of their treehouse. "Though it's starting to look like that'd be an improvement, I'll admit."

"I'm going too," Vanessa said, standing close to Quint. "There's a chance that whoever it was might have been in the Navy, blown way off course and shipwrecked here. Might be I'd have a better chance at talking to them, if so."

That logic struck Quint as flimsy; he suspected that spending years marooned on distant shores would erode even Vanessa's sense of patriotic loyalty. But he also suspected that Vanessa might have other reasons for wanting to accompany him, so he kept his mouth shut.

"Anyone else?" he asked, glancing about the circle. None of the gathered pirates volunteered themselves, which felt somehow dishearteninging. He tried to console himself that they were taking the safer option by remaining here amongst their fellows than they would be striking out into the wilderness in search of an unknown thief. Yet a small, childish part of him felt like they were choosing sides in a game, and that Ophelia was the overwhelmingly more popular choice.

"Rusty?" he asked, fixing his onetime crewmate with an encouraging smile. "Up for one last adventure with your captain?"

"I..." Rusty rubbed his head, his gaze fixed firmly in his lap. "I don't think I should. Cap'n. Not when the Jewels are at stake."

Those Jewels had led him to betray his captain once already. Quint could not find it in himself to fault Rustbucket for wanting to avoid falling prey to the same temptation a second time.

"I will go," Tarja said, standing abruptly. "Meaning no offense, but I have the greater expertise when it comes to animals, ja? And where this monkey is there may be more."

"I certainly hope not," Margherita said, lips puckering. She turned to Ophelia. "We'll get packed up and headed out shortly, then."

"But you only just got back," Ophelia pointed out, her gaze roaming over the four of them. "You sure you don't need a while longer to recover?"

"That means we're the ones who've explored the island the most," Vanessa pointed out. "So we'll have the less chance of getting lost. Hopefully we'll find some clue as to which way the thief went—"

"Captain!" Adewale poked his head up over the side of the treehouse platform, peering brightly up at them. "I think I've found a clue as to where our thief is headed."

"Where?" Vanessa demanded, at the same time as Margherita frowned and asked "How?"

"Well." Adewale took a deep breath and glanced between the two women. "You know how I said I would search for tracks?"

28

"Rabbits leave tracks," Quint said, staring down at the impossibly broad, five-toed depression sunk deep into the riverside mud. "Foxes leave tracks. Deer, even. This is a crater."

"Craters," Adewale corrected, stepping carefully around the next footprint, some several feet away from the one in which Quint stood.

Both of his own feet fit comfortably within the footprint, which belonged to no animal Quint could identify. It was broader than it was long, with five almost perfectly triangular toes. Standing within the shape of it made Quint feel at once very small and very young, as if whatever had left this enormous track had crawled its way up from some primordial depth of time to march upon the newcomers to its island.

Like a crocodile, he thought, and wondered what kind of footprints a croc might leave. And how big could crocodiles get, anyway?

"The tracks are heading away from here," Vanessa said, nodding upriver. She squatted and touched two fingers to the footprint in which she stood, then held them up, thick with mud. "Fresh, too."

"So we probably just missed them," Quint said, glancing at Margherita. "They were probably leaving these tracks when you found the treehouse in disarray."

"Seems so," Margherita agreed, striding forward with one hand on the hilt of her cutlass. "How fast do you think this big lizard or whatever it is can walk?"

"Not very far," Adewale said, shaking his head. "But swimming is another question. Look."

He pointed a little way further upriver, where the tracks detoured into the shallows.

"It can *swim?*" Quint asked, disbelieving that anything as large as the unknown creature would be able to haul its bulk through the water.

"Ja," Tarja said, bending low over a pair of prints that had been partially obscured by long, wide furrows. "These are marks left by the creature's tail. I think it would be likely the beast uses it to propel itself through the water."

"Great," Quint grimaced. "How are we supposed to follow it, then?"

"It ain't exactly hard to track," Margherita pointed out, gesturing at the crushed remains of shrubs and undergrowth that the creature had trampled underfoot. "Wherever it comes out of the river should be pretty obvious, so long as we're looking closely."

"That doesn't give us a whole lot of lead time," Quint remarked, shouldering his pack. Frederick and Darby had ensured that each of the four travelers was well-supplied for the journey, their sacks laden with mangoes, coconuts, and even some hardtack Lurk had managed to salvage from a watertight crate aboard the *Marigold.* And so long as they were following the river's course, they'd have plenty to drink.

Nor were they unarmed. In addition to Margherita's sword, each of them had been equipped with cutlasses that Lurk had dredged up from the *Marigold* in the intervening days. Privately, Quint doubted that even those blades would be much use against whatever monster had left its footprints in the riverbed, but he supposed it was better than nothing at all.

"You won't make it very far today," Adewale advised, glancing up at the afternoon sun. "Perhaps four hours, if you're going slowly enough to track the creature. The shade cast by the trees will turn the jungle dark well before nightfall, and you might pass even the most obvious of tracks in the gloom."

"Four hours is better than nothing," Margherita said, coming to stand beside Quint. "We'll make camp the moment the shadows grow long."

"Sure you won't come with us?" Vanessa asked Adewale. "Five might be better than four, especially when there's a...giant lizard-thing involved."

"Thank you, but no," Adewale said, shaking his head. "In truth, I do not think the crew can spare more than four, at present. There is still a great deal of cleanup and repair that will need doing after today's incident."

"Understood." Margherita nodded. "Good fortune to you, Adewale. And to Ophelia and the others."

"Good hunting, Captain." Adewale saluted, then turned and headed back downriver, towards the hill with the treehouse. As they watched him go, Quint felt an unexpected pang of longing at the prospect of returning to their little makeshift settlement, rather than braving the unknown wilderness a second time.

"Almost wish I was going, too," Vanessa murmured, glancing at him as Margherita and Tarja shouldered their packs and started heading upriver.

"Me too," Quint admitted. "Funny how quickly a place starts to feel like home."

Only what was it Lurk had said? That home was where your people were?

He looked at Vanessa, who gave him a wan smile. "Still time to head back, if you want."

"What, and let you pirates make off with the Crown Jewels a second time?" Vanessa shook her head, still smiling. "Not on your life."

She nudged him with her elbow and took off after Margherita and Tarja, who were already trekking along the narrow game trail that ran along the river's edge. Quint waited a moment before following, smiling to himself.

So long as Vanessa was along for the adventure, home would never be so far away.

⚓

They followed the river for several hours, their eyes scanning both the far bank and the nearer one for any sign of where the mysterious creature must have emerged from the water. Such careful inspection slowed their progress, so that by the time the shadows began to lengthen over the water and they were forced to call a halt none of them felt fully satisfied with the day's progress.

"Anyone else getting déjà vu?" Vanessa asked, glancing about the little hollow they'd made their camp in, sitting once again on a familiar log.

"What, you mean about this being the same place we camped two nights back?" Margherita asked, toying with her ostrich feather. For reasons known only to the pirate queen herself, she'd insisted on taking it with her.

"Is a good spot," Tarja pointed out, digging in her pack for their dinner. She began passing mangos around the little circle they'd formed, each seated upon a fallen log. "Far enough from the water that crocodiles will not bother us, yet near enough that we will not lose time once we set off."

"Aye," Margherita nodded, accepting a mango from her. "Which we'll do as soon as it's light enough to see. Our monkey and monster already have enough of a head start."

"Monkey, monster, and master," Quint said, flicking the gold doubloon into the air. He caught it, slapped it onto his wrist. Tails. "Someone's giving them orders—oh, *angels*."

All three women turned to look at him.

"What?" Vanessa asked, speaking for all three.

"I just remembered," Quint said, thinking hard. "Last time we were here, when I had watch. I saw—I thought I saw a person."

"Who?" Vanessa asked.

"Not sure," Quint said, rubbing his beard. "Just a shadow in the dark, really. Eyes staring at me in the gloom."

"And you're only just telling us this *now?*" Margherita demanded.

"I thought I was dreaming!" Quint said, annoyed at how defensive he sounded. "What, like you haven't seen things that weren't there while on watch duty?"

Margherita's lips puckered, as if she was trying to physically contain whatever retort was straining to leap from her mouth.

"I saw something, too," Vanessa said. Quint threw her a grateful glance. "We didn't know there was anyone else on the island, other than whoever it was that left the doubloon. If we had..."

"We might have been more watchful," Tarja nodded. She rubbed the back of her neck with the curved edge of her hook. "I...also may have seen something."

"Right, then," Margherita said, unbuttoning her lips. "That settles it. We'll take the watch in pairs. That way if one of us starts seeing things, the other can say if it's really there or not. Fair?"

"Aye," Quint said reluctantly. The thought of halving his sleep ahead of what promised to be another long day's march was not an enticing one, but he couldn't fault Margherita's logic. "I'll take first, in that case."

"We both will," Margherita said, and to Quint's surprise, offered him a conciliatory smile. "Captains' duty, and all that."

⚓

"Ask you a question?" Quint asked, some hours after night had truly fallen and the sounds of Tarja's snores filled the hollow.

"Can't guarantee I'll answer," Margherita shrugged. They stood side by side, each facing the opposite direction into the darkness of the surrounding trees. "But seeing as there's nothing else to while away the hours, you may as well ask."

"Fair enough." Quint took a deep breath. "Why is it that you hate them so much? The Empire, I mean."

Margherita stiffened beside him. "You don't exactly have cause to love them either, Captain Redbeard."

"The Navy's an occupational hazard in our line of work," Quint admitted. "But it ain't like fishermen hate sharks the way you hate the Empire."

Margherita was silent a moment. Quint held his tongue, sensing that she was weighing whether or not to confide in him.

"You wore the purple jacket at one point," she said, "back before you flew the black flag. I'm guessing something happened to compel that trade?"

"Aye," Quint admitted, though he did not relish the thought of rehashing his experience of the famine on Jasper again. "Let's say that I saw the Navy wasn't the force for good it claims to be and leave it at that."

"That's underselling it," Margherita said, chewing her lip. "Suppose you wouldn't be the first to be taken in by the shiny buttons and big parades."

"No," Quint said, glancing down at Vanessa's sleeping form, her head resting against her pack. "I knew plenty of folk who signed on just like me. Young lads and lasses with dreams of honor and adventure and doing good."

"Everyone's the hero of their own story," Margherita agreed. "Just happens that mine was always on the other side from the Empire."

Quint glanced at Margherita Elena Rossini's profile, taking in her aquiline nose and dark, straight hair. He did some mental math, gauging her age. "The Emerald Rebellion?"

"Aye," Margherita said, turning to stare at him with obvious surprise. "My family's from Beryl. Least, they were."

"I'm sorry," Quint said quietly. He'd learned about the Emerald Rebellion, and the terrible cost of life it had entailed—primarily upon the rebels' side.

"The Empire burned down half the island," Margherita said, as if he hadn't spoken. Her voice was quiet, distant. "I was only a little girl, but I still remember the sound of the bombs going off. The smell of burning hair, the way the bodies..."

She trailed off.

"I'm sorry," Quint began. "I shouldn't have—that is, you don't have to..."

"No." Margherita's voice was firm. "You asked, and so I'm telling you. Like I said, I was only a girl at the time. Was on my way back from the marketplace with a basketful of apples when the Navy started shelling the harbor. I ran all the way home, only when I got there home was just...gone. Nothing but a pile of bricks and rubble, and bodies..."

She swallowed, hard. "Funny what you remember. I dropped the basket and apples went spilling all over the place. I haven't touched an apple since."

"I'd lose my appetite for them, too," Quint said.

It wasn't really a joke, but Margherita let out a shallow laugh anyway. "The bombs didn't stop, not that day or the one after, nor the one after that. Beryl was a ruin by the time the governor sued for peace."

"What did you do?" Quint asked.

"Survived." Margherita's nails made soft clicks as she tapped them against her cutlass. "Lived on the streets, if you could call it living. Picked pockets and robbed shops, until one day I picked the wrong mark."

"Who?"

"Doesn't matter," Margherita said, shaking her head. "I made it off Beryl, is the point. And the day I did I made two promises to myself."

She counted them off on her fingers. "One, that I would never set foot there again, so long as the Imperial flag still flew above her shores. And two, that I'd spend my life tearing down that flag wherever I could."

"Can't fault you for trying," Quint said, imagining how deep his own sorrow and rage would run if the Navy had laid waste to his precious Ember Bay. The thought of his parents' tavern in flames alone was enough to turn his stomach.

She glanced at him, the darkness making her expression unreadable. "I don't need your approval."

"Never said you did. I just..." He rubbed his beard, trying to think of the most delicate way to phrase it. "It's just that my folks always wanted me to make my own path. Not be bound by their expectations, y'know? If I'd gone through what you had, I don't know that it'd make them happy to know that I spent the next forty years trying to avenge them."

“That’s where you miss the mark,” Margherita said, looking away. “It’s not about revenge. It’s about making sure that no little girl ever has to endure what I went through again.”

She turned to face him, peering up at him through the gloom. “Not even if I have to burn down the whole Empire along the way.”

Quint looked down at Vanessa’s sleeping form and prayed silently to all the angels that it would never come to that.

29

—•—

They hiked well into the afternoon the following day, keeping close to the river. By now they were once again climbing into the low foothills surrounding the island's central mountain. On the opposite bank the river was bordered by low shale cliffs, each of them rising above the rushing water like stepstones. In places the cliffs gave way to sheltered little bays and coves, shaded by overhanging trees.

"How are we going to tell whether they came ashore in one of those?" Quint asked, shading his eyes and peering across the river for any sign of the monster's passage. "It's not like we can tell very well from here—"

His next words were drowned by a sudden whoop of triumph from Margherita. Bemused, Quint watched as the diminutive pirate queen darted forward and seized a tattered scrap of fabric from a nearby branch.

"Sailcloth," she said, holding it up and waving it before him like a flag. "Can't be from whatever ship tossed our ghost onto these shores; that's sure to have rotted away long since."

"And Frederick *did* say that some of ours was missing," Vanessa said, nodding. The quartermasters' inventory had revealed that a handful of supplies had been taken, along with the Crown Jewels. "They've come this far, at least."

"Ja," Tarja agreed, ambling down to the shallows and pointing her hook at the soft mud. "Look!"

Footprints—not those of the massive creature, but ordinary, barefoot human footprints, baked dry by the sun.

"Whoever it was must've come ashore to stretch their legs," Quint said. Vanessa nodded her agreement. "Probably they didn't think we'd follow so far upriver."

It was an assumption that was soon proven correct. Throughout that day and the one following, their little search party continued to find signs of their quarry's passage as they made their way along the riverside. There were more sailcloth scraps, presumably torn loose by the dense jungle, as well as dropped mango pits from the last fruiting tree they'd passed, and (in one notable instance) a discarded bottle that must have come from Margherita's store of tequila. Quint and Vanessa hastily kicked this into the undergrowth before Margherita could catch sight of it.

"Not exactly concerned about leaving a trail, are they?" Vanessa pointed out as the group paused for an afternoon break beneath a tree, the trunk of which bore several long, deep cuts.

"Why would they be?" Quint shrugged. "Living on this island for angels only know how long, I'd probably forget to cover my tracks too."

"It could be we are being led into a trap," Tarja pointed out.

"Should have thought of that when you volunteered to come along," Margherita pointed out, taking a sip from her waterskin. It froze, halfway to her mouth.

"What?" Quint asked, following her gaze. But then he saw.

There, on one of the cliffs directly across the river from where they sat, something stood framed against the trees. At first glance Quint had taken it to be an odd rock formation, though admittedly a squat and ugly one. Only it was not quite the same color as the brownish gray cliffside, and bits of it stuck out at odd angles.

Bits that were, in places, perfectly straight lines.

"It's a..." Vanessa started, then frowned. "...fort?"

"Ship?" Margherita suggested.

"Enclosure," Tarja guessed.

The details were difficult to discern from this distance, but it looked to Quint as if someone had attempted to assemble the main cabin of a modest sailboat atop the cliffside, become bored halfway through, and then used the leftover bits to form a crude wooden barricade around the main body of the structure.

"Trumpets," Vanessa murmured, sounding awed. "I wonder how long whoever built that's been living there."

"Centuries, for all I care," Margherita said, stowing her waterskin and hefting her cutlass. "I've got some choice words for whoever built that eyesore. Come on, let's go introduce ourselves to the neighbors."

The pirate queen set off towards the river. Quint wondered how she intended to ford it and then scale the cliffs, but before he could ask Margherita suddenly slapped her hand against her neck.

"Sea devil's suckers," she cursed, drawing her hand away. Something brightly colorful fell from it and fluttered downwards, disappearing into the riotous underbrush. "What kind of bugs—"

"Eep!" Tarja squealed, surprisingly high-pitched as she smacked at her neck. "I am stung also!"

She withdrew her hand, showing it to the others. But in her palm lay not an insect, but a bright blue feather like those Quint had seen in the plumage of the birds that had flitted overhead as they hiked. And affixed to that feather was a—

"Dart," Margherita croaked, all color draining from her face. Her eyes rolled backwards, and she toppled to the ground.

Or she would have, had Quint not instinctively rushed forward to catch her. Margherita did not weigh much, but she had already gone completely limp. Quint grunted as she fell against him, sinking to his knees to keep her from falling. A few feet away, Vanessa was experiencing the same difficulty with Tarja, though her strain was considerably greater than his.

"I am sorry, friend Vanessa," Tarja said, swaying where she stood. "Perhaps it is best if I just...sit...for a moment..."

Her knees folded beneath her, and the best Vanessa could do was help guide her to the ground, settling the big Trechtish pirate's head in her lap.

"Quint," Vanessa said, her curls tossing as she turned to face him. "We've got to get them out of here. Whoever shot them—"

There was a soft *puff* of air from someplace in the undergrowth, not far off. A blue feather materialized in Vanessa's neck.

"Shot us," she corrected, then promptly joined the other two in unconsciousness, her head drooping on top of Tarja's.

Quint flinched, awaiting the inevitable fourth dart.

None was forthcoming.

"Well?" he called, looking about at the little clearing where they'd stopped to rest. "You out of ammunition, then? If you're looking to parlay..."

He trailed off at the abrupt realization that something in a thick patch of underbrush was moving. No, not something *in* the underbrush, but the brush itself, an entire section of tangled roots and fallen leaves and vines churning and roiling and lifting itself from the ground like some primeval monster waking from untold eons of slumber.

One of the branches protruding from the apparently mobile vegetation rotated towards Quint, peering directly at him like a spyglass. There was another soft *puff*.

"Ow," Quint said, looking down at the bright blue feathers of the dart protruding from his forearm. "That really stings something awful."

He was going to say more, but found his tongue would not cooperate. Neither was his torso much interested in remaining upright.

Quint collapsed into a heap, his head landing by some stroke of mercy not on a loose stone or upturned root, but on the familiar pillow of Vanessa's thigh. Already his vision was growing blurry around the edges.

He wondered whether that had anything to do with the fact that the bit of undergrowth that had assaulted him was now standing fully upright, and coming towards him. It halted above him, blocking out the sunlight filtering down from the trees overhead.

Quint tried to get a better look, but found he could not lift his head any higher than the pair of gnarled, calloused, impossibly weathered feet standing inches from his face. The cracked toenails were yellow and incredibly long.

"Ahoy," Quint greeted the island's ghost, and then promptly passed out.

30

Sailor that he was, Quint Thatch had awoken under the influence of enough hangovers to know that each had its own particular flavor of agony. This one felt as though a clan of tiny miners were hammering away at the inside of his skull with miniscule pickaxes, desperately trying to force their way out into daylight.

His first coherent thought was that it seemed monumentally unfair that he was experiencing the aftereffects of a night of revelry without having enjoyed the pleasures thereof. Not that he could have articulated it in such terms at that moment.

"Ugh," Quint said instead. The inside of his mouth felt like someone had poured sand down his throat.

He was answered by a splash, which, curiously, seemed to come from above him. Even in his current state, that struck him as odd.

Quint forced his eyes open, fighting through the lance of pain that even the dim light of his current surroundings sent flashing through his brain. There was another splash, again from somewhere over his head. He craned his neck and looked up, and saw an impossibility.

A pool of water hung a dozen feet above him, dark in a way that suggested impressive depth beneath its placid surface. Or mostly placid, anyway. There were shapes moving at its edges, though his vision was still too bleary to fix on them properly.

Quint moved his neck experimentally, and in doing so discovered that the pool lay not above him, but below. He was hanging upside down, arms bound to his sides with ropes, dangling from knots tied securely about his ankles.

Nor was he alone. Margherita and Vanessa hung similarly trussed beside him, both looking to be in various stages of awakening from their dart-induced sleep.

"Ahoy, friend Quint!" Tarja called from his other side. As the largest of the four, whatever toxin ran through their veins had clearly departed her system the quickest. "I am quite glad you are awake!"

"Pleasestopyelling," Quint groaned. The tiny miners were still assaulting him with their pickaxes, their efforts aided by his slight swaying from side to side.

"Apologies," Tarja said, somewhat quieter. "It has been boring waiting for you to wake, is all."

Drawing upon his long experience mitigating seasickness, Quint forced his nausea down and took stock of his surroundings as best he could, trying to move only his eyes.

They seemed to be in some sort of cave or grotto, not very much larger than the *Marigold's* poop deck had been. The deep pool which lay directly beneath the captives abutted one of the gently sloping walls, and was bordered on the other side by a shelf of rock the same brownish grey color as the cliffs lining the river.

Which made sense, Quint supposed. The half-glimpsed ghost of the island had not struck him as being particularly tall, and it would have taken no small amount of effort to haul four people into...wherever they were now.

"Quint?" Vanessa's face was hidden from him by the slow turning of her rope, but her voice sounded as cracked and dry as his throat felt. "You...wake?"

"Aye," he called back, wetting his lips with his tongue. "What about you, Margherita?"

A grunt of assent came from the pirate queen, followed by the reflexive gurgling sound of someone trying very hard to keep down their lunch. Quint felt a pang of sympathy; as the smallest of their group, Margherita had doubtless gotten the worst of whatever they'd been poisoned with.

"Where...we?" Margherita managed to spit out, turning on her swaying rope to look at him. Her unbound hair streamed towards the pool beneath them.

"Cave," Quint said, swallowing. The effects of the dart seemed to be receding somewhat, so he decided to attempt a complete sentence. "Our ghost was hiding in the bushes. Darts."

"'member," Margherita mumbled, making a jerky motion that might have been an attempt to touch her hand to her neck. The effort set her rope to swaying more erratically, almost bumping her into Vanessa.

"Where...ghost?" Vanessa said, looking around with greater care than Margherita had. "Not here?"

"Not yet," Quint said.

"Going to kill us," Margherita grunted.

"Don't think so," Quint said, shaking his head and immediately regretting it. "If he was, why leave us hanging like this?"

"Could be cannibal," Tarja pointed out helpfully.

Margherita groaned.

"Suppose I'd..." Quint swallowed, refusing to let his dry mouth conquer his power of speech. "...be willing to try new foods, if I was on this island so long."

"If that's so," Vanessa pointed out, "why leave us hanging over water?"

Before any of them could postulate an answer, they were interrupted by a faint, rhythmic tapping, one that seemed to be drawing steadily nearer.

"Is that..." Margherita cocked her head to one side. "Not footsteps. Rhythm's wrong."

"It sounds...familiar." Vanessa's brows furrowed, then lifted—or dropped, considering their present orientation. "Trumpets, that's a Navy parade march."

Quint was dumbstruck to realize that she was absolutely correct. Only the familiar *rat-tat-tat-tat-a-rat-tat-tat-tat* beat was not being played upon a drum.

The four captives watched as a shadow loomed against the far wall of the grotto, cast by daylight streaming in from the unseen entrance just beyond. It stretched against the stone, clapping its unnaturally elongated arms together over its grotesquely misshapen head in time to the rhythmic beat.

Then it rounded the corner, revealing itself as—

"That thrice-bedeviled monkey!" Margherita growled, writhing and straining against her bonds. "Give me back my hat, you evil little miscreant—"

The monkey, who was indeed still wearing Margherita's battered and now-featherless hat, grinned its toothsome smile up at her without so much as a break in the rhythm of its drumming. This, Quint now saw, it was performing by banging two sticks together above its head with impressive dexterity.

"What—" he started, but was silenced by the monkey letting out a high, fearsome screech as a second shadow darkened the grotto entrance. The clacking of sticks rose to a crescendo, then stopped altogether with a final, decisive *clack*. The little creature continued standing on its hind legs, its posture as upright as its anatomy allowed.

The second shadow rounded the corner, the ghost of the island finally making its appearance.

Quint's first impression was of hair, long and matted, though in places it looked as if it had been roughly trimmed with a dull pair of scissors. The ghost's beard and sideburns were in a similar state, though somewhat shorter. Quint met the ghost's gaze and found that one eye was a startlingly vivid blue, while the other lay partially obscured behind a cracked monocle.

"Who—" Quint started, but the monkey screeched again.

"Atten-*shun*," the ghost of the island boomed, his voice hoarse but surprisingly deep. His heels tapped together with military exactitude, straightening his posture. Quint realized with a daze that the tattered jacket he wore bore the threadbare ruins of a Navy officer's epaulets. "Commanding officer on deck!"

The monkey squawked a reply, saluting with one of the sticks it had been holding.

"At ease, Lieutenant," the ghost said, returning the salute. The monkey dropped to all fours and scratched at its belly, while its master returned his gaze towards the prisoners dangling from the ceiling of the grotto.

"I am Commodore Sir Edward Wilson of His Majesty's Imperial Navy," he said, his aged voice low. "And you four cutthroats are going to tell me exactly what it is you're doing trespassing upon this island."

Out of the corner of his eye Quint saw a spasm of what might have been recognition flicker across Margherita's face.

"We've met before," she said slowly. "Only you were Captain Wilson, then, and we were both a good deal younger."

Wilson peered hard at her, then blinked. "Aye, I remember you. You were just a slip of a thing in those days A skinny little orphan pirate girl, always hanging about—"

"And you had a ship and a crew," Margherita fired back, "Instead of a lice-ridden monkey."

The monkey let out a hurt sound and scratched at his armpit.

"Lieutenant's cleaner in his habits than you, pirate," Wilson said, offended on his pet's behalf. "And you're in no position to cast aspersions. Now, as to your trespassing upon this island—"

"Trespassing?" Quint blinked. Judging from the tattered state of the man's clothes and his matted hair, this Commodore Wilson had to have been stranded upon the island himself for angels only knew how many years. "Listen, mate, we're all castaways here—"

"I am *not,*" Wilson objected, the last word echoing off the walls of the grotto, "your *mate.* You are trespassing upon the sovereign territory of His Imperial Majesty the Emperor Justinian IV—"

"Justinian?" Vanessa repeated, her jaw somehow falling open even while upside-down. "It's been nigh on thirty years since Justinian went to his celestial reward. His daughter's Empress now—"

"*Lies*!" Spittle flew from Wilson's mouth as his shout echoed around the grotto, surprisingly loud. Quint flinched at the unexpected vehemence, as did the others.

"Lies," Wilson repeated, regaining a touch of his former composure. "Someone would have sent word. My absence at the state funeral would not have gone unremarked. Not after so many years of loyal service."

"Sir?" Vanessa's voice was uncharacteristically timid, yet when Quint looked at her he saw that the slight frown at the corner of her mouth that appeared whenever she made a risky maneuver on the chessboard. "Permission to speak?"

The old commodore looked up at her through narrowed eyes. "Granted, Miss...?"

"Commander, actually," Vanessa said quickly. "Commander Vanessa Delacort of Her—of the Imperial Navy."

"You're out of uniform, Commander," Wilson reprimanded her, plucking at one of the fraying gold threads that were all that remained of his epaulettes. "And fallen in with lawless company, from the looks of it. You know what the regulations say about fraternization with enemies of the Empire."

"Lawless—" Vanessa started, but Wilson cut her off with a gesture.

"Don't dissemble," he warned, wagging a gnarled finger. "I've conducted enough reconnaissance upon your crew of cutthroats to know that you've thrown your lot in with a band of marauders and renegades. You're practically a pirate now yourself, *Commander.*"

"You—" Vanessa stared down at him, astonished. Quint watched as she visibly fought to compose herself. "We're castaways, *sir.* What should I have done, if not ally with them for survival?"

"Deliver the Emperor's justice upon them, of course." Wilson frowned up at her with the unmistakably disappointed air of a stern schoolmaster whose favorite student had just given the wrong answer. "Or died in the attempt."

Vanessa seemed to have no good answer to that. Margherita did, however.

"Bilgewater," she spat. "If you really thought that, why not kill us instead of hanging us up like a bunch of plucked chickens?"

"It's better to take captives when possible," Wilson said, shrugging. "Corpses are rather difficult to interrogate, for one thing."

"We shall tell you nothing," Tarja declared firmly. "Not if you pull our fingernails out, or heap hot coals upon our feet, or make us drink saltwater until we retch—"

"Tarja," Margherita sighed. "Stop giving him ideas."

Tarja's mouth snapped shut with the finality of a trapdoor closing.

"Listen," Quint began, hoping he sounded more reasonable than his companions had. "There's no need for this to be so...confrontational. So why not just cut us down—"

"And let you overpower me?" Wilson tugged at the tattered sleeves of his jacket. "Not bloody likely, boy. I've got you right where I want to."

"You're bluffing," Margherita said suddenly, a fierce light in her eyes. "Those darts are poisonous, but they ain't deadly. And you've no other weapons. You ain't going to kill us because you haven't the nerve, nor the means."

Wilson's chapped lips peeled back in a cold, cruel smile. "I don't, don't I?"

He let out a high, sharp whistle, piercing in the grotto's confines.

The pool, never entirely still, suddenly came to roiling, bubbling life. Water sloshed over its edges, flooding the grotto's stony floor so that the monkey leapt scrambling onto the nearest rock, shrieking his dismay.

Directly beneath him, Quint glimpsed a titanic bulk rising from the black depths of the pool.

A bony mountain broke the surface, water sloughing from its sides as it rose. The mountain split, revealing its peak to be a huge, beaklike mouth, its edges toothless but serrated like a woodcarver's saw. A long, snaky tongue the color of raw meat lolled inside.

The pirates' screams echoed off the grotto walls.

It rose and rose towards the captives, until the gaping maw seemed to threaten to devour not only them but the entire world. Quint felt a blast of stale breath upon his face, stinking of seaweed and rotting wood.

Then the titanic creature sagged, defeated by gravity, and fell away.

The mountain sank back into the pool, sending another bow wave out from its massive bulk. It let out a disappointed *huff*, sending blasts of water from the nostrils on either side of its beak, and began to paddle around the pool.

"That's what we were tracking?" Vanessa breathed, eyes wide. "Trumpets, it's a *turtle?*"

It *was* a turtle, but only in the same way that a minnow and a whale shark were both fish. The creature's legs looked as long as Quint was tall, and its broad shell could have comfortably carried an entire jollyboat upon its back, though no vessel subjected to such a conveyance would ever be seaworthy again. The turtle's shell, face, and limbs were all covered in countless bony spikes and protrusions. Even its tail, which lashed paddlelike from side to side as it swam, was armored.

"You see?" Wilson asked, taking evident satisfaction in their shocked expressions. "Carrying out His Majesty's justice in payment for your crimes remains well within my power. So you'd best get to talking."

Quint exchanged a glance with the others. Their eyes told him that all four of them were thinking the same thing: ancient and half-crazed though their captor might be, there was no longer any doubt in their minds that he would carry out his threats if provoked.

"Alright," Quint said, finding his voice as he turned his attention back to Wilson. "I'll admit you've got us well and truly over a barrel, Commodore. Ask your questions, and I swear on all the angels that I'll answer as best I know how."

He was somewhat gratified to see that Wilson's bushy eyebrows lifted, seemingly taken aback by this easy acquiescence. Doubtless he'd anticipated more resistance from the obstinate pirates, even after displaying the primordial beast that, like the monkey, lay apparently at his beck and call.

"Well," the commodore muttered, digging in his threadbare jacket and producing—incredibly—a battered but intact long-stemmed pipe.

Wilson stuck it in his mouth without lighting it, chewed contemplatively, and then met Quint's gaze.

"How long," the castaway commodore asked, "have you pirates been members of Captain Wolf's crew?"

31

—•—

"What?" Quint heard himself ask, as if from a remote distance. A strange feeling that resembled both déjà vu and vertigo was washing over him.

Captain Wolf, the pirate hero of his pop's every bedtime story all throughout Quint's childhood. Captain Wolf, who had turned out to actually *be* Quint's pop, in a life that he and the closest members of his crew had all turned their backs on years before Quint was born, retiring themselves to the quiet life in the sleepy little hamlet of Ember Bay.

Captain Wolf, who apparently had crossed paths with the very man responsible for their current predicament.

Quint wracked his brain for any mention in his pop's bedtime stories of a man fitting Wilson's description. He found none, though he was forced to admit to himself that the passing of several decades must have wrought quite a change upon the castaway commodore.

"Wolf—" Quint started, but Margherita beat him to the punch.

"Captain Wolf disappeared," she said. She wore an odd, tight expression Quint couldn't readily identify. "Better than forty years ago, now. No one's seen nor heard tale of him ever since."

"Really," Wilson said, sounding wholly unconvinced. "And I suppose that it's pure coincidence that one of his crew just happened to arrive on the same island he left me marooned upon, all grown up and with her own band of cutthroats?"

Who? Quint wanted to ask, only to realize that Wilson's gaze had never left Margherita.

"I told you," she said steadily. "I haven't seen Captain Wolf since the day I left the *Howler.*"

The words hit Quint like a blow. He opened his mouth, a million questions on his tongue, but could not seem to find a way to force them past his lips.

"You're a poor liar, lass." Wilson's teeth ground against the stem of his pipe in agitation. "Now tell me why Wolf sent you to these shores, or I start feeding pieces of you to Bosun here."

He knelt and patted one of the turtle's spikes. The great beast's belch echoed off the grotto walls.

"Hold on," Quint said, finally recovering the power of speech enough to voice his question. He turned as much as his bonds permitted, facing Margherita. "You were a Sea Dog? One of Captain Wolf's crew?"

"Aye," Margherita nodded, looking curiously at him. "I wasn't more'n ten, maybe eleven years old, picking pockets and cutting purses in Beryl. One day I found a big man with a big beard, deep in his cups. Easy mark, I thought, until his hand clapped around my wrist, tight as any iron. Thought he'd twist the hand right off."

"He didn't, though," Quint said, recovering his voice.

"Obviously," Margherita snorted, "or you'd see me askin' Tarja for fashion advice more often. Nah. Wolf was softer than he let on. Took a little orphan girl onto his ship and taught her how to sail. By the time he disappeared, I was old enough to start my own crew."

"So, Wolf's built himself a fleet of his own by now, has he?" Wilson spat into the pool, eliciting a deep bellow of complaint from Bosun.

"He hasn't," Quint said, finding his voice. "I can promise you that."

He looked at Margherita, wanting to ask her so many different things. How long she had known his pop. What he had been like as a younger man, before retirement and parenthood had softened his edges.

But now was not the time.

"Listen to me," Quint said, returning his gaze to Wilson. The eye not occluded by the cracked monocle stared steadily back at him. "Captain Wolf isn't coming for you. He left the pirate's life behind years before I was even born. Retired to a small island called Ember Bay. Started a tavern, got married."

He swallowed hard. "Became a father."

Quint watched as Margherita's blank stare became a look of dawning comprehension, swiftly transmuting into denial.

"No," she said, shaking her head. "Not possible."

"Hm," Wilson muttered, adjusting the frame of his broken monocle as he peered hard up at Quint, "perhaps you *do* look a bit like old Wolf..."

"Except the red hair," Margherita said slowly, reluctantly. "And the nose."

Quint smiled weakly. "Got those from the other side of the family."

"The other..." That one took a moment to register, but when it did it struck Margherita like a lightning bolt. "Lola Read's your *mom?*"

"Ma," Quint and Vanessa corrected in unison.

"Can't be," Margherita said weakly, shaking her head. "I mean, they always talked about giving up the life and finding someplace quiet, but..."

"You didn't think he'd actually do it?" Quint guessed.

"Would you?" Margherita shrugged as much as her bonds allowed. "Turn your back on the pirate's life and scuttle the *Bloody Angel?*"

It was a question he'd asked himself more than once following the revelation of his father's former career. What had it cost his ma and his pop to hang up the black flag, to abandon a life of danger and adventure for their quiet, sedate existence on the sleepy island of Ember Bay? Faced with the same choice, would he be able to stop being Captain Redbeard and just be Quint Thatch?

Quint felt Vanessa's eyes on him, awaiting his answer.

"No," he said at last, shaking his head. "There's a reason I took up the black flag. There's folks with no place else to run but the *Angel*, and I owe it to them to keep flying those colors. But that's me. My parents were made differently. Wanted different things."

"This is as fine a production as the Imperial Theatre's ever performed," Wilson interrupted, looking back and forth between Margherita and Quint. "But I don't buy it any more than I buy that old Wolf gave up on the pirate's life. Now, one of you is going to start answering questions, or I'm going to start feeding the others to Bosun—*what?*"

This last was directed at Vanessa. Though she was bound as tightly as the other three, one of her hands lay outside the ropes and vines Wilson had tied them with, and she was waving it with the frantic desperation of a schoolgirl trying to get the teacher's attention.

"Sir," Vanessa said, and though Wilson was still scowling around his pipe his expression softened fractionally. "May I ask *why* you're so certain that it's Captain Wolf who's sent us?"

"You should answer her," Quint said before Wilson could object, thinking quickly. "We captured Commander Delacort and turned her to our side on the way here. She doesn't know anything about—about Captain Wolf."

"Hm," Wilson grunted, pulling his pipe from his mouth and rubbing it on the tattered lapel of his jacket. "Traitor or not, I suppose the young commander at least is owed some explanation."

He perched upon a low, oddly square rock, rubbing his hands together. Quint realized with a start that it was no rock, but the chest containing the Crown Jewels, unnoticed until now in the gloomy grotto. A glance to either side showed him that his companions had seen it, too.

"Well," Wilson began, staring meditatively down at the pipe in his hand. "There was a time, long ago, when I tangled with old Captain Wolf on a regular basis."

He stuck the unlit pipe in his mouth, took a deep drag of imaginary tobacco. "I chased that buccaneer from the highlands of Trecht to the mountains of Cuprite, from the scattered islands of the Reach to the alleyways of Port Solace. We traded blows and bullets. Crossed blades as often as we crossed paths, and left marks upon each other."

Wilson peeled back the neck of his jacket, revealing an ancient, faded scar running from one collarbone to the center of his hollow chest. The sight of it recalled to Quint's mind a similarly faded scar that had run along his pop's jaw, missing his artery by half an inch. The old man had always claimed it was due to a bowline coming loose in a bad storm, but now Quint had his doubts.

"Aye," Margherita said softly. "You were a thorn in the old man's side, that's for certain."

"And he in mine," Wilson said, less vehemently than he might have.

"I remember," Margherita said, her voice distant and a little sad. "That was part of why Wolf encouraged me to split off and start a crew of my own. The Navy was closing in, and he didn't want me on the *Howler* if they ever caught up to us."

"Canny old blighter," Wilson said admiringly. "But not canny enough to flee from me forever. It took months, yet I finally managed to trap him 'tween a rock and a hard place. A full squadron of Navy frigates on one hand, me and my flagship *Concord* upon the other, and the storm-wracked Sea of Tears before him. No place to flee, or so I thought."

"Only you underestimated him," Quint said, earning a monocled glare. "Wolf braved the Sea of Tears, didn't he?"

"Aye," Wilson said, packing as much bitterness into that single syllable as he could. "With nowhere else to run, Wolf turned his *Howler* south, into the storms. He fled south, and I gave chase. Across the Sea of Tears, into the worst monsoon the angels had ever loosed upon this mortal coil—"

"Why?" Vanessa demanded. Quint was taken aback by the raw anger in her voice. "When you'd already driven Wolf towards his own destruction? Why would you risk the lives of your crew in the pursuit?"

"Because, Commander," Wilson said slowly, as if speaking to an exceptionally stupid child. "I had my orders. Direct from the Admiralty Board itself, and theirs came straight from His Majesty. 'Find the Pirate Wolf and Deliver Unto Him the Emperor's Justice,' they said. I spent better than two years in pursuit of that mission, and I'd be damned if I'd permit a storm to finish what I'd begun."

"Even at the cost of your crew's lives?" Vanessa challenged.

"I had my orders," Wilson repeated. The stare he fixed her with was made of flint. "And my crew had theirs. If you can't grasp that, then it's little wonder you've thrown in your lot with a band of pirates."

"If it was you giving me orders," Vanessa said steadily, "I'd have taken up the black flag years ago."

Her defiance lit a fierce, prideful sort of joy in Quint's heart, but now was not the time to indulge in such a feeling.

"So," he said, swaying in his bonds and attempting to draw Wilson's attention back to himself. "Wolf fled across the Sea of Tears, and you followed?"

"Aye," Wilson said, grimacing as his gaze dropped to the pool. "I in my *Concord*, with an escort of two frigates upon our flanks. I swore before men and angels that Wolf wasn't escaping the noose that day."

"Oh," Vanessa breathed, dread weighing her words. "You didn't. All those people aboard all those ships—"

"Lost with all hands, every one." Wilson looked down at his pipe, his face clouded. "Taken in the same storm that spat me out upon these very shores. The angels heard my vow and decided to make mock of it, it seems, for not only did I lose everything and everyone in that storm, but days later a ship appeared upon the horizon. White sails 'neath a black flag."

"The *Howler*," Margherita said quietly.

"Aye." Wilson chewed on his pipe. "She hadn't escaped the storms unscathed either, but she was seaworthy. I hid in the jungle, not far from the very place you've made your camp, and watched as they sent a party ashore to resupply. I caught sight of Wolf himself, along with the redhaired quartermaster and that big first mate, and that little smuggler woman who kept their books—"

"Ma?" Quint asked, blinking. "And Uncle Jun and Miss Rosa?"

"Angels," Margherita muttered. "You really *are* their kid."

"Them," Wilson nodded. "I followed them while they explored the jungle I'd spent days in. Crept up when they laid themselves down for the evening. My plan was to take one of them hostage, force them to give me passage back to the Empire so that I could deliver the whole crew to my superiors. I had my orders."

"Only I'm guessing it didn't work out that way," Quint said, privately reflecting upon the absurdity of a lone man holding an entire vessel hostage for the weeklong trip back to the Archipelago. "Considering my existence and all."

Wilson shook his head. "Nah. The redhead—your mother—"

"Ma," Quint and Vanessa corrected automatically.

"—she wasn't as fast asleep as I'd thought," Wilson said, sounding as though that admission had cost him something. "Had a knife in one hand before I could so much as tie the other down."

"Guessing you wound up being their prisoner instead, then," Margherita said.

"Hardly," Wilson said with a contemptuous snort. "I slipped free and was clear on the other side of the river before the rest of them could so much as rouse from their bedrolls. My point was made, though. This island's territory of His Majesty the Emperor, and no pirate scum were going to trespass there on my watch. Wolf and his crew set sail the following morning."

"Hold up," Quint said, wrinkling his nose. "I can't imagine my pop leaving even his worst enemy alone and marooned on uncharted shores."

"Oh, he hunted for me all through the night and into the next day," Wilson said, jabbing the stem of his pipe up at Quint. "Your mother had caught sight of my face, so they knew it was me that was after them. They hunted for me all through the night, calling my name and trying to entice me back to their ship with promises of clemency and safe passage."

"That sounds like Wolf," Margherita said softly, and if Quint had harbored any remaining doubts that she had truly known his pop, the gentle reverence in her tone shattered them.

"Aye," Wilson nodded, scratching at the stubble under his chin, "he was always a wily one. But not so clever as to catch me in so blatant a ploy. He turned tail and fled back to the Archipelago, and I've kept watch against his return ever since."

"For forty years?" Vanessa stared down at him, incredulous. Quint concurred.

"Aye!" Wilson pounded his fist against his thigh. "I'd claimed this island for Emperor and Empire, under the eyes of all the saints and angels. Just as I'd sworn to defend that Empire from whatever threatened it. I might have been shipwrecked and marooned here, but that doesn't absolve me of my duties."

Vanessa stared at him for a long moment, then over at Quint. He met her eyes, and knew they were thinking the same thing.

Commodore Wilson was not wholly sane.

The man had survived the storm that had drowned the three ships under his command, but a part of him had died with his crews that day. The guilt over their senseless loss must have eaten away at him during his decades of isolation, until he'd convinced himself that the only way he could atone was to carry out the duties he'd been entrusted with, Empire or no Empire.

We may be the ones tied up, Quint thought, straining uselessly against his bonds, *but we're not the real prisoners here.*

And there was no reasoning with a man like this, he realized. How then would they escape?

"Just a minute," Margherita said, very slowly. "If Captain Wolf sent us here to deal with you, why would we bring the Crown Jewels with us?"

For a moment that seemed to stump Wilson. He stuck the pipe in his mouth and chewed so furiously that Quint feared he would bite clean through the ancient wooden stem.

Quint glanced over his shoulder at Tarja, who had been quiet throughout most of this encounter. To his surprise, her gaze was fixed not on their captor, but upon the monkey sitting beside him.

"Well," Wilson said abruptly, recalling Quint's attention. A slow, crazed smile spread across the old maroon's features. "It'd be just like old Wolf to kill two birds with one stone, wouldn't it?"

He hopped off the chest. The locks had been shattered by the mermaids, so he had no difficulty unlatching it and throwing it open. Even in the dim light of the grotto, the Crown Jewels gleamed.

"Aye," Wilson repeated, more to himself than his prisoners. "That'd be the old rascal's plan, no doubt. Send you lot here to bury the Crown Jewels safely out of harm's way, until the time came for him to retrieve them. Only he didn't plan on you getting shipwrecked. And maybe he didn't reckon on old Commodore Wilson still being here, did he?"

"Wolf didn't send us," Quint cut in. Out of the corner of his eye he saw Margherita staring at him. Not daring to break eye contact with Wilson, he sent a silent prayer that she would forgive him this. "He's gone, Wilson."

For the first time, a shadow of doubt passed over the aged commodore's face. "Gone? Gone where?"

Margherita made a small, broken sound.

"Dead," Quint said, forcing himself not to look at her. "A few months back, now."

"No," Wilson said, shaking his head after a moment's consideration. "He can't be. This is another ploy—"

"It's not," Vanessa said, her voice nearly as heavy as Quint's heart. "I visited Ember Bay. The place where Wolf's crew settled down. They were all there, all mourning him."

"Can't be," Wilson said, more to himself than to them. He began pacing around the lip of the pool, gnawing at his pipe and muttering to himself. "Otherwise I've been here all this time for...could have gone with him...and why the Jewels...? No. No, I won't—don't believe it. Don't believe *you*."

He jabbed his pipe towards Quint. "You've inherited his likeness, lad, surely enough. His cunning too, no doubt. Enough that you nearly had me fooled."

"I'm not lying," Quint said, glancing at Margherita's stricken face. "Angels, I wish I was."

"No," Wilson said again, firmer this time. "Wolf *has* to have sent you here. To bury the Jewels. But when you don't return, he'll get to wondering what's happened to you and to them."

A small, vicious smile lined the old castaway's wrinkled face. "And when he comes looking, I'll be here waiting."

He returned to the treasure chest and shut its lid with a final, definite *thunk*. "Help me with this, Lieutenant."

The monkey hopped off his rock and clambered across the grotto floor to seize one handle of the heavy chest in his nimble little fingers. Wilson bent, not without effort, and the two of them began hauling the chest towards the grotto entrance.

"Hold on," Quint called down, feeling as if he'd missed part of the conversation. Or maybe that was the inevitable result of so much blood draining into his head. "What are you doing with the Jewels?"

"Setting a trap," Wilson grunted, pausing in his labors to glance up at them. "I'll leave the chest on the beach. When Wolf and his cutthroats arrive, I can pick them off one by one."

"Not before our crew catches you," Margherita pointed out. "They're still at our camp, waiting for us to return. By the time you get there they'll know we've been gone too long."

"They'll be no obstacle." Wilson reached into his jacket, produced the blowpipe he'd used to incapacitate them. "I've spent forty years stockpiling frog venom and making darts. I could set each of your crew to drowsing a hundred times over."

"There's more of them than there are of you," Vanessa said in a desperate last attempt to keep him from going after their companions. "You think you can take on twenty seasoned pirates alone?"

“A score’s hardly more than four,” Wilson said dismissively. “And I’m not alone. Speaking of...”

He gave a high, sharp whistle. Beneath the prisoners the pool sloshed and roiled as the great turtle plunged beneath the pool, disappearing into its inky depths with alarming suddenness.

“Bosun can deal with any stragglers who escape my darts,” Wilson said, looking up at them. “As for you four, you’ll have plenty of company in a few days. Until then...”

His teeth split in a yellow grin. “Hang tight.”

The old castaway turned his back on them and resumed dragging the chest from the grotto, his pet monkey dutifully assisting. In moments he was gone, leaving the four pirates dangling above the pool.

“That,” Tarja said in the wake of his departure, “is a very odd man.”

32

—•—

"There's got to be a way out of here," Vanessa muttered, looking up at their feet. "Can anyone tell what these ropes are fixed to?"

"Looks like some kind of pulley," Tarja said, squinting into the gloom. "Look. The ropes are strung through holes in the rock above, then tied off onto that...what is it called? The cave rock like a pointy tooth."

Quint followed her gaze. "Stalactite."

"Stalagmite," Vanessa corrected. "If there was a way to untie it, or to cut the rope, we'd fall into the pool. If it's deep enough for that turtle, then at least we know we won't break our necks in the fall."

"How are we to swim with our arms and legs bound?" Tarja pointed out. "That is, if the ropes were loosened first it might be that I could cut through the rest with my hook..."

As Tarja and Vanessa began discussing plans for an escape that already seemed like it would require several miracles to successfully enact, Margherita turned to Quint, her eyes boring holes into him.

"Angels," she said softly. "You really are their kid. Clarent's and Lola's, I mean."

"Yeah." Quint managed a tired smile. "Though you were hardly more than a kid yourself when they took you on. Guess that makes us kind of like siblings?"

"Don't get familiar," Margherita sniffed, but something in her seemed to soften. "You said it's been how long, since...?"

"A few months now," Quint forced himself to say.

"Months," Margherita murmured. "What was it that finally did for him?"

"It was his heart," Quint said, echoing the words his ma had spoken to him months ago. By some minor miracle his voice did not break. "That's what took him, Margherita. The only thing that could've, I think."

"The best part of him," Margherita said, and for a moment Quint could hear the lost little orphan girl she must have been when his pop had taken her into his crew. Into his home. "And your Ma? How is she holding up?"

"As well as you'd imagine," Quint said. "Helps that she's got good folk around her. Many of whom you'd recognize, I'm certain."

"Aye." Margherita smiled, a touch wistfully. "Your pop had a talent for attracting gentle souls, pirates or not. Sounds like your ma hasn't changed, neither."

"She's like she's always been," Quint agreed. "She's steady as ever, dependable as ever. If Pop's the North Star, Ma's the wind in your sails."

"Aye." A gentle smile crept across Margherita's features. "That was always the way those two were. Your pop was the idealist, your ma the practical one. It was her that encouraged me to split off and start my own crew, in truth."

"You told Wilson that was Pop's doing," Quint said, brows furrowing.

"It was," she admitted. "He thought I should get out of the Empire's sights, leastaways as long as Wilson was after them. I wanted to stay and fight, but..."

Her gaze drifted down to the dark pool beneath them. "Wolf never quite approved of my vendetta against the Empire, even if he understood my reasons well enough. Wanted to keep me from danger, I 'spect. Not that I appreciated it at the time. You can probably imagine how well a seventeen-year-old took an adult's concerns for her safety."

"I can," Quint agreed, thinking of how he had been only a scant few years younger when he'd similarly disregarded his pop's warnings of the fraught dangers of life in the Imperial Navy.

"Funny, isn't it?" Margherita's voice was wistful. "How small those arguments look after so many years have passed. After all the headbutting we did, I was just glad to finally strike out on my own. Wish I'd gotten over myself enough to give him a proper goodbye."

The sincerity in Margherita's voice was a blade to Quint's gut. And while he and his pop had managed to mend their bridges in the years following Quint's departure from home, the regret of not saying a proper goodbye was one he and Margherita shared.

"He—" he started to say, but was interrupted by Tarja's sudden, delighted shout.

"Look!" she called, struggling against her binds and nodding her head towards a shadow darkening the grotto entrance. "Help has come!"

They watched as the shadow drew nearer, growing smaller, resolving itself at last into the form of—

"You again?" Margherita growled as the monkey trotted into the chamber, adjusting Margherita's hat as it drooped low over the beast's eyes. "Give me that hat, or I—"

"*Captain*," Tarja interrupted, so authoritative that Margherita unexpectedly clamped her mouth shut. "I will do the talking, if you please."

Talking to who, Quint was about to ask, but the question was answered before he could. Tarja took as deep a breath as her bonds allowed, her round cheeks growing rounder, then let out a series of hoots, screeches, and grunts, startlingly similar to the monkey's own vocalizations. The little creature stood straight on its hind legs, staring at her as monkey sounds echoed about the grotto.

"Is she..." Quint stared at the monkey's attentive posture. "Angels, is she *talking* to it?"

"She's trying to," Margherita said, skeptical. "She does this with most of the animals she and Frederick rescue. Says it helps soothe them—"

"Hush, you two," Vanessa ordered. "Look."

The monkey cocked his head sideways, glancing from Tarja to the stalagmite to which their ropes were bound and back. He clambered onto it and patted the ropes, while letting out a low, inquiring series of noises.

"What's he saying?" Quint asked Tarja. An hour ago he might have shared Margherita's skepticism, but at this point he was ready to believe anything if it meant they'd escape this mess sooner."

"That he is willing to set us free," Tarja said, turning her head to one side. The monkey added a growl, raising both his front paws. "But that he has conditions."

Margherita snorted. Vanessa shushed her, then turned to Tarja. "Such as?"

Tarja turned to the monkey, which flapped its arms before gesturing towards the light spilling in from the grotto entrance, then adjusted Margherita's hat to keep it from falling over his eyes.

"He wants to come with us when we leave the island," Tarja said. She turned to Margherita. "And...I am sorry, Captain. But he wants to keep your hat."

"Absolutely not," Margherita said, scowling. She began wriggling against her bindings, trying in vain to free herself by force alone. "Tell that pint-sized primate that he'll let us down, or—"

"Margherita," Quint said, more calmly than he felt. "It's your hat, or our crew."

She looked at him, grimacing. "Maybe there's another way to free ourselves. If you swing towards me, might be we can grab each other's ropes with our teeth—"

"Captain," Tarja said, grinding her teeth in a rare show of impatience.

"Fine," the pirate queen nodded to her first mate. "Tell him we accept, Tarja."

Tarja hooted down at the monkey atop the stalagmite, who again patted his front paws on the frayed old rope they'd been bound with. Before he began untying it, he chattered something up at them, opening and closing both arms like a trapdoor snapping open and shut.

"What was that?" Quint asked.

"He says that if we renege on our deal he will feed us to the crocodiles," Tarja said, sounding unperturbed by the prospect. "That or give us each a firm spanking. It is hard to tell."

"Noted," Margherita sighed. "Now will you please tell him to let us down?"

Tarja relayed this, earning an affirmative hoot from the monkey as his nimble little fingers began untying the rope with surprising speed.

"Wait a minute," Quint said, craning his neck to peer at the deep pool beneath them, then up at the ropes tying his arms to his sides. "How are we getting out of—"

The line holding him went slack. The monkey shrieked and jumped from the stalagmite as the rope whipped past it towards the grotto ceiling, sending all four of the captives plummeting to the pool below before they could so much as scream.

Shockingly chill mountain water closed in around and over Quint as he plunged in, pouring into his nose. He tried to right himself, but struggled with his arms still pinned against his sides. A stream of bubbles escaped his mouth, drifting up past his booted feet. He forced his eyes open, looking from side to side for some glimpse of his comrades, but it was so dark down in the depths that he could scarcely see his own hair floating in front of his face.

He drifted down, down, until his shoulder bumped roughly against the smooth, sandy floor of the pool. Something cold and damp wrapped about his neck, causing him to jerk violently away before realizing it was just some kind of weed, not a strangling eel.

Where were the others? Had they too sunk to this lightless depth, or were they even now gasping for air on the surface? Had the monkey promised them a false escape, intending all along to finish what its master had begun?

All of this flashed through Quint's mind as his lungs burned. He kept his jaw clenched firmly shut, knowing that the first swallow of water would lead to more, as he reflexively gasped for air that was not there. He tried to position himself so that his feet were against the pool bottom, but everything seemed turned around, and he could no longer say with complete certainty which direction was up and which was down...

A shadow moved in the depths. A burly arm wrapped itself around Quint, followed by another. He struggled instinctively, then forced himself to calm as he felt the cold hoop of Tarja's hook loop itself through the ropes holding him. Suddenly they were rising upwards, up past the streaming bubbles towards the glimmering light of the surface—

Moments later he was lying on his side, face pressed against the cool stone of the grotto floor. Another shadow rose above him, but this time he recognized her straightaway.

"Vanessa," he croaked, and was relieved not to vomit up any water.

"Hold still," she ordered, kneeling above him and swiftly loosening his bindings. Over her shoulder Quint glimpsed Margherita staring daggers at the monkey, who was wisely perched on a rock just beyond her reach.

"What happened?" Quint asked, wondering at how much more swiftly the other two had recovered.

"Bad luck," Vanessa said, undoing the last of the knots tying him. "You were over a deeper part of the pool than the rest of us. When we went in you sank like a stone to the bottom."

"I would have dove in for you sooner," Tarja said apologetically, coming over and offering him her hand. "But first I needed to undo my own bonds, and then grab these two before they could drown. I went for you as soon as I could."

"Thanks," Quint said, accepting both her outstretched hand and Vanessa's as the two women pulled him to his feet. He looked about, blinking as his eyes adjusted to the grotto's dim light after the sudden plunge into total darkness. "Think we can catch up to Wilson?"

"We have to try," Vanessa said, setting off towards the grotto entrance. "We owe it to our crew."

They emerged blinking into the late afternoon sunlight. Quint's stomach growled at the realization that they had been unconscious for nearly an entire day. Whatever venom Wilson's darts contained was frighteningly potent—small wonder he was so confident in his ability to singlehandedly subdue the remainder of their crew.

"How are we going to get back to the beach?" Margherita asked, looking around. "It took us days to reach this place, and he's probably riding that big turtle."

"He can't rely on that creature to ferry him around all the time," Vanessa reasoned, brushing her hair from her face, her eyes fixed on the distant northward horizon. "He must have some other means of navigating the island—"

The monkey screeched, loudly and abruptly, and went shooting past them along the edge of the river, towards a low tree overhanging the cove in which they had emerged from the grotto. It turned and beckoned them forwards with one paw, adjusting its hat with another.

"I think you are right, friend Vanessa," Tarja said, approaching the monkey. Sure enough, a small canoe lay moored beneath the tree, its narrow keel scraping the sandy bottom.

"It will be tight quarters," Tarja grunted, wading in and pulling the little craft into the shallows. The monkey clambered onto her shoulder and stayed there. "But it should be able to carry all four of us down the river."

Together they pushed the canoe out from the cove and into the river. This far into the highlands, the water ran swiftly downstream, and soon they were rushing along, the brown cliffs and green jungle blurring past at either hand.

33

Two rough paddles lay in the hull, and the four of them took turns rowing to conserve their strength as they traveled downriver.

As the largest and heaviest of the group, Tarja sat cramped in the stern, the monkey perched on her shoulder. Occasionally he would chatter something into her ear and point a wizened finger downstream, which Tarja would relay to the others as navigational directions. Even Margherita's skepticism soon died away as the simian companion's instructions unerringly guided them through rapids and around hidden rocks, and—in one notable instance—past a sluggish inlet teeming with what Quint at first took to be logs, but swiftly revealed themselves as dozens of crocodiles.

"Guess that wasn't an idle threat," he remarked as they skirted a wide arc around the nearest of the crocs, who blinked a lazy eye at them as they passed. The sun had already dipped below the unseen horizon, and the strange gray twilight cast all the world in stark shadows.

"Don't worry," Margherita said, hefting her paddle over her head. "I'll bop 'em if they get any closer."

"My hero," Quint said. Behind him, Vanessa stifled a snort.

"Pity that old lunatic took my cutlass," Margherita said, patting her hip where her sword was customarily sheathed. "It'd add some weight to our argument when we finally catch up to him, I can tell you."

"Hopefully it won't come to that," Quint said, glancing over his shoulder at Vanessa, who nodded her agreement. "Maybe we can still find a way to settle all of this without anyone else getting hurt."

"Quint," Margherita said, frowning at him. "That Wilson's already showed that he ain't the kind of man who can be reasoned with."

"I know," he said, rubbing his beard in agitation. "But that doesn't mean we shouldn't still try to solve things peaceably. Killing's only ever a last resort."

Margherita turned to face him, settling her paddle across her lap. The current was doing most of the work at present, anyway.

"Angels," she said after a moment. "Now that I've put two and two together, it's downright spooky how much you take after your old man. I swear I'd heard him say exactly those words in exactly that voice, at least a dozen times."

"Thanks," Quint said around the lump that had spontaneously formed in his throat.

"There's something I need to ask," Margherita said suddenly, her voice small. "Was he...did it hurt?"

"I don't think so," Quint said, as gently as he could. He had wanted to know the same thing, when he'd first heard. "By all accounts it was quick. He probably didn't even know it had happened."

"That's a mercy, I guess." Margherita looked up at the sky, where the first stars had just begun to glimmer. "I wish I'd gotten to see him again, before."

"He'd have liked that, I think," Quint agreed. "I'm sorry I didn't tell you about him sooner."

"You didn't know," she said, very quietly. They lapsed into silence, watching the stars wink into being overhead.

"Even in Trecht we heard tell of the exploits of Captain Wolf," Tarja said softly from behind them. The monkey chittered, as if in agreement.

"Of his piratical adventures and daring deeds. Yet he must been even a better man than he was a pirate, to have left behind such a legacy as you two."

Vanessa made a noise of agreement, rubbing Quint's back.

"Aye," Margherita nodded, looking over her shoulder at Tarja, then at Quint. "I'm betting he was a good father, too."

"You'd win that bet." Quint nodded. "He was...angels. He was the best. Any room he walked into, it was like he carried the sun with him. Always smiling, singing, talking, laughing. Always had a joke or a story to tell, or a kind word for those that needed it."

"Aye." Margherita nodded, and in her distant gaze Quint saw she too was retreading the paths of old memories. "Cap'n...Clarent. I remember thinking, after I'd known the man a while, that he was like a mirror. Never focused on himself, always turned outwards. Reflecting the best part of whoever he was with back at them. Making them better."

"That he did," Quint said. "He lifted up everyone he ever met, just by being around them. Made us want to live up to the example he set. Harps and bells, I built my whole life around that example, and I didn't even realize I'd followed in his footsteps."

"What?" Margherita stared at him, uncomprehending.

"That he was a pirate," Quint clarified, and watched her incomprehension turn to disbelief. "No, really. I had no idea."

"You can't be serious."

"He really didn't," Vanessa chimed in, and Quint knew without looking that she was smiling. "I clocked it within a half hour of meeting his ma. Beat Quint's record by a solid three and a half decades."

"It's not like I grew up *looking* for clues that my folks had led a secret life before I came along," Quint protested, but found himself smiling anyway. "They kept it from me my whole life. Same with Jun and Manish and the rest of them."

"Now I know you're lying," Margherita snorted, but she too was smiling. "No way old Manish could keep a secret that long."

"He nearly gave it away a time or two," Quint admitted, grinning fondly as he considered all the near-slips Manish Anand had made throughout the years, which now seemed obvious in hindsight. Growing up, he'd just assumed his best friend's dad was absent-minded.

"That sounds more like him," Margherita admitted. "Did he ever—your pop, I mean. Or your ma. Did they ever mention me?"

"You have to understand," Quint said, after a few moments' careful consideration. "They kept their history from me. For my safety, I suppose, but also because that part of their lives was over, I think. Because they wanted me to have a future of my own choosing, not one shadowed by who they'd been."

"Oh." Margherita's shoulders slumped.

"But," Quint said, "like you said. My pop loved telling stories."

Margherita looked quizzically at him.

"And his favorites," Quint continued, "were the exploits of the legendary Captain Wolf and the daring crew of the *Howler.* Stalwart First Mate Jun, capable quartermaster Rosa, Hawkins the suicidally brave—"

"Hold on," Margherita said, a wry smile tugging at her lips. "He told you their names and you still didn't know?"

"Of course not," Quint said. "He changed them in the telling, so that I wouldn't figure it out down the line. Which is why I never realized who he meant when he told me stories about the youngest of Wolf's crew. Of the clever, courageous thief named Margie."

Margherita let out a small, breathy sound that was at once a laugh and a sob.

"Angels," she said, shaking her head. "No one's called me Margie since I was seventeen."

"That is because you do not approve of nicknames," Tarja pointed out. "Unless they are from Ophelia, at least."

"She gets a pass," Margherita acknowledged with a shrug. "Can't let the rest of the crew get too familiar, though."

She turned her attention back to Quint. "Now, let's hear some of those stories your pop told you about clever young Margie."

"Only if you'll tell me a few about Clarent and Lola," he countered. "I've a feeling there's a few even my pop didn't want to tell his son, even with the names changed."

"I reckon I've got a few of those," Margherita said, grinning. She ran a hand through her hair, thinking. "Let's start with the time your folks went spearfishing in a sea serpent's lair..."

Quint closed his eyes and listened, relaxing into the rhythm of Margherita's storytelling and the gentle rocking of the boat as the current pulled them downstream, listening as she began to weave a story of comic accidents and near-fatal mishaps. When she finished, he knew, it would be his turn, and together they would piece together a fuller picture of the man who had shaped them both into the people they'd become.

People, Quint reflected, opening his eyes to gaze at the star-studded sky, were multifaceted as any gemstone.

Perhaps you could never fully know someone, in all their aspects and identities. But the more sides of them you saw, the closer you came to understanding the greater whole. It had been that way with his parents, who had turned out to be so much more than the proprietors of a humble tavern. As it was with him and Margherita, each finally seeing the other's finer qualities after so many years of what now seemed a petty and vindictive rivalry.

But perhaps that was the joy of people, he thought, glancing sternwards as Tarja scratched the monkey behind his ears, eliciting a satisfied cooing sound. They could surprise you. And they could change, and change you in their turn.

Vanessa caught him looking in her direction. Brushing aside a curl that had blown into her face, she held his gaze, her brown eyes peering steadily into his green ones.

And then, Quint thought, and found he was smiling, there were the people you would happily spend a lifetime discovering. To learn each and every facet of them, their hard edges and their soft spots, the faces they showed to the world and the ones they hid from even themselves.

Vanessa returned his smile, and Quint wondered whether her thoughts followed a similar path to his own. Perhaps it was true that you could never know the other person in their full, incredible complexity.

But he was willing to try.

34

Riverine travel was much faster than overland, especially downhill. In their haste to catch up to Wilson before he could attack their companions, they traveled through the night, taking turns rowing in pairs while the other two got what little rest they could while sitting upright in a rocking canoe.

"Wilson can't have gotten that far ahead of us," Quint muttered as the faint threads of gray dawn filtered down through the trees. "Even with a head start, I doubt he could've made his turtle swim all through the night without stopping."

"No," Vanessa agreed, dipping her paddle into the river, which was flowing more slowly now than it had at the start of their journey. "But Bosun—the turtle, I mean—must swim a lot faster than we can row. Probably they made good time, then stopped for the night and resumed before we caught up."

"So he'll be well-rested and fresh," Margherita said sourly, rubbing sleep from her eyes. "Meanwhile we've been rowing all through the night, with hardly a wink between the four of us."

"Five of us," Tarja corrected, patting the monkey's hat. It chirped a protest, adjusting the hat that had previously been Margherita's. "Lieutenant has also been helping."

"Haven't seen him pulling an oar," Margherita muttered sourly, throwing a dirty glance in the monkey's direction. Quint suspected she was never going to forgive him for the theft of her hat.

"He's kept us from danger so far," Quint pointed out. "And who knows? Maybe he'll be of some use when we confront Wilson."

"Speaking of," Vanessa said, squinting ahead at a bend in the now-sluggish river. "We should probably come up with a plan for when that confrontation *does* occur. Unless you think we should take our chances on hitting that turtle with our paddles."

"Right," Quint said, looking uncomfortably between them. He suspected they had put off doing exactly that all night, precisely because none of them had been able to think of an answer to their predicament. "Seeing as we haven't been able to outrace Wilson, he'll have gotten to the camp before us—"

"Not by much," Vanessa said, taking a deep breath. "Smell that?"

Quint sniffed, and was rewarded with the sharp, salty tang of a fresh sea breeze stinging his nostrils. Dazed at how far they'd come overnight, he looked ahead and realized that they were nearly to the lagoon. Once they rounded the bend up ahead, they'd catch sight of the hill on which the treehouses stood, and then the lagoon beyond.

"And still no sight of Wilson," Margherita muttered, frowning. "Maybe he overnighted someplace further upriver?"

"Afraid not," Vanessa said, pointing towards the near bank. "Look."

Quint shaded his eyes. His heart gave a sudden lurch as he saw two familiar figures slumped against a tree, eyes shut and mouths open.

"Ginger," he murmured, fear stabbing through him like an icicle. "Simon. No—"

Simon's head drooped further onto his chest, and he let out a snore that carried across the river.

"Just darted," Quint said, relieved. A closer look revealed a pair of fallen buckets lying in the sand beside them. "They must have come here to get water when Wilson ambushed them."

"From where, though?" Margherita frowned, her gaze sweeping the river. "While he was traveling, or did he slip off the turtle and travel overland—"

Her speculation was interrupted by a sudden, frantic screeching from Lieutenant, who scrambled from Tarja's arm to the top of her head, tugging at her hair with his paws.

"Ow!" the big Trectish pirate shouted, wincing. "Easy, little friend! I am not a horse for you to steer—"

Just ahead of them the water began to bubble and roil, as something huge came rising from the depths towards the surface.

"TURTLE!" Margherita bellowed, standing and throwing herself clear of the canoe. Tarja followed with considerably less grace, falling into the water with the shrieking monkey still clinging to her.

Quint gripped the side of the rocking canoe with one hand, reached for Vanessa with the other. Her hand found his as the turtle came roaring to the surface, the first spikes of its shell rising like mountains being dredged from the depths.

"On three!" Vanessa yelled over the splashing cacophony. "One—"

The turtle's head broke the surface like a breaching whale, its triangular jaws opening large enough to swallow the world.

"Two, three!" Quint shouted, and flung himself over the side, pulling Vanessa along with him. As he hit the water the sound of wood splintering filled the air, the turtle's jaws snapping shut on the prow of the canoe.

For the second time in as many days water closed in around him, but this time Quint did not panic. Hands still clasped together, he and Vanessa kicked clear of the wreckage, towards the bank where Ginger and Simon lay in their envenomed sleep. They swam and swam, until they felt sand beneath their boots and stood, wading from the shallows onto the bank. Behind them, the turtle thrashed against the canoe, shattering it into matchsticks.

"He seems rather upset," Tarja said, frowning out at the river. Lieutenant let out a disconsolate sound of agreement, clambering from her shoulder onto a low-hanging branch.

"Where's its master, though?" Margherita asked, looking about, as if Wilson might come out of the trees at any moment.

"Simon and Ginger," Quint said, kneeling beside his fallen mates. Sure enough, blue-feathered darts emerged from both their necks, their chests rising and falling in the deep, even rhythm of gentle sleep.

"Simon," Quint said. He shook him, hard. "Hey, Simon!"

But Simon only let out another snore, one that was soon deafened by the now-familiar roar of the great turtle. Quint looked over his shoulder to see the huge beast had finished destroying the canoe, and was now turning towards the bank, beady yellow eyes fixed on them.

"We have to move," Vanessa said, pulling Quint to his feet. "Got to find Wilson before he can hurt anyone else."

"Not without them," Margherita argued, jabbing a finger at Ginger and Simon. "Who knows what that turtle will do to them—"

"They will be fine," Tarja said, without even a hint of fear in her voice. "I will see to it."

She stood, feet planted wide apart in the sand, rolled her neck like a prizefighter warming up before the big match, and stared at the oncoming turtle.

"Tarja," Margherita said, but was silenced by a wave of her first mate's hook.

"Take care of the crew, Cap'n," she said, a fierce smile spreading across her broad, honest features. "I will take care of this beast."

Margherita swallowed whatever objection she'd been about to voice. Instead she nodded, saluted her first mate, then turned to hurry through the jungle, up the hill to where their crew must even now be under attack by the mad old commodore and his darts.

Quint and Vanessa followed, sparing one last glance over their shoulders to watch as Tarja raised fist and hook against the tidal wave of the charging turtle, grinning like a madwoman.

Her laughter followed them as they sped through the jungle.

35

Trees whipped past them in a blur of greens and browns as they sprinted up the hill, bent nearly double to avoid both trailing vines and flying darts. Quint's pulse roared in his ears as he fought to ignore his knees' pounding protests against such frenetic motion after so long confined in the canoe.

A high, angry buzz like a hornet's rang through the trees. Ahead of him Vanessa dove for the undergrowth, pulling a yelping Margherita down with her. Quint followed suit, throwing himself flat just as a blue-feathered dart hurtled through the space where his head had been half a moment earlier.

Quint exhaled sharply, then began hauling himself forward on knees and elbows, wary of rising and making himself a target once more.

A boot stuck out of the undergrowth just ahead of him—Vanessa's he thought, but wasn't certain.

"Ahoy," he said softly, reaching out and shaking the heel of the boot.

The answer was a snore too high and too nasal to belong to Vanessa. Peering closer, Quint saw that the inch or so of exposed skin between the boot and the tattered pantleg was several shades too light to be hers, either.

He crawled forward and saw that it was Frederick. The diminutive quartermaster lay curled in a ball with his head pillowed by his hands, a bundle of blue feathers protruding from just above his collarbone. His spectacles lay in the dirt a few feet away. Quint retrieved them and carefully placed them on Frederick's nose, feeling at once relieved and guilty that he would not have to tell the little Trechtish pirate that his wife had stayed behind to battle a monstrous turtle.

"Quint!" This time it was unmistakably Vanessa's voice hissing at him from just ahead, higher up the slope. "Catch up!"

He did, wincing as another dart buzzed past somewhere overhead. Wilson himself remained unseen, but if the unconscious forms of Simon, Ginger, and now Frederick were any indication, he could easily dispatch any of them if they broke from the cover of the undergrowth.

Quint hauled himself forward towards the base of the bunkhouse, ignoring the stones digging into his elbows and roots scraping over his sides, his eyes half-shut as creepers and leaves brushed across his face, until his shoulder bumped against something hard and unmoving, which turned out to be Margherita's elbow.

"Ow," he breathed, hoping he'd said it softly enough not to draw Wilson's fire.

"Ow yourself," she fired back, wincing and rubbing her elbow. "He hasn't got you yet, eh?"

"Not yet," Quint acknowledged. "I found Frederick back there under a bank of ferns, though."

"Hurt?" Margherita's tone turned anxious.

"Sleeping like a babe," Quint assured her.

"We came across Vigo slumped against a tree a little ways back," Vanessa said from the other side of Margherita, jerking her head over her shoulder. "And Darby just a few paces on from him."

"Looked like he'd tried to go for help," Margherita said, then cursed and pressed herself as flat against the dirt as she could as another dart went buzzing past only a few feet ahead of where they sheltered. "And Wilson picked him off, same as he'll do to us if we stay here."

"Ahoy!" someone called from the trees. Quint looked up to see Adewale appear from the main bunkhouse, his arm already in motion as he hurled a spear into the jungle behind Quint. It had scarcely left his hand when an angry buzz flitted past Quint, a blue-feathered shaft sprouting like a macabre flower from Adewale's outstretched arm.

He teetered for a moment, swaying drunkenly on the edge of the treehouse platform, the roots beneath him hard and unforgiving as stones.

"Adewale!" Margherita cried, charging straight ahead, no longer concerned with evading the oncoming darts.

Adewale's eyes rolled back in his head, and he began to fall from the treehouse—until a pair of heavily tattooed arms wrapped around his chest from behind, hauling him back into the shelter of the main bunkhouse.

Ophelia, Quint thought, grinning, but there was no time to celebrate. Vanessa reached out and grabbed Margherita by the shoulders, hauling her backwards as another volley of darts came flying just ahead of them. One of them caught Margherita in the wrist.

The pirate queen slowed, looking dumbfoundedly at the blue feathers sprouting from her sleeve. Quint caught up to her and Vanessa both, and together they hustled Margherita up the last few paces of the slope, towards the sheltering safety of the trees' waist-high roots.

Vanessa and Margherita leapt behind the nearest of these. Quint followed, only for a smaller root to catch his boot. He let out a huff of surprise as he tripped, the larger root slamming into his middle and forcing him into an impromptu somersault over it.

He was saved from faceplanting directly into the dirt by a pair of rough hands catching him under the shoulder, easing him down into a reclining position behind the sheltering root as another dart passed between them and the treehouses overhead.

"Easy, Cap'n," a voice muttered in his ear, leaning him against the low wall of the root. Rustbucket stood crouched beside him, looking up at his former captain with undisguised concern.

"Rusty?" Quint asked, dazed. "Why aren't you up in the bunkhouse?"

"Was off doing my business when all the commotion started," Rustbucket admitted. "Ran up here when darts started flying but couldn't make it all the way up to the bunkhouse. Anyone who tries climbing the trunks or ladders is too easy a target."

Adewale had proven that much. Quint turned to Vanessa and Margherita. They too had pressed themselves against the root, shielding themselves from Wilson's barrage, which seemed to have tapered off now that no easy targets were in sight.

"How bad is it?" Quint asked Margherita, who was miraculously still awake, and still staring fixedly at the blue feathers sprouting from her wrist.

"I..." she shook her head, disbelieving. "He didn't get me. Look."

She pulled back her sleeve, revealing that the dart had pierced cleanly through the fabric without brushing the skin. An oily sheen of venom glistened on the dart's tip.

"Here," Vanessa said, pinching Margherita's sleeve and gently removing the dart with two fingers. "Before one of us accidentally gets a scratch from that."

Margherita let out a shaky laugh, looking at Vanessa with a curious expression on her face. Had the Navy commander not pulled her from the line of fire, the pirate queen would have been pierced by at least three of those same darts.

"Hang onto that," Quint said, beginning to feel his way around the faint outline of a plan. He turned his attention back to Rustbucket. "How long has this been going on?"

"An hour, maybe?" Rustbucket shrugged. "Or maybe two. Time gets funny once the blood's pumping. This the work of our ghost, then?"

"Aye," Quint nodded. "How'd it begin?"

"Folk started disappearing," Rustbucket said. "Ginger and Simon went down to fetch water, then never came back. Ophelia sent Darby and Vigo to look for them, then Frederick when *they* didn't come back, neither. He at least managed to shout a warning, first. That's how we knew we was under attack. How many of them are there, anyway?"

"Just one," Vanessa said.

"One?" Rustbucket's brows rose towards his nonexistent hairline. "We figured on at least a dozen, the way those darts have been flying. Where's Tarja, by the way?"

"Stayed behind to buy us time," Margherita answered, sparing Quint the necessity of doing so. "How many of us are left?"

"Counting you three?" Rustbucket did some math. "Eleven—no, ten, since Adewale just got hit—wait, forgot myself. Eleven. Four of us down here, Ophelia and six others up there. The rest were out in the woods or down at the beach when the attack started. "

Nodding, Quint took a deep breath and looked up at the floorboards of the bunkhouse above them. "Ophelia!"

A moment passed. Then Ophelia's somewhat muffled voice came drifting down, sounding as if her face was pressed close against those floorboards. "That you, Quint?"

"Aye," he called up. "Rusty says there's eight of you in there and still awake. That right?"

"Eight," she confirmed. "Listen, mate. Don't try and come up here, it's too exposed—"

"I know," Quint called back. It occurred to him that the jungle had fallen oddly quiet without the near-continual buzzing of Wilson's darts flying through the air. He caught himself hoping against hope that the old castaway had grown bored of his sport and wandered off—wishful thinking, he knew.

"Was staying in the bunkhouse your idea?" he asked.

"Aye," Ophelia said slowly after a moment. "Doesn't feel too great, though—staying cooped up in here while our friends get shot. Did they...are they...?"

"They're all right," Margherita called up. "We got hit with the same stuff a few nights back. Leaves you with a powerful hangover, but nothing you don't wake from."

"Thank the angels," Ophelia breathed, and Quint could easily picture her running her hand through her thin stripe of hair. "I keep on wanting to go out there and check on them, but—"

"Better that you haven't," Quint assured her. "You made the right call getting as many into safety as you could."

"Maybe," Ophelia's muffled voice came a moment later. "It's just...if we'd all charged out there at once, maybe we could've overwhelmed—"

"Lia," Margherita said, and it was only when a small sound carried down from overhead that Quint realized this must be Margherita's pet name for Ophelia, never before spoken in his hearing. "Captain's first obligation is to the lives of her crew. You made the right call. Ain't none of us down here who could've done better."

"Thanks, Rita," Ophelia said after a moment had passed, uncharacteristically quiet. "Think I'm about ready to set down the reins of command now that you two are back, though."

"You can hold onto them just a hair longer," Quint assured her, looking at Vanessa. She was twirling Wilson's dart between her fingers, carefully to keep well clear of the envenomed tip. Her lips were pursed in a way that suggested she was about to declare six moves until checkmate. "We're coming up with a plan."

"Aye-aye," Ophelia said, followed by the sound of feet tramping across the floorboards above as she moved about the bunkhouse—shoring up any gaps in their defense, Quint suspected, or taking stock of what few weapons they might have on hand.

"What're you thinking?" he asked Vanessa.

She looked at him, then nodded in the direction of the beach, where the glittering blue lagoon lay just barely visible through a gap in the leaves.

"The Crown Jewels are somewhere in that direction," she said. "Wilson told us he planned to use them as bait for Captain Wolf's supposed arrival, and they weren't with the turtle when it attacked us."

"What?" Rustbucket frowned, looking between the three of them.

"Our ghost is a lunatic old Navy maroon riding a turtle the size of a warship," Margherita told him in frank, clipped tones. "He also thinks that it's Captain Wolf who sent us here to do him in."

"*What?*" Rustbucket said again, more faintly.

"Not important," Quint assured him, then nodded at Vanessa. "You were saying?"

"If we act like Wolf's nearly here," Vanessa said, glancing around at the three of them, "and that our main concern is getting the Crown Jewels back to him, we can flip the script. Use the Jewels to lure Wilson to the beach, and away from the bunkhouses."

"It's a pretty long run from here to the beach," Margherita pointed out. "What's to stop him from picking us all off at once?"

"We split up." Quint's guess was confirmed by Vanessa's nod. "There's four of us, so we all take a different path to the beach. Keep well away from each other so that he's forced to choose one target at a time. We won't all make it down there, but at least some of us will."

"And more importantly, we'll free up Ophelia and her lot," Margherita caught on, gesturing upwards. "Then once Wilson's down at the beach, they can come up from behind him and take care of him."

"Right," Quint agreed, internally still hoping that there was a peaceable means of resolving their dilemma. Assuming Tarja had managed to escape the giant turtle, no one had been seriously hurt yet, and Quint was reluctant to escalate the situation any further than necessary.

"All in agreement?" Vanessa asked, looking around at them. All three nodded.

"Ophelia!" Quint called up, and was answered by the sound of boots tramping across the floorboards overhead.

"Made progress on that plan, have you?" Ophelia's muffled voice asked.

"Aye," Quint nodded. "We're going to make a break for it. Remember that bar fight in Solace?"

"Which one?"

"The one about five years back," Quint said, ignoring the way one of Vanessa's eyebrows had transformed into a geometrically perfect arch.

"The one at the Diving Bell?" Ophelia asked after another moment's consideration. "Or do you mean that time at the Cracked Clam? Or—"

"The Cracked Clam," Quint said. "You recall how it went?"

"Surely do," Ophelia said, then: "Ah. You want us—"

"Aye," Quint nodded, peeking over the edge of the root in case Wilson was listening. There was a faint *puff* from somewhere in the distant trees, and Quint ducked back beneath the root before the inevitable dart buried itself in the thick wood. *Definitely listening.*

"On three," he said to the others, pulling himself into a crouch. The rest of them did likewise, nodding at each other. "Ready?"

"Hold up a moment," Rustbucket said, raising his hand. The others looked at him, bemused, as he cleared his throat. "I just wanna say. If this all goes belly up, I mean."

"Stow that talk," Quint ordered, but Rustbucket gave him a thin smile and shook his head.

"Nah," he said. "You ain't my Cap'n no more, remember? But even so, I wanted to say. I'm glad you saved me from the gallows. And I'm glad to have been on your crew."

He looked meaningfully from Quint, to Vanessa, to Margherita. "*Our* crew."

"Aye," Margherita nodded, also looking about. "Same here."

"It's been an honor," Vanessa agreed, smiling.

"One we'll have a good long laugh about over a round of drinks in the Queen's Arms," Quint assured them. "Ready?"

They nodded, as one, faces set. Quint held up his hand, counted off on his fingers. *Three, two, one.*

Then they were off, pelting in four separate directions, as once again the air was filled with the whirring of darts.

36

"This way!" Quint shouted as he raced downhill, opting for the straightest path from the treehouses. To his left and right the other three peeled off, zigzagging in disparate directions as they called out similar fictions, their voices echoing through the trees:

"Sail on horizon!"

"Make for shore!"

"Captain's gonna be PISSED!" This last from Rustbucket, in what Quint considered an impressive display of improvisation.

Air puffed from the unseen blowgun, sending darts buzzing through the air with frightening rapidity. Quint could have sworn that some of them passed so close that he felt the blue feathers tickle his cheek.

The trees ahead of him opened up onto the broad white sands of the beach, and the glittering lagoon beyond. Quint ran, heartbeat pounding against his chest, until suddenly he was out of the trees, loose sand shifting beneath his feet. He stumbled, another dart speeding through the space where he had been not a moment before.

Quint kept running.

His feet pounded against the golden sand, whipping his head from side to side in search of—*there.*

The treasure chest lay just above the tideline, remarkably close to where the merfolk had deposited it mere days ago, its lid open and facing the lagoon. The sight of it sent an odd feeling of déjà vu washing over Quint, as if any moment now Lurk might rise from the waves with her pod in tow, just as she had saved him from Rustbucket and his more vicious cousins mere months ago.

"Quint!" Vanessa's voice, echoing over the sands as she came running from the trees halfway between where Quint had emerged and the firepit. At the same moment Margherita came pelting from the other side of the beach, making a beeline for the chest. Where was Rustbucket?

Darts came flying from the jungle, burying themselves in the sand at Quint's heels. Out of the corner of his eye he saw more volleys flying for his companions. Vanessa let out a curse that echoed across the sands, backpedaling until she landed with a startled, undignified yelp in the firepit.

"Stay down!" Quint yelled at her, knowing if that if she tried to climb up from the pit, she'd be too easy a target for Wilson to miss.

He was closing in on the chest, now only a few feet away. From the trees behind them came a rapid series of *puff-puff-puffs*. The darts' buzzing grew louder, closer, and Quint knew a moment before they hit that this time Wilson would not miss.

"DOWN!" Rustbucket's roar echoed across the beach as he came sprinting towards Quint from the direction of the dunes, tackling him around the middle. Sand scraped against Quint's shoulder as he fell, Rustbucket let out a grunt as he landed atop him.

"Go," he growled, disentangling himself from Quint and rising woozily to one knee. A blue feather protruded from his neck.

"You're—" Quint started, but Rustbucket shook his head and shoved him weakly forward.

"Go," he said again, voice already heavy with venom as he shook his head. His bleary eyes focused on the chest ahead of him. "'sides. I told you, that treasure's no good for me..."

Then he pitched headfirst into the sand, already snoring.

Quint scrambled half on his feet, half on his knees, fingers digging into the suddenly damp sand as he crawled past the tideline, throwing himself behind the shelter of the chest. Within the Crown Jewels lay glittering in the sun, brightly unconcerned by the drama playing out around them. Margherita joined Quint a moment later, breathing hard, sweat plastering her hair to her brow.

"Vanessa?" she asked.

"Safe for the moment," Quint said, gasping in air. "She took cover in the firepit."

Margherita nodded, sneaking a glance past the edge of the chest. No sooner had she done so than a dart came hurtling towards them. It fell short, landing in the sand a few feet from the chest.

"Now what?" she asked, looking at Quint. "Wait for the rest to get here?"

"That was the idea," Quint said, but a troubling thought had occurred to him. Their plan had been predicated on luring Wilson away from the treehouses and onto the beach, allowing Ophelia and the others to close in on him from behind. But Wilson had yet to emerge from the trees, and if he heard the other castaways approaching, surely he would slip away through the jungle and back to his grotto in the highlands, to remain a thorn in the castaways' sides for as long as they remained upon his island.

This had to end now.

"Commodore!" Quint yelled, raising his voice to carry across the sand and through the trees. "We want a parley!"

There was silence on the beach, save for the quiet murmur of the tide lapping against the sand.

"Pirates ain't got no right to parley," Wilson's voice called from the trees. But Quint thought he sensed a dubious note in his tone.

"Maybe not," Vanessa allowed from her place in the firepit. "But I haven't been stripped of my rank yet, Commodore. And under the articles of the Navy, you're obligated to honor *my* request for parley."

A pause. Quint waited, not daring to say anything lest doing so should sway Wilson in the other direction.

"Make your case, Commander," the old maroon said gruffly. "Though I'll warn you straight off, I'm unlikely to accept any offer less than your unconditional surrender."

Beside Quint, Margherita let out a huffing sound of disbelief. Quint motioned for her not to interrupt.

"You've been here forty years, Commodore." Vanessa's voice carried clear and high through the morning air. "In all that time, the Navy's never sent a vessel to search for you. Haven't you ever wondered at that?"

Wind sighed softly through the palms above as they awaited Wilson's response.

"I'm sure they sent someone, sometime," he said after several moments' consideration. "But the Sea of Tears is perilous. Doubtless they never made it so far south. But I'm certain they *tried.*"

"Commodore." Vanessa's voice was gentle, lowered just enough that Wilson was obliged to stop talking in order to hear her. "Do you know that I read about you in the Navy's history books?"

"You did?" Wilson's voice was flatly astonished.

"You're not mentioned by name," Vanessa interrupted, gentler still. "Only a passing reference to three ships lost in the Sea of Tears while pursuing a fleeing pirate."

A dim memory from his midshipman days rose in Quint's subconscious. He had read that selfsame passage, which been included not in an historical tome, as Vanessa indicated, but in a textbook on maritime disasters.

"...you're saying they don't know that I'm here," Wilson said, his flat disbelief undercut by the faint tremor in his voice. "That they thought I was dead all this time."

"Three ships lost with all hands," Vanessa said, not even faintly accusatory. "No one knew there was an exception. The Navy forgot you, Commodore."

"They wouldn't. Not after all I'd given them."

Wilson sounded closer now. Quint chanced a glance around the corner of the chest, and thought he saw a glimpse of a figure stalking through the shadows of the trees. This was confirmed a moment later by a puff and buzz as another dart came flying towards them, but it fell short, burying itself in the sand inches from the sleeping Rustbucket.

"That's what the Navy does, Wilson," Vanessa said quietly. "At its worst, anyway. It chews folk up and spits them out when it's done with them, unless it still has a use for them."

Wilson narrowed his eyes. "That's treason you're talking, Commander."

"It's not treason to see the failings of the nation you serve," Vanessa said, and Quint found himself silently applauding the saintlike patience she was displaying. "To have a clear eye to its faults, its misdeeds. To grapple with the injustices it perpetuates. How else can we make it better?"

To that, Wilson had no ready answer.

"Wilson!" Margherita called, coming to her feet. Quint tried to pull her back down, but she shook him off, muttering in an aside, "We're out of range down here."

As if to prove her point, a dart came flying for them, landing a foot in front of the treasure chest.

"Wilson!" Margherita repeated, cupping her hands to her mouth. "Why'd you join a Navy that was so ready to forsake you, anyway?"

"They did *not*," he called back with a snarl, stepping forward so that he was now fully visible, though still shaded by the trees overhanging the beach. Quint peered around the corner, watched as the old castaway visibly mastered himself. "To serve, of course. With honor and integrity—"

"Serve who?" Margherita demanded.

"The Empire, of course. Its people—"

"Not the same thing," Margherita said, shaking her head. "It's like Vanessa said, Commodore. Empire and Navy both, they exist to perpetuate themselves. Protecting the folk who pay them tax is just a neat excuse they can wave whenever they split apart a family, or bombard a town that just happens to sit on a diamond mine—"

"Lies!" Wilson sputtered. "They—we would *never*—"

"I've seen it," Margherita said, less angry and more weary. "Time and time again, on any island you'd care to name from here to Trecht. You want to know the ironic thing, Commodore?"

Silence answered her question, which Margherita interpreted as assent. "By staying here on this island all these years, you may have done the people of the Empire more good than if you'd stayed on serving the Navy. Or at least less harm."

"No." Wilson stepped out from the trees and into the sunlight, blowpipe raised to his chin. Quint realized with a start that it was the first time he'd ever seen the man in full daylight. Blinking beneath the bright tropical sun, Wilson no longer looked like the crazed, paranoid soldier he had seemed within the confines of his lair. Instead Quint saw an old man looking lost and afraid, clutching the blowpipe to his chest as if it could defend him from the coldness of the world that had abandoned him years before Quint was even born.

"No," Wilson said again, shaking his head. "You're...you're lying. It can't all be for nothing. They..."

He trailed off, but not before Quint heard the sorrow weighing down that final word.

"Your crew," he said, rising from his place behind the chest. Wilson pressed the blowpipe to his lips but did not fire. "You're afraid they died for nothing."

Wilson's eyes widened above the blowpipe, then narrowed.

"They can't have," he said, lowering the length of bamboo just enough to speak over. "Don't you see? It's because of me. I ordered them into the storm. There has to be a *reason* the angels spared me, elsewise—"

"Sometimes there is no reason," Quint said gently, crossing the sands in slow even steps, as if he were approaching a spooked animal. "No reason some of us live and others die. All those of us who survive can do is keep on living, and do it in a way that honors the ones we've lost as best we can."

He was within range of Wilson's blowpipe now, he knew. All it would take was one dart to send him toppling to the sand, snoring alongside Rustbucket. Out of the corner of his eye Quint saw Vanessa begin to rise from the firepit where she'd been sheltering, the dart she'd plucked from Margherita's sleeve gripped firmly between her fingers. Without taking his eyes from Wilson, Quint motioned for her not to risk an attack.

"You weren't lying," Wilson said after a moment, as Quint drew steadily nearer. "About Captain Wolf, I mean. Your father."

"I wasn't," Quint agreed, spreading his empty hands wide. "He's gone, and all I can do is carry on his legacy as well as I know how."

"Plying the pirate's trade," Wilson scowled. "Terrorizing the sea lanes and laying hands on honest folk."

"Those weren't the lessons he passed onto me," Quint said, smiling despite himself as he shook his head. "Believe it or don't, Wilson, but he hung up the black flag of his own volition. Might be you even had something to do with that."

Wilson's line face grew even more wrinkled. "He wouldn't."

"He did," Margherita said, closer than Quint was expecting. She too had emerged from behind the treasure chest, drawing up alongside Quint. "He turned over a new leaf, Wilson. Settled down to a quiet life and never did any further harm to anybody."

The words hung between them like an offer, punctuated only by the soft sighing of sand as Vanessa scrambled up from the firepit.

"Forty years is a long time, Commodore," she said. "Well past time you stopped punishing yourself."

A snapping branch from the jungle caused Wilson to turn, raising his blowpipe. Beneath the branches Quint glimpsed Ophelia's silhouette creeping closer, several others behind her.

"It's alright," Quint called before either party could make a move, both his palms outstretched. "We're working things out."

Wilson turned back to him, looking dubiously at Quint over his blowpipe. "You're not going to throw me in the brig and hold me for ransom?"

"No," Quint said, shaking his head, deciding against pointing out that the commodore had been presumed dead for longer than Quint had been alive. "We'll give you passage back to the Archipelago, if that's what you want."

"Or you can stay here," Margherita said, surprisingly conciliatory. "If this place is home and not a prison, we won't take you from it."

Wilson turned in a slow circle, peering intently into Quint's face. Into Margherita's, Vanessa's, Ophelia's and the rest as they formed a ring around him. He looked down at the blowpipe in his hands, his shoulders slumping.

"It's been so long," Wilson whispered, closing his eyes. "I don't even know if there'd be anyone back in the Empire waiting for me."

"Only one way to find out," Quint said.

Wilson drew in a deep breath, and let the blowpipe fall to the sand.

When he opened his eyes it was to see Quint's hand extended towards him, a smile on the bearded pirate's face.

"Peace?" Quint asked.

Wilson let out another long breath, then nodded. "Aye, lad. You're right."

His weathered old hand clasped Quint's, his grip surprisingly strong, his eyes a startling blue as he gazed intently at the son of his long-ago nemesis.

"It's time I stopped warring with ghosts."

37

—•—

"All that's well and good," Ophelia said a moment later, stepping out into the sunlight, "but what about all our folk you shot with those darts?"

"Oh," Wilson said, looking suddenly abashed. "Right. Hold a moment."

He fumbled in his jacket, pulled out a wineskin and held it up demonstratively. "Got the antidote right here. I've pricked myself enough times with those darts to keep it on my person."

"You're saying you could have woken us up at any time?" Margherita asked, frowning.

"It took a long time to get the four of you into the cave and tied to the roof," Wilson said defensively. Over his shoulder, Ophelia shot Quint a quizzical look, which he waved off with a mouthed *Later.* "I needed a lie-down after."

"Right," Quint said, making to pat the old castaway on the back but thinking better of it. "If you wouldn't mind..."

He jerked a thumb over his shoulder towards Rustbucket's sleeping form.

"Oh, aye," Wilson said, coloring a little as he ambled across the sand towards their fallen crewman. "I'll, ah. See to the rest of them as well."

"Much appreciated," Quint said, following him. "Were you really going to feed us to your turtle?"

"Bosun?" Wilson's brows crinkled. He stopped where Rustbucket lay and turned him over. "She don't eat meat. I was just trying to give you a scare."

"She attacked us," Margherita said, hurrying to catch up. "This morning. Smashed your canoe to splinters. One of my crew..."

"She likes to play rough, I'll admit," Wilson said, pouring a generous serving of antidote into Rusbucket's open mouth. Rustbucket's eyes fluttered open, choking and sputtering. Quint knelt beside him, helping him up. "But she'd never hurt anyone on purpose."

Margherita frowned. "Then what happened to—"

As if in answer, Tarja's voice echoed across the beach.

"Ahoy, Cap'n!" she called, drawing their attention to the lagoon. The enormous turtle—Bosun, Quint mentally corrected himself—was rounding the bend where the river fed into the lagoon, Tarja sitting astride her shell just behind her trunk-like neck. The monkey Lieutenant was perched on one of Tarja's own shoulders, while on her other perched—

"Jimmy?" Quint blinked, staring hard at the little green parrot, wondering if hallucinations were one of the aftereffects of Wilson's darts.

"Jimmy good bird!" Jimmy called, launching from Tarja's shoulder and winging her way across the beach towards Quint. He stuck out his arm instinctively, a grin spreading over his face as she flapped to a halt, talons digging into his wrist, sharp and real.

"Jimmy very good bird," he assured her, scratching under her chin. Jimmy preened in delight, giving his finger an affectionate nibble. "But I'm guessing you didn't get here all on your lonesome, did you, girl?"

"All hands on deck!" Jimmy said proudly, and Quint grinned. As yet no sail had broken the blue line of the horizon, but if Jimmy had made it here, rescue could not be far behind.

A groan from the sands drew Quint's attention. He looked down to see Rustbucket blinking blearily up at him.

"Cap'n?" Rustbucket mumbled, voice still heavy with Wilson's venom. "Wha...happened?"

"*Cap'n on deck!*" Jimmy squawked, spreading her wings wide as she balanced on Quint's forearm. "*Cap'n on deck, look alive!*"

Rustbucket rubbed his eyes, no doubt wondering whether he was hallucinating the reappearance of Quint's pet. When Jimmy did not disappear from his vision, a slow, dreamy smile spread across Rustbucket's face, softening his features.

"I love that bloody bird," he said.

Quint had scarcely helped Rustbucket to his feet when Tarja's voice rang out along the beach once more, calling out the two most blessed words Quint had ever heard in his life.

"SAILS AHOY!" the big Trechtish pirate bellowed, thrusting her hook lagoonwards. "SAIL ON HORIZON!"

Sure enough, white sails had crested the horizon, growing seemingly larger with every passing moment. A deafening cheer rose from the castaways assembled on the beach, some of the more eager of whom raced into the shallows, shouting and waving their arms.

"Guessing it's not the Navy, then," Margherita said, coming to stand alongside Quint. She held out a finger to Jimmy, who permitted Margherita to scratch her chin. "Lurk must've gotten to Ember Bay alright."

"I knew she would," Quint said, though beneath his assumed air of confidence he knew he would not rest easy until he set eyes on their mermaid friend.

Margherita smirked, as if she saw through his façade. "You really do look like him."

"Who?" Quint asked, then realized. "My pop?"

"Aye," Margherita said. "Just now. That 'I'm quite concerned but trying to hide it' look. He made the same face anytime the crew had to split up for one reason or another."

Quint rubbed his beard. "Runs in the family, I guess."

For a moment they were silent, watching the *Bloody Angel's* sails grow steadily larger above the horizon. Jimmy launched herself from Quint's shoulder and fluttered over the heads of the excited crowd of castaways crowding the beach in eager anticipation of their rescuers. Only Wilson stood apart from the rest, looking dazed at the prospect of rescue so soon after his decades of isolation.

"Commodore," Vanessa said, striding over and offering the old officer a salute. "Would you mind if I accompanied you while you woke the rest of the crew?"

"What?" Wilson started, unused to being addressed in a friendly manner after so long alone. "Oh. I mean, aye. I can do that."

"Thank you," Vanessa said, offering him her arm as she turned towards the jungle. "And while we're at it, I can tell you a bit about what's happened back home while you've been away..."

They strolled off into the trees, Wilson clearly relieved at escaping from having to meet so many new people at the same time.

"There's still one thing we have to decide," Margherita said, looking out across the waves at the approaching ship, arms folded across her chest. "Before your lot shows up and things get complicated."

"Don't tell me you're still holding us as prisoners," Quint said.

"Not that," Margherita said, refusing to be amused. She rested her hand on the top of the treasure chest, looked down at the Crown Jewels glittering within. "We need to figure out what we're going to do with these."

"Aye," Quint said, sobering. He looked down at the Jewels, the sun shining off the countless facets of rubies and emeralds, the gleaming silver and burnished gold. Something hungry stirred in his heart, and for just a moment he thought he grasped what had led Rustbucket to betray him.

He looked up, into Margherita's eyes, and saw something of that same avarice reflected in her own gaze.

"You said you misjudged me," he said, breaking the spell. "About being a greedy, selfish thief. But you weren't entirely wrong, either."

He nodded towards the *Bloody Angel,* now grown large enough that he could make out the dark wood of her hull beneath the white sails. "I wanted to make a home. For myself, aye, but also for everyone else who couldn't find a place for themselves under the Empire. But I suppose I never paid enough thought to those that couldn't just flee aboard a ship."

Quint looked at the pirate queen beside him. "You did, though."

"Maybe." Margherita chewed her lip. "Or maybe I've just spent these forty years fighting a war that can't be won. Maybe I got so wrapped up in the fight that somewhere along the way I stopped caring about who got hurt in the process."

"It's not too late to change," Quint said, then paused, wanting to ensure he chose his next words with care. "For either of us. And I have an idea of where to start."

He bent, scooping a handful of rings and bracelets from the chest. Any single one would have been enough to buy a ship larger than the *Angel.*

"You were going to use these to lure the Empire into a trap," Quint said. "I was going to sell them."

"Now you've a third option in mind?" Margherita asked, sounding genuinely curious.

"I do," Quint said, handing her a silver ring inset with a brilliant yellow stone. "One of the Queen Mother's Rings. Recognize the gem?"

"Beryl," Margherita said after a moment, her eyes widening.

"Aye," Quint said, holding up another ring—this one gold set with a deep green gemstone. A tourmaline. "The Empire plundered these stones from across the Archipelago. I think it's about time they were returned."

"How?" Margherita asked, still staring at the beryl ring. "Just dock at the main island and toss its native Jewel to whoever's loitering around the port?"

"That's where you come in," Quint said, clapping her on the shoulder. "I'm willing to bet you've made a fair number of allies who've grudges of their own against the Empire. Doubt you could've survived this long otherwise."

"You're suggesting I give it to them?" Margherita asked.

"Only those you think would use them for their people," Quint clarified. "I don't want some governor who turns a blind eye to your ventures in exchange for a cut of your profits to get even richer by claiming to have recovered one of the Jewels, for example."

A guilty look stole across Margherita's countenance, confirming that Quint had been right in at least one of his suspicions as to how Margherita had eluded the Empire for so long.

"But if you give them to community leaders," he continued, "those who would use the Jewels as a symbol to rally their people around...wouldn't that do more good for the people of the Empire than whatever you'd originally planned?"

Margherita looked at the beryl ring, ruminating on the idea.

"There's no guarantee that at least some of them won't sell the Jewels instead," she said slowly. "A lot of the communities these treasures came from are still hurting under the Empire's yolk."

"All the more reason they should have them back, then," Quint said, carefully putting the tourmaline ring back into the chest. "At least that way they'll get some coin where it can do the most good."

"Restitution," Margherita said slowly. "Rather than revenge. You're right."

"Like I said," Quint said, smiling at her. "It's not too late to change."

38

—•—

By the time the *Bloody Angel* had safely anchored well beyond the reefs dividing the lagoon from the Sea of Tears, Wilson and Vanessa had succeeded in rousing those who'd fallen victim to the old castaway's darts. Thus it was that, when their rescuers arrived at last, every soul who'd been aboard the *Marigold* when it went down stood assembled on the beach, eager to greet the new arrivals. Quint watched as the *Bloody Angel* began lowering a jollyboat onto the waves, though they were too far off for him to tell yet which of his crew would be the first ashore.

The first of their rescuers arrived well ahead of the jollyboat, leaping from the depths to fly in a glittering arc of spray and scales above the white breakers. A whooping cheer rose from the watchers on the beach as the mermaid dove gracefully over the whitecaps and into the lagoon.

Something inside Quint seemed to unclench as Lurk came snaking through the water towards the shore. His feet moved without conscious thought, carrying him towards the lagoon. The other castaways parted before him, and he reached the waterline just as Lurk slithered up from the surf.

"*Quint*!" she shouted, giving him a smile that displayed every last one of her shark's teeth.

"Lurk," he said, grinning nearly as widely as he clasped her shoulders. "Lurk, mate, you did it. You saved us."

"I had help," she said, though her spinal ridge stood tall and proud. "The Deep Shadows took me across."

"They must have swum awfully fast," he said, trying to count off how many days it had been since the mermaid tribe had appeared in this very spot. "You practically just left."

Lurk made the hissing sound of mermaid laughter. "Your crew was already looking for you. Jimmy told them you'd been taken to the Sea of Tears."

"Aye," Quint nodded, silently vowing to stock up on Jimmy's favorite treats—papayas and macadamia nuts—as soon as they made landfall. "Is...did everyone make it through alright?"

"They did," Lurk assured him. "They'd been searching the Sea for a while when I came across them. They were only a couple days' journey away from here when I found them, and we had fair winds the whole way back."

"Some good fortune at last," Quint said. "I'm proud of you, mate. More than words can say."

"You're my pod," Lurk said, though she couldn't suppress the happy tremor that rippled through her ridge.

"Speaking of," Quint said, gently squeezing her shoulder. "Once we're back in the Archipelago and we've resupplied, we'll set a course straight for the Great Reef. It's time we got you home."

"I'm already home," Lurk said, looking from him to the castaways waiting to greet her once she'd finished reuniting with their captain. "But...it will be good to see my parents again. My pod."

"You'll see them soon," Quint assured her, still smiling. "I promise."

⚓

Lurk lingered on the shore just long enough to accept the congratulations and thanks of the other castaways before she had to excuse herself, diving back into the lagoon to help guide the jollyboat through the narrow pass between the reefs.

Another chorus of cheers went up from the castaways as the jollyboat crossed into the lagoon. Quint's heart surged as he saw the familiar faces of his crew dipping their oars into the glittering blue waters: quartermaster Bonnie Kate, her hair tied up with a vivid orange headscarf; the boatswain Fillbrick, a rare smile gracing his ordinarily stoic countenance at the sight of his comrades gathered on the beach.

But it was not only the crew of the *Bloody Angel* manning the jollyboat, Quint saw.

"I'll be damned," Margherita said, coming up beside him and letting out a low whistle. "Lola Read."

Quint's ma stood in the prow of the jollyboat, the wind tugging insistently at her short hair, her gaze staunchly fixed on her son and the rest of his crewmates gathered on the shore. With a cutlass thrust through her belt, Quint found it easy to imagine Ma as the fearsome pirate she had once been.

Nor was she the only member of Captain Wolf's Sea Dogs who had volunteered for the rescue mission. Quint's Uncle Jun sat in the stern of the jollyboat alongside Fillbrick, the two of them powering the little craft across the waves with broad, powerful strokes of their oars. Just behind the bow sat Manish Anand, the father of Quint's childhood best friend Hari, his arms wrapped about—

"*Ahoy, Cap'n!*" came a high, piping voice. Quint stared as a slight figure wriggled his way out of Manish's grasp, grinning a gap-toothed grin at Quint as he stood and waved both hands above his head. One of those hands held a hammer.

"Angels," Margherita swore, dismay stealing across her features. "They brought a *kid* with them?"

"*Mani*!" Quint shouted, cupping his hands to his mouth at calling across the waves at Manish's grandson. "Sit down, before—"

Too late. A wave hit the jollyboat, rocking it from side to side. Mani lost his footing and slipped towards the water, still waving.

Lurk broke the surface, wrapping her scaly arms about the youngster and depositing him back onto the jollyboat. Manish bound his grandson in a more secure grip and thanked Lurk.

Moments later the jollyboat was in the shallows, the entire crew of castaways surging forward to help pull the little vessel ashore.

"Cap'n!" Mani yelled again, saluting with his hand. Not the one holding the hammer, thankfully. "We came to rescue you!"

"And a fine job you've done of it, mate," Quint said, nodding to Manish. "Do your parents know where you are, Mani?"

"I think so," the youngest of the *Bloody Angel's* crew said brightly. "At least, I told my brothers to let them know where I was going. They probably told them. I think."

"Our little stowaway," Quint's ma said, stepping over the rail of the jollyboat. "Nobody knew he was aboard until we were a few days into the Sea of Tears. Would have sent him home if a storm hadn't blown up behind us. That gale raged for days and days before the winds finally calmed, at which point we were on the verge of turning back anyway so we could send him and Manish home when Lurk found us."

She looked her son up and down in that appraising way mothers looked at their children. "Good thing she did, too. You've gotten too thin, Quentin."

Quint barked out a laugh, then bent and swept his ma up in a tight hug. She wrapped her arms around him, holding him close.

"Thanks for coming," he said into her ear. Ma patted his back.

"Like I was going to sit around at home once I heard you'd been captured by the pirate queen," she said as they broke apart. "You still her prisoner, or am I going to have to crack some heads before you're well and truly rescued?"

"That won't be necessary," Quint assured her, glancing aside to where Margherita was lingering nearby, her posture unmistakably apprehensive. "Right?"

"Aye," Margherita nodded, smiling weakly at Quint's ma. "We've put all that behind us. Hi, Lola."

Lola Thatch, once Lola Read, stared at Margherita Elena Rossini, the self-proclaimed pirate queen of the Archipelago. Quint watched as recognition dawned across his mother's lined face.

"Margie?" she said, half-disbelieving. "What in all the heavens...?"

"It's a long story," Margherita said, still with that weak smile. "About forty years long."

She stepped forward and reached out a hand, as if to embrace the other woman, then seemed to think better of it at the last moment. "I'm so sorry. About Clarent. I always meant to ..."

What she had meant to do, Quint never found out, for his ma threw her arms around Margherita and pulled her into a bone-crushing embrace. The two women stood that way, swaying a little, both of their shoulders shaking.

"It's all right," Lola said at last, sounding like she was coming up for air. "It's all right, lass. He knows."

"If you say so," Margherita said, wiping her eyes.

The mood was abruptly shattered by Mani squealing "*TURTLE!*"

Quint turned and watched the young boy sprinting across the beach, his heels kicking up sand as he dashed towards where Bosun sat sunning herself, half in and half out of the surf. The enormous turtle turned her head and watched with what seemed to Quint like an expression of bemusement as Mani clambered onto her back, wholly unafraid. Jimmy fluttered over his head, then settled herself on one of the bony spikes protruding from the turtle's shell.

"Ma," Quint said, gently disentangling her from Margherita. "There's someone else you should see."

He took her by the arm and led her over to where Wilson stood beside Bosun, watching in confused fascination as a small boy climbed all over the back of the titanic turtle that had been his only companion for much, much longer than Mani had been alive.

"Commodore," Quint said, throwing a lazy salute. "This is my ma."

Wilson stood a little straighter, adjusting the tattered lapels of his threadbare jacket, and nodded to her. "Miss Read."

"It's Thatch, now," Quint's ma said, looking hard at him. "Do I know you from someplace?"

"This place, in fact." Wilson gestured broadly at the island upon which they stood. "Though last time we spoke you had a knife at my side.

"Angels above," Ma swore, recognition stealing across her face. "*Wilson?*"

"Aye," Wilson nodded, looking abashed. "Suppose I should have taken you up on your offer of safe passage all those years ago."

"You've been here all this time?" Ma asked, looking past him towards the mountaintop which crowned the island, just visible above the treetops.

"I have," Wilson admitted, taking a deep breath. He held out his hands, wrists pressed together. "If the offer still stands, I'd like to offer you my surrender."

"Consider it accepted," Ma said, taking his hands in hers, and gently lowering them. "I'm certain we can find you a spare bunk for the voyage home. "

"Thank you," Wilson said, his hoarse voice scarcely louder than a whisper. "And...your boy here told me about...about your husband. I know it isn't much, but you've my condolences, for whatever it's worth."

For a moment there was no sound save the wind and the waves.

"Thank you," Ma said, a little stiffly. Then she softened. "How long's it been since you shared a drink with someone, Wilson?"

"Too long," he said wistfully.

"Well," Ma said, nodding towards the firepit, where Ophelia and Margherita had broken out the remaining tequila bottles, and were busily toasting their rescuers. "Let's remedy that, shall we?"

"Aye," Wilson said, a slow grin spreading across his features. "I've worked up a powerful thirst these last forty years."

With that he ambled across the beach, towards the gathered pirates whom he had regarded as his sworn enemies only hours ago. Quint watched him join them, the tequila being passed freely from hand to hand, and felt a curiously bittersweet feeling stir in his heart.

How strange, he thought, that after so long stranded in this place dreaming of rescue, he should suddenly be afflicted by a reluctance to leave. That once they were across the Sea of Tears they would disperse, each group going their separate ways. That this was the last time they would all be together like this again.

"How's the *Angel* doing on provisions?" he asked his ma.

"More'n sufficient," she answered, glancing out at the ship anchored beyond the reef. "We should be able to make it back across the Sea of Tears with victuals to spare. That quartermaster of yours is meticulous with her inventory."

"Kate's the best," Quint said fondly. "In that case, think you can linger for one more day? Give Wilson a bit of time to adjust to the prospect of leaving."

“We could,” Lola allowed, casting a weather eye to the horizon. “Storms should hold off long enough that another day won’t make much difference.”

“In that case,” Quint said, throwing an arm around his Ma’s shoulders, “let’s give you a proper island welcome.”

“Aye,” she agreed, letting him guide her up the beach towards the firepit. “And you a proper farewell.”

“Speaking of...” Quint said, as the two of them strode over to where their fellow pirates’ celebration of their rescue was already shaping up to be as riotous a party as any Quint had taken part in. “...have you ever tried a margherita?”

Epilogue

Several weeks later, the *Bloody Angel* lay anchored off a sandbar on the edge of the Great Reef, surrounded as far as the eye could see on every side by a veritable forest of brightly colored corals lying just beneath the surface. The air was full of the high, ethereal strains of merfolk song as Lurk's pod called to one another from across the waves.

It was a calm day without a breath of wind, the shallow waters so clear that Quint could see the sinuous forms of the merfolk gliding gracefully between the coral formations, slipping in and out of sight as they wove through subaquatic grottos and magnificent arches of old-growth coral.

Quint leaned against the *Angel's* aftcastle rail, watching as a trio of mermaids streaked like shadows beneath the waves. The one in the lead suddenly dove deep, disappearing from sight just beneath the *Bloody Angel's* hull. The other two circled around where she'd dove, then scattered as she came rocketing up, breaking the surface in a powerful leap.

"Hi Quint!" Lurk yelled up at him, her mouth set in her wide shark's grin as she curved gracefully through the air beneath him.

"Ahoy, Lurk!" Quint said, raising the bottle he'd been nursing in salute as the two smaller mermaids leapt from the waves after their sister. "Ahoy, Bask! Ahoy, Seek!"

"Hi Quint!" Lurk's two younger sisters chorused back at him, before all three of them fell splashing back to the waves, laughing their hissing merfolk laughter.

"Don't tell me you're planning on recruiting the little ones, too," Ophelia said, coming to lean alongside Quint.

"I didn't *know* Lurk was just a kid," Quint said, rising to the bait even though he knew he really shouldn't. He'd been the victim of much good-natured ribbing on the subject ever since they'd left Wilson's Isle, as they'd ended up naming the island. "I wouldn't have given her the tattoos if I had."

"You certain of that?" Ophelia asked. "Because I saw Mani doodling on his arm with a fountain pen the other day..."

Quint groaned and looked back out at the mermaids frolicking in the waves. Seek and Bask had managed to corner their elder sister, but Lurk twisted away from their grasping webbed hands with a nimble corkscrew, and the chase began again.

"I can see why their pod comes here," Ophelia said, shading her eyes as she gazed out at the vast expanse of coral spreading to the horizon. "Not a landfolk within a hundred leagues, excluding ourselves. I'm glad we got her here."

"Me too," Quint said, watching as a distant group of Lurk's kinfolk leapt from the waves, their musical voices carrying across the water. "I tell you what, though. I'm going to miss her something awful."

"Same," Ophelia nodded. "But she'll come back to you, one day. We all do."

Quint turned, studied her too-casual expression. "You're still set on leaving, then?"

She'd first broached the subject back at Port Solace, where the *Bloody Angel* had parted ways with Margherita and all her crew, save two. The news had not come as a complete surprise, but it had stung all the same.

"It's nothing against you," Ophelia assured him, not for the first time. "It's just...when you and Margherita were gone, it was up to me to get both crews to work together. I just didn't expect that I would like it as much as I did. Being in charge, making decisions. Having folk look to me for answers. It felt..."

"It felt right," Quint suggested. Ophelia nodded gratefully. "Have you decided where you'll go?"

"Aye." She looked at him, almost shyly. "I talked things over with Margherita. She's willing to loan me one of her ships for a time. Said to consider it a parting gift."

She trailed off into silence, and Quint knew that, however casual her relationship with Margherita might have been, it had reached its end.

"Aw, mate," Quint said, putting an arm around her shoulder. Ophelia leaned against him, and for a time they stood like that, taking comfort in the familiarity of their long companionship.

"I won't be gone forever," Ophelia said after a while. Quint wasn't sure if it was him she was trying to convince, or herself. "It's just...something new. For me to try and see if I like it. Captaining a vessel of my own, even if it's a loaner. If I don't..."

"Then you'll always have a place here," Quint said, ruffling her hair. "You know that."

"'course I do," Ophelia said, waving him off. "You couldn't keep me away from the *Angel* if you tried. Besides, Margherita's gonna want her ship back eventually."

"That she will," Quint nodded. "You have a crew in mind?"

"Already picked them out," Ophelia said as she clambered to her feet. "Tarja's gonna be my first mate."

"That explains why she and Frederick came along," Quint said, glancing over to where the Trechtish pirate couple were sunning themselves on the quarterdeck. "You couldn't have chosen a better first mate, Cap'n Price."

Ophelia blinked, then grinned.

"I like the sound of that," she said.

"Aye," Quint grinned back. "Me too."

"Ahoy, Cap'n!" Mani's high, piping voice shouted from somewhere off the port rail of the quarterdeck. Quint threw Ophelia a brief salute, then hurried forwards.

"Thought you two were supposed to be watching him," he said to Tarja, who lay reclining on the deck in a red and white-striped bathing suit, head pillowed by her hand. Frederick leaned against her in a matching one piece, absorbed in a book.

"I have delegated the task to Lieutenant," Tarja said, waving her hook. "Or the merchildren, failing that."

Quint looked over the rail. Mani sat astride Bosun's neck, the great turtle lazily paddling around the *Bloody Angel* while a gaggle of merfolk close to Mani's own age chased after him. As Tarja had promised, the monkey stood balanced on one of Bosun's protruding spikes, looking uneasily about at the great stretch of water surrounding them. Jimmy perched atop one of the turtle's other spikes, apparently enjoying the ride considerably more than her simian counterpart.

"Ahoy, Mani!" Quint called back down to him. "You make certain not to let any of those merchildren drown you, you hear?"

"Lurk already promised that they won't!" Mani assured him, and patted the turtle's shell. "And I don't think that Bosun would let them, either."

"Likely not," Quint agreed, musing on how gratifyingly odd his life was, that the friendship between an ancient and enormous turtle and an eight-year-old boy was not even the strangest one he'd witnessed.

For her part, Bosun seemed to be enjoying her sojourn away from her home island—significantly more than her master. Wilson had spent the first stage of the journey belowdecks, cowering in his bunk as they crossed the Sea of Tears, no doubt fearing that the drowning death he had escaped forty years past would claim him at the last. Once they had reached the Archipelago he had begun to emerge from belowdecks more frequently, staring out at the islands passing by and speaking little.

"It'll be an adjustment," Ma had told Quint one night when he'd broached the subject. "The man was alone for a long time. But once we get him settled in Ember Bay he'll have all the time he needs."

"You're sure that's wise?" Quint had asked her, not for the first time. "Letting him live in the same place as Pop's old crew?"

But Lola Thatch had only shaken her head and smiled. "It's a forgiving place, Ember Bay. Full of forgiving people. Might be that's just what the commodore needs. And besides..."

She had leaned in, winked. "I tossed his blowgun overboard our first night at sea. Just in case."

Grinning at the memory, Quint glanced over to the starboard bow, where Ma and Wilson were playing dice with Bonnie Kate and Rustbucket, who had decided to join the *Bloody Angel* on one last voyage. Though he had not said as much, Quint suspected that Rustbucket wanted to make sure that Lurk made it safely to her family before he retired from the pirate's life altogether.

The booming laughter of Quint's Uncle Jun rang out across the deck. He sat in the *Angel's* prow beside Vanessa, a chessboard between them. Quint watched as Vanessa darted out a hand, capturing Jun's rook with her knight. Quint watched her lips form the word "check."

Jun hesitated, then after careful consideration placed his king—only for Vanessa's next move to bring the game to an end. "Checkmate."

Jun laughed again, bowing his head in gracious acceptance of his defeat. Quint detached himself from the bow and made his way towards them.

A broad smile spread across Jun's jovial features as he waved at Quint.

"Seems you've got a new contender," he said, turning to Vanessa. "Take it easy on my nephew, will you?"

"This is a pirate ship, isn't it?" Vanessa replied, one corner of her mouth twisted into a smirk. "No quarter."

Jun barked out another booming laugh and strode passed Quint, clapping him on the shoulder as he went.

"So," Quint said, as Vanessa clambered to her feet. "Does that mean you finally decided to hoist the black sails after all?"

"Well," she said, her smirk widening into a smile. "Ophelia *did* sentence me to a life of piracy, after all. Plus, you're still my prisoner."

"Lucky me," he grinned. "That why you didn't disembark with Margherita and the others at Solace, then?"

Vanessa looked away, but not before Quint caught sight of her smile fading.

"It's tempting," she said, glancing up at the black flag fluttering idly in the breeze. "A life with you, out here on the open waves, with no one to answer to but ourselves. I could be happy with that, I think."

Quint heard what she did not say. "But it isn't for you."

"No." Vanessa tucked a stray strand of hair behind her ear. "Not as things currently stand."

Quint nodded, trying to swallow this bitter pill with as much grace as he could muster. "Back to the Navy, then?"

"Yes." Vanessa's gaze turned southwards, as if in recollection. "Margherita told me about your plan, you know. To redistribute the Crown Jewels to the people of the Archipelago."

"You don't approve?" Quint asked, thrown by this apparent non sequitur. They had loaded the Crown Jewels onto Margherita's *Wildflower* at Solace before parting in friendship.

"On the contrary," Vanessa said. "I think it's brilliant. You and her are both outside the Empire's law. That gives you avenues of repairing the harm the Empire's done that I don't have."

"Because you're still in it," Quint surmised. Vanessa nodded.

"The Empire's responsible for a lot of hurt," she said, her voice growing heavy. "A lot of wrongs in need of righting. I can't deny that. But I have to believe that the whole institution isn't so broken that it can't be fixed. I have to believe that someone in the right position, with the right influence, can still change things for the better from the inside. Do you...does that make sense?"

She was looking up at him with such honest, fearful vulnerability that Quint wanted to wrap her in his arms and pull her close.

"Aye," he said, forcing himself to nod instead. "I take it you have a plan?"

"You know me," Vanessa nodded, a smirk tugging at the corner of her mouth. "There are a few Navy higher-ups I know who I think would be open to discussing reform in the way we handle certain situations. Some friends from my academy days as well. And Estelle has connections in the academic world..."

She trailed off, eyes gleaming with the same eagerness that Quint had first fallen in love with across a chess table. He smiled at her.

"If there's anyone in the Eight Seas who can make the Empire do better, it's you."

"Thank you," Vanessa said, her shoulders relaxing as she let out a long sigh. She gave him a grin. "But all that can wait until we get back to civilization. For now, I'm still officially missing, possibly dead. And that's on top of all the shore leave I've accumulated."

"I think you've earned a vacation," Quint nodded, looking out at the sea of rainbow coral all around them.

"Or several," Vanessa agreed. "Speaking of...Yuletide's not too far off. You going to spend it with your Ma?"

"Hadn't thought about it," Quint said, glancing over his shoulder at where she was playing dice. "If I do, you'll have to promise to come along, though. Ember Bay goes all in when it comes to the holidays."

"I wouldn't miss it," Vanessa smiled.

"It's a date, then." Quint smiled back, but something still nagged at him. "Ask you a question, though?"

"Sure."

"What happens if you can't fix it?" Quint asked. "What if one of your higher-ups—or hell, the Empress herself—gives you an order your conscience can't countenance? The kind you can't follow and still live with yourself afterwards?"

Vanessa regarded him steadily, the sun illuminating golden flecks in her brown eyes.

"Then," she said, as calm as the waters surrounding them and just as clear, "I become an enemy of the Empire."

A slow grin spread across Quint's face. "In other words, a pirate."

"If you like," Vanessa said, amused.

"In that case..." Quint put both hands on her hips and drew her close, pressing her against the *Angel's* aft rail. Vanessa's breath caught, but she did not resist. "There's still one thing we need to do."

"Oh?" Her voice was low as she looked up at him, brown eyes huge and expectant. "What's that?"

Quint kissed her forehead, fingers tightening around her middle as he leaned in and whispered in her ear:

"Buccaneer's baptism."

Then he picked her up and flung her over the rail. Vanessa fell from the *Angel* to the water below, shrieking out *"Quint!"* just before the waves closed over her head.

Grinning, Quint Thatch leaned over the rail, watching as Vanessa surfaced, sputtering and rubbing water from her eyes. Quint dove in after her, the cool sea closing in around his head as he jackknifed into the waves, surfacing just beside Vanessa.

"You bloody *pirate!"* she yelled, laughing as she put both hands on his shoulders and pushed down, dunking him. Quint's hands found hers, pulling her down with him.

Underwater, he opened his eyes, looking around at the rainbow forest of corals in every direction. At the great black hull of the *Angel,* solid and real beside them. And at Vanessa, looking back at him beneath the waves.

They surfaced together, both drawing in the same breath, legs kicking to stay afloat as they held each other.

"Well, Ness," Quint said, brushing her cheek with his thumb as they floated in the shadow of the *Angel.* "How's it feel, now that you're secretly one of us?"

"What's that thing you lot say?" Vanessa asked, laughing. Before Quint could answer she leaned in and kissed him.

When they finally broke apart she was grinning. "A pirate's life for me."

To be continued in ENEMY OF THE EMPIRE

Acknowledgements

My first and greatest thanks goes to my wife, Megan. Throughout this process her keen eye has made sure the pacing doesn't drag, the jokes land, and that the romance scenes are sweet and flirty. Thank you, my love, for seeing this story through from rough idea to outline to the final draft, even if it took a few tries to get there.

Another huge thanks to Emily, whose live reactions and immaculate GIF choices while beta reading had me laughing to the point of tears. I am beyond thankful for both your emphatic love of the final story and the insightful critiques and changes you suggested.

Thank you to my other incredible beta readers: Steve for finishing the book at a breathtaking pace and confirming that it was, in fact, good; Cameron for talking me through the epiphany that unstuck the plot when the book was stalled; Lauren for correctly predicting every romance trope in the book; Li for your constant support and encouragement in every aspect of my writing.

Thank you to every ARC reader who took the time to read this sequel, review it, and spread the word. I couldn't do any of this without you all.

And lastly a huge thank-you to my mom and my brothers: our adventures on remote tropical islands together are what inspired the latter half of this story.

About the Author

Marshall J. Moore is a writer, traveler, and martial artist who was born and raised on Kwajalein, a tiny Pacific island. He is the author of *Son of a Sailor: A Cozy Pirate Tale* and the Rites of Resurrection trilogy, a fantasy series about a necromancer soldier who investigates murders within his city. Marshall has trained a professional mercenary in unarmed combat, once sold a thousand dollars' worth of teapots to Jackie Chan, and on one occasion was tracked down by a bounty hunter for owing $300 in overdue fees to the Los Angeles Public Library. He lives in Atlanta, Georgia, with his wife Megan and their two cats Delilah and Furiosa.

marshalljmoore.com

www.ingramcontent.com/pod-product-compliance
Lightning Source LLC
Chambersburg PA
CBHW030637260626
47157CB00007B/2361

9798988267034